the Raven
SAINT

Charles Towne Belles / Book 3

M. L. TYNDALL

the Raven
SAINT

Charles Towne Belles / Book 3

BARBOUR
PUBLISHING

IF
Tyndall

© 2009 by M. L. Tyndall

ISBN 978-1-60260-158-1

All scripture quotations, unless otherwise noted, are taken from the King James Version of the Bible.

Cover design: Kirk DouPonce, DogEared Design

Published by Barbour Publishing, Inc., P.O. Box 719, Uhrichsville, OH 44683, www.barbourbooks.com

Our mission is to publish and distribute inspirational products offering exceptional value and biblical encouragement to the masses.

 Member of the
Evangelical Christian
Publishers Association

Printed in the United States of America.

DEDICATION

To the bit of Pharisee in all of us.

ACKNOWLEDGMENTS

My deepest appreciation to all the wonderful people at Barbour Publishing, who not only believe in my writing, but treat me as if I were family.

To my agent, Greg Johnson, who works hard on my behalf, and who also lends a shoulder to cry on when I need one.

And what would I do without my incredibly talented critique partners: Laurie Alice Eakes, Louise M. Gouge, Ramona Cecil, and Paige Dooly, who are not only great authors, but good friends.

To my editor and partner through all my books, Susan Lohrer. You're the best!

And to Traci DePree for making me work harder than I ever have on a book, and for making it the best it can be. Thanks, Traci!

To all the writers at HisWriters Yahoo group, a plethora of historic knowledge and Christian kindness. Love you guys!

Special thanks to Angela Robinson for winning the contest on my blog to name the cat in this story Spyglass!

My fondest appreciation goes to Cathi Hassan for help with all the French phrases which I conveniently forgot from high school French class.

And last but not least, to my dearest husband and my children who put up with my long hours in front of the computer and that glazed look in my eye when I'm off in my story land somewhere.

Finally, all praise and glory to my Savior, my friend, and my King, Jesus Christ.

But he that received seed into the good ground
is he that heareth the word, and understandeth it;
which also beareth fruit, and bringeth forth,
some an hundredfold, some sixty, some thirty.
MATTHEW 13:23

CHAPTER 1

Outside Charles Towne,
Carolina, October, 1718

Black, menacing clouds snarled a warning from the Carolina skies. Clutching her skirts, Grace Westcott trudged down the muddy path. A shard of white light forked across the dark vault, and she glanced up as thunder rumbled in the distance.

"I hope the rain doesn't catch us, miss." Alice's shaky voice tumbled over Grace from behind.

"Never fear, Alice, we are almost there." Grace pushed aside a leafy branch that encroached upon the trail. As the wind picked up and raindrops began to rap on the leaves above them, the wall of greenery arching overhead provided a shelter that brought an odd comfort to Grace.

"Look, miss. This plant. Isn't it bloodroot?" Alice squeaked. "To heal afflictions of the skin?"

Grace huffed. Her legs ached from the mile-long journey from Charles Towne. She could hear the rush of the Ashley River in the distance. They were close to the Robertses' cabin, to poor little Thomas, sick with a fever and in desperate need of the medicines they brought.

Whirling around, Grace examined the leaf in her maid's hands. "Nay. 'Tis not bloodroot, as you well know." She searched Alice's eyes, but the maid kept her gaze lowered. "Whatever is the matter with you today?"

The maid cast a quick glance over her shoulder and shrugged. "I am only trying to help, miss."

"You can help by hurrying along. Thomas may be failing as we speak." Grabbing her skirts, Grace turned and forged ahead. A drop of rain splattered on her forehead, and she swiped it away.

"But the rain, miss. Shouldn't we return home and don some proper attire?"

"Mercy me, Alice. We are nearly there. A bit of rain will not harm us. We've been in far more dangerous situations." Grace hoisted the sack stuffed with herbs, fresh fruit, and rice farther up her aching shoulder. "Besides, we are going about God's work. He will take care of us."

Grace heard Alice's shoes *squish* in the mud. "Indeed, miss."

Her maid's voice quivered—a quiver that set Grace's nerves on edge, along with the dark tempest brewing above them. Something was bothering the woman, Grace couldn't guess what.

Another flash lit up the sky. Releasing her skirts to the sticky mud, Grace pushed aside a tangled vine that seemed to be joining forces with Alice in attempting to keep her from continuing. Musky air, heavy with moisture and laden with scents of earth and life, filled her nostrils. Thunder bellowed, closer this time, and raindrops tapped upon the canopy of leaves overhead. Plowing ahead, Grace ignored the twinge of guilt at her most recent expedition. One of many expeditions she'd been strictly forbidden to embark upon—both by her father, before he set sail for Spain, and more recently, her sister Faith and Faith's new husband, Dajon. But Grace could not allow anyone or anything to stop her from doing what God had commissioned her to do: feed the poor, tend to the sick, and spread the good news of His gospel.

She glanced up at the dark clouds swirling like some vile witch's brew. Perhaps she should have left a note informing Faith of her whereabouts. No matter. She would drop off the food and herbs, attend to Thomas, and be home before sunset.

Grace emerged from the green fortress into a clearing. Thunder bellowed, and she shivered as a chill struck her. In the distance, the wide Ashley River tumbled along its course. A cabin perched by the water's edge, smoke curling from its chimney. Squaring her shoulders, she took a deep breath and quickened her pace. "Here at last. And, as you can see, Alice, all is well."

A nervous giggle sounded from behind her.

Hoisting the sack higher up on her shoulders, Grace clutched her skirts and climbed the steps of the cabin, but before she could knock on the door, it swung open. Mr. Roberts, a burly red-faced man with unruly dark hair, stared curiously at her for a moment then cocked his head and smiled. "Miss Grace. A grand pleasure to see you." His glance took in Alice standing on the steps behind Grace. His forehead wrinkled. "What brings you this far from home on such a rainy day? Helen, Miss Grace has come for a visit," he yelled over his shoulder. The scent of smoke and some sort of meaty stew wafted over Grace.

"Why, we've come to help Thomas, of course." Lightning flashed, casting a momentary grayish shroud over Mr. Roberts's normally ruddy face.

"Thomas needs help?" He scratched his thick, dark mane.

Alice's boots thudded on the steps, and Grace turned to see her maid inching away from the cabin, her chin lowered.

Shaking her head, Grace faced Mr. Roberts. "Yes, you sent Alfred yesterday to inform us of Thomas's fever and ask for my help, did you not?" The man looked puzzled. Grace slid the sack from her shoulder and set it down on the planks of the porch. "I've brought elder root and dogwood bark for his fever and some fresh fruit and rice for you and your family."

Mrs. Roberts appeared in the doorway, her infant daughter cradled in her arms. "Grace, what a wonderful surprise. Henry, don't just stand there. Invite her in out of the rain."

"Thomas isn't sick." Mr. Roberts's nose wrinkled. "And Alfred was here with us all day yesterday."

Grace swerved about to question Alice, but the girl was nowhere in sight. Descending the stairs, she dashed into the clearing, her heart in her throat as she scanned the foliage for any sign of her maid.

A *swoosh* of leaves and *stomp* of boots reached her ears, then a band of five men materialized from the foliage. Armed with cutlasses and pistols, they stormed toward Grace. She tried to move her feet, but the thick mud clung to them like shackles. Mr. Roberts cursed and ushered his wife inside. The baby began to howl.

A tall, sinewy man halted before her. A burst of wind struck him, fluttering the green feather atop his cocked hat and the tips of the black hair grazing his shoulders. He shifted his jaw, peppered with black stubble, and gazed at her with eyes the color of the dark clouds churning above them. A slow smile crept across his lips, lifting his thin, rakish mustache. "*Mademoiselle* Grace Westcott, I presume." His thick French accent turned her blood to ice.

Grace met his gaze squarely. "I am, sir."

With a snap of his fingers, two of his men flanked her. "You will come with us."

"I will not." The men wrenched her arms behind her back. Pain shot across her shoulders.

The snap of a rifle sounded, drawing the man's attention to Mr. Roberts pointing his musket in their direction. "Leave her be."

A flicker of relief eased over Grace, quickly fading when she examined the man before her. Instead of fear, amusement sparked in his eyes. The men on either side of Grace chuckled as if Mr. Roberts had told a joke.

"*Quel homme galant*, but I fear I cannot do that, *monsieur*." The leader crossed his arms over his gray waistcoat and scraped a finger along his lean chin. "With a bit of fortune and a good aim, you may shoot one of us. *Mais* that would leave you and your family completely at our mercy. *Comprenez-vous?*"

Mr. Roberts stared at him for a long moment, obviously measuring the man.

"Toss your weapon to the ground, monsieur, and go into your house. If you come out, we will shoot you. If you fire another weapon at us, we will kill your family."

A short, barrel-chested man beside the leader drew his pistol and leveled it at Mr. Roberts. The sneer on his face suggested he would love nothing more than to shoot the man where he stood.

The musket quivered in Mr. Roberts's hands as he perused the band of ruffians, but still he did not relent. Grace shook her head, sending her friend a silent appeal. She would not allow him to put his family in jeopardy for her.

Mr. Roberts swallowed, threw his weapon into the mud, and gave her an apologetic look before slipping inside the cabin and closing the door with an ominous thud that echoed Grace's fate.

She faced the leader. Thunder roared across the clearing. "What have you done with Alice?"

"Alice? Hmm." His eyes lit up. "*Votre servante?* I merely paid her well for leading you to us." He grinned.

The skies opened and released a torrent of rain upon Grace as if

God Himself shed the tears that now burned behind her eyes. How could Alice have done such a thing? She had been Grace's personal maid for the past five years—had traveled with her in the crossing from Portsmouth to Charles Towne.

The rain bounced off the cocked hat and the broad shoulders of the man before her. Drops streamed down Grace's face, her neck, soaked into her gown, and befogged the scene before her. If only the fresh water from heaven could wash away these devilish creatures like holy water sprinkled upon evil.

The black-haired man turned and marched away as though her desperate wish had reached God's ears. But then his two minions wrenched her arms again and dragged her behind him. Panic seized her. This couldn't be happening! She dug her heels into the mud but her captors merely lifted her from the ground. Pain scorched across her arms and neck.

"Please, sir. Please. What do you want with me?"

But the only reply came from the rain pounding on the leaves and the thunder rumbling across the sky.

They plunged back into the thick forest. Grace struggled against the men's meaty grips. Even if she did manage to break free from them, tree trunks rose like prison bars on either side of her, holding her captive within the dense thicket. They trudged down the path for what seemed an eternity. Each step dug the knife of fear deeper into Grace's heart. Silently, she appealed to God for her salvation, begging to hear His comforting voice, but her petitions were met with the same silence her captors afforded her. Finally, they emerged onto a secluded shore, and the men shoved her onto the thwart of a small boat then launched the craft into the rushing river. In the distance Grace saw a two-masted brig swaying with the rolling tide.

Lord, where are You? She clasped her hands together and tried to catch her breath.

The black-haired man locked a smoldering gaze upon her. He did not look away as propriety demanded but perused her with alarming audacity. Rain streamed off his hat onto his black breeches, and a smirk creased one corner of his mouth. Averting her gaze to the agitated water, she considered leaping overboard. She couldn't swim. At least not well enough to fight the strong Ashley current. Besides, surely God would rescue her from these brigands. He was simply testing her faith by waiting until the last minute when things were at their worst. Lifting her chin, she cast a defiant look upon her captor, but it only caused his smirk to widen.

Within minutes, they reached the ship and thudded against its hull. Shouts pitched upon them from above as faces popped over the bulwarks to peer down at her. Grace glanced about for the rescuer God should have sent by now. The leader pulled her to her feet, and before she could make a move, he hoisted her over his shoulder like a sack of grain and climbed the rope ladder without effort.

Grace could no longer feel the fear or even the damp chill. Numbness gripped her, born of shock at her predicament. Blood rushed to her head, and she closed her eyes, breathing in the musky scent of the man's damp wool waistcoat and praying for the nightmare to end.

Once aboard, he carried her across deck as he issued a string of orders in French, sending his crew scrambling in every direction.

"Welcome back, Captain," a deep voice shouted, then a shock of brown hair appeared in Grace's vision. "I see you found her."

"*Oui, bien sûr.*" His tone carried the haughtiness that excluded any other possibility as he tapped her on the rump.

"How dare you!" Grace shouted and tried to kick her legs, but the captain's arm kept them pinned to his chest. The two men shared a chuckle.

"Weigh anchor, away aloft, and raise the main, Mr. Thorn. We set sail immediately."

Raindrops bounced over the wooden planks, pelting her from all directions. Her head bumped against his damp coat. His hard shoulder pressed into her aching stomach as he carried her down a ladder. She stretched her hand to grab the hilt of his rapier, but it taunted her from its sheath at his other side, out of her reach. She pounded her fists against his back. Muscle as unyielding as steel sent pain through her hands.

With a chuckle, he sauntered down a hallway and kicked open a door. Grace tensed, fearing the man would toss her to the floor. Instead, grasping her waist, he gently set her down inside the tiny cabin.

Gaining her balance, Grace wiped the matted strands of wet hair from her face and faced him. "Who are you and what do you want with me?" she said in a stalwart tone that surprised her.

He doffed his feathered hat and banged it against his knee, sending droplets over the floor. Tucking an errant strand of wet hair behind his ear, he bowed. "Captain Rafe Dubois at your service, mademoiselle. I welcome you aboard *Le Champion*. And regarding what I want with you"—he raised one brow and allowed his gaze to scour over her—"I am to deliver you to Don Miguel de Salazar in Colombia."

"Colombia?" Grace took a step back and gripped her throat.

"Oui, he has promised to pay quite handsomely for you."

"For me? But why? I don't even know the man." A shudder ran through her.

"Ah, but your father does apparently. The two men are not...how do you say? Agreeable? Don Miguel holds him responsible for the death of his son in a skirmish with a galleon. He thought you would be adequate payment for the transgression."

"Payment!" Grace's fear gave way to anger. "I am no one's payment. How can you take part in such a wicked scheme?"

The captain shrugged as if her words rolled off him. "Like I said, he's willing to pay handsomely." He offered her a devious grin then donned his hat and closed the door with a resounding thud.

CHAPTER 2

Rafe stormed up on deck, struck by both the rain in his face and the vision of the lovely Mademoiselle Westcott staring incredulously at him as he slammed the door of her cabin. He took the quarterdeck ladder in two vaults and positioned himself by the helm. Arms across his chest, he surveyed his crew as some of them climbed aloft to loosen sail, while others hauled in the cock boat. Monsieur Thorn stormed the planks, braying orders to keep the men at task. Soon fore- and mainsails were lowered and drawn taut, catching the wind in deafening claps.

"Take her out, Mr. Atton," Rafe shot over his shoulder at the helmsman.

"Oui, *Capitaine*," came the quick reply.

The ship bucked, and Rafe braced his feet against the deck and doffed his hat, allowing the rain to pound down upon him. Closing his eyes to the pellets, he hoped their crisp sting would douse the heat that had taken over his senses after his encounter with Mademoiselle Grace Westcott. He could not keep his eyes off her. No matter where he tried to focus them, they always landed back on her as if drawn by some invisible bowline. It was not so much her *beauté*, although she possessed a comeliness ranked above most women. There was an aura about her, a presence that reached out through those emerald green eyes and grabbed hold of his senses, his reason. He rubbed his belly. Perhaps it was the weevil-infested biscuit he'd eaten for breakfast that morning. Just a case of indigestion, *sans doute*. Oui, that must be it. Once out upon the open sea and in possession of an empty stomach, he'd be his normal dispassionate self again.

"Let fall," Mr. Thorn bellowed from the main deck. "Hoist storm staysails and main topsail!"

The ship picked up speed as the thunder of the sails accompanied the roar of the skies. The bow rose and plunged over a swell, sending foam upon its deck. Before long, they rounded the tip of the peninsula and Rafe spotted O'Sullivan's Island.

"Hard alee, Monsieur Atton," he ordered.

"Hard alee, Capitaine."

Once free of the Charles Towne harbor, Rafe had only to deliver the girl unscathed to Colombia. Although Don Miguel had never met Mademoiselle Grace, Rafe was confident he would be pleased with his purchase. The mademoiselle was well worth the five hundred pounds in gold the loathsome Spaniard had offered for her. *Peut-être,* Rafe could bargain for more doubloons for such a valuable prize.

His first mate appeared beside him and gripped the railing. Doffing his hat, he shook the water from it then plopped it back atop his head. The rain had lessened to a sprinkle. Releasing a sigh, Thorn grinned at Rafe. "Quite an alluring woman Grace Westcott turned out to be, eh?" he remarked as if reading Rafe's thoughts.

Rafe shrugged. "I take no notice. She is cargo to me."

"Cargo, eh?" Monsieur Thorn chuckled. "Much more appealing than those crates in the hold, I'd say."

A vision of the mademoiselle stretched across Rafe's mind. Rain dripping from her skirts, her black hair clinging in saturated strands to her face, her shoulders arched back in a regal stance of superiority. The way her bottom lip quivered, belying the imperious defiance burning in her eyes. She'd handled herself with more bravery than he would have expected from a lady born to comfort. An admiral's daughter. Perhaps she'd gotten her stout heart from her father. *Sacre mer,* why was he thinking of her again? He shook his head, sending droplets flying, then ran a hand through his wet hair.

"More appealing only in the gold she'll bring me."

Monsieur Thorn fingered the whiskers sprouting on his chin and gave Rafe a look of censure. "I trust this particular cargo is not to be handled? You may want to remind the crew—and yourself—of that. 'Tis been awhile since we anchored at port."

Rafe nodded and lifted his gaze to the angry clouds. "She will not be touched, *je t'assure*, but not due to any of your lofty principles, *mon ami*."

"You should try living by some of my lofty principles, Captain. You may find them agreeable." Instead of the expected lift of sarcasm in his first mate's voice, the clamor of disdain rang loud and clear. Thorn's jaw tightened and a look of spite flared across his eyes that set Rafe aback. Rafe returned the look with one of his own, hoping to remind the man that he rarely suffered impertinence, even among those close to him.

Thorn raised his hands in surrender and looked away. But the man had given Rafe an idea. It had been a long time since he'd felt the warmth of a woman beside him. Perhaps that was what ailed him, what caused his strong reaction in Miss Westcott's presence. Though he knew better than to allow his mind to wander in her direction again, not if he was to deliver her to the don unspoiled.

Mr. Atton navigated the shoals of the bay with expertise, and soon *Le Champion* plunged from the narrow Charles Towne harbor onto the open sea. The dark clouds lifted from the horizon, allowing the setting sun to spread its bright wings of crimson and gold across the western tree line. *C'est bon.* It would be a clear day tomorrow.

Thorn tugged his cocked hat further upon his head. "Where should I point her, Captain? Colombia?"

Rafe flattened his lips. "Perhaps a side trip to Port-de-Paix is in order, Monsieur Thorn. I need to offload the cargo in the hold, and the men could use some diversion."

"Aye, Captain." Thorn winked, touched his hat—a habit he picked up during his two years serving in His Majesty's Navy—and sped off, barking orders as he went.

Rafe smiled. Oui, a quick stop in Port-de-Paix would do everyone good. And he would welcome a chance to see his old friend Armonde again. Afterward, all he had to do was deliver the lady to the don in Rio de la Hacha, and his pockets would be lined with enough gold so that finally, after all these years, he could keep his promise to Abbé Villion—a promise that would save many lives. A promise that was worth the kidnapping of one insignificant lady. Rafe winced beneath a pang of guilt that was quickly assuaged when he brought to remembrance the lady's heritage. She was British and therefore his enemy.

He shoved his hat back onto his head and thrust his face into the wind. What could be so hard about delivering one small woman to Colombia?

⌒

Creak, creak, slosh, slosh. The sounds of strained wood and rushing water crept uninvited into Grace's consciousness. She pushed them back, preferring the ignorant repose she'd fallen into during the night. A chill ran across her back. Her legs trembled. Where was her goose-feather coverlet? Had she kicked it off in the night?

"Oh, mercy me." She reached down, groping for the warm covering but found only a stiff counterpane beneath her hand instead of her feather bed. She rolled on her side. A splinter stabbed her arm. Grace bolted up and she opened her eyes, her heart crashing into her ribs. The room that met her gaze was not her bedchamber at home but a ship's tiny cabin. A bowl, mug, and lantern perched upon a small table that was bolted to the wall. Beside it, a green gown draped over a stuffed leather chair. A large ornamented chest guarded one corner while an empty armoire with open doors filled the other.

Throwing a hand to her throat, Grace squeezed her eyes shut as memories of yesterday flooded her wakening mind. *Lord, make it go away.* But when she opened her eyes, the same sordid scene filled her vision.

Don Miguel de Salazar. The name slunk around the cabin. Her throat tightened. She could not go to Colombia. Her life was in Charles Towne. Her work was in Charles Towne. People depended on her for food, for clothing, for medicine. God depended on her to share His love and truth with those who would listen.

She sprang from the bed. Rays of sun spiked through a tiny porthole like daggers. Trembling, she hugged her gown, still damp from yesterday's storm, then eyed the dry one strewn over the chair. Sometime in the night, an old man had ambled in with a bowl of stew, a mug of rum-infused lemon juice, and a gown he tossed over the chair. He'd stared at her for a minute, grunted, and then stormed out. The meaty odor of the food still permeated the cabin, but her churning stomach could not accept the sustenance any more than her propriety could accept the unseemly gown. After the man had left, Grace had spent most of the night upon her knees, begging God to rescue her, begging Him to protect and save her, but the Almighty had been silent.

Finally, when her eyes had swelled from crying and her knees ached from the hard wood floor, she had dropped onto the narrow cot attached to the bulkhead and was finally lulled to sleep by some ribald ballad slinking through the planks from below.

Grace covered her mouth with her hands as tears burned behind her eyes. She thought of her sister Faith and her brother-in-law Dajon. They would be so worried about her, along with the household servants, Lucas, Molly, and Edwin. And what of her other sister, Hope? They still had no idea where she was after she'd run way with Lord Falkland. How could Grace honor the promise she made on her mother's deathbed to ensure the salvation and spiritual well-being of her sisters if she were lost to them forever? *Oh, what am I to do? Where are You, Lord?*

Boot steps thumped outside the door. The latch lifted. Grace swiped the tears from her cheeks and she took a step back. The thick oak slab crashed open against the bulkhead, and in stomped Captain Rafe Dubois with all the authority of a king and the swagger of a brigand. Behind him, the old man who'd brought her food the night before entered, followed by a gray cat, which bounded in and leapt upon the table.

Captain Dubois's presence filled the room, shrinking its size and draining it of air. Dressed in a loose-fitting white buccaneer shirt, with a gold and purple sash strung about the waist of his black breeches, and heavy jackboots, he approached her, the silver hilt of his rapier gleaming in a ray of sun.

He raised a brow. "Do you shiver from fear, mademoiselle, or is it because you prefer your wet attire?"

Grace drew a deep breath to steady her nerves. "A bit of both, I believe."

The captain cocked his head and studied her. "Honesty. *Comme c'est rafraîchissant.* Do the garments Father Alers provided not meet with your satisfaction?"

"They dip far too low in the collar." Grace felt a blush rising on her cheeks. "Only a woman of questionable morals would wear them."

Captain Dubois' jaw tightened, and the mirth slipped from his gaze. "They belonged to my sister."

Grace gulped. The old man who'd entered behind the captain chuckled and took a seat in the chair.

"I thank you for the dry attire, Captain, but I cannot in good conscience wear that gown."

The captain snorted in disdain. "Of all the women to kidnap, I get a *prude pieuse*. Fortune has fled me once again."

Wincing beneath his insult, Grace lifted her chin. "I believe 'tis I whom fortune has deserted."

"Hmm," was the captain's only reply, but a glimmer of appreciation for her honesty shone from his eyes.

The sound of lapping drew his gaze to the gray cat, partaking of Grace's dinner. Raising her head, the feline licked her whiskers and stared at Grace with one eye. Naught but fur covered the spot where the other eye should have been, and Grace wondered what had happened to the poor creature.

Sails flapped above as the ship careened. Grace stumbled backward. Captain Dubois reached out for her, but she jumped out of his reach and laid a hand on the bulkhead to steady herself.

He frowned. "You will eat what is provided for you. Unlike *l'excès* you are accustomed to, we cannot afford the luxury of wasting food."

"I am not accustomed to excess, Captain." Grace's anger rose up. "'Tis but my stomach which protests at the moment. Surely you can understand that?"

The captain's eyebrows arched, and he gave a quick snort of unbelief. "*C'est-ça.*" He gestured toward the old man still sitting in the chair. "Nonetheless. This is Father Alers. He will bring you food and whatever you need."

Grace blinked. A father? Or was it just some odd pirate name? Father Alers nodded, briefly meeting her gaze, as he pressed down a mass of gray hair coiling around his head like a silver spiderweb. Years of hard work lined his ruddy skin, but Grace found naught to fear from his amiable expression.

"He is the ship's cook. You can trust him," the captain said.

"Trust?" Grace snapped. "How can I trust anyone aboard this ship? Are you all not complicit in my abduction?"

He grinned and slid the back of his finger over her cheek before she could stop him.

She jerked away from him. "I am the daughter of Admiral Henry Westcott. And I assure you, sir, he will come looking for me."

"I know who you are, mademoiselle."

"If you do, then you know I speak the truth." Grace squared her shoulders even as her insides began to crumble beneath his haughty disregard. "And you are as good as dead for kidnapping me."

Not a speck of fear crossed the captain's features. Instead, he broke into a chuckle, soon joined by Father Alers. "We shall see, mademoiselle."

Anger dried the tears burning behind her eyes, anger at this beast before her, anger at his arrogance, his audacity. "I insist you release me at once!"

He cocked his head and studied her, and she thought she saw a flash of admiration cross in his gaze, but then the hard sheen returned. "But of course." He waved a hand toward the entranceway. "The door remains unlocked. You may wander freely through the brig, though I must warn you, avoid going below deck. My crew may not be as, shall we say, *courtois* as I."

"Courteous, faugh, I've been treated better by savages."

Father Alers coughed a laugh into his hand.

Captain Dubois gripped his baldric. "If it is savages you want, mademoiselle, there are plenty aboard." He smiled. "Regardless, I encourage you to stay above deck. The don will not accept soiled goods."

Soiled. The word sent a flood of horrifying visions into Grace's mind. She cringed.

Captain Dubois leaned toward Grace until she could smell the brandy on his breath and the sea in his hair. "I will not have you ill when you arrive in Colombia. You will take off your wet gown and put on this dry one by the time I return, or I will do it for you." A lewd flicker crossed his eyes, and she knew he meant it. He turned to leave, gesturing for Father Alers to follow him.

Anger seared through Grace, stealing the chill from her bones. "You're naught but a pirate."

He halted. The skin on his face grew taut. "You are mistaken, mademoiselle. I am a mercenary."

Grace's stomach tightened. A soldier for hire. "Which nation do you serve?"

"Whichever one pays the most." He grinned.

"Then you are a pirate, indeed."

His brooding eyes narrowed. "Take care, mademoiselle. *Gardez vos lèvres.* I give no quarter to the weaker sex."

Grace swallowed and raised a hand to her chest.

"Come, Spyglass." He swerved about and the gray cat leapt into his arms. "There is no way off this ship, mademoiselle. If you behave yourself, things will go pleasant for you. If not, well." He shrugged, a twinkle of deviant mirth in his expression. "The gentleman in me will not permit the utterance of such atrocities."

CHAPTER 3

The door to her cabin creaked open, and Grace turned her aching head to see who had entered. Father Alers offered her a smile from the entrance before he shut the door and set the tray he carried atop the table. "How are you feeling, mademoiselle?"

Grace rubbed her forehead and winced at pain that pounded beneath her fingers. "Not well, I'm afraid." Blurred images drifted through her feverish mind. Images floating on the shadows of night and the glare of day as they passed like specters through the cabin, images of Father Alers and the captain entering and leaving, their whispers lingering in the stale air. The last thing she remembered with any clarity was the captain's threats before he had stomped out, leaving her to face the night alone. She had cried herself to sleep that night and awoken to a body in complete rebellion, expressing its dissent at her predicament with a fever and a seething stomach. Why did she have to get sick at a time like this, when she needed all her strength to plan an escape? She forced back her hatred toward this unknown don and the scoundrel who had kidnapped her, knowing it was wrong. "How long have I been ill?"

"Five days, mademoiselle." Father Alers lifted a bowl from the tray and sat in the chair beside her cot. "You must eat something." The rank odor of some type of fish caused her nose to wrinkle and her stomach to convulse.

She pressed a hand to her mouth. "Forgive me, Father, I cannot," she mumbled. "But I thank you for the food. You have been most kind."

He returned the bowl to the tray with a huff then faced her, leaning back into the chair. "The fever has lessened, mademoiselle. You should feel better soon." A look of concern softened the lines at the corners of his eyes. He started to rise.

"Father." Grace held out her hand. "Please stay a moment. I feel as though I shall go mad all alone in this cabin." She moaned. "Especially not knowing what is to become of me."

He settled back into the chair but averted his eyes from hers.

The momentary glimpse of shame she saw in them emboldened her to ask the question that had been burning on her lips ever since she had discovered kindness in Father Alers. "Father, why do you sail with such a villain?"

Father Alers shifted in the seat and folded his hands over his belly. "*Le* capitaine has some villain in him, I admit, but he does much good *aussi*."

Grace's head pounded as she tried to make sense of his words. "I do not understand. He has kidnapped me. How is that good?"

Releasing a deep breath, he glanced toward the window but said nothing.

"Why do they call you Father?" Grace remembered praying for an ally aboard this ship, a friend, someone who would help her. Truth be told, she remembered praying for many things. None of which had been answered.

Father Alers grimaced. "I used to be of the Jesuit order."

"Used to be?"

"I am no longer a priest, mademoiselle." Anger pierced his tone.

"But surely you still have faith." Grace struggled to rise. How could anyone turn away from God? "My faith is all I have," she said. Although even as she said the words, she wondered at their truth.

He nodded. "You spoke of God often in your dreams these past few days."

Grace's cheeks heated at the intimacies this stranger must have heard her utter in her delirium. She was afraid to ask what she'd said, but he continued nonetheless.

"Oui, something about the Catawbas and Alice and a boy named Frederick and the Hendricks." Father Alers scratched his beard and smiled. "Ah, and always a praise to God. That is how I knew of your faith."

The sound of familiar names washed over Grace like a refreshing mist, bringing with them memories of a time when God walked with her daily. " 'Tis what I do back in Charles Towne. Alice"—pain sank into Grace's heart as she remembered the girl's betrayal—"my lady's maid and I often visit the Catawbas, a local Indian tribe, to bring them blankets and kettles and other cooking utensils, and to tell them about God. And little Frederick." Grace smiled as she remembered the ragged, starving orphan boy she had found on the streets of Charles Towne. "He's an orphan I placed with a couple who couldn't have children. And the Hendricks are a poor family who live on the edge of town. I take food and medicine to them when their children are sick." Relaying the stories out loud brought memories of God's faithfulness to the forefront of her mind, chipping away at the despondency she had built up over the past days.

Father Alers cocked his head and gave her a knowing grin. "And why would a young lady do these things when you could be attending *les soirées* and be courted by beaus?"

"To share God's love and truth with others and help those in need. Isn't that what we are supposed to do?" Unlike her sisters, parties and courtship had never appealed to Grace overmuch.

A beam of admiration glimmered in the father's golden-brown eyes. "A worthy goal, mademoiselle. Your faith is admirable, and the many prayers you offer during your *maladie* have, sans doute, risen straight to heaven."

Horrified that this man had also overheard her intimate conversations with God, Grace fought the tears that filled her eyes. "Yet He does not answer them. Can you explain to me why?"

Father Alers shook his head. "If I could, mademoiselle, than peut-être, I would still be a priest."

Grace swallowed against the anger and fear clogging her throat. "Why are you with Captain Dubois? You are nothing like him."

"Le capitaine and I. . .have a long *histoire* together."

"That still doesn't explain why a man of God would lower himself to partake of such iniquity."

Father Alers pressed down the coils of his silver hair and glanced out the window. He hesitated and seemed to drift to another place and time. "I had a nephew, Armonde." He shifted in his seat. "A bright boy, full of life and love. A bit of a rebel at times, like any boy his age." A slight smile alighted upon his lips but then disappeared. "He was a Huguenot."

The word struck a chord of sorrow within Grace, for she had heard that the Huguenots had undergone horrific persecution in France.

"When Louis XIV issued the Edict of Fountainebleau, Armonde was captured, tortured, and put to death." Father Alers's jaw tightened and he glanced down at the deck.

Grace reached out, but he made no move to accept her hand. "I am so sorry, Father."

He shrugged. "After that I gave up on all religion. It causes men to fight and kill each other. It causes death. I want no part of it. So, I sailed to Saint Dominique where I met Rafe, I mean Captain Dubois." He grinned and finally took her hand. "He reminds me of Armonde."

Her heart filled with compassion, and she placed her hand atop his knobby fingers. "Do not give up on God, Father." Yet her words seemed to drift away for lack of true conviction in her voice. For it appeared God had, indeed, given up on her as well.

The door burst open and in stomped Captain Dubois bringing with him a gust of wind, laden with the smell of salt and damp wood. His dark eyes latched upon her and then shifted to Father Alers, and then to their clasped hands. His jaw stiffened, and he gripped the hilt of his rapier.

Rafe grimaced at the stupidity of his friend and took a step forward. He had told the father not to get too close to the mademoiselle during her maladie. He knew the man's heart and how easy it would be for him to take pity on her.

But Rafe certainly did not expect to find their hands clasped together. *L'idiot.* Sans doute *la femme* attempted to charm Father Alers into helping her escape. "I see the mademoiselle is recovering. There is no further need for your ministrations, Father."

Father Alers lifted one defiant gray brow his way then gently placed the mademoiselle's hand back on the cot.

Grace flattened her lips. "Father Alers was just informing me why he sails with a man such as you." Though weak, her voice spiked with disdain.

"*Vraiment?*" Rafe shifted his stance and jerked his head toward the door in an attempt to get Father Alers to leave.

Rising, the father pressed a hand over his back. "Mademoiselle Grace was also informing me how she spends her time in Charles Towne helping to feed and clothe the poor and take care of the sick." He faced

Rafe and gave him a taunting look. "Who does that sound like?"

Rafe huffed. The daughter of a British admiral feeding the poor. Not likely. "It sounds like la femme has poisoned your mind, *mon vieux*. Now, attend to your duties."

The mademoiselle shook her head and took a labored breath as Father Alers brushed by Rafe, gave him a grunt in passing, and headed out the door.

Coughing, Mademoiselle Grace lifted her emerald eyes to his. Gone was the glassy shield of courage and defiance he had seen five days ago. In its stead, a pleading innocence stared at him and seeped through the cracks in his armor headed straight toward his heart. But he wouldn't allow it entrance. Not again. Was it true she cared for those less fortunate than her? Was it true she spent her life caring for others? *Non*. He would not believe it.

He could not believe it.

A drop of sweat slid down the back of his neck, and he wiped it away as he stared at the deck and conjured up a vision of what the British navy had done to his mother. It was the only way to combat the rising guilt those green eyes stirred within him.

He found the anger. He welcomed it and allowed it to burn away any tender spots on his heart, crusting them over until they were once again hard.

Mademoiselle Grace must have sensed his fury, for when he lifted his gaze to hers, she flinched and her face drained of color.

So she *was* afraid of him. When he had first brought her on board, he had expected either a swooning female, begging for her life, or a ferocious wildcat, clawing and hissing at him. What he had not expected was a woman with the courage of a soldier and the heart of an angel.

She struggled to get up on one arm, her chest rising and falling, either from the exertion or from her fear, he didn't know. "Why are you doing this?" she said. Her bottom lip trembled, and Rafe felt that tremble down to his soul.

He planted his fists upon his waist and tore his gaze from her. "As I have said, for the money."

"What will the don do with me?"

Rafe shook his head. His anger began to retreat again. He must get away from her before it left him defenseless. "You can ask him when you see him." Turning, Rafe stormed out the door and slammed it behind him.

CHAPTER 4

Rafe burst into his cabin. Grabbing the decanter of brandy from his desk, he poured himself a swig and snapped it toward the back of his throat. The sharp liquor burned a soothing trail down to his belly and radiated a numbing heat through his body. Just what he needed. He poured himself another and strode to the stern window, watching as the sun's orange glow slipped behind the horizon, tugging a curtain of black in its wake. He felt like kicking something—or someone—and what bothered him the most was that he didn't know why.

A *tap* sounded on his door and at his *entrez*, Father Alers ambled in with a tray. "I thought you would want to eat in your cabin tonight." The old man's eyes took in the empty glass in Rafe's hand.

"And why do you assume that?"

"The crew says you are in a foul mood, Capitaine."

Rafe emitted a sinister chuckle.

The man set the tray on Rafe's desk. "And they know you well enough to leave you alone." The plate of salt pork, beans, and a hard biscuit stared back at Rafe, taunting him with the scent of spice and molasses, though he could find no yearning for the food in his belly.

He huffed. "What, no drink to accompany this savory *mélange?*"

"What need? You have supplied your own." Father Alers glanced at the decanter of brandy and raised a haughty brow.

Rafe turned on his heel and stared into the growing darkness outside. The ship groaned beneath a swell and a bell rang above deck, announcing a new watch.

Father Alers grunted, and Rafe heard the shuffle of his shoes retreating over the wooden planks.

"*Asseyez-vous*, Father. I wish to speak to you." Turning, Rafe gestured toward one of the high-backed *fauteuils* in front of his desk and set his empty glass down.

The cook scratched his beard as if contemplating whether or not to obey, then he dropped into the chair. "What has soured your *humeur*, Capitaine? Seeing me holding hands with the mademoiselle?" He chuckled.

Ignoring him, Rafe opened a desk drawer and chose a French cheroot from within a lined case. Then lighting it from the lantern, he inhaled a draft, allowing the pungent smoke to fill his lungs and calm his fury. He would not give his friend the pleasure of seeing his inner turmoil. "She has no affect on me, mon vieux. I simply want her well." Rafe circled the desk.

Father Alers leaned back and clasped his hands together over his portly belly. "She will survive. Since that is all you care about, non?"

"Oui. I mean, non. I do not want her emaciated." Rafe crossed his arms over his chest. "Does she take in fluids?" He'd seen many a stout sailor die from fever and nausea aboard a ship, especially if they refused to drink.

"She will not partake of the lemon juice—it contains liquor, she says—so I have brought her the water we collected in the last rain storm."

"She *will not*?" Rafe gave a humorless snarl.

"Quite politely refuses." Father Alers crossed his buckled shoes at the ankles and smirked. "With sincere apologies. *En fait*, she treats me more as a friend than a captor."

"As I saw." Rafe puffed on his cheroot, masking the annoyance bristling his nerves.

Father Alers shook his head. "I admire the woman. Despite her malaise, she spends hours in prayer. A true testimony to her faith." He chuckled. "Be careful, Rafe, you may find that God answers her supplications."

Rafe snorted. "Strong words coming from a man who has spent the last four years hiding from God." He poured himself another swig of brandy.

"If I am hiding from Him, then you are surely running."

"You cannot run from someone who does not exist, Father. I run from no god and no man." He downed the liquor.

"Perhaps not. Yet you have proclaimed war upon both." Father Alers's golden eyes sparkled with playful humor. "And if you would, please abstain from addressing me as Father. I am no longer of the order."

"From Jesuit priest to ship's cook." Rafe smirked. "How far you have fallen."

"And you. From wealthy planter's son to abductor of virtuous ladies."

Rafe puffed upon his cheroot, more annoyed at his friend's continual approbation of Mademoiselle Westcott than the insult. "That you find the lady *agréable*, you have made quite clear."

"She has a humble, kind spirit and her mood is always pleasant— which is more than I can say of you."

"You live and die by my grace, *mon vieux*." Rafe waved a hand through the air. "Why should I be pleasant?"

Father Alers leaned forward in his chair and directed a patronizing gaze at Rafe. "Because it is in you to do so, Capitaine. You can call me *old man*, but I have known you since you were a boy, and the only reason I remain in your service is the charitable acts you perform." He sighed. "Now what of *la dame*? Surely you do not intend to deliver her to this don."

"Mais oui. That is my exact intention." Rafe poured another swig into his glass.

Father Alers shook his head, his chin sinking to his chest. "It is not like you. Never have you dealt in innocent human flesh. You've escorted prisoners, dealt in espionage, battled enemies in time of war, even thievery, but never this."

Guilt assailed Rafe's already bruised conscience, and he downed the brandy. That was the problem. He had grown soft over the years. "Innocent? A lady?" He snickered. "None in her gender can claim such a state."

"They are not all like Claire."

Rafe slammed his fist on the desk, unsettling its contents. "I told you never to speak her name."

Unmoved by Rafe's outburst, Father Alers held up a wrinkled hand in acquiescence.

Rafe ground his teeth together. "Besides, Grace is the daughter of Admiral Henry Westcott. Eye for an eye. Does it not say that in your Holy Book?"

Father Alers rose. Muffling a moan, he placed a hand on his back. "It is not *my* Holy Book, and what would you know of it anyway?"

"I know more than I care to." Rafe took another puff of his cheroot, hoping the tobacco would calm his temper. "But to appease your sense of righteous mercy, the price I get for her will save many lives."

Father Alers flapped his hand through the air as if arguing with Rafe was a waste of his time. "And put out that cheroot. You will light the ship aflame."

Rafe scowled. Why did he allow this old man to play the father to him? He only taunted him with his inadequacies. "I am the capitaine of this ship, and I'll do as I please!" he shouted in a tone that sent most men cowering.

Father Alers guffawed. "What has pricked your nerves tonight if not la dame Westcott?"

"*C'est absurde.*" Rafe sat back against his desk and rubbed his chin. "But I will not have her waste away and lower my profits. Force her to eat, if you must, and inform me when she fully recovers."

Father Alers turned and waved a hand through the air. "Force her yourself, Capitaine. You forbade me to attend to her further, did you not?" And with that, he hobbled out and closed the door.

Rafe put out the cheroot in the empty brandy glass and avoided the temptation to toss the glass across the cabin. They'd been at sea barely a week, and Mademoiselle Westcott was already proving to be more of a problem than he expected.

Grace climbed the companionway, her legs trembling with each step. Whether from weakness or fear, she didn't know, and she no longer cared. After doing naught but retch and pray for days—she'd lost count of how many—all she had to show for it were a pair of bruised and scraped knees. Not to mention her spinning head which continually induced her to lose the contents of said stomach—which of course was already empty, making the action all the more painful.

To make matters worse, nightmares from long ago attacked her feverish mind with ferocity. One nightmare in particular—a nightmare that had been so terrifying, she'd never spoken of it to anyone. A nightmare that had changed the course of her life forever. The night she had seen a vision of hell.

Even now she couldn't bring herself to think of it, but its memory always lingered at the edge of her thoughts, prompting her with greater and greater urgency to save those who were heading down a path that led to the horrifying place. Finally, pushing aside the hellish vision, she decided to venture on deck for some fresh air and to see if perhaps God could hear her pleas more clearly out in the open. Perchance this ship and its occupants were so evil that they blocked her prayers from rising to heaven. But now as she rose above hatches and slid her shaky foot across the deck, she questioned the wisdom of her actions. Instantly, a dozen pairs of eyes fastened upon her as tightly as the hooks on the bodice she'd been forced to squeeze into.

Her sister Faith had always told her never to cower before bullies, so she lifted her chin to meet their gazes. A cacophony of whistles flew her way.

"Shiver me soul, if it ain't the captain's piece," one portly sailor in a red shirt said.

"An' a handsome petticoat she be." The man next to him elbowed his friend and grinned.

A lanky man with a pointy chin licked his oversized lips. "Don't she look as tasty as a sweet berry pie."

"Come join us, mademoiselle," another sailor gestured toward her. "We haven't had our dessert yet." The men all joined in an ear-piercing chortle.

Grace lowered her chin, flung a hand to cover her bare neck, and made her way to the railing, hoping not to topple to the deck from weakness and humiliation. Perhaps this had not been a good idea, after all.

Trying to erase the vision of the ribald men behind her, she gripped the railing and gazed across the sparkling turquoise sea. She drew in a deep breath of the heavy salt-laden air, hoping it would chase from her lungs the moldy staleness that had taken residence there from her confinement below.

Movement caught her eye, and she turned to see three sailors peering at her from the bulwarks on her left. One of them, a tall man attired in a modish style that belied the crude look in his eyes, spoke passionately to the man beside him. His companion, a rotund fellow made all the more large by the third man's wiry frame beside him, chuckled and raised an inviting brow her way. His wide mouth stretched into a wet smile.

Grace's stomach lurched.

A deep voice she recognized as the captain's bellowed over the ship, immediately sending the men scampering and silencing the salacious onslaught. "Back to work, *crapaud stupides!*" The stout man did indeed look like a toad.

Grace glanced over her shoulder to see Captain Dubois standing by the companionway, fists on his waist. His unfettered black hair blew behind him in the hot ocean breeze, and his dark smoky eyes latched upon her, an inscrutable emotion brewing within them.

Grace faced forward and tugged upon the chain at her neck, pulling out the gold cross tucked within her bodice. Gripping it with both hands, she slid her fingers over the jewels. She wanted to pray, to plead with God for help, but she had no words left. Why wasn't God answering her? She had spent her life serving Him, and now when she needed Him the most, He seemed to have disappeared.

The thump of the captain's boots faded across the deck, and she released a deep sigh. At least for the time being, it appeared that he would leave her be and keep his men away from her as well. She had come up here to spend time with God, but as she gazed over the huge expanse of blue, she felt more alone than ever. The ship bucked, and she released the cross to grab the railing. The ornament struck the wood with a clank, and she stuffed it down her bodice again. A gift from Reverend Anthony at St. Philips for her exemplary charity work in and around Charles Towne. It was all she had left to remind her of God's love and faithfulness.

Closing her eyes, she gripped the ship's railing lest she collapse from the lightness of her head and weakness of her knees. She must regain her strength. She must plan her escape. If she could discover what this don planned to do with her, perhaps she could convince the captain to appease him in some other way. Her heart pounded slow and heavy in her chest as if it pushed through molasses, reminding Grace that she needed sustenance.

Something furry tickled her arm. Grace shrieked, jumping back, and opened her eyes to find the gray cat balancing on the railing. The feline stared at Grace curiously through one eye. Laughter tumbled over her from behind.

A man approached, retrieved the beast, and held it in one hand. "Now, Spyglass, don't go scaring the lady." He scratched the cat behind the ears. The feline's loud purrs could be heard even over the purl of the waves against the hull. The man bowed. "Justus Thorn, miss."

"You are British." Grace studied him. He could be no older than her own twenty years. Brown hair the color of almonds danced wildly in the wind and brushed the top of his pristine gray doublet. A swath of white lace bounding from his neck matched the lace at the cuffs of his white shirt. A bulbous nose and a thin red scar that ran from his left cheek to the middle of his neck were the only deterrents to an otherwise flawless countenance.

"Born in Wellingborough, Northamptonshire." Mr. Thorn set the cat onto the deck. "Have no fear. Spyglass may look fierce, but she is harmless."

" 'Tis not the cat that worries me, Mr. Thorn."

His gaze rose to Captain Dubois standing on the quarterdeck amidst a group of crewmen, and for a moment Grace thought she saw a spark of bitterness cross his hazel eyes. "Aye, 'tis a most perilous situation in which you find yourself." He said the words as if remarking about a rainy day or a pair of lost tickets to a play.

"Most perilous, sir, when you consider what my future holds." Grace reached up to clasp the buttons at the top of her gown, but her fingers met bare skin instead. She'd forgotten about the low-necked bodice and spread her hand across her naked flesh in horror. "But then, why do I complain to you? You are an accomplice in the captain's nefarious scheme."

"I am a member of his crew only."

"Then you disagree with his plans?"

He swerved his gaze to the sea and clenched his fingers around the railing. "Often."

The spite ringing in his tone ignited a spark of hope within Grace. Had she found an ally? Or like Father Alers, did this man hold some affection for the French captain? "Perhaps the captain reminds you of some fond relation?" She could not help the sarcasm in her voice.

Mr. Thorn's brows shot up and he gave a humorless laugh. "I have no affection for the captain, I assure you."

"Then why do you remain in his service?"

"It serves my purpose for the time being."

Grace shook her head, as confused with Mr. Thorn's excuses for wickedness as she was the father's. "A grand purpose it must be to implicate yourself with such atrocious deeds."

Mr. Thorn drew in a deep breath. He swallowed hard, and Grace sensed her accusation had struck a nerve of shame within him. The man appeared to possess some measure of honor. But could she trust him? "Do you not care that an innocent woman is being led to the slaughter?"

He faced her, and she detected a hint of moisture in his eyes. "I am not a man without a heart, miss."

Desperation tossed propriety to the wind, and Grace laid a hand on his arm. "Then save me, sir, by all that is good and holy."

"I cannot." He turned away. "There are bigger forces at work here than you realize, miss."

Grace's head began to spin, and she felt as though it would dislodge from her body and float into the cloudless sky. "Then you are equally duplicitous in this heinous act and will be punished accordingly." She regretted her harsh tone, but how could anyone choose to join the side of evil with such deliberation?

He chuckled, all traces of concern fleeing from his tone. "And who, might I ask, will execute the sentence?"

"God's justice will suffice." Grace rubbed the perspiration from the back of her neck.

"God's justice is too long delayed. Therefore I fear it not." Mr. Thorn stiffened his jaw, and he slid a finger over the scar lining his neck.

" 'Vengeance is mine; I will repay, saith the Lord.'" Grace quoted from Romans, hoping the word of God would soften this man's heart.

Mr. Thorn snorted. "Begging your pardon, but I have yet to see that promise fulfilled. Not in this life, anyway."

Dismayed by his lack of faith, Grace closed her eyes to a blast of hot wind. She was surrounded by miscreants and unbelievers. Yet as she allowed the muggy air to swirl around her, a glorious idea began to form in her mind. Perhaps she had been sent here by God to convert the poor souls on this ship? Perhaps the Almighty could find no other dedicated servant willing to do the task, so He had allowed Grace to be kidnapped in order to bring her on board.

The ship rose and plunged over a swell, showering Grace with a salty mist. Thankful for the momentary reprieve from the heat, she dared a glance over the deck and found most of the crew hard at their tasks. A menacing band of men, if ever she saw one. Composed of all ages and sizes, most wore faded checkered shirts and stained breeches, while others attempted—but fell woefully short of—a semblance of nobility with their gold-trimmed waistcoats and frayed satin neckerchiefs. All were armed with pistols slung about their chests as if they didn't trust the man beside them.

She felt Captain Dubois's gaze upon her from his position upon the quarterdeck. A shiver ran through her, and she turned around. Doubts assailed her, drifting atop her fears.

How, Lord, will I ever be able to reach such miscreants?

She grew dizzy, and her knees buckled. Mr. Thorn reached out for her, but she latched onto the railing instead.

"Are you ill, Miss Grace?" Mr. Thorn asked.

"Oui." The captain's heavy voice filled her ears as his massive frame filled her vision. "She has been indisposed below with a stomach ailment and has not eaten much in six days."

"Zooks. Six days? No wonder she's weak," Mr. Thorn exclaimed.

"I am feeling better today." Grace managed to sputter out the words as she caught her breath. But in truth, her nausea was returning.

"Get back to work," Captain Dubois ordered Mr. Thorn. The man bowed toward Grace, cast a look of scorn at his captain, and stomped away.

The wind whipped the captain's ebony hair about his shoulders, bringing with it the scent of brandy and tobacco. Cocking his head, he narrowed his gaze upon Grace. Her throat went dry. That the man invoked fear in those around him was evident. That he invoked it in her, she would not give him the satisfaction of knowing.

"You must eat something, mademoiselle, or you will never get well." Rafe crossed his arms over his chest to stop the urge burning in them to hold her, lest she fall.

Her brilliant green eyes stared at him from beneath a fan of dark lashes. An innocence beamed from them, a purity, coupled with a strength he had rarely seen in a woman.

"And why, pray tell, do you concern yourself with my health, Captain?" she asked.

He offered her a playful grin. "You know why."

"I know you are a thief, a kidnapper, and only God knows what else." A sail snapped above them as if sealing her words. Her raven hair glistened like onyx in the sunlight, though not a strand could escape the tight bun she had formed at the back of her head.

"The Bible says that neither thieves, nor the covetous, nor drunkards, nor revilers, nor extortioners will inherit the kingdom of God." Mademoiselle Grace lifted her chin; then her eyes softened. "But that does not have to be your fate, Captain."

"My fate is not your concern." Rafe flexed his jaw in irritation and leaned his elbow on the railing. "I may be a thief, mademoiselle, but I am also a man of my word, and I promised to deliver you to Rio de la Hacha, Colombia, in one piece." He said the words as much to remind himself of his task as to inform her of it.

"A man cannot be held to a promise of evil."

"I make no such distinctions."

"That much you have spoken in truth." She released a sigh of disappointment that jabbed his conscience. "But please be warned, Capitaine"—her attempt at the French pronunciation sent a shiver of delight through him—"evil begets evil."

"Is that so? Then you must have done something quite wicked to deserve such a fate as this"—he grinned and slid a finger over his mustache—"while I on the other hand must have done something admirable to have fallen into the fortune you will surely bring me."

Mademoiselle Grace's bottom lip began to quiver, and she looked away, but not before he saw tears fill her eyes. An unexpected pinch of remorse caused him to shift his stance and clear his throat.

"What does this don want with me?" she asked, still staring out to sea.

Rafe allowed his gaze to wander to the swell of her bosom above the lace of her bodice. "I suppose what all men want with beautiful women."

A noticeable shiver passed through her, and Rafe forced down another wave of regret. Sacre mer, what was wrong with him? She was merely a woman, a spoiled, wealthy woman encased in a pretense of saintly propriety and feminine beauty that would suck the life out of a man's soul if given the chance.

She splayed her fingers across the bare skin above her bodice as if she knew where his gaze wandered. "Men and their wars. What care have they for their innocent pawns?" she said to no one in particular as she gazed across the sea.

Disgust and hatred stole the sparkle from her eyes and left him cold.

The ship pitched over a wave, and she staggered but quickly righted herself.

Another urge to place a hand on her back to steady her overcame Rafe, and he fisted his hands and folded them across his chest. The blood of a certain British admiral flowed in her veins. That alone had been enough to persuade him to accept the don's proposal. That and fulfilling a promise to Abbé Villion that would save hundreds of lives.

"How can you do something so cruel?" The look in her eyes cut into his heart.

Rafe stiffened his back. "For a greater cause, mademoiselle."

"Everyone has a choice, Captain."

"Not everyone, mademoiselle. Choices are often stolen from us. As, unfortunately, yours has been."

"I have no choice in my current situation, 'tis true, but I can choose the direction my heart takes, and I choose to continue to pray for God to deliver me. And I will pray for you, Captain. That you will repent of your evil ways and seek life in the arms of the Almighty."

Rafe ground his teeth together. Did these religious zealots follow him everywhere? "You have been praying for six days, mademoiselle. Perhaps God is too busy." Sarcasm filled his tone.

She glared at him below heavy lids. "Be on your guard, Captain Dubois. God is on my side."

Rafe opened his mouth to tell the exasperating woman that God was on no one's side, but her eyes fluttered shut, and she collapsed.

CHAPTER 5

Hot fluid seeped into her mouth. Spicy, bitter. It slid down her throat, stealing her breath. Grace jerked her head away. Her cheek brushed against something soft. The pungent scent of meat intermingled with the sting of brandy that bit her nose. Vague, nightmarish memories lurked like shadows in her mind, taunting her. Memories of her capture and a tall Frenchman with a heart of stone.

A hand gripped her chin and forced her face forward. Fingers that felt like rough rope and tasted of salt pried her lips apart. More hot liquid burned her tongue, poured down her throat, and she gagged. Raising a hand to her mouth, she sprang up, coughing. Dark eyes peered down at her, the spark of concern in them instantly hardening.

"Drink this, mademoiselle." Captain Dubois inched the bowl toward her mouth.

She pushed it away, shaking the fog from her head. "Can you not wait until I am conscious?"

"When you are conscious, you do not eat." A shadow of a smile played around his mouth. He rose from the bed and set the bowl atop a table.

Only then did Grace realize she lay upon a real bed. She scanned her surroundings. Two massive wooden chests ornamented in gold and bolted shut with iron locks guarded the wall opposite her. Upon the plush Persian rug at the room's center sat three colorfully upholstered armchairs. Beyond them, a cabinet housed a haphazard assortment of books, swords, pistols, and bottles. A large carved mahogany desk perched before a span of windows that stretched across the stern of the ship. Two guns, perched in their wheeled carriages, flanked either side, ready to be shoved through portholes should an enemy dare to approach from behind.

She was in the captain's cabin.

In the captain's bed.

With the captain looming over her, wearing that sardonic smirk upon his lips.

Her chest tightened. "Why am I in your bed? What day is it? How long have I been here? And why are you feeding me instead of Father Alers?" She glanced down at the loosened ties of her bodice, and a flush of horror heated her face. "How dare you?" She cowered away from him.

Captain Dubois raised his brows. "Which question would you like me to answer first, mademoiselle?"

"None." Grace swung her legs over the side of the bed. "I wish to leave this instant." But her body would not cooperate. Her breath caught in her throat. Her head spun like a waterspout upon the sea, and her legs quivered like pudding. She lifted a hand to her forehead.

A warm hand gripped her arm. "I suggest you lie back down, mademoiselle, and eat something. It has now been seven days since you have partaken of a full meal."

Grace shifted from beneath his touch and gazed out the windows where the rays of the morning sun angled across the captain's desk, setting the brass lantern aglitter. The glow lit the quadrant, backstaff, charts, and quill pen and beamed off a rapier, setting aglow the amber liquid in a half-empty bottle.

"Mercy me, I slept here all night?" She snapped her gaze to Captain Dubois. The possibility sped through her mind, seeking an alternative, any alternative besides the one that her purity could never consider.

He grinned, yet a spark of playfulness flitted across his dark eyes. Remembering the loose bindings of her bodice, Grace threw a hand to her chest. "What have you done?" Terror crowded in her throat.

He gave a derisive snort then shook his head and gripped the baldric strung over his white shirt. "Never fear, mademoiselle. I prefer *mes conquêtes* to be awake." He sauntered to his desk.

Conquests. Grace swallowed, praying he told the truth, praying she had not become one of his conquests during her unconscious stupor.

He picked up a chart, examined it, then tossed it back to the desk, sending dust particles floating within a ray of sunshine into a frenzy that reflected on his face. Danger hung on his broad shoulders like a well-fitted cloak, but there was a depth to this man that went beyond the baseness of a common brigand, a depth that lurked behind those dark, smoky eyes. He spoke of a greater cause—what had he meant by that?

"You should not treat women as property to be conquered or sold to the highest bidder," she finally said. Grace clasped her moist hands in her lap, trying to stop them from trembling. "Intimacies"—her voice squeaked and she cleared her throat—"between a man and a woman should remain within the sanctity of marriage."

He turned, crossed his arms over his chest, and chuckled as if she'd told a joke. "Do spare me your proverbs, *mon petit chou pieuse.*"

"Did you just call me a shoe?"

A smile broke across his lips and widened. He chuckled. "Non. A little pious cabbage."

"A cabbage? Of all the. . ."

"It is a term of endearment." He waved a hand through the air, then settled his gaze upon her.

Endearment, indeed. More likely an insult to her intelligence. Fidgeting, she looked away beneath the warmth in his eyes. She'd never been alone in a room with a man other than her father. And Father Alers. What would Reverend Anthony say? Her reputation would be besmirched beyond repair. But what did it matter? Where she was going, she would not require a reputation.

He approached her. "You slept here because I feared your fever would return, and I loosened your bindings to allow you to breathe."

Graced fiddled with the ties. "Though I am appreciative of the clothes, Captain, the bodice is far too tight."

"Perhaps you are too fat." He grinned.

"Fat?" She jumped to her feet. The cabin spun around her. "You are no gentleman."

"And it took you only seven days to reach that conclusion?"

Grace sank back down to the bed, studying his cavalier attitude with curiosity. "You seem proud of your boorish behavior."

"I am proud of many things that would not engender your good opinion."

"Of that we are in agreement, Captain. But as I am sure you know,

'Pride goeth before destruction, and an haughty spirit before a fall.'"

He chuckled. "So, do you chastise me for being proud or being a boor?"

"Both."

"Yet you are the one who has fallen."

"I have not fallen," Grace snapped. "I am here for a reason."

"Oui, to line my pockets with gold." He smiled.

Grace's stomach knotted. She hated this man. She knew hatred was wrong. She knew it was as bad as murder, but at this moment, if she had a pistol, she would probably shoot him where he stood. "You are naught but a French rogue." She struggled to her feet. "I will leave now."

Captain Dubois blocked her exit. "This French rogue demands you eat something first, mademoiselle." He advanced toward her.

Grace sucked in her breath and retreated. Her foot struck the bed, and she collapsed back onto it.

Placing one hand on the edge of the mattress, he leaned toward her and laid the other upon her forehead. She flinched. "C'est bon. No fever." His warm breath wafted over her, bringing with it the smell of brandy. He righted himself. "Never fear, I have no interest in you, mademoiselle. My tastes lie in women *plus* agréables."

Grace tore her gaze from his and stared at the gold and purple sash tied around his waist and the leather baldric cutting across his chest. "I have no doubt in what direction your tastes lie."

"I have every doubt that you do, mademoiselle." He retrieved the bowl and handed it to her. "Now will you drink this, or shall I continue to pour it down your throat?"

"If I drink it, I fear it may end its journey upon your boots." Grace took the bowl and offered him a cautious smile.

The taut lines on his face faded. "I shall take that chance."

A tap on the door sounded, but the captain did not break the lock his gaze had upon her—an admiring, hungry gaze that set her nerves on edge.

The door creaked open and footsteps sounded. A man cleared his throat. "Capitaine, *s'il vous plaît.*"

Captain Dubois's features instantly stiffened, and he turned to face the cook. "Father." He cleared his throat and stepped back from Grace. "See to it that the mademoiselle drinks all of the broth, then escort her back to her cabin."

The captain grabbed his rapier from the desk, slid it into his sheath with a metallic *chink*, and stormed out the door.

Father Alers shifted sympathetic eyes her way. A stained red shirt hung loosely over his corpulent frame, dangling below his waist where it met black breeches that spanned down to sturdy buckled shoes. He huffed out a sigh of impatience but finally took a seat and scratched his thick beard. "Come along, mademoiselle, finish your broth."

With the captain's exit, Grace's heart returned to a normal beat. She sipped the meaty soup. The warm broth slid down her throat like an elixir and plunged into her ravenous stomach.

"His methods may be a bit severe, mademoiselle," Father Alers said. "He only wishes you to keep your strength so you do not fall ill again."

Grace took the last sip and then tested her legs. Though still shaky, she felt her strength returning. "You have been too long at sea, Father, if you think there is an ounce of kindness in that man."

Father Alers chuckled and stood with a moan, then offered her his arm.

She placed her hand in the crook of his elbow. "He only wishes to fatten me up for the slaughter."

Father Alers's only reply was a grunt as he escorted her out the door and into the dimly lit companionway.

The ship canted, and Grace was thankful for Father Alers's support as they made their way down the hallway and around a corner to her cabin—especially when they were forced to squeeze past several crewmen who ogled Grace as if she were the evening meal.

"I will bring you some more food soon. *Pour maintenant,* you should rest." He turned to leave and Grace, feeling light-headed again, sank into the only chair in her small cabin.

Halting, Father Alers faced her, a pensive look on his aged face. "The capitaine is not as bad as he seems."

Grace blinked. "He is selling me as if I were cargo to an enemy who will subject me to a life of pain. How much more evil can he get?"

Father Alers rubbed the back of his thick neck. Compassion softened the lines on his face.

Struggling to her feet, Grace took a step toward him. "You are not like him. You don't agree with what he's doing. I can see it in your eyes. Will you help me, Father? Will you help me escape?"

Golden eyes snapped to hers, hesitant, sympathetic, but then they froze like two ponds beneath a winter's frost. "Non, I could never deceive him. He has seen too much betrayal in his life." His curt tone slammed a heavy door on her hope. He shrugged. "I am hoping he will figure this out on his own."

"You cling to a hope of the captain's redemption while my life is being destroyed." The blood rushed from Grace's head, and she crumpled into her seat. " 'Tis a sin to know the right thing to do and not do it, Father."

"Peut-être, mademoiselle, but I've seen greater sins perpetrated every day in the Church." With a jerk of his head, he waddled out and closed the door.

Dropping to her knees, Grace leaned over the chair. "Why do You close all the doors to my rescue, Lord? If it is indeed my task to bring these nefarious men to redemption, please show me how. Give me the words to say. Please do not let me be handed over to this Don Miguel." Yet no answer came, no feeling of peace, no assurance of God's presence. Tears slid down her cheeks onto the chair just as droplets of her hope continued to seep from her heart with each passing day.

Rafe stood at the bow of *Le Champion* and closed his eyes against the hot, raging wind, allowing it to blast away the memory of Mademoiselle Grace: her scent that reminded him of the sweet pastries his mother used to bake, the silky feel of the mademoiselle's skin beneath his fingers, and those sharp green eyes that sliced right through his soul into his heart. *Femme exaspérante!*

He had barely slept two minutes all night. It wasn't the hard floor that kept him awake. He had slept on far worse in his day. It was the sound of her deep, restless breathing, her occasional quiet moans, and his concern that she would fade into a perilous fever and die during the night.

Finally, before dawn, he had risen, lit a lantern, and watched her as she slept. The way her lips twitched and her eyelids fluttered as if she were dreaming, the strands of raven hair curling across her cheek like feathers spanning a creamy river. Her delicate fingers coiled around her arms in a protective embrace. She appeared as fragile as a tender flower in the field, yet possessing enough tenacity to push above the others in her quest for the sun. Honesty coated her lips like honey. He doubted a lie would survive among its sweetness. And in a world where lies were commonplace, her candid jabs brought him more amusement than insult.

That she was innocent, he could tell from her reaction to him. That she possessed a gracious heart was evident from the errand in which he found her engaged when he'd captured her. That she nudged awake a long-dormant spirit of protectiveness within him caused his blood to boil.

He did not want to protect her. He did not want to admire her. He wanted to hand her to the don as planned and get his money. Why could she not have been pompous, churlish, and deceitful like the women to whom Rafe had grown accustomed among high society?

The ship rose and plunged over a wave, drenching him with salty spray. He opened his eyes and shook it from his face. Spyglass pressed against his boots. He picked her up and laid the damp cat across one shoulder. She purred her approval, and he ran his fingers through her fur.

Zut alors, why was the mademoiselle always in his thoughts? He flexed his muscles as if strengthening his defenses. He must. He must hand her over. The money she would bring would save hundreds of lives. What was the fate of one pretentious girl compared to that? And pretentious she was, full of the same religious banalities he had been beaten with all his life. She was more like his father than he realized. He must look beyond his reaction to her, beyond her admirable qualities, and remember that fact.

A slap on his back startled him from his thoughts. "What brings you here to the fo'c'sle, Captain?"

Rafe turned to see his friend, Monsieur Thorn, smiling at him. He had been a good friend, Rafe's only friend this past year. "Clearing my head."

"Ah, the lady is quite enchanting."

"My thoughts were not directed toward her." Rafe grimaced at his friend's discernment.

"Indeed?" A coy grin lifted the lad's thin lips. "Has she recovered from her illness?"

"Oui." Rafe laid a hand on Spyglass and braced his boots on the deck as the ship plunged over another swell.

"Captain." Thorn cleared his throat and adjusted his hat. "Has the lady's family laid some unpardonable insult upon you? For I've yet to see you barter in human flesh."

A spark of shame seared Rafe, but he drowned it under his rising ire. Had his whole crew gone soft? "She is a woman, and her father is an admiral in the British navy. Need I say more?"

"I was in His Majesty's service, Captain, as were several of your crew. And yet you do not despise us."

Spyglass ceased her purring, and Rafe began caressing her again, resurging her soothing tones. "You quit the navy, as did they, because your conscience could not bear their cruelty. How can I fault you for that? Instead, I applaud you."

Monsieur Thorn rubbed the scar on his neck and gazed across the choppy sea. "We should be coming alongside Inagua Island soon."

"*Bien.* Only a few more days to Port-de-Paix. I could use some time ashore." Where he could seek comfort in the arms of one of the town's many willing females. And distance himself from Mademoiselle Grace.

"What of the men? They haven't been paid since we sank the Dutch merchantman and delivered her crew and cargo to Monsieur Franco." Thorn fingered the feathery whiskers on his chin. "We wouldn't want a mutiny on our hands."

The sprinkle of glee in Thorn's tone bristled over Rafe's nerves, but he shrugged it off. They had all been on board this ship far too long. "The crew never complains about enjoying les *plaisirs* de Port-de-Paix. Besides, we will be there only a few days."

Dropping his hands to his sides, Thorn began clenching and unclenching his fists. He shifted his stance then gripped the railing.

Rafe frowned at his friend. Thorn was usually the essence of unruffled composure. "What has you so skittish, mon ami?"

His first mate's gaze darted over the horizon as if searching for something. He gripped the hilt of his sword, then scratched his chin before dropping his hands again. He shook his head and turned to Rafe. "What did you say?"

"You are jumpier than a cat on hot coals."

"Me? No. Just anxious to get to port." Thorn rubbed his hands together.

Rafe shook his head. As long as he had known Mr. Thorn, the man had never enjoyed the amenities of port, had often opted to stay on board when the rest of the crew went ashore. Especially in Port-de-Paix. No matter. Perhaps the man's long days at sea had changed his appetites.

Sunlight set the peaks of waves aglow in silvery strips that glittered as far as his eye could see. The smell of oakum, pitch, and salt filled his nostrils, and Rafe took a deep breath. He loved the sea. The ultimate playing field for those who craved danger, excitement, and freedom. They were the outcasts of society—those who did as they pleased and answered to no man.

A speck appeared on the horizon just as "A sail, a sail!" bellowed from the masthead. Setting Spyglass upon the deck, Rafe plucked the telescope from his belt and leveled it upon the intruder, wondering if perhaps the mademoiselle's family had pursued them. Thorn coughed beside him. Two red sails glutted with wind filled his vision, and from the white foam clawing the bow of the ship beneath them, she appeared to be rushing straight for them.

"Who is she?" Thorn asked as Rafe handed him the glass.

"Have a look."

Mr. Thorn peered toward the ship. "I can't make her out yet, Captain."

"Only one ship I know of has crimson sails."

"Captain Howell." The first mate lowered the glass. "Isn't he one of Roger Woodes's men? I wonder what he's doing out here."

"Oui, one of his *laquais*, and he searches for pirates is my guess. Those who did not accept the king's pardon or who have since broken the accord."

"Then we have nothing to fear from him." Thorn slammed the glass shut and handed it to Rafe, but not before Rafe heard the slight tremble in his voice.

"I trust no one." Rafe crammed the spyglass into his baldric. "Ready the guns, but do not run them out. And send the men aloft in case we need to unfurl topsail."

"Aye, Captain." The first mate touched his hat, spun on his heel, and marched away.

Within an hour, Rafe could easily make out the schooner *Avenger* crowding every stitch of her red canvas and housing a full tier of guns fore and aft. Captain George Howell stood regally at her helm.

Rafe's gut churned. What did Howell want with him? He glanced upward where the flag of France flapped regally from *Le Champion*'s foremast. There were no hostilities between France and Britain, unless some war had broken out of which he was unaware.

But he didn't have to wait long for an answer as the *Avenger* veered to larboard and ranged up alongside *Le Champion*. One by one gun ports popped open, and the charred muzzles of twelve guns bade him welcome.

A thunderous boom roared across the sky and shook the sea.

CHAPTER 6

Boom! Grace jerked awake. A colorful pattern blurred in her vision. She rubbed her eyes. The pattern came into focus, and she realized it was the upholstered back of the chair she knelt beside. The bulkhead quivered. The planks shook beneath her legs. Her heart seized. She sprang to her feet. Ignoring her dizziness, she bolted for the door. A gun had been fired. That meant an enemy was in sight. And that carried the possibility of her rescue. She darted down the companionway and up the ladder, praying that perhaps her sister Faith had somehow found her. *Oh, Lord, let it be so!*

Pushing aside her fear, she rushed across the deck, weaving among the sailors dashing here and there as they obeyed their captain's orders. Gripping the railing, she batted away the smoke and peered toward a two-masted ship bearing down upon them off their larboard bow. Red sails, stark against the blue sky, gorged with wind as they pushed the vessel onward. Her heart sank. 'Twas not her sister Faith's ship, the *Red Siren*. But perhaps the ship's captain might still be noble enough to save her from these villains. She coughed as the dissipating smoke stung her nose.

"Sacre mer, what are you doing? Get below, mademoiselle!" Captain Dubois clutched her arm and dragged her to the companionway hatch.

"Who are they?" Grace could not keep the hope from her voice.

"Ah, you think they are your *sauveteurs*, your champions, eh, mademoiselle?" He raised a brow then released her arm. "Je t'assure, they will not save you. Now get below. I have no time for this."

"The *Avenger* wishes a parley, Captain," Mr. Thorn shouted from the quarterdeck.

Swerving away from Grace, Captain Dubois darted to the bulwarks. His men ceased their frantic activities and formed an audience upon the main deck. Grace slunk into the shadows beneath the quarterdeck. She would not allow her fear to send her below when a possible rescue was at hand.

The schooner ranged up alongside them keel to keel within twenty yards, and her captain, a brawny man with a full beard and plumed tricorne hailed them in a powerful voice. "I am Captain Howell of the *Avenger*."

Captain Dubois leapt upon the gunwale and grabbed a backstay for support. "I know who you are, monsieur." His deep tone full of cheerful insolence held not an ounce of fear. With his tricorne atop his head, his gray coat flapping in the breeze behind him, and the sun glinting off the long rapier at his side, he appeared every bit the pirate he claimed he was not.

"We come with the compliments of Captain Roger Woodes," the man bellowed, waving his plumed hat through the air, "who bids you to haul down your colors and surrender your ship."

Coarse chuckles bounded over the sailors, and Grace wondered what they found so amusing. She had heard of Roger Woodes, the ex-pirate turned governor of New Providence—a man who thought nothing of rounding up his one-time colleagues and stringing them upon the scaffold.

"For what reason, monsieur?" Captain Dubois asked.

"For the crime of piracy," boomed the captain of the *Avenger*, who replaced his hat atop his head and began fingering the hilt of his sword.

Snorts of derision replaced the laughter among the crew, and Mr. Thorn broke away from the agitated mob and retreated toward the starboard side of the ship as if frightened of the altercation. But when his eyes met Grace's, only malevolence brewed within them.

"With my compliments," Captain Dubois shouted, "you may tell Governor Woodes that I am no pirate and as such, am in no position to surrender anything." He turned and whispered something to a sailor behind him, sending the man scampering below.

"Most unfortunate, Captain, for I have been instructed to blast you from the sea should you resist." Howell's laughter bounced over the sapphire waves between them, silencing all within its hearing upon the deck of *Le Champion*.

All save Captain Dubois.

"By all means, I beg you to try, monsieur." Captain Dubois swept his hat out before him, hand on his heart.

Seeing that she only had a few moments before the battle began, Grace rushed to the railing, waving her hands through the air. "Captain Howell! Captain Howell!"

The man halted and squinted in her direction. She continued, "I am a prisoner aboard this ship. I am the daughter of Admiral Westcott. Please save me!"

Instead of the expected look of horror on the captain's face, followed by his quick action to save her from these scoundrels, the man chuckled, put his hands on his waist, and replied, "What is that to me, miss?"

The crews on both ships broke into coarse laughter as Grace's heart sank to the deck. One of the sailors fired a pistol into the air, initiating the battle, and Grace attempted to go below but found her feet would not move—no longer from curiosity, but from pure terror. Instead she uttered a prayer for the souls on both ships, herself included.

Captain Dubois, on the other hand, stormed the deck with all the confidence and courage of a man born to lead, his crew close on his heels awaiting his commands.

"Haul foresheets to the wind!" he bellowed, and seconds later the ship lurched and sped on its way.

A gust of hot air struck Grace, bringing with it the smell of salt and wood and the sweat of the crew as they readied for battle. Managing to pry her shoes loose from the deck, she crept toward the companionway just as the air reverberated with the thunder of guns. Streams of dark gray smoke spurted from the *Avenger*'s hull as the ship sped by their larboard quarter. Grace braced herself for the impact of their broadside. But instead of the jarring crunch of wood, the snap of coiled lines, and the screams of the injured, only hollow splashes met her ears.

"Bring her about, Mr. Thorn!" the captain shouted, planting his hands upon his waist and staring at the enemy as if they were naught but a temporary annoyance.

The ship yawed widely to starboard, and Grace flung herself against the mainmast to keep from tumbling across the deck. She gripped the rough wood. Splinters jabbed her tender skin. Above her, the sails clapped as loud as a cannon blast. Sailors darted around her, some jumping into the ratlines with muskets in hand, others hauling shot to the various guns positioned about the deck. Curses filled the air and took flight on the wind, burning her ears, but the men took no notice of her.

As *Le Champion* veered on her tack, the *Avenger* slipped from Grace's sight. She lifted a silent prayer that the ship had slunk away in cowardice. But no such luck. The threatening red sails appeared again on the horizon like bloated demons flying through the sky. In minutes, the ravenous schooner swooped down upon *Le Champion*'s lee quarter with her rigging full of men and white foam salivating over her bow.

"They hope to board us." Captain Rafe chuckled. Doffing his coat, he laid it over the capstan and rolled up his sleeves as if he were commencing a day's work. The sash strapped about his waist whipped upon the gleaming metal of his rapier, whose pommel he now gripped with a tight fist.

"Load the swivels," he shouted. "And arm yourselves with hand grenades, men."

A furious rumble filled the air, and Grace clapped her hands over her ears. Small shot from the *Avenger*'s swivel guns whistled through *Le Champion*'s shrouds, ripping holes in her canvas and sending the sailors into a frenzy.

Grace threw a hand to her throat to still her chaotic breathing then swept a gaze over the deck for injured men. But she saw none. *Thank You, Lord.*

"Strike their rigging only," the captain ordered.

Before her eyes could locate him, Mr. Thorn shouted, "Fire!" and the air was set aquiver with the roar of guns.

Sooty smoke blasted over Grace, stinging her eyes and nose. She gasped for air, then peered through the haze. The men aboard the *Avenger* staggered back beneath the onslaught and made haste for the stern of their ship. Their captain stood by the helm, spewing a string of unending commands.

The *Avenger* continued on its tack, cruising by *Le Champion*, its occupants scurrying back and forth across the deck like ants upon an upturned anthill.

Rafe nodded to Mr. Thorn, who in turn yelled to a man standing at the entrance to the companionway. "Fire the crossbar!" A second later, a gun exploded in a thunderous *boom* that shook *Le Champion* from truck to keelson. Grace squeezed her eyes shut, fearing the ship would be rent apart by the force.

A massive crunch filled the air, followed by the eerie snap of wood.

A shout of victory ensued, and Grace opened her eyes to see the rigging upon the main and top mizzen sails of the *Avenger* fold into a tangled mass of rope and spar. Without their mainsail, the *Avenger* groped listlessly through the sea. Their captain charged toward the stern as if he would jump the distance between the ships and pummel Captain Dubois to the deck. Instead, all he could do was raise his fist in the air and assault them with his foul mouth. Captain Dubois leapt upon the gunwale and gave a mock bow. "Another time, perhaps, Capitaine. *Mes compliments à* Woodes." Chuckling, Captain Dubois slipped down to the deck where he was engulfed with cheers from his men.

His white shirt flapped in the breeze. The tanned skin on his chest and neck glistened with sweat in the noonday sun. He ran a hand through his coal-black hair, and his eyes latched upon Grace—dark eyes, flashing from the heat of battle. A shiver ran through her, the cause of which she could not explain. Fear, perhaps? More likely disgust at how easily he resorted to violence.

Tearing her gaze from him, Grace released the mast, ignoring the pain in her hands, and took a tentative step with her trembling legs. Her stomach lurched, and she was thankful the broth had long since digested, or she feared she'd lose it upon the deck. She'd never been in a gun battle. Everything had happened so fast, she hadn't time to consider that she could have been torn to pieces by a twelve-pound ball of metal. But now as relief flooded through her, she began to shake uncontrollably. She made her way to the companionway, hoping to manage a quiet exit, when she saw a gray mound rising out of the sea off their larboard side.

"Sir," she called to one of the crewmen who was passing by—a young, lanky lad with a braid of brown hair hanging halfway down his back. He turned to her, surprise and delight brightening his sun-baked face.

"What land is that?" She pointed to the sight on the horizon.

"'Tis the island they call Inagua, miss."

"It appears so close."

"A mile or two, aye." He started to leave.

Grace grabbed his shirt, but quickly released it, not wanting him to think her wanton.

"What is your name?" She attempted a coy smile as a sour taste filled her mouth. How did her sisters feign such coquettish mannerisms?

"Andrew Fletcher, miss."

Grace leaned closer to him. "Mr. Fletcher, may I ask where we are heading?"

Huzzahs and hurrahs blared from the crew. The young sailor glanced nervously across the deck as if seeking his captain's permission.

Grace wondered if he or any of the crew were aware of the reason she'd been brought on board. "I am a prisoner, Mr. Fletcher. What harm would it do to tell me?"

He faced her and nodded. "We should arrive at Port-de-Paix in two days' time, miss. I'm told we'll anchor there for only a short while before setting sail again."

"Thank you." Grace smiled.

He gave her a curious look before being whisked away by his companions who passed around bottles of some vile alcohol in celebration of their victory.

Port-de-Paix? That would mean they'd be anchored close to land. Close enough to swim—or float—to shore. A daring idea began to form in her head.

CHAPTER 7

Grace released Father Alers's arm and entered the captain's cabin. The desk and chairs had been pushed aside, the Persian rug rolled up, and in its place sat a long wooden table laden with steaming platters of food, mugs filled to the brim, decanters of wine, and brass candlesticks. Pewter plates shimmered in the flickering candlelight, and the spicy scent of pork and the pungent smell of cheese swirled about her. At the head of the table sat Captain Dubois and lining each side were members of his crew, some of whom Grace recognized, and all of whom jumped to their feet at her entrance. Including Captain Dubois, looking rather dashing in his black silver-embroidered coat and gold and purple sash tied about his waist. He had tamed his unruly mane into a slick style which he tied behind him, revealing a strong jaw which flexed beneath a sprinkle of black stubble. His white shirt, devoid of its normal stains and wrinkles, appeared oddly out of place upon his broad chest. And without his pistols and knives draped across it, he could almost pass for a gentleman attending a soirée.

Almost.

Behind him, through the stern windows, the sea and sky melded into a smoldering curtain as dark as the captain's gaze.

Father Alers gestured to an empty seat at the opposite end of the table. All eyes remained fixed upon Grace as if the men had never seen a woman before, and she began to regret accepting the captain's invitation to dine with him and his officers.

She stepped forward and raised her chin. "Have I been invited to partake of a meal, or am I to be the meal itself?"

Chuckles rumbled around the table. Mr. Thorn coughed, and one side of Captain Dubois's lips lifted in a sly grin that sent an uncomfortable quiver through her belly.

"Whichever you prefer, mademoiselle."

"I prefer that you turn this brig around and take me back to Charles Towne at once."

"That is not one of your choices." He raised a brow.

"Then what exactly are my choices?"

"To dine with us or return to your cabin hungry." Cocking his head, he sent her a lazy grin.

Grace bit her lip and scanned the men. A chill pricked her skin. She'd never envisioned herself dining with such depraved characters without benefit of chaperone, without a proper escort—without protection. And though she'd love nothing more than to turn and make a mad dash down the companionway, if God had placed her aboard this ship to convert these men, she couldn't accomplish that task alone in her cabin. Which was why she'd accepted the captain's invitation. And why she must now stay.

"I will remain, but not because it pleases you." She didn't want to inflate the captain's already billowing pomposity. Nor did she want to hide her loathing for him, God forgive her.

Captain Dubois rubbed his chin and gave her a haughty look. "Mademoiselle, I find no pleasure in your company. En fait, it was Father Alers who suggested you join us."

Heat flushed up her neck at his insult. *Insolent cad!* She'd like to tell him that she found no pleasure in his company either, but she knew that wouldn't be a very prudent thing to say.

Nor a very Christian thing to say.

"Our food grows cold." He waved a hand as if brushing her away.

Father Alers gestured again toward her chair. "S'il vous plaît, mademoiselle?"

Gathering her courage along with her skirts, Grace slid onto the wooden seat. Without hesitation, the men sat down and began piling food onto their plates as if it were their last meal.

"Please, gentlemen. Shouldn't we ask God's blessing first?" Grace raised her voice over the clank and clatter of silverware and plates.

Groans filled the room. Hands halted in midair. Looks of derision shot her way as one by one, the men lowered themselves back in their chairs and dipped their chins.

Grace sought some measure of support from Father Alers but found only a hint of surprise mixed with curiosity lifting the lines on his face.

Captain Dubois, on the other hand, shifted his jaw in impatience and nodded for her to continue.

Grace bowed her head. "Father, we thank You for the bounty that You have provided this night. Please bless it, and may we always be thankful for Your goodness."

The clank of spoons resurged like a rising swell before a storm.

"And Lord," she shouted. "I ask You. . ." Huffs and moans rippled across the cabin, ending in silence. "To open the eyes of these men so that they may see You and know You. Amen." Grace lifted her face.

The men stared at her, their mouths agape as if she'd asked for lightning to strike them.

Ignoring them, she swallowed a lump of fear and nodded toward a steaming platter in the center of the table. "The pork, if you please, Mr. Alers."

He smiled and handed her the tray as the men resumed their feast, rudely grabbing platters and bowls without discretion and shoveling food onto overstuffed plates, reminding Grace of pigs before their slop.

She took a bite of the meat and though it was tough, the spicy, rich taste burst in her mouth and was welcomed gladly by her stomach. Having consumed three meals yesterday, she found her strength returning in full force. "Did you prepare this feast, Father?"

Captain Dubois chuckled and poured amber liquid into his glass from a flagon.

"Address me as Monsieur Alers, s'il vous plaît," Father Alers said. "Mais oui, mademoiselle. I did."

"It is quite good." Grace grabbed a biscuit from a platter in front of her. "Thank you for all your hard work."

Again the men stared her way, and Father Alers smiled. "Finally I receive some recognition for my hard work." He glanced across the table. "You could all learn manners from this lady."

The man to Grace's left belched in reply and poured himself another mug of what Grace assumed was ale. The bitter, grainy smell rose to join the fruity scent of wine, overpowering the savory aromas that filled the cabin. Grace lifted her own cup and found Mr. Alers had provided her with lemon-flavored water to drink.

Spyglass leapt onto the captain's lap, but instead of pushing her aside, Captain Dubois set down his glass and offered the feline a morsel of his food. His expression softened as he coddled the animal, and Grace found his affection for the cat curious. She scanned her other dinner companions, who were too busy scooping pork and peas into their mouths to converse with one another. Captain Dubois took a bite of a biscuit and leaned back in his chair.

Grace shifted in her seat. "Captain, would you introduce me to your men, please?"

He narrowed his eyes and lifted his lips in pretense of a smile that seemed to hurt his face. "Mais oui." He flung out his arm and beginning with the man seated to her left, he introduced each sailor in turn: the ship's bosun, the carpenter, Mr. Thorn, then to her right, the helmsman, the second mate, and finally Father Alers.

Grace nodded at each man, her stomach tightening when her gaze landed upon the second mate, Mr. Weylan. She recognized him as the foppish man she'd seen on deck with two other sailors—the ones who had gawked at her with such alarming bawdiness. Even now, in front of his captain, Mr. Weylan took such brazen liberties with his gaze that Grace felt soiled by proximity.

She looked to the captain for assistance, but he busied himself refilling his glass. Why should she assume the captain could control his men's passions any more than he could his own?

⟡

Heat stormed through Rafe, and he poured himself another drink. Why was Mademoiselle Grace being so courteous? One would assume she was attending a soirée at a friend's estate rather than eating alongside dissolute, reckless sailors who held her captive. And now, those green eyes bored into him, condemning, slicing through him like emerald ice. He wouldn't have invited her at all, save to answer Father Alers's challenge that Rafe was somehow uneasy in the girl's presence. But in truth, his gut had been in a knot since she entered the room.

"Pleased to meet you, gentlemen." Mademoiselle Grace smiled, but the slight tremor in her bottom lip gave her unease away. She wasn't at all pleased to meet them. Then why ask for introductions?

She took a bite of cheese then washed it down with the lemon juice Father Alers had provided. Her rosy lips puckered, and Rafe had trouble keeping his eyes off them. Setting down her glass, she met his gaze briefly, then she gripped a chain that hung around her neck and glanced over the men. "May I inquire, gentlemen, what brings you into the captain's service?"

Monsieur Atton thought for a moment then raised a glass toward Rafe. "The captain's a fair man, a good seaman, and he's lined me pockets wit' many coins."

Rafe returned his helmsman's salute.

"Yet I have seen none of those coins in quite a while," Monsieur Weylan grumbled beneath his breath, and exchanged a quick glance with Thorn.

Rafe eyed the two with suspicion, hearing only pieces of the exchange.

Monsieur Maddock halted his spoon, overloaded with potatoes, halfway to his mouth, "Aye, 'tis been some time, now that I think about it." He tossed the mound into his mouth, dropping some onto his lap.

Rafe continued petting Spyglass, but his insides tightened like a sail beneath a hard wind. "You were all paid handsomely for our last job. I heard no complaints." He eyed each of the men but none would meet his gaze. "And we stand to make a fortune on our current mis—" He froze and glanced at Mademoiselle Grace.

Her face blanched and she bit her bottom lip. "Mission, as in me." Simmering green eyes rose to meet his. "No need to mince words, Captain. Everyone at this table knows what heinous future awaits me so that all of you can—how did you say it, Mr. Atton—line your pockets?"

Spyglass leapt from Rafe's arms to the deck, sans doute to escape the hatred firing from her eyes. Brushing away the twinge of pain caused by her scorn, Rafe preferred to focus on her courage and forthrightness, qualities he had not expected in a British admiral's daughter.

"Regardless." She squared her shoulders and glanced over the men. "You all should be ashamed of yourselves. Surely there are far more worthy and honorable ways to make a living!"

Rafe chomped on his biscuit, knowing he should be angry at her insult, but instead found himself amused by her audacity. His crew was not in agreement.

Monsieur Maddock, the carpenter, choked on his food. "Honorable, lud." He set down his spoon with a clank. "Beggin' yer pardon, miss, but what does honor have to do wit' anything?"

She leaned forward, spreading her fingers over the bare skin above her bodice. "Honor, sir, is doing the right thing, living the right way. Obeying God and those He places in authority over you. Honor has to do with everything."

"Honor never did me no good." Monsieur Atton, the helmsman sitting to Rafe's left, spewed crumbs over his plate.

The bosun, Monsieur Legard, pointed his spoon at her. "Honor is for the weak minded."

Her face crumpled. "But what does a man have, what can he acquire that can truly satisfy? 'Tis only what he does in the name of goodness, what he does for God that counts in the end."

"I quite agree, Miss Grace." Monsieur Thorn dropped a slice of cheese into his mouth and gave her a nod that grated over Rafe. His friend's pious prattle had become quite bothersome lately. And now, with the encouragement of a like-minded zealot, no doubt it would become far worse.

"Then pray tell, Mr. Thorn." Mademoiselle Grace's reprimanding tone rang through the cabin. "Why do you partake of such wickedness?"

Monsieur Thorn faced his captain, a supercilious smirk on his face, and Rafe leaned his elbows on the table. "Do enlighten us, Monsieur Thorn. Why *do* you keep such nefarious company?"

Monsieur Thorn hesitated and his face paled, but then he winked at his captain. "Perhaps to shine as a beacon of sanity amidst this treacherous mob. Or"—he shrugged—"perhaps I was in need of a holiday from the rigidness of society."

Rafe settled back in his chair, relieved that the brandy began to spread its numbing fingers through his senses. "Then you and Father Alers have that in common. He, too, feels the need to take a *répit* from the shackles of religious obligations."

"They are not shackles, Captain." Mademoiselle Grace shifted a gaze to Father Alers as if seeking an ally, but the father's focus remained on his food. "In truth, the love of God will set you free."

"Yet you are not free now, mademoiselle. Neither physically nor, it appears, in any other way." Rafe moved his chair back from the table, his stomach disinterested in the food he'd heaped upon his plate. "You do nothing but point a finger of condemnation on everyone around you. If this is freedom, you may keep your religion, mademoiselle."

"You mock me, Captain." Mademoiselle Grace hung her head, one delicate strand of ebony hair feathering over her cheek. "God is but a joke to you."

"That there is a God who created this world of pain and injustice would indeed be a joke—a joke upon us," Rafe shot back. When Mademoiselle Grace lifted her head and he saw the moisture that filled her eyes, he instantly regretted his tone.

"Such strong faith is quite admirable, mademoiselle." Monsieur Weylan said, drawing her gaze to him. He steepled his fingers together.

"Ye don't believe in God, ye cockerel." Monsieur Maddock chortled. "Don't listen to Weylan, miss. He'd say anything to win a lady's affections."

Rafe studied Weylan and the way he ogled Mademoiselle Grace as if she were a morsel of food on his plate. The vain peacock had a reputation with the ladies. His good looks, fashionable dress, and cultured tone deceived them into believing he was a gentleman, when nothing could be further from the truth.

Yet, much to her credit, Mademoiselle Grace seemed undaunted by his flirtations; *en effet*, she seemed more repulsed than enamored.

Turning from him, she faced the men and spoke in a voice urgent with sincerity, "Mercy me, don't any of you believe in God?"

Monsieur Thorn finished the food in his mouth and took a sip of his wine. "I do."

"Mais oui," Monsieur Legard grunted.

"Haven't really taken much thought of it." Monsieur Atton shoveled a spoonful of peas into his mouth, sending one shooting across the table like a miniature cannonball.

Monsieur Maddock shrugged while Father Alers focused a convicting gaze upon Rafe.

"God is real." The pitch of her sweet voice rose. "He created this world, and He created you. He does not approve of such licentious living, wasting your talents on dissipation and thievery. There will come a judgment one day, gentlemen, and my hope, my desperate prayer, is that you will not be found wanting." Her eyes flamed with sincerity and true concern.

And Rafe knew she meant every word she said.

But he didn't have the heart to tell her she was a fool for putting her hopes in such nonsense.

Monsieur Legard took another swig of ale. A trickle ran down his bearded chin, and he wiped it with his sleeve. "You are fair to look at, mademoiselle, but you should pray the don is deaf. Your religious jabbering will drive a man *fou*—even a devout Spaniard."

Chuckles of agreement spanned over the table.

Rafe winced beneath Monsieur Legard's insult, and he opened his mouth to reprimand the man, but then he hesitated, his gaze shifting to Mademoiselle Grace, curious to see her response to the injurious affront.

Her cheeks reddened, and she glared at the man as if she would shoot him where he sat. But then her features softened like the settling of waves upon the sea, and she gave him a sweet smile. "I have been told I talk overmuch, Monsieur Legard. Please forgive me if I have offended you."

The man blinked then shook his head. "No offense, mademoiselle."

Rafe sipped his brandy, trying to quell the unease gripping his belly. Such charity in the face of insult and hostility. *Incroyable.*

Spyglass jumped into her lap, and she ran her fingers over the cat's fur. She met Rafe's gaze but quickly lowered her lashes. This evening could not be easy for her. Yet she'd accepted his invitation, and not only that, she had engaged the men in a discussion of what was important to her, no matter the cost to her dignity.

"D'ye think we'll see more of Captain Howell?" Monsieur Maddock shifted uncomfortably in his seat and faced Rafe.

"Non. I'd say he's been sufficiently humbled." Rafe chuckled, eager to follow the conversation on its new tack.

"He'll have to assemble a fleet next time to catch you, Captain." Monsieur Thorn lifted his mug in salute.

Monsieur Atton scratched his head. "I still can't figure out what sent 'im after us."

Monsieur Thorn coughed and poured himself more wine.

Rafe couldn't make sense of it either. He'd never committed piracy, and his reputation as a mercenary was well known throughout the West Indies. That Capitaine Howell sailed the Caribbean in search of him only made Rafe's job more difficult. As soon as possible, he would send a dispatch to Governor Woodes to inquire after the matter.

"How long will we anchor at Port-de-Paix, Capitaine?" Monsieur Legard scooped another helping of pork onto his plate.

"*Je ne sais pas.*" Rafe shook his head. Mademoiselle Grace continued to pet Spyglass, the cat's purrs filtering over the table. The woman had not eaten much of her food. Her shoulders slumped, and she seemed to have detached herself from the conversation. Rafe felt the loss immediately.

"Long enough for me to visit Mademoiselle Bertille?" Monsieur Legard asked, his eyes aglow.

"That trollop." Monsieur Weylan snickered.

"She's no more trollop than the women ye frequent."

Mademoiselle Grace cringed.

"Jealous?" Weylan grinned.

"*Assez!*" Rafe slammed down his mug. "Hardly proper conversation with a lady present."

"If you'll excuse me, gentlemen." Mademoiselle Grace rose from her chair, cuddling Spyglass in her arms. "My absence will surely allow you to continue your engaging discourse without censure." She offered the men a weak smile.

Father Alers pushed his seat back, its legs scraping over the wooden deck. "I will escort you back to your cabin."

"Non. Allow me." Rafe stood, feeling the brandy swirl in his head. Steadying himself, he wove around the table and held out his arm while Father Alers gave him a curious look and resumed his seat.

Fear dashed across Mademoiselle Grace's eyes. She hesitated then set Spyglass down, nodding her assent but refusing to take his arm.

"C'est-ça." Rafe hid his disappointment beneath a shrug.

With a swish of her skirts, she followed him out the door and into the dark companionway.

"My men have not had opportunities to polish their social graces. My apologies if they offended you."

"They did not offend, Captain. I merely wished them to see the peril of their souls so they can choose God's love rather than continue in a life of sin." They passed beneath a lantern hanging on the bulkhead. Rafe noticed how its light sought her out and showered over her as if she were the only thing worthy on board the vessel.

"I would leave the fate of their souls up to them, mademoiselle, if I were you. They do not take kindly to religious reprimands. En effet, most left their homes to avoid such castigation."

He rounded the corner, opened the door, and ushered her inside.

She turned to face him. "I fear for your soul as well, Captain. I urge you to flee from this sordid life you have chosen before it is too late."

Yet no urgency or concern could be found in either her tone or in her expression.

Rafe cocked his head. "Before I sell you to the don, you mean?"

She looked down. "If that is my destiny, I accept it. But that is not why I warned you."

"I do not believe you care for my soul, mademoiselle. In fact, I think you despise me. Am I right?" Rafe laid a finger beneath her chin and tipped her head up to face him, longing to see a glimpse of emotion, a spark of feeling, anything that would prove him wrong.

But her eyes were as hard as glass. She stepped back, breaking their contact and sending a chill through him. "What do you expect?"

Rafe studied her. What *did* he expect? Nothing but the hatred he received. Why then, did he long for something else? Longing made him weak. And weakness was not to be tolerated. So, he attacked her where he knew it would hurt. "Are not Christians supposed to love everyone? Even your enemies?"

Sighing, she clasped her hands together and hung her head. "I love you as a fellow human being and a lost soul in need of God." She lifted narrow, spiteful eyes upon him. "But in truth, I loathe you and what you've done to me."

He tore his gaze from her hatred and feigned a chuckle. "Ah ha, mademoiselle has a crack in her holy armor. But at least you speak the truth and not lies."

She flattened her lips. "I am only human." Stuffing a loose strand of hair into her tight bun, she shifted her gaze to his, then away, then back again. "Why do you stare at me like that?" She retreated a step. "'Tis impertinent and rude."

"What do you expect from a French rogue? Is that not what you called me?" He leaned on the door frame and folded his arms over his chest. "I stare at you because you are beautiful." She was *la belle femme*, but in truth he did not stare at her for her comeliness. He stared at her because she hated him and he wanted to make her uncomfortable for it. He stared at her because a devilish idea began to hatch in his brandy-drenched brain.

"Outward beauty is fleeting, Captain."

"Perhaps. But while it is here, I will admire it if I please." He lifted his brows and tossed any propriety he still possessed to the wind. "Most women would offer themselves to me in the hope of buying their freedom."

The mademoiselle's face flushed to a deep shade of burgundy. Her chest rose and fell. She retreated even further and raised her chin. "I am not most women, Captain Dubois."

"But you do want to go home?"

"Of course." Her bottom lip trembled. "But not at the cost of compromising everything I hold dear."

Rafe studied her, desire and admiration warring within him. He nodded, conceding to admiration, then walked out and shut the door behind him before he gave in to the stronger emotion.

Suddenly five hundred pounds didn't seem a large enough sum for such an exquisite treasure. En fait, he wasn't sure any amount would be.

CHAPTER 8

Grace crept down the lower deck ladder, cringing with every creak of the wooden steps. She didn't know whether to hold her free hand to her nose to block the stench of rot, mold, and waste or to cover her mouth to stifle her nervous breathing that seemed as loud as the sea purling against the hull. She had hoped that perhaps her second trip to the hold wouldn't be as horrifying as the first, but as her heart cinched in her chest and her feet rebelled with each shuffle forward, she realized she'd probably never possess the courage of her sister Faith.

She took another step, and her shoes met the layer of muddy rocks covering the bottom of the ship. In the hold, heat seemed to take on its own persona and cling to whoever dared venture below as if in hope of escaping with them when they ascended. With the sleeve of her gown, she dabbed at the perspiration on her forehead, surprised at the damp chill seeping from the rocks through her shoes.

Lifting her lantern, she allowed its glowing circle to create a barricade of light around her. Perhaps a false barricade, for she knew not what crept beyond its borders, save for the rats she heard pattering away. But within its lighted walls sat an assortment of crates, barrels, and sacks broken from their bindings and scattered haphazardly wherever the sea had tossed them. She moved forward. More pattering caused her to shudder. At least the tiny beasts were afraid of the light. She'd have no such luck if she happened upon a sailor. Since it was well past midnight, most of them should be asleep, an assumption she confirmed by the barrage of snores that had assaulted her as she descended past the crew's berth.

All she needed was one more slab of wood to match the one she'd retrieved the night before. Just one piece of wood and she could return to her cabin.

She coughed and bent over, trying not to breathe too much of the foul air, focusing her thoughts on something else, anything else besides the stench suffocating her and the roast pork now roiling in her stomach. After the captain had deposited her in her cabin, she'd waited for hours as the ship drifted into slumber, pondering the sanity of her plan. But the captain's mention of bartering her purity for freedom only increased the urgency of her escape.

Standing tall, she threw back her shoulders. *Be strong and of a good courage; be not afraid, neither be thou dismayed: for the Lord thy God is with thee withersoever thou goest,* she thought, quoting from Joshua. But the bold words sank to the deck beneath the dank, weighted air. Did she believe them anymore? Truth be told, she did not feel God's presence at all. Which is why she must take measures into her own hands. She took a step forward and scanned the cargo for the broken crate she'd stumbled upon—or stumbled over—the night before.

A gray streak flashed across her vision, and before she could swerve the lantern to see what it was, it sprang at her and landed on her chest. Sharp claws and soft fur scrambled over her skin. *A rat! A large rat!* She screamed. Stumbling backward, she tried to swat the beast away. The lantern slipped from her hand, struck a crate, and hit the deck with a clank. The flame flared, sputtered. . .then went out. Thick, inky darkness molded over her. The eerie creak and groan of the ship grew louder as if it were laughing at her misfortune. Her feet went numb.

The furry animal clinging to Grace's chest began to purr.

"Spyglass, is that you?" The cat nestled beneath her chin, her pleasing rumble soothing Grace's nerves. Releasing a sigh, she ran her fingers through the cat's fur and waited for the thumping of her own heart to slow and her feet to regain their feeling. "You frightened me, little one."

The ship pitched, and Grace braced her shoes on the uneven pebbles to keep from falling. She peered into the darkness. Not a speck of light. Not a glimmer. Nothing but charcoal black met her gaze. The hair bristled on her arms.

"Now look what you've done," she whispered to the cat. "Hold on, let me find the ladder, and I'll take you up to my cabin." Where she'd have to grab another lantern and come back down again.

A thump sounded. Her ears perked. Was that a boot step? Another thud. She turned toward the sound. A glimmer of light appeared from above, streaming down the ladder. Grace slunk backward, petting Spyglass, more to comfort herself than the cat. Her stomach tightened. *Lord, please help me.*

Spyglass continued to purr. "Shhh." Grace ceased stroking the cat, but the rebellious feline only rumbled her approval louder.

A man descended the ladder. Handsomely dressed in a laced waistcoat, gray sash, and trousers, with silver-plated pistols and a dagger in his belt, he raised his lantern above his head and squinted into the darkness.

Mr. Weylan.

A scrawny man in a checkered shirt and torn breeches slinked behind him, casting his gaze this way and that. A third man wobbled down the ladder after them, the wooden steps bowing to near breaking beneath his considerable weight.

The three men who had leered so blatantly at her on deck two days ago.

"We know yer down here, mademoiselle," Mr. Weylan said with a sneer.

Grace's knees quivered. How did they know where she was? She backed up and hit a stack of crates. One of them toppled to the deck with a bang. The men jerked their gazes her way, and all three grinned simultaneously. "There she be."

Mr. Weylan started toward her, his eyes gleaming with malice. He reminded her of her sister Hope's latest beau, Lord Falkland—the one she'd run away with. The same striking features, same debonair mannerisms, yet for those with discernment a facade covering the corruption within. The other two men came alongside her, the third one holding his lantern up to her face. Brown sweat streamed from the folds of his neck. Two yellow teeth perched along his bottom gums, like sentinels guarding an empty cave.

Spyglass leapt from Grace's embrace and darted up the ladder. *Traitor.* Grace swallowed and gathered her resolve. "What is it you want?"

Mr. Weylan chuckled and raised his brows at his friends. He reached out to touch her cheek. She jolted away.

He frowned. "We thought ye might want to accommodate us lonely sailors who've been out to sea far too long. We don't often come across *une femme si belle*."

A sickening wave of terror washed over Grace. "I don't know what you mean by accommodate, sir." Her voice came out in a rasping squeak. "But I seem to have lost my lantern and would appreciate an escort back to my cabin." Perhaps if she appealed to their male instinct of chivalry, they'd rise to the occasion.

Again she seemed to have said something amusing.

"We'd love to escort you, mademoiselle, wouldn't we, *messieurs*? That is, after you do us a favor." Mr. Weylan fingered the lace atop her neckline then dropped his hand to the ties of her bodice.

Grace slapped the offending appendage. "Shame on you, sir." Anger burned hot, snuffing out her fear. She eyed each one in turn. "On all of you! To take advantage of an innocent lady. The Bible says, 'As ye would that men should do to you, do ye also to them likewise.' Would you like someone to accost you?"

Again their chuckles filled the room. The man who was beginning to look more like the huge barrel he stood beside leaned toward her and drew a deep breath of her hair. "I'd love to be accosted, miss, if ye'd oblige me."

Grace's mind reeled. She must get through to these men. Were they so depraved that no goodness could be found in them? "Look inside of you, gentlemen. You are better men than this." She gave them an affirming nod. "God has made you to be better than this."

Mr. Weylan cocked his head and studied her while the other two snickered beside him. For a moment, Grace thought she had pierced the evil crust around his soul.

"God has nothin' to do with this," he scoffed.

Grace's hopes plummeted to the sharp pebbles beneath her feet. "On that I will agree." The metallic taste of horror filled her mouth. Her heart felt as though it would crash through her chest. "Do you wish to spend eternity in hell?"

"Hell don't scare me, miss. I'm livin' in it already." Setting down his lantern, Mr. Weylan approached her, devouring her with his gaze.

"I assure you, sir, you know nothing of hell." A chill bristled over her at the memory of her vision—a vision that if these men caught even a glimpse, they'd fall to their knees and repent right here. But at the moment, with their wicked intent toward her screaming from their eyes and dripping from their salivating lips, she wished them all the eternity they deserved.

Grace squeezed her eyes shut and screamed, but Mr. Weylan's hand smothered the sound. She tasted dirt and sweat and fish on his rough skin and braced herself for the assault. Seconds passed. The creaks and moans of the ship taunted her from all around. And something else. The thud of boot steps reached her ears, then gasps and curses. Weylan's hand left her mouth.

Slam. Thud. Crash.

The sounds of a brawl pounded in her ears, and she pried her eyes open to see Captain Dubois dragging Mr. Weylan through a pile of sacks. The captain slammed him against the hull then gripped the man's throat until his eyes bulged and his face purpled. The other men struggled to rise from the deck, where they'd obviously been tossed, and rushed to the aid of their friend.

Grace shrieked, and Captain Dubois released Mr. Weylan, swung about, kicked the scrawny man in the stomach, sending him crashing backward into a stack of barrels, while he drew his rapier and leveled the tip upon the other. Fury stormed from the captain's dark eyes. His hair hung in black strands about his face. "You dare attack your *capitaine*, Holt?"

Mr. Weylan groaned from his spot on the deck, gripping his throat and gasping for breath. "*Et vous*, Monsieur Weylan?" Rafe shot over his shoulder.

"We jest wanted some female companionship, Cap'n." The portly man that Dubois held at the tip of his rapier offered a conciliatory grin and shrugged. "We's lonely men."

"You'll be even lonelier when I toss you overboard." Captain Dubois pressed the blade upon Holt's chest, drawing a drop of blood that stained his brown shirt.

The lanky man emerged from the barrels, pressing a hand against his back.

Grace's fear resurged. Could the captain handle all three?

"Ye shared the last woman on board." Mr. Weylan rose to his feet, still clutching his neck.

"*You* shared the last trollop, not lady, and she came aboard willingly. I never touched her." The captain lowered his blade and wiped the sweat from his brow.

"What do it matter?" Holt jerked a thumb in Grace's direction. "This one's ending up a Spanish whore anyway."

Without hesitation, the captain slammed his fist across the man's jaw. Holt spun around beneath the blow and stumbled backward, crashing to the deck. Grace threw a hand to her mouth, both in shock at the violence she witnessed and the speed with which the captain came to her honor. But why would he? When he was the one leading her straight into dishonor?

The captain turned on Mr. Weylan, who fingered the handle of a knife stuffed in his belt.

"Make sure you know what you are doing, mon ami, before you draw that." Captain Dubois snapped his hair from his face. Behind his back, the skinny man shook his head at Weylan, his eyes wide.

Mr. Weylan released the handle with a huff. "This isn't a British warship, nor even a pirate ship, and we have signed no articles." His jaw tightened beneath eyes alight with fury. "Someday you'll regret this, Captain."

"I never regret," came the captain's sharp reply. "Now off with you. And if I see you so much as glancing at the lady, I'll string you up on the yardarm."

Amidst a cacophony of grunts and curses, the men eased by Captain Dubois, Mr. Weylan rubbing his neck, the skinny man his back, and Holt his jaw. They disappeared up the ladder.

Sheathing his rapier, Captain Dubois ran a hand through his hair and faced her. "*Allez-vous bien?* Are you all right?"

Grace tried to find her voice, but her heart still hung in her throat. The harsh lines on the captain's face softened, and she found herself mesmerized by the way the lantern light flickered across his dark eyes. It was the concern burning within them that set her aback. Could the man actually have some goodness in his heart? She rubbed her own eyes. Perhaps she was too tired or the light too dim. He had saved her for no other reason than the protection of his property. Hadn't he?

He took a step closer, so close she could smell the brandy on his breath. "Did they hurt you?" He eyed her from head to toe.

Grace lowered her gaze. "No. I am fine."

His countenance stiffened. "Sacre mer, what were you doing down here, mademoiselle?" He backed up and snorted. "If you wish to be ravaged, then by all means, let me know and next time I shall remain in my bed."

In his bed. Now that her mind no longer reeled in fear, she noticed he wore no boots and his shirt hung loose instead of being tucked into his breeches. Even the belt housing his blade hung haphazardly about his hips. "How did you know I was down here?"

"Answer my question first." He cocked his head.

"I was looking for something." Grace bit her lip, not wanting to lie.

"*Qu'est-ce que vous recherchez?*"

Grace squared her jaw. "*You* must answer *my* question now."

A hint of a smile lifted his lips. "Spyglass woke me. She clawed into my cabin and would not stop meowing. The last time she did that, a thief snuck on board and had captured one of my crew. So I thought I should *enquêter sur*"—he paused and flattened his lips—"how do you say, investigate."

Grace blinked and let out a tiny chuckle, amazed she found anything amusing amidst her subsiding terror.

Captain Dubois swept a hand toward the ladder. "May I escort you back to your cabin, mademoiselle, or do you prefer to spend the night in the hold?"

Grace allowed him to lead her up the two decks to her cabin, reluctantly taking his proffered arm lest she collapse beneath her still-trembling legs.

Sweeping open her door, he ushered her inside, and then he set down his lantern. Spyglass slipped in after them, perched upon the table, and began licking her paws then wiping them over her face as if pleased with a job well done.

The corner of the slab of wood Grace had retrieved the night before stuck out of the open armoire. She hastened to stand in front of it and whirled around, her stomach tightening. If the captain saw it, he'd no doubt remove it from her cabin, and with it, her last hope of escape.

Rafe studied the baffling woman. She possessed an intriguing mixture of courage, purity, and strength in the midst of delicacy he had not seen in any lady he had encountered. And he had encountered quite a few ladies in his day. Such pluck, such bravado in the face of certain assault. He could still hear the admonition she'd expounded to the trio of brigands as they were about to ravage her. He'd been barreling down the ladder, following Spyglass, when those words drifted up to him, halting him in his tracks, jarring him to his soul—that God had made them to be better men—that they *could* be better men. Even now, he couldn't shake the words from his mind. But then she had spewed her pious condemnations upon the men, jolting Rafe back to reality—people who professed to follow God sat in judgment on others.

Mademoiselle Grace splayed her fingers over the skin above her gown and looked away. "You are staring at me again."

Rafe's heart leapt at her innocence. "Next time you find yourself in such a precarious situation, mademoiselle, might I suggest you avoid the moral censure. Men who would accost a lady have no care for what the Bible says. You will only infuriate them. Your God will not save you upon your insult to others."

"I was not insulting them. I was telling the truth. And God did save me. He brought me you." She swept her green eyes back to him—sharp, clear, convicting.

"I accept your gratitude." He bowed, longing to see some spark of appreciation for him on her face.

"You do not have it, Captain," she snapped. "Why should I thank you? You deliver me from the wolves only to feed me to a lion."

He winced inwardly, unable to deny that truth. Yet at the moment, deep down, he wished he had met this lady in a different time, in a different place, and that she was not the daughter of Admiral Henry Westcott. He ground his teeth together. What was wrong with him?

She seemed to sense his conflict, and the haughty veneer fell from her face. "Captain, return me to my home. I beg you." Her eyes moistened. "There are so many who depend on me. Not the least of whom are my sisters. Faith is so new to her beliefs, and Hope, my other sister." The mademoiselle sighed and wrung her hands together. "She ran away and we do not know where she is, but she will need me when she returns." She clasped the chain around her neck and stepped toward him. The vulnerability, the desperation, the appeal in her eyes softened the shield around his heart. "Surely you have family somewhere that you love?"

At the mention of family, Rafe's armor stiffened once again. "I have no family."

"But I heard Father Alers make mention of your father."

"My father is a beast." Rafe's back stiffened. "A man who beats innocent children and preys on young women. To me, he is dead." Why was he telling her this? he thought. What was it about her that made him want to tell her?

Her forehead wrinkled and she looked at him curiously. Heat stormed through him as he realized the irony of what he had just said. He clenched his fists. "Contrary to what you might think, mademoiselle, I am nothing like him." He turned to go, displeased with the course of the conversation and the way it made him feel.

She laid a hand on his arm, drawing him back by her touch. "Then behave differently, Captain. Take me home. I promised my mother, don't you see? I promised her I would keep my sisters close to God, that I would keep them on the straight path."

Rafe knew of promises. Promises that had been nothing but smoke and dust, here one day and then blown away with the trade winds the next. But something in her eyes made him want to believe that some promises could be kept, that some people could be trusted.

And that angered him all the more.

"Stay in your cabin, mademoiselle," he snapped, "or the next time I may allow the men their play."

She winced, but Rafe steeled himself against caring. He could not care. Would not care. "I will have Father Alers bolt a lock and chain to this door tomorrow, so that by the time we arrive at Port-de-Paix, you will be unable to cause any further trouble." He patted his chest, looking for the cheroot he usually kept in his waistcoat pocket, but he had not donned his waistcoat. He needed a smoke. A brandy. Anything. He needed to get away from this woman. "Come, Spyglass."

The cat shifted her one eye from Rafe to Mademoiselle Grace but did not move.

"Spyglass." He snapped at the rebellious feline, yet the cat remained. "Zut alors!" Rafe stomped out and slammed the door with a *bang* that echoed down the companionway. Even his cat was under her spell.

❧

Grace jumped as the door slammed. She sank into the chair. Spyglass leapt into her lap and began to purr. Petting the cat, Grace drew a deep breath and then released it, hoping to ease the tightness in her chest. Not just tight from the harrowing events below but from her time in the captain's presence. He befuddled her. She wanted to hate him. Did hate him. But then he had rescued her and the look in his eyes when she pleaded for her freedom. . .it was almost as if he cared. Regardless, she did not fear him as she did the men in the hold. Though he was as wild as the sea he sailed upon, she didn't believe he would hurt her. Sell her, but not hurt her himself. Instead she sensed an overwhelming sorrow in the captain, a hopelessness, and a passion so deep it seemed fathomless.

"I suppose I should thank you, little one, for saving me." She snuggled the purring feline against her chest. "A smart one, aren't you? Leading the captain to my rescue." She scratched beneath the feline's chin, and Spyglass nestled against Grace's cheek. "But I would go with the captain next time he summons, if I were you. From what I've seen, his temper is not to be trifled with."

A temper that flared at a moment's notice. Every time Grace saw a softening in his eyes, every time a hint of goodness crossed his face, he'd stiffen, as if being held at musket point. And he became hard as stone, unfeeling, uncaring, volatile—like a ship bracing for an enemy attack.

The chipped corner of the slab of wood peeked at her from the open armoire. She didn't dare risk another trip below tonight. Not with Mr. Weylan and his minions on the prowl.

She gulped at the fear clawing at her throat. "Lord, why have You thwarted my last hope for escape?" Releasing Spyglass, Grace rose and crossed to the tiny window. Darkness as black as coal blanketed the sky and sea so thick it seeped into her soul. But she couldn't let it. Grace must continue forward with her plan to escape—a plan made all the more pressing by the captain's threat to lock her in her cabin, and all the more harrowing if she couldn't procure another piece of wood. Regardless, she was willing to face anything in order to avoid the fate Captain Dubois had planned for her—even her own death.

CHAPTER 9

Rafe stood at the quarterdeck rail and watched as the island of Hispaniola blossomed on the horizon. *Home.* At least the only home he knew. Though a foreigner by descent, Rafe had been born on this island. His family had hailed from Bordeaux, France, but Rafe possessed no memory of the land of his heritage, and from what he'd heard of her atrocities, he was glad for it.

He gritted his teeth, still enraged at Mademoiselle Grace for putting herself in such a precarious position last night, and equally enraged at Weylan, Holt, and Fisk for daring to assault her, but most of all enraged at himself for allowing the woman to affect him so.

"You care for her." The words startled Rafe as Father Alers slipped beside him, two mugs in his hand. Rafe shook his head. The priest's uncanny ability to read Rafe's mind had, of late, become more of a nuisance than a wonder.

The smell of coffee rose and swirled beneath Rafe's nose. "C'est absurde. You've grown blind as well as deaf, old man. Is that for me?"

Father Alers handed him the cup. "Yet you knew exactly to whom I was referring."

"There is only one woman on board the ship." Rafe gave his friend a look of dismissal.

The priest huffed. "Drink it. It will dull the effects of the brandy you have been drowning yourself with."

Embracing the cup, Rafe allowed its warmth to penetrate his hands. "And why would I want to do that?"

"Because the liquor transforms your few redeeming qualities into demons. Because it hides what you truly feel inside."

The snap of canvas above Rafe muffled his chuckle. "I feel nothing inside but a desire to assist those who cannot provide for themselves."

"Ah." Father Alers sipped his coffee and stared across a rippling sea transformed into ribbons of diamonds by the rising sun. "The grand Captain Dubois, champion of the poor and downtrodden."

Rafe gripped the baldric strapped over his chest, wondering why he tolerated his friend. "Be careful, mon vieux. Your taunting words may be the death of you."

Father Alers grinned, revealing a bottom row of crooked teeth.

Rafe shook his head and glanced aloft. "Furl topsails, Monsieur Thorn!" He bellowed over the deck, and his first mate echoed his command, sending sailors scampering. They should make port in a few hours, and Rafe found himself unusually anxious to get off the brig.

"But what of Mademoiselle Grace? Is she not one of the downtrodden aussi?" A gust of wind lifted the father's gray hair until it circled him like a halo.

Rafe clenched his jaw, no longer wishing to speak of the lady below deck. "She is Admiral Westcott's daughter."

"Guilty by birth?" the man raised an eyebrow.

"*Précisément.* You know what His Majesty's Navy did to my mother. Do you think I would have accepted this job if the mademoiselle were an innocent?"

"On the contrary, she seems to be more innocent than you expected. Besides"—Father Alers waved a bony hand through the air—"you cannot punish the entire British navy for the actions of one commander."

Rafe grunted. "And why not? How many innocent people have they slaughtered?"

"How many of theirs have we?" Luis shrugged. "It is the way of war."

"My mother was at war with no one."

"Many suffer who are not soldiers during war."

Rafe slid a finger over his mustache. The brig crested a wave and spray came sweeping over her bow. He drew in a deep breath of the salty wind, seeking the sweet scent of earth and hibiscus that reminded him of home. Anything to assuage the anger, the bitterness, the guilt warring within him.

"You care for Mademoiselle Grace." The priest repeated the words that sliced through the air like a sharp blade.

"So you have said." Rafe feigned a nonchalant response.

"Then deny it."

Rafe took a swig of coffee, its soothing elixir sliding down his throat and warming his belly. "Care? I hardly know her, but I will admit she is a surprise. She intrigues me." He snorted. "The sentiment will pass."

"What will you do?" Father Alers rubbed his back and turned toward him.

Rafe narrowed his eyes against the glitter of the sun that reflected off the turquoise sea, then he glanced over his shoulder at the helmsman. "Veer three points to starboard, Monsieur Atton. Keep your luff."

Ile de la Tortue rose off their larboard bow like a giant sea turtle as its name denoted. Across from the once famous pirate haven, distanced by the Canal de la Tortue, the lush green mountains and white sands of Saint Dominique came into focus.

Father Alers cleared his throat and raised a gray brow, reminding Rafe of his question, though he needed no reminding; it had haunted him ever since he had brought Mademoiselle Grace on board.

What *would* he do?

Grace pressed her face against the porthole glass and peered at the harbor. The commands to bring the brig about and shorten sail blaring from above alerted her that they had reached Port-de-Paix. That and the splash of the anchor as it plunged into the shallow bay and the thud of boots and the clamor of excitement as the crew amassed on deck for their journey to shore. Ships of all sizes and shapes rocked idly in the sapphire water of the harbor. Grace squinted against the glare of the sun as she made out merchant brigs, slavers, barques, schooners, an East Indiaman, and other vessels she didn't recognize. Beyond them, docks jutted into the water, peppered with dark-skinned slaves carrying the goods from ships to warehouses and shops. Blue-green mountains loomed in the distance while the leaves of a multitude of trees glinted myriad variations of green in the noonday sun.

Grace rubbed the blurry glass but could get no clearer view. A knot formed in her belly. She'd heard Port-de-Paix had once been a notorious pirate haven. And although most of the seafaring brigands had moved their home base across the narrow channel to Tortuga and then to

Petit Goave, she wondered what remnant of debauchery had been left behind. Whatever villainous activities remained, Captain Dubois would no doubt be an avid participant. Though a small part of her doubted that assessment.

Early that morning, before they had sailed into the harbor, Mr. Maddock, the carpenter, had strung a chain through the latch on her door and clanked it shut with a padlock. True to his word, Captain Dubois had imprisoned her in this muggy fortress. For how long, she couldn't know. For as long as it took the crew to commit as many wicked acts on land as their depraved minds could conjure up, she supposed.

Stepping away from the porthole, she blew out a sigh. That was as close a look as she'd get at Port-de-Paix. Perhaps it was for the better. Even if she made it to the port floating on her broken crates without drowning—or worse, being picked up by some sailors—what would she do once she got there?

Hugging herself despite the heat, Grace began to pace across her tiny cabin. She reached the bulkhead in three steps and swerved about. A million fearful questions assailed her. Had Captain Dubois joined his men ashore? And who would keep his remaining crew at bay? Her heart took up a frenzied pace as the cabin closed in on her. She gasped for a breath in the stagnant air and perspiration streamed down her back.

"Oh, Lord." She sank onto the bed and dropped her head into her hands. "Please help me." Prayer was such a habit with her that she momentarily forgot God wasn't answering her pleas as of late.

I will never leave thee, nor forsake thee.

Grace looked up and batted the tears from her face. It was the first time she'd heard the Lord's voice since her capture. "Where have You been, Lord?"

I will never leave thee, nor forsake thee. The words repeated, and Grace bowed her head.

"I know Your Word says that, but I've had such a hard time believing it, Lord." Grace tucked a loose strand of hair back into her bun and gripped her stomach. Fleeting memories dashed through her thoughts— memories of the time when she brought medicine to the Jacobs family on the edge of the frontier and the Yamassee Indians attacked, memories of her father taken ill with smallpox, of her sister Faith in the Watch House dungeon about to be hanged for piracy. And all those times, God had answered her prayers and delivered her and those she loved.

"Forgive me, Lord, for doubting You. You have always been with me before. I just don't understand. Why is this happening to me? Why am I here? I have done no good. No one listens to me, especially the captain. They all continue in their wicked ways. They deserve their fate, but I have done nothing to deserve mine."

She glanced over the cabin. "Please help me understand." Her thoughts drifted to Hope, her sister who had run off with Lord Falkland over a month ago, much to their family's shame and disgrace. Too angry at her sister's foolish and licentious behavior, Grace had given up praying for her, for she had believed Hope also deserved whatever fate she received. Year after year, Grace had tried to instruct Hope in righteous living and turn her sister away from the path of sinfulness she'd so ardently chosen to follow. But to no avail. The silly girl would not listen. Yet, why was the vision of her sweet face ever before Grace? Haunting her, just as another vision haunted her. A vision of fire and a barren land and an unrelenting hot wind that brought no relief.

Shame pulled her to her knees beside the cot. She would use this time to pray. Not only for herself, but for Hope, for Faith and Dajon, for her other sister, Charity, and her father. And for Captain Dubois. Leaning her forehead against the scratchy counterpane, she poured her heart out to God.

Hours later, the chain upon her door clanked against the wood. Lifting her head, Grace tensed as the door opened, and Mr. Thorn entered with a tray of food.

He smiled. "It isn't much. Some dried beef and a hard biscuit. And the rum-sweetened lemon juice Father Alers insisted I give you." He set the food down onto the table as Spyglass pranced inside and darted to Grace. The scent of meat and butter jolted her stomach awake, and it began to growl.

"Looks like you've made a friend." Mr. Thorn nodded toward the cat and straightened his freshly pressed dark blue waistcoat, looking more like a gentleman about town than a sailor.

"Where is Father Alers?" Grace nestled Spyglass beneath her chin and slowly rose.

"He went ashore with the captain and most of the crew."

"And why have you not joined them, Mr. Thorn?" Spyglass nudged her chin, begging for more caresses.

He shifted his polished boots over the deck planks and shrugged. "I take no pleasure in the nefarious diversions the port has to offer."

She studied him, noting that the frequent smile he offered her rarely reached his eyes. "And yet you do not swear allegiance to God?" The ship creaked over a tiny roller, sending a splash of waves against the hull.

"I do not believe He requires it." Mr. Thorn stuffed a lock of his brown hair behind his ear and rubbed the scar on his neck with his thumb. "I fear, Miss Grace, He has left us to our own devices."

"I am sorry you believe so." Grace nuzzled her nose into the cat's furry neck.

"Your own situation is a testament to my belief, is it not?"

Grace set Spyglass down on her cot and crossed her arms over her waist, unable to find a suitable answer to the question she'd wrestled with for days. That God was with her, she now believed, but that He was not helping her as she wished was only too plain.

"Humph. I thought so." Mr. Thorn glanced over the cabin. His brows rose at the sight of her open armoire. "Ah, what is this?" He pulled out the piece of broken crate and a coil of rope and examined them.

Grace's heart clenched. " 'Tis nothing."

He arched a brow and gave her a devious look. "Methinks the lady has a plan."

Grace huffed. What did it matter if she told Mr. Thorn of her foolish scheme? "I did, but it was ruined when the captain put a lock on my door."

"And what precisely were you planning on doing with this?" He set the crate down with a thump. "Hitting the captain over the head?" He chuckled.

"Nay." Grace stifled a laugh. "But I wish I had thought of that."

He smiled, revealing a set of unusually straight, white teeth, and fingered the whiskers on his chin. "Zooks, quite bewildering. I don't believe the captain expected to find such a wildcat in an admiral's daughter."

"I don't know what being an admiral's daughter has to do with anything."

Mr. Thorn lowered himself into the only chair in the room, adding to Grace's uneasiness. Did he intend to keep her company all day? She eyed the open door and wondered how many crewmen were on board.

He seemed to notice the direction of her gaze. "I have a better idea, Miss Grace."

"Than what, Mr. Thorn?"

"Than your swimming ashore. I doubt you'd have made it to land without being picked up by even more unsavory sorts than you'll find on this brig."

A flicker of playfulness sparked in his brown eyes, and Grace wondered if his proposal involved the same thing the captain had in mind last night. But no, there was no desire in his expression—at least not for her. "What are you proposing, Mr. Thorn?"

"I am proposing to grant you your freedom."

CHAPTER 10

R afe leapt from the longboat onto the quay and ordered his men to shoulder the crates and follow him. He strode down the wobbling dock onto sturdy ground, bracing himself as he switched from sea legs to land legs. Doffing his hat, he wiped the sweat from his brow.

"Monsieur Dubois!" A familiar voice hailed him, and Rafe turned to see his old friend Armonde waving and heading his way. "We did not expect you so soon."

"*Bonjour,* mon ami. I did not expect to be here either." Rafe met his embrace. "But I needed some time ashore"—Mademoiselle Grace invaded his thoughts once again, but he shook them away—"and I have brought some goods for Abbé Villion. Have you seen him?"

"Oui, this morning at the church." Armonde dabbed at the sweat on his neck with his cravat. "How long will you stay? Let us have a drink together before you sail again?"

"*Absolument.* I'll speak with you later." Rafe watched his friend saunter away. Turning, he snapped at his crew to hurry behind him as the other longboat made dock, and Weylan led the men and the crates down the wharf.

Cheerful hails and greetings swarmed over Rafe as word spread of his arrival and people ran out to greet him. Smiling faces bobbed all around like waves lapping against a buoy, assailing him with their admiration and approval. Precisely what he needed to erase the memory of a pair of convicting emerald eyes and the shame that sliced through him in their wake. He was doing something good here, something worthwhile. His life had meaning, purpose, unlike so many who squandered their time, wealth, and energy on pleasing themselves.

His father, for one.

The thought of the man who'd sired him put a sour taste in Rafe's mouth. He hoped to avoid him during his stay at port. But then again, his father rarely tainted himself with the stench of poverty that lingered down by the docks.

"God bless you, Captain Dubois!" one old man yelled.

A haggard woman pushed through the crowd. "What have you brought for us this time, Monsieur Rafe?"

"Many good things." Rafe ordered his men to set down one of the chests. "Take the rest of the cargo to Abbé Villion, Monsieur Weylan, and tell him I'll be along shortly."

"Aye, Capitaine," Weylan snarled, obviously still angry over their altercation the night before. Turning, he barked orders to the men behind him who hoisted the remaining crates, chests, and barrels onto their backs and followed him down the muddy street.

⟋⟍

Shoving the tip of the oar against the hull of *Le Champion*, Thorn pushed the tiny cockboat away from the ship. A roller struck the bow and splashed over him, and he glanced at Miss Grace sitting among the thwarts behind him. "Hold on."

The lady, appearing much smaller in her new attire, smiled at him from beneath the floppy hat that perched atop her head as she gripped the sides of the small boat.

Thorn faced forward and continued rowing toward shore. This would trouble the captain sorely. Losing his precious cargo and the fortune that went with her. No doubt the crew would be furious, perhaps even mutinous when they discovered they were not to be paid anytime soon. He grinned and shoved the paddle through the swirling turquoise water, urging the craft onward.

The sun beat down upon him, and sweat began to trickle beneath his waistcoat. But nothing could sour his humor today. Finally something was going his way. A seagull cawed overhead and then dove toward the water, spreading its wings across the surface to scan for a delectable morsel.

Bells rang and voices brayed from the port as they drew near. Making his way around an anchored schooner, Thorn plunged his oar on the other side and pushed the water back. His muscles ached from the strain.

After spending a year with Rafe, Thorn had concluded that the only thing the man cared about was his precious ship and his ability to make money for the poor. Thorn hoped the captain had developed affection for his prisoner. It would make his revenge all the sweeter. Though Thorn wondered if Captain Dubois was capable of caring for anyone.

It was better this way. Miss Grace did not deserve the fate which the captain planned for her. Now she could return home. Tugging his hat down further on his forehead against the bright rays, Thorn thrust the oar through the choppy water. The sounds of splashing and gurgling rose like the guilt bubbling in his stomach for leaving her alone in Port-de-Paix. Wasn't he using her as a pawn to further his own agenda just as the captain was? No. He would give her enough money to convey her safely home. And since Rafe would be spending his days and nights in town in his usual manner—saturating himself with alcohol and women—and Thorn had volunteered to attend to Miss Grace's needs himself, no one would be the wiser. Thorn felt the heavy pouch hanging from his belt and smiled. If Rafe only knew that he was the one funding the mademoiselle's journey, no doubt he would be even further enraged.

Hot wind blasted over Thorn, cooling the sweat on his neck and forehead, and taking his guilt with it. There was no other way. When Thorn took Rafe's ship from him, everything that was important to the captain would go with it. Having Rafe arrested for piracy would have proved simpler, but Woodes had sent that imbecile Howell to do the job. The only other option was mutiny, but most of the men were loyal to the captain. Even so, Thorn had heard mumblings of discontent recently that gave him hope. Without the mademoiselle to sell, Rafe's position would become precarious.

Quite precarious indeed.

❧

Grace braced her oversized boots against the thwart in the wobbling boat and stared at Mr. Thorn's outstretched hand. "'Tis best if I do not accept your assistance, Mr. Thorn." She gave him a playful glance. "If I am to pass myself off as a boy, I must behave accordingly."

"Indeed." He withdrew his hand, his face reddening, and busied himself tying the bowline onto a piling. Gripping the rough wood of the dock, Grace struggled to hoist herself upon it but instead tumbled back into the boat. On her second attempt, she managed to extract herself from the rocking vessel but paid for her clumsy efforts with splinters in her hands, adding to the collection already planted there when she'd clung to the mainmast.

Mr. Thorn flipped the dock master a coin and led the way toward the main street as Grace did her best to strut behind him. Yanking upon the waist of her baggy breeches, she hoisted them so the hems wouldn't drag through the dirt. But her cumbersome clothes, coupled with the muddy street that seemed to wobble up and down as if the whole island were afloat, sent Grace nearly tumbling to the ground. Which she would have done if not for Mr. Thorn's quick reach and firm grip.

"It takes a while to get used to solid land again, miss." He quickly let go of her.

"Thank you, Mr. Thorn." She stopped to catch her breath. Tugging the brim of her hat lower over her forehead both to shield her eyes from the blazing sun and to hide her gender, she surveyed the port town.

The scene that met her gaze made her stomach fold in on itself. Worse than anything she'd seen in Charles Towne or Portsmouth. On a platform to her right, Africans—including small children—were being auctioned off. The obnoxious voice of the auctioneer spouted their strength and breeding capability as if they were naught but animals, while a bevy of boisterous planters vied for their bids to be heard above the uproar. Open taverns lined the street, filled to the brim with men laughing and sloshing their drink and half-naked women sprawled over their laps.

In broad daylight!

A mob of people in tattered clothes swarmed around something in the center of town. Somewhere in the distance a musket fired, and a scream pierced the air. Yet no one seemed to notice. An African woman with a basket of fruit atop her head sauntered by. Pigs and chickens ran freely through the streets. Grace's nose stung with the fetor of animal dung, human sweat, and rotten fish.

She was struck by an overwhelming urge to dash back to the boat and return to the ship at once. But no. God had finally heard her prayers and had offered her a way of escape. She would not turn her back on His gift of freedom simply because of her fears.

Mr. Thorn gave her a sorrowful look. "Sorry, miss. I know these sights must shock you."

She pursed her lips and shifted her shoulders beneath the overcoat. Perspiration trickled down her back, but she dare not remove the heavy wrap lest the curves of her figure betray her gender. And from the looks of things, enduring discomfort would be preferable to being discovered as a lady alone in such a place as this. " 'Tis not your fault, Mr. Thorn."

"I'll take you as far as the port master, miss." He handed her a pouch that jingled in her hand. "This should be enough to procure passage back home on one of the merchant brigs." He ran a hand over the back of his neck and gazed nervously about the street.

"Why are you doing this, Mr. Thorn? I sense it is not purely out of kindness for me."

"I'll admit it serves more than one purpose, miss." Tiny green flecks burned in his brown eyes, and he brushed a speck of dirt from his otherwise clean coat as if somehow his kind deed was ridding him of something troublesome.

Grace didn't want to know what. "Regardless, I thank you. I know you risk the wrath of Captain Dubois."

They headed down the street, weaving among the crowd of sweaty humanity and repugnant farm animals. "I can handle his wrath, Miss Grace," Mr. Thorn said. "What I fear is being left in some port with no job and no prospects."

As if offering them a vision of such a future, a man appeared on their left, slouching beneath a huge calabash tree. Before Grace drew within three yards of him, his fetid smell nearly stole her breath away, and she covered her nose. His scraggly beard hung down to his belly, and the dirt smudging his face made it difficult to ascertain his age. She started toward him, intending to see if there was something she could do for him, but Mr. Thorn nudged her in the other direction. "What are you doing, miss?"

"Who is that man?" she whispered.

"Naught but a lazy beggar, a thief."

Grace glanced over her shoulder in disdain as Mr. Thorn ushered her past him.

"Nay, he's young and fit enough to work. He prefers to steal his food." Disgust stained Mr. Thorn's tone. "There are many like him in town."

They had no sooner made it to the fringe of shops and taverns edging the road when Mr. Thorn halted, then slipped behind a horse tethered to a post.

"What is it, Mr. Thorn?" Grace stared at him wide-eyed.

"'Tis Captain Dubois." He inclined his head toward the center of town where there was a crush of people.

Ducking behind the horse, she crept along its side then peered around its neck. The captain conversed with a woman and her child. He leaned over, retrieved articles of clothing from an open chest, and handed them to her. The woman kissed his hand and bowed to him as if he were royalty before grabbing her child and dashing away. Grace shook her head to jar the perplexing vision from her mind. An old man shuffled forward, and the captain dipped into the chest and pulled out two bags, which the man immediately received with a gap-toothed grin.

Grace slunk behind the horse. "What is he doing?"

"He gives gifts to his adoring masses." Mr. Thorn's tone hissed with disgust.

"What do you mean?"

Mr. Thorn huffed out a sigh of exasperation. "After the captain pays the crew their allotment, he distributes the rest of his plunder to the poor here at Port-de-Paix."

Grace lifted a hand to her brow to quell the shock reeling through her head. She peeked back at Captain Dubois as he embraced an older woman, then back at Mr. Thorn. "Are you telling me that he doesn't pocket the money he receives for his nefarious deeds?"

Mr. Thorn flattened his lips and nodded. "Odd, isn't it?"

"Then he is some sort of Robin Hood of the seas?" Grace could not believe it. Every word the captain had spoken, every threat, every evil glint in his dark eyes, all led to the conclusion that he was as greedy as he was heartless and wicked. But this. . .this changed everything.

"Sickening, isn't it?" Mr. Thorn rubbed his bulbous nose and snorted.

Grace flinched at the man's disdain. "Why do you find it so?"

"The act is kind. The motivation may not be, miss." Mr. Thorn took one last peek at his captain, then glanced toward the brig. "But I fear I must leave you before he sees me."

Grace's heart clenched. Alone? In this riotous bedlam?

He pointed past the grappling mob. "See that building by the docks?"

Grace nodded as her gaze found the clapboard shanty surrounded by sailors.

"You should have no trouble bartering there for passage on the next ship leaving port." He gave her a reassuring nod. "There are always ships heading to the colonies loaded with sugar and coffee. I'm sorry I cannot help you any further. The captain hates nothing worse than betrayal and surely would toss me from his ship should he discover I have done this much."

Grace bit her lip. Her palms began to sweat. "But I do not speak French."

"Most merchantmen know a pinch of English, miss. Never fear. You shall be well." He tipped his hat and abandoned her to her spot behind the horse.

The horse's tail whipped through the air and struck Grace in the face. Jumping back, she coughed and swiped at her cheeks as laughter tumbled over her from the storefront to her left. Three men and one lady, who'd just exited the store, enjoyed the moment at her expense. The man spewed a few sentences in French, which caused more laughter.

Face hot, Grace tugged her hat farther down on her head. Then skirting the horse, she made her way across the street. At least they had not seen past her disguise. All she had to do was procure passage on a ship, and if it didn't leave right away, purchase a room in a tavern and hide away until it did. How hard could that be? But with each step, her boots sank deeper into the mud—a sticky black ooze that made it as difficult to move forward as it did to have faith that all would be well, as Mr. Thorn had said. Her chest tightened, and she plucked one boot from the sludge and forged ahead.

Grace stepped away from the trail of shops and into a web of people and horseflesh darting this way and that as they went about their business. And like a fly caught in a web, she got the distinct impression she was about to be devoured by its occupants. She threaded her way through the crowd, bumping shoulders with a bare-chested sailor and barely missing being crushed beneath the wheel of a carriage. French words shot toward her from all directions, some tickling her ears with their beauty, while others jarred her with their harsh tones. She had no idea what the words meant and from the looks of their source, she preferred it that way.

The clank of chains drew her gaze to a black man clothed only in tattered breeches, bent beneath a huge barrel that balanced on a back striped with the punishing marks of his master. Iron shackles bound his feet together.

Grace swallowed the burning in her throat. *Lord, such misery.*

Music bounced over her from an open tavern to her left. The smell of roast pig and bitter alcohol mixed with human sweat saturated the air.

Careful to keep her head down, she edged past the center of town and peeked at Captain Dubois, who had concluded his charitable business and was instructing his men to pick up the chest and follow him. She shook her head at the dichotomy. A rogue, a villain by all inspection, yet possessing a heart for the poor? She could make no sense of it and found herself staring at him as if the answer would come by her perusal.

He glanced up and stretched his back, their eyes locking. Heart in her throat, Grace tugged her floppy hat down and darted to her left.

And barreled into the iron chest of a massive man.

"*Garçon stupide! Regardez où vous allez!*" He shoved Grace aside and she tumbled into the mud. The man spat on the ground beside her then snorted and swaggered off. Passersby wove around her, staring at her, but no one stopped to help. Placing one hand into the warm mud, she pushed herself to her knees and tried to collect her emotions. Fear threatened to crush her resolve to go on.

Then she saw him. Captain Dubois headed her way. His men proceeded along the street without him. She glanced over her shoulder to see what had captured his attention, but when she faced forward again, those smoky dark eyes were locked directly upon her. Did he know who she was, or was he only trying to help a boy? She didn't intend to stay and find out.

Leaping to her feet, she planted a hand atop her hat and dashed in the other direction, shoving her way through the crowd. Her breath strained in her lungs. Her legs burned. She bounded around the side of the tavern and into an alley littered with garbage and puddles of slop. Coughing from the stench, she splashed through the refuse, splattering it over the bottom of her breeches. She darted behind a stack of barrels and backed up against the wall of the tavern, listening for the sound of footsteps. Her breath heaved in her throat.

No thump of boots, no deep smooth voice. Just the clamor of the town. She peered around the barrels. The alley was empty. Leaning her head back onto the wall, she closed her eyes, caught her breath, and offered a prayer of thanks.

The click of a pistol cocking jarred her from her silent worship. She froze as every nerve within her tightened. The cold press of metal against her forehead forced her to open her eyes to the greedy sneers of two men. They spouted a string of French at her. Though she didn't understand the words, she knew what they wanted.

And she had no choice but to give it to them.

CHAPTER 11

Rafe strode up to the front of the stone church, shouldered aside the wooden door, and entered the dim vestibule. A haze of smoke lingered in the air from the candles burning in their sconces upon the walls. Wind slammed the door shut behind him, echoing through the room and enclosing him in its shadows. He doffed his plumed hat. The odor of beeswax, mold, and aged parchment tickled his nose as the air, kept cool by the stone walls, refreshed his heated skin. As his eyes grew accustomed to the shadows, stained glass windows appeared on either side of another massive door that separated him from the sanctuary. Taking a step toward the glass, he peered at the blurred shapes of several people sitting upon wooden pews or kneeling at the candlelit altar, praying to a nonexistent God.

A waste of time, to his way of thinking—sending appeals upward in the hope some powerful being would hear and answer them. En fait, it was a selfish act. Better to spend one's days helping the poor and needy as he did. He took a step back and gripped his baldric. If everyone would follow his example, the world would be a better place, and there would be no need for useless prayers.

The side door swung open and in walked Abbé Villion. The elderly priest's eyes lit up, and he opened his arms, the sleeves of his long gray robe swaying in the candlelight like apparitions. Taking Rafe in a hearty embrace, he smiled, his blue eyes sparkling. "Rafe, how good to see you! I did not expect you for another month."

Still unaccustomed to his displays of affection, Rafe stiffened beneath the man's enveloping grasp. "My crew needed some time ashore before our next stop. And I have brought you some more supplies." The door opened, and Father Alers peeked his gray head inside amidst a stream of sunlight.

"Come in, Father." Abbé Villion waved his hand. "Unless of course you will burn in hell for entering a haven of heretics." He grinned.

Father Alers chuckled and proceeded within. "I am no longer a Jesuit, *Révérend*, and even so"—he glanced around the vestibule, taking in the wooden cross atop the sanctuary door and the open Bible on a table to his left—"I believe we worship the same God."

"Well said, Father." Abbé Villion folded his hands over his gray cowl. "I wish King Louis held the same belief." He shrugged. "But I suppose if his father had, I wouldn't have fled here. None of us Huguenots would have. And who then would help the poor on this island?"

Father Alers shifted his stance and looked away.

Rafe ground his teeth together. Would things have been different if his father had not also fled the persecution and brought his family to the West Indies? Non, sans doute, his father would have been the same hypocrite, the same monster, in France as he was here.

Abbé Villion grabbed Rafe's shoulders. "I am glad you have come, my boy. And you bring gifts just in time." He exhaled a sigh of exhaustion, reflected in the deep lines on his face. "There are so many needs."

"I will have my men take the crates around back. There are clothes, grain, corn, dried peas, as well as pearls, silver, and gold jewelry, which should bring you a good price."

"I won't ask how you came upon such wealth." The reverend's sharp blue eyes flashed a silent reprimand.

"It is best you do not." Rafe grinned.

Father Alers coughed and lifted a look of repentance upward.

"But regarding the other matter I promised you." Rafe scratched the stubble on his chin.

Abbé Villion's brows lifted. "The hospital?"

Guilt assaulted Rafe at his friend's exuberant look. Then anger burned in his gut—anger at Mademoiselle Grace and the spell she'd cast upon him. "Oui. There may be a delay."

Abbé Villion turned and stared out the front window to the swaying palms and beyond to a group of mulatto children playing in the sand. "We lose so many each day. Sometimes up to five."

Rafe clenched his jaw. "I promised I would build you a hospital, fill it with supplies, and bring a qualified apothecary from the Continent, and I will. Just not by the end of the year, as I had hoped."

"It is not your fault, son." The reverend's brows pulled into a frown. "I meant no dishonor. You have done so much for us. And all at great risk to yourself. My disappointment lies only in the thought of those who will die in the meantime." He forced a smile. "Only God knows how many lives you have already saved with your generosity."

Pride swelled within Rafe. In the three years he had known him, Abbé Villion had been more a father to Rafe than his own had been in six and twenty. "I wish I could do more." He had to do more. He could not let this kind, gentle man down. His thoughts drifted to Mademoiselle Grace—five hundred pounds' worth of sweet cargo sitting aboard his ship, all his for the taking. Then why couldn't he take her to the don and collect it? Every fiber within him longed to do so, to tell Abbé Villion he would have his hospital by year-end.

But he could not.

The reverend laid a hand on his arm. "God will indeed bless you."

Rafe winced as if God Himself had spoken to him—sealing His approval on Rafe's silent decision. A sense of peace, of acceptance, came over him so strong it felt as if someone else had entered the room. "I do not want His blessing. I wish only to help those in need, those whom the grand blancs have deemed unnecessary and unworthy."

"He will bless you anyway." Abbé Villion lifted one shoulder and smiled.

Father Alers snickered and reached for the door.

Suddenly Rafe was equally as anxious to leave the sacred place. "My men wait outside. Show me where you would like the goods stored, and I will be on my way."

"Oui, you are no doubt tired from your journey."

Rafe turned. "I promise I shall find a way to build the hospital."

"We need it, oui." Abbé Villion's eyes burned with concern. "But not at the cost of your life and not at the price of innocent blood."

Father Alers coughed, and Rafe squirmed beneath another wave of guilt but said nothing. Better to not add lying to his list of sins.

Especially not in a church.

⤝

Grace huddled beneath an old ripped tarpaulin she'd found discarded by the docks and crouched against the back wall of the warehouse to shield herself from the wind. *Pound pound pound.* Rain dropped like round shot on the cloth, begging entrance to her makeshift shelter. But when not granted it, the water slid down to seek an opening, quickly found among the tarpaulin's abundant rents. The rain dripped onto Grace, saturating her already damp breeches. She sneezed and held her stomach against another grinding roar of hunger.

Three days had passed. Three days since all her money had been stolen by the two thieves, three days since she'd lost all hope of getting off this evil island, and three days since she'd had a bite to eat. Now she must endure another long sleepless night, hiding from both the small rats, as they rummaged through the refuse piled up in the alley, and the big drunken, two-legged ones—far more dangerous.

At least the thieves had not seen through her disguise, or she would have lost more than the livres Mr. Thorn had given her. She supposed she should be thankful for that. Although, covered with bug bites, consumed by a fear that left her numb, and a stomach that rebelled at every scent of food that remained ever out of her reach, she found it difficult to offer any thanks to God at all.

Hugging her knees to her weak body, she leaned her head atop them and allowed her tears to fall. "Why, God? Why have You abandoned me? I've served You my entire life. I've done naught but try to please You." She waited, listening for the answer amidst the *pitter-plop* of the rain. Yet this appeal seemed to dissipate in the air above her.

She had contemplated sneaking aboard one of the ships, but she shuddered at the stories of what happened to stowaways. Out at sea, if she were caught, she'd be trapped with nowhere to run. She had even thought of signing on as a crewmember, but she couldn't speak French and had no idea how to work a ship. It wouldn't take long for the sailors to notice her incompetence. Not to mention what the crew would do with her should they discover she was a woman. She trembled at the thought. She had also searched for Mr. Thorn, but he must have remained on the ship, and she could find no one willing to row her back out to it for less than a livre. One tiny spark of hope ignited when she had convinced a young French sailor, who spoke a modicum of English, to take a post to her sister Faith in Charles Towne. Yet Grace was unsure of whether he understood her or even if the ship he sailed upon was actually going toward home.

She could, of course, try to find Captain Dubois, but she wondered if life as a slave to a Spanish don would not be worse than dying in the filthy alleys of Port-de-Paix. At least if she died here, she'd end up in a much better place.

A rat poked his twitching, whiskered nose beneath her covering, and Grace booted him away. "Find your own shelter."

A crack of thunder hammered through the night sky, and she jumped. Puddles formed around her and began to soak through the bottom of her breeches. She hugged herself against the chill. "Lord, help me. Please help me. . . ." The petition faltered on her lips as she drifted into a nightmarish half sleep.

Grace dragged her boots through the mud, wincing as pain from the blisters covering her feet shot up her legs. The sun drooped in the western sky, sinking behind the mounds of green that bordered the nefarious port town. And nefarious it was. Worse than the worst parts of Charles Towne, worse than she ever imagined possible. The things she'd witnessed in broad daylight—brawls, drunkenness, lewdness, thievery—were nothing compared to the nighttime activities. If she hadn't had a clear vision of hell some years ago, she'd swear Port-de-Paix was indeed that place.

But she knew what hell was like. And the memory of her vision never ceased to send her heart racing and her skin crawling in terror. If only these people could witness it as well, if only for a second. Surely, they would fall on their knees and never commit another shameless act. Grace spent her days seeking either a friendly face among the crowd or a morsel of food—both of which rarely appeared. Even the scraps tossed from the taprooms and boardinghouses were quickly gobbled up by dogs roaming the street. Grace was beginning to feel like one of the hairy beasts and could soon envision herself on all fours, growling and fighting for a bone alongside the pack of mongrels.

Winding her way through the crowded street, she searched the passing faces for any sign of compassion, any flicker of kindness. Yet most of them looked beyond her as if she didn't exist. Some of the ladies pressed a handkerchief to their noses and glanced back over their shoulders in disgust. Grace dropped her chin and sniffed her clothing. Damp linen and an odd sour odor met her nose. Certainly not offensive enough to garner such a snobbish reaction. Yet perhaps Grace had simply grown accustomed to the smell.

Lifting her chin, she met the gaze of a haggard man sitting in the shade of a tree beside the road, and she recognized him as the beggar she and Mr. Thorn had seen when they first arrived in Port-de-Paix. But this time, she did not shift her gaze away as she had done then. This time, she did not cover her nose from the smell, nor send him a look of disdain. This time she knew exactly what he suffered day after day, and a sudden remorse for her judgmental attitude consumed her. She nodded her greeting and offered him an understanding smile as she passed, and he tipped his floppy hat at her in return.

The scent of fish swirled around her, taunting her and sending her belly into a ravenous growl. Pressing a hand against it, she allowed her nose to lead her down the street to a cart laden with fresh fish and mangos. The owner, a woman with spiny hair and a flat face that seemed in a perpetual frown, stood braying out the value and price of her wares. "*Poissons frais, mangues pour la vente, deux denier.*"

Grace ambled up to the cart and offered the woman all that she had—a kind smile.

"Qu'est-ce que vous *voulez*?" The lady ceased her calling and laid a knotted hand on her wide hip.

Pointing toward the mangos, Grace gave the woman a pleading look.

"Deux denier." The woman produced an open palm, but Grace shrugged and held out her own empty hands.

The woman's mouth puckered into a dark hole that reminded Grace of a cannon. "*Allez-vous-en!*"

Grace shrank back even as her stomach shriveled at this latest denial. Turning, she gazed out over the glittering bay, watching the ships swaying with the incoming waves. A blast of wind struck her, tearing away the putrid stench of the port and replacing it for a moment with the fresh smell of the sea—the vast, deep, magnificent sea, and all that stood between her and her home. She sighed. It might as well be a bottomless pit, for she had no way to cross it. Her gaze landed on *Le Champion*, and she was surprised to see Captain Dubois had not set sail. Had he discovered her missing? If he had, she'd seen no evidence that he had made any effort to find her.

Loud French words shot over her, and she swung around to find the cart lady in a heated argument with a man and his small son. The woman circled around her cart and with a pointed finger, spit a string of harsh words toward the man, who returned them with equal fervor. Numb and weak from hunger, Grace eyed the altercation as if in a dream. Her eyes finally latched upon the mound of mangos in the cart.

And not a soul around to guard them.

She glanced over the crowd and found everyone's eyes focused on the ensuing argument.

Just one mango. Would it matter if she took just one mango? She could almost taste the sweet, pulpy fruit. Her stomach lurched at the thought, and before she could ponder it another second, she dashed toward the cart, plucked a mango from the pile, slid it beneath her shirt, and sped away.

"*Voleur! Voleur! Ce garçon a volé mes mangues!*" came the condemning shout behind her. Followed by the thudding and squishing of shoes on the muddy ground. Grace clutched her treasure as if it were gold and wove through the startled crowd with more speed and agility than she'd have thought possible in her weakened condition. A whistle blew. Behind her, boot steps drummed a guilty sentence like the pounding of a judge's gavel. A man reached out to clutch her as she passed, but she pushed him aside and barreled forward.

Her eyes darted up and down the street as she went, seeking a hiding place. Heart pounding, she leapt up a span of stairs, barreled through an open door, and dashed across a dim room before she realized she'd entered a tavern. The stench of rum and moist wood assailed her as she sped past a group of men, tripped over a chair, and landed face-first in a sticky puddle on the floor. As if in final salute to her stupidity, her hat tumbled off and landed beside her head, spilling her matted hair into the slop.

"*Où est le garçon?*" A booming voice shouted behind her.

Grace's head began to spin. The putrid smell of whatever she'd fallen into saturated her hair and shirt, and she coughed, unable to rise, unable to even consider what the punishment was for thievery in this horrifying town.

Gentle hands gripped her arm and dragged her to her feet then wiped Grace's hair from her face. A lady with eyes the color of the sky and hair as light as honey stared at her with concern. Then gasping, she threw a hand to her mouth and bent over to retrieve Grace's hat from the floor. She shoved it atop Grace's head and tugged it down around her eyes and cheeks. "Keep your face hidden," she whispered. Boot steps thundered their way, and the lady whirled around to face the oncoming men, nudging Grace behind her.

"What's all this fuss over one young lad, gentlemen?" She placed her hands upon her hips.

"Step aside, Nicole. The boy stole a mango," the taller of the two men growled.

"A mango, is it? Sacre bleu, what a beastly crime." Sweet sarcasm chimed in her voice. "Why, most of the men in here have stolen far more than that, and you know it." She opened her palm behind her back, and Grace plucked the mango from within her shirt and gave it to her. All the while lifting a prayer of thanks heavenward for this unexpected protector.

The woman thrust the mango toward the men. "Here, take it and leave the poor lad alone." She sashayed toward the obvious leader, a man who looked more like a pirate than a magistrate. "Surely you have more important villains to catch, Pierre." She kissed him on the cheek, and a hint of a smile broke on his lips before he grunted and took a step back.

"*Très bien.* I suppose no harm was done," he muttered. "But only for you, Nicole." He winked at the lady, sent a harsh glare toward Grace, then turned and stomped out, the other man following him close behind.

As soon as the men left, the tense silence that had descended upon the place dissipated, and the patrons returned to their drink and cards with groans of disappointment. No doubt a hanging would have provided a pleasant diversion. Thankful she'd not become the afternoon's amusement, Grace took a deep breath as her heart settled to a steady beat.

The lady swerved around. Mounds of creamy skin burst from within a low-cut bodice that was far too tight for her voluptuous figure. Gaudy beads jangled from her ears and hung around her neck, but beneath the paint adorning her face beamed a caring smile. Taking Grace by the arm, she led her toward a stairway at the back of the tavern.

Tugging from her grasp, Grace halted, worried she'd escaped one danger only to find herself in another. "Where are we going?"

"Shhh. . .someplace safe." Lifting her skirts, she escorted Grace up a narrow set of creaking stairs, down a hall, and into a room not much bigger than Grace's cabin aboard *Le Champion.*

"I thank you for saving me from those men, mademoiselle." Grace shook the terror from her arms and neck where it stubbornly clung as if portending new dangers within this room. "But I. . .but I cannot impose upon your kindness, Miss, Miss—"

"Nicole. You may call me Nicole." She closed the door and bid Grace sit upon the bed at the room's center. "You are not imposing."

Though kindness sparked in the woman's gaze, Grace had learned these past four days to trust no one. Especially not someone with questionable morals. "I offer you my thanks, for I can offer you no more than that, but I shall take my leave now, if you please."

"Sit down, and I will bring you something to eat," Nicole commanded in a maternal tone, although from the looks of her she could not be much older than Grace.

Although Grace knew she should remove herself from this woman's presence as soon as possible, her stomach leapt at the mention of food, keeping her feet in place.

Approaching her, Nicole placed a finger beneath Grace's chin and lifted her face to examine it. "How long did you think this charade would last? You are très belle to be a boy."

Grace sighed and removed her hat, freeing her hair from its stale, matted confinement. The raven locks matted with dirt and slime fell to her shoulders like a rock, and she took a step back. "It has kept me unscathed until now."

Nicole ran a glance over her and chuckled, and Grace looked down at her torn, muddy breeches, her soiled, damp coat, and dirt-smudged hands and face.

"Unscathed? Perhaps. But you could use a bath." Nicole sniffed and raised the back of her hand to her nose. "What happened to you?"

Grace knew it was true, but the insult jarred her nonetheless. "I've been on the streets for four days," she said. "And how do you come to speak English so well?" Though the woman's French accent was strong, her words told of an education that defied her profession.

"I spent a few years in the acquaintance of a British sailor." She looked away for a moment, her expression drawn. But when she snapped her gaze back to Grace, her face pinked. Only for a second. "What is your name?"

"Grace Westcott."

"From where do you come, *ma chérie?*" Nicole batted the air. "Oh, never mind. Let me go get you some food." She swept a gaze through the room. "Madeline, *viens ici.*"

A shuffling sounded in the corner behind the dressing screen and out crept a little girl, no more than seven, with long, curly blond hair like Nicole's and large brown eyes. Grace smiled at such innocence amidst such wickedness, and the girl beamed at her in return.

"Keep our guest company until I return with your dinner," Nicole said.

Madeline nodded and trustingly took hold of Grace's hand while Nicole swept out the door, leaving Grace in a state of confusion, not only at the presence of the girl but at the ease with which Nicole entrusted her to Grace.

"Why are you dressed like a boy?" Madeline eyed Grace's clothing and wrinkled her nose.

"Because I don't want anyone to know I'm a girl." The shock at seeing such a small child in a tavern subsided, immediately replaced by fear for the little girl's safety.

"I like being a girl." Madeline plopped onto the bed.

"I usually do, too." Grace sat down beside her.

Grace glanced across the tiny room, which contained only the bed she sat upon, a wooden engraved chest, a dressing screen, and a small vanity upon which sat a bottle of perfume, a mirror, comb, hair pins, and jars of what Grace assumed to be face paint. A tiny open window—too high to peer out of—allowed a faint breeze to enter the room, not enough to cool the sultry air or to sweep away the putrid smells drifting in.

Madeline swung her legs back and forth over the side of the bed and began humming a tune, still holding onto Grace. Grace squeezed the girl's hand. She knew she should probably leave, should not remain in this woman's room, should not even be in this tavern, but the temptation of a meal was too much for her to resist.

Perhaps God had sent her here to help this little girl. "Is Miss Nicole your mother?"

The little girl nodded.

"And you live here? In this room?"

Releasing Grace's hand, Madeline lifted the coverlet on the bed and pulled out a straw doll. She held it to her chest. "Oui."

Grace cringed. "Do you stay here all alone?"

"Only when Mama works." Madeline's brown eyes lit up. "But when she does not work, she takes me outside to play, and to the market, and sometimes we walk along the shore."

Grace eased a wayward curl behind Madeline's ear as she remembered her own childhood and the many hours she had spent without her father and mother. But of course, there had always been a governess or a servant or her sisters around to look after her.

Nicole soon returned with two plates of fried fish, baked sugared plantains, and corn. After handing them to Grace and her daughter, she sat at her vanity for a moment to squeeze color onto her cheeks, pin up a loose strand of her hair, and dab perfume on her neck.

Then kneeling beside her daughter, she kissed her on the forehead. "Mother won't return until late. Be a good girl and keep Mademoiselle Grace company and go to sleep when you get tired."

"I will, Mama." The sweet obedience nipped at Grace's heart.

Nicole rose and gestured toward the bed. "You may stay here tonight if you wish."

Grace hadn't the strength to decline the invitation. "Thank you. . . *merci*. You've been so kind."

Nicole smiled then turned and flounced out the door.

Grace took to her meal with such desperation and lack of propriety, she nearly laughed at herself. Never had food tasted so good. Finishing her plate, she longed to lick it but resisted the urge, lest she appear rude.

Madeline also made good work of her dinner and afterward, Grace, stomach bursting, lay back on the bed and closed her eyes, unable to hold them open another minute. Sometime later, she jolted when Madeline crawled into bed and snuggled against her. Wrapping an arm around the little girl, Grace drew her close and faded back to sleep to a discordant French ballad meandering over them from below.

Sometime in the middle of the night, a lurid thought seeped into Grace's mind, jarring her consciousness. A picture of a ripe yellow mango danced through her mind. Lifting her hand to her throat, she gasped as tears of shame burned behind her eyes.

I am a thief.

CHAPTER 12

Rafe leaned back in the wooden chair and inhaled a deep breath, trying to still the spinning in his head. He immediately regretted doing so as a vile brew of malodorous fumes stung his nose and throat. Flanked at the table by Monsieur Atton and Monsieur Legard, Rafe cast his dizzy gaze around the tavern as curses, threats, and ribald laughter blended in a devil's chant that further goaded his ill humor. The throng of humanity twisted in odd shapes before him, even as it seemed to retreat to the long end of a tunnel.

Monsieur Legard grabbed a passing woman and pulled her onto his lap. Disgusted by the display and confused by his disgust—since he'd done the same thing a hundred times—Rafe grimaced and looked away.

He'd been in Port-de-Paix four days now, but it had not provided the diversion he hoped it would. Even Abbé Villion's deep appreciation for what he was doing for the hospital and the praises the people continually cast his way as Rafe strode through town had not provided him with the satisfaction and pleasure they normally did. Even spending every night in his favorite taverns, enjoying his brandy and an occasional game of faro, had not lifted the burden weighing upon his humors. En fait, his mood had grown fouler, and he found himself snapping at his men for no reason.

Mais, he knew the reason. The same reason that kept barging unbidden into his mind—and his heart. The lovely Mademoiselle Grace Westcott. The captive aboard his ship. Yet why did it seem as though he were the one being held captive? For no sooner did he begin to enjoy himself than a vision of those convicting green eyes appeared before him and stole all his pleasure like a schoolmaster with a ruler.

He poured himself a sip of brandy and tossed it to the back of his throat then drew a puff of his cheroot, allowing the spicy smoke to fill his lungs. He had no choice. He would return Mademoiselle Grace to her home. Admiral's daughter or not, he could not sacrifice such an innocent, kindhearted, brave lady to the wolves, or the lion, as she had put it. He smiled as he remembered how her bottom lip quivered when she was nervous and the way her raven hair made her skin look like porcelain.

But lives will be lost.

Rafe winced. He must find another way to procure the fortune he needed. He could not let Abbé Villion down. He could not allow more people to die when it was within his power to prevent it. Sacre mer, why couldn't the woman have been a shrew?

"What's wrong, Capitaine? You look as though someone died." Monsieur Atton leaned toward him, his wiry, spiky hair reminding Rafe of a sea urchin.

Rafe snorted. He felt as though someone had died—or something— some part of him that had the courage to do the sensible thing even if it meant doing the wrong thing.

The blurry shape of a man sauntering up to their table drew Rafe's gaze, and he ground his teeth together, hoping the haze of brandy deceived him. Unfortunately it hadn't.

Monsieur Gihon halted before the table like a king before his subjects. One hand pressed firmly upon the pommel of his rapier, he fingered his pointed, brown beard and shifted eyes as cold as steel onto Rafe.

"If it isn't Monsieur Dubois, the paladin of the poor. Come to receive the praises of your admirers?" He waved his hand through the air, the lace adorning his sleeve flapping in equal alacrity with his lips.

Monsieur Legard's wench abandoned his lap and melted into the crowd that settled into an unusual hush. Like pigs to slop, they no doubt smelled an altercation as their hungry eyes darted toward the men.

Rafe poured himself another drink, raised his glass in mock salute, then gulped the burning liquid. "Monsieur Gihon." The man had been a nuisance since Rafe's childhood. The bully who because of his unusually large size and position in society had hounded the other children. But he'd never been able to bring Rafe into subjection, for even before Rafe grew to his present size, he'd used his wits to defeat the half-masted brute.

Monsieur Gihon flung curled strands of his periwig over his shoulder. "Perhaps you should appoint yourself governor, or better yet, king, and set up a throne where you can receive a continual stream of your adoring masses."

"Thank you for the suggestion, monsieur. I may do that." Rafe grinned and took a puff of his cheroot.

Laughter rumbled across the mob.

Rafe leaned back in his chair. "What do you want?"

"You know, monsieur."

Messieurs Legard and Atton pushed their chairs back and stood, the smirks upon their lips evidence of their confidence in their capitaine. They backed away from the table to join the growing throng of bodies that undulated like waves upon the sea.

Frustration boiled within Rafe. He squeezed the bridge of his nose, trying to clear his head. "How many times must you come for retribution only to depart in humiliation?"

"I will have my revenge, monsieur." The ogre of a man narrowed his slit-like eyes upon Rafe.

"All you will have is a headache in the morning from your overindulgence in drink and a wound in your arm where my rapier will make its signature." Rafe batted him away. "Now, go and leave me be."

A fly landed on the rim of Rafe's glass and he swatted it, wishing he could rid himself of this man as easily. It was then that he noticed from whence the fly had come as the insect buzzed to join his companions in a swarm about Monsieur Gihon's wig.

Quelling a chuckle, Rafe downed his drink, resigned himself to trouncing this boor yet again, and studied his opponent: the way his beefy fingers twitched upon his sword's pommel, the apprehension flickering across his glassy eyes, the swagger of his massive frame caused by either an excess of alcohol or his overinflated pride.

Rafe yawned, patting his hand over his mouth, confident in the knowledge that his display of boredom would spark his longtime nemesis's capricious temper. As expected, Monsieur Gihon drew his rapier in one sweep and leveled its tip upon Rafe's gray waistcoat.

Cheers and howls surrounded them like a pack of hungry wolves while his own men stood to the side wearing expressions of abject tedium as if watching a play to which they knew the ending.

Rafe lowered his chin to examine the sharp point denting his fine cambric. "Tear this waistcoat and you shall pay, monsieur."

"It is you who shall pay. For ruining Mademoiselle Rachelle." The man's nostrils flared like those of a horse that had been run too hard.

"Mademoiselle Rachelle." Rafe scratched his chin thoughtfully. "Do remind me. Who is she again?"

The raucous mob brayed in laughter.

"The woman I was to marry, you scoundrel!" Monsieur Gihon's rapier point pressed deeper into Rafe's waistcoat.

"Ah, oui, I do recall her now." Rafe nodded and gazed off in pretense of remembering the lady. "Hair the color of mahogany and skin the color of fresh cream." He snapped his gaze back to Monsieur Gihon, whose face resembled an inflated pig skin. "Mais I also recall the betrothal of which you speak was only in your mind. The lady denied even knowing you."

Chortles sped through the rabble, and several women pushed their way through the crowd toward the front to watch the impending battle.

Monsieur Gihon's jaw expanded until Rafe thought it would explode. Something besides fury appeared in the man's eyes that set Rafe aback. Pain, real pain and sorrow. And the glimpse he caught of it sobered him instantly. The insolence that had taken over Rafe at the man's presence faded beneath a rising burst of sympathy. For Rafe understood well the agony of losing someone he loved.

He puffed upon his cheroot. "She came to me willingly, monsieur. How was I to know the depth of your interest in her?" When he had discovered Gihon's affections for the lady, Rafe had truly felt bad about the incident. He was not a man to meddle with another man's woman, not even Gihon's. "I offered you my sincerest apology at the time, non? And if I remember correctly, I returned her to you, mon ami."

"Soiled." Gihon spat and then slid his hand within the flap of his coat. "And I take no man's castoffs."

Rafe let out a ragged sigh. "Oui, neither do I." A pinch of pain stabbed his heart as a memory resurged from long ago—a memory of a lady he had hoped to marry who had been stolen by another. Shrugging it off, he faced his adversary, searching for the anger he knew he would need for a fight. "But can I help it if the ladies find me *irrésistible?*"

At this remark, one of the women batted her lashes and cooed at him, igniting more laughter from the mob.

"Will they find you so with my rapier through your heart?" Monsieur Gihon seethed.

Rafe cocked his head. "Even then I believe they would prefer me over you."

The man's hand trembled with rage. His face grew a deep shade of purple and he began sputtering nonsense. The tip of his rapier tore through Rafe's waistcoat, and Rafe heaved a sigh. He had no desire to fight Gihon. There was nothing to be done about the past—for either of them. But to back down in front of this crowd would be a death sentence. "Now you have angered me, monsieur." He stamped out his cheroot upon the wooden table.

A hush consumed the crowd.

Rafe inched his boot to the leg centering the table and gave Monsieur Gihon his most sardonic, confident stare—the one that had melted many men's resolve—hoping he would forsake this foolish squabble. Beads of sweat sprang upon the man's forehead, and he lunged at Rafe.

Rafe kicked the leg. The table slammed into Gihon. He stumbled backward, dropped his rapier, waved his arms through the air, then tumbled into the crowd. They caught him and threw him back toward Rafe. Booting the table aside, Rafe stormed toward the man, shaking the spin of brandy from his head and allowing all of his frustration and anger of the past weeks to flood into his clenched fists.

Monsieur Gihon recovered, eyed his rapier on the floor, and slid his hand into his waistcoat, no doubt in search of a pistol.

Rafe slammed his fist across the giant man's jaw, sending him reeling to the left. He didn't want to hurt him, just make him stop his foolish quest for revenge.

Turning, Rafe bent over to retrieve the man's blade. A punch to his back forced him to the floor. Burning pain seared across his shoulders. He gasped for breath.

"Get up, Monsieur Dubois," one man shouted.

"Can't let 'im beat ye," another chimed in.

"Rafe, Rafe." Female voices chanted his name.

Rising, Rafe whipped around to see a hairy fist fill his vision and flatten against his eye. He bolted backward. His anger boiled and his eye began to throb. The man's skill at fighting had improved.

While Monsieur Gihon lifted his arms to encourage the cheers of the crowd, Rafe charged toward him, barreling into his waist. Together they plunged into the agitated mob. The stench of sweat showered over Rafe as hurrahs filled his ears.

Grabbing the man's coat with both hands, Rafe lifted him off the floor then slammed him down. Before Gihon could recover, Rafe leveled a punch into his stomach followed by another across his jaw, snapping the man's head to the side and sending his periwig flying through the air. The giant toppled over like a felled tree and landed in a heap on the crusty floor. His moan echoed throughout the tavern.

Rafe plucked Gihon's rapier from the floor and tossed it at the man. It landed beside him with a *clank*.

The mob roared their approval, fists in the air, but Rafe felt no relief from the burden weighing upon him. He waved away the crowd, righted his chair, and dropped into it as his men picked up the table and snapped their fingers for more drink.

"Bravo, Capitaine!" Monsieur Atton slapped Rafe on the back. "Though ye had me scared for a moment."

Monsieur Legard took his seat and the trollop who had occupied his lap last slid back into place as if nothing had happened. "*Moi non.* I never seen the capitaine lose a fight."

Rafe touched the swollen tissue around his right eye. "He's a clod. I merely toyed with him."

A blond woman emerged from the throng and headed his way, carrying a bottle of brandy and a cloth. The brandy she set upon the table, the cloth she dabbed upon his eye. He brushed her hand aside. "Nicole. What are you doing here? I thought you worked at *Le Cochon Doux.*"

"I missed you, too, Rafe." Perching on his lap, she continued her ministrations. "Quit behaving the imp and allow me to attend to you."

Though Rafe hated being coddled, he didn't mind the close view of her curvaceous figure nor the sweet smell of her lilac perfume that helped to drown the reek of the men beside him. "I heard you saved a boy today from the noose."

She flattened her lips. "He stole a mango. Poor thing was starving to death." She dipped some brandy onto the cloth, then continued dabbing around his eye.

Rafe winced as the alcohol stung his wound. "Quit wasting good brandy." He pushed her hand away. "You are a good woman to help the lad."

She dropped her hand into her lap. "Can I tell you a secret?" Before he could answer, she leaned toward his ear, her honey curls tickling his cheek. "The lad turned out to be a lady."

"Vraiment?" Rafe's brows shot up. Pain etched across his forehead.

Nicole put a finger to her lips. "You mustn't tell anyone."

"Dressed as a boy?"

"Oui, and she had not eaten for days, by the looks of her. I have her upstairs in my room now."

As long as Rafe had known Nicole, she was always taking in strays. Once, she'd even forfeited some of her earnings to help Rafe feed a hungry family. "You amaze me, Nicole. Are you sure you are not an angel in disguise?"

Her blue eyes the color of the sky glistened beneath his praise, and he thought he detected a slight blush coloring her cheeks. She giggled. "Sacre bleu. An angel? Far from it, I am afraid." Despite her profession, Rafe had once considered pursuing something permanent between them. If not for one tiny obstacle.

"Has my father visited you lately?" His tone edged with more anger than he wanted.

She gave him a sideways glance. "Do you wish to know or are you just expressing your disapproval?"

"Neither." Rafe reached for the bottle of brandy. "Never mind."

She clicked her tongue. "So much anger, Rafe. You are just like one of your cannons about to explode."

"Yet you do not keep your distance, as wisdom would dictate."

"You would never do me harm." Nicole kissed his bruised eye then ran a finger over his stubbled jaw. "I can make it all feel better, Rafe." Her voice grew heavy with the sultry invitation.

Rafe grimaced. "You know I cannot." He gently nudged her from his lap, amazed her closeness evoked no reaction from him. In fact he had no appetite for any woman since he'd landed at port, much to the dismay of his usual flock of *jeunes femmes*.

Nicole huffed and planted her hands upon her waist. Her comely face lined in disappointment. "I have not seen your father in months."

"It matters not." Rafe tipped the bottle to his lips and allowed the spicy liquor to slide down his throat. Leaning the flagon atop his thigh, he raised his gaze to hers. "It only matters that you have been with him at all." A wounded look crossed her expression, and Rafe stood, set the bottle onto the table, took her hand in his, and kissed it. "I thank you for your care, mademoiselle."

Nicole smiled so sweetly, it seemed to wipe the stain of her profession from her face. Then turning with a swash of skirts, she sashayed away to the next customer.

Rafe faced his men. "Gather the crew. We set sail tonight."

"Mais, Capitaine," Legard complained, pulling back from the woman nibbling on his neck.

"One more night?" Monsieur Atton pleaded.

"I said tonight!" Rafe barked, and the men jumped to their feet. Monsieur Legard's woman nearly fell to the floor.

Rafe could no longer remain in this port. His life would never return to normal again until he returned Mademoiselle Grace safely to her home. Then he could get back to his mercenary work without her convicting presence dangling over him like a hangman's noose over a criminal's neck.

CHAPTER 13

A stream of light danced across Grace's eyelids and scattered into tiny diamonds. She stretched and savored the soft feel of a dry coverlet beneath her instead of cold, wet mud. Quiet, steady breathing filled the air, and the tiny warm body molding against Grace reminded her of the odd predicament in which she found herself.

On the bed of a trollop, snuggling beside the woman's illegitimate child.

Movement in the distance brought Grace to full attention. Slipping her arm from beneath Madeline, she rose on one elbow and glanced across the room, smoky in the dust-laden rays of the sun streaming through the window. In the far corner, with woolen shawl about her shoulders, lay Nicole, whose open eyes met Grace's.

She smiled. "How did you sleep?"

Grace blinked. "You slept on the floor? Why did you not come to bed?"

Nicole pushed herself to a sitting position and brushed the hair from her face. "I did not wish to disturb you. You and Madeline slept so soundly."

"When did you come in?" Grace swung her legs over the edge of the bed.

"Late," Nicole replied with a smile that seemed to carry a trace of shame. Then Grace lowered her gaze to Nicole's wrinkled gown, her disheveled coiffure, and the smeared paint on her face. A sudden embarrassment flooded Grace at the realization of what the woman had undoubtedly subjected herself to during the long night.

Grace clutched the top of her shirt and held it tight over her chest in fear that the condition might be contagious. She gazed down at the sleeping child, a beacon of innocence amidst this haven of debauchery. "Madeline is a lovely girl."

Nicole's eyes moistened, and she crawled over to sit beside the bed, gazing at her child. "She is my life." She took the sleeping girl's hand in hers, and from the look in her eyes, Grace knew she meant it.

Grace bit her lip, wanting to ask the woman why she subjected her daughter to this sordid existence, but feared to insult someone who'd been naught but kind to her.

Lifting her gaze to Grace, Nicole brushed a curl of her golden hair aside, and sighed, her blue eyes stinging with pain. "You look at me with such reproach."

Grace looked down, regretting that she wore her opinions so blatantly on her face. Or so her sisters had told her. "Forgive me. I mean no offense."

Rising, Nicole trudged to her vanity and sat down. "You forget, I am accustomed to the looks of disdain I receive from proper ladies. And even some men." She grabbed a cloth, dipped it in a basin of water, and attempted to wipe the paint from her cheeks. But after a few seconds, she faced Grace again, a grin forming on her lips. "But I didn't expect it from"— she chuckled—"a woman who dresses like a man and steals mangos."

Grace smiled at the ease with which this woman cast offense aside. Her sweet spirit transformed their conversation from one of strain to one of enjoyment as if they'd been friends for years. Which gave Grace the encouragement to ask the question that had burned on her tongue ever since she'd met Nicole. "Why do you. . .why do you—?"

"Sell myself for money?" Nicole raised her brows. "For her." She gestured toward the still-sleeping child. "To feed her. Keep her warm and off the street." She tugged the lace bounding from her bodice in an attempt to straighten it. "Otherwise we would both be wandering the alleys as you were yesterday and would probably die, hungry and alone."

"Surely there is another way." Grace thought of her sister Faith who had resorted to pirating to garner much-needed wealth. A shudder ran through her, and she thanked God that situation had turned out well in the end.

"What would you suggest?" Nicole snickered as she faced the mirror again.

"A trade of some sort, perhaps?"

"A woman in business on her own? Here in Port-de-Paix?" Her laughter bubbled through the room, and she waved away the thought. "Besides, I have no skills."

Grace clutched the chain around her neck. What did a woman do if she had no family, no husband, no money? In Charles Towne, some women had been permitted to run millinery shops as long as they were widowed or deeded the right to do so by their husbands. But apparently here in Saint Dominique that was not the case. "How did you come to this town? Where is your family?"

Nicole set down the cloth, shook her head at her appearance in the mirror, then swerved in her chair to face Grace. "I grew up an orphan on the streets of Creteil. At seventeen, I was rounded up by King Louis XIV's men and sent here to be a wife to one of the local planters." Her nonchalance gave no indication of the horror she must have endured. She chuckled. " 'Daughters of the King,' they called us. Simply a polite way to say *prostituées*."

Grace's heart sank. How atrocious. How could any woman have endured such a thing? She glanced at Madeline, and Nicole seemed to read her silent question.

"I was ravished by one of the sailors on the crossing, and when I arrived with my belly full of a child, no one wanted me for a wife." Nicole pressed a hand over her stomach as if remembering the incident; then she released a heavy sigh.

A sour taste filled Grace's mouth. "I am sorry."

"*C'est la vie.*" Nicole shrugged. "That sailor left me with two precious things: the ability to speak English and ma Madeline chérie. Besides, we have done well. Madeline lacks for nothing. And"—Nicole's blue eyes sparkled with hope—"I am saving money so that she and I can escape this place and sail for the British colonies in America. I hear they accept everyone, and there are opportunities for women that are not found here."

" 'Tis true. There are some." Swiping away a tear, Grace fingered the little girl's curls as shame sank into her chest. Grace had judged this woman—had spent a lifetime judging all women like her. And she'd never once considered the path that led them to such a life. She'd never considered the situations forced upon them by the world and its kings and its men, and the difficult choices they had to make. And as she stared at the little girl, she wondered for the first time if she wouldn't have chosen to do exactly the same thing Nicole had done. Anything to protect and provide for this precious child sleeping so peacefully. "Forgive me, Nicole, I have judged you unfairly."

Nicole tilted her head and smiled. "I may be a trollop, but you are a thief, remember?" She laughed and Grace joined her.

"Indeed."

When their laughter died down, Grace studied her new friend. This woman did what she had to in order to survive. Just as Grace had done when she had stolen the mango. It didn't make either action right. They were both sins. But for some reason, understanding the cause removed the guilt just a bit.

"I will go get us some breakfast." Nicole rose and patted down her wrinkled skirts. She opened the door then swung her gaze back to Grace. "And then you shall tell me all about how you came to Port-de-Paix and why a lady like yourself was running around town half starved and dressed like a boy." She gave Grace a look that said she wouldn't take no for an answer. "And I have a feeling it will be quite an interesting tale." She winked then stepped into the hallway and closed the door.

Interesting, indeed. Grace took a deep breath of the room's stale air as shouts and bells and the sound of horses' hooves drifted in through the open window. The port awoke to another day. Only this day, Grace would have a belly full of food and the strength of a good night's sleep.

Thank You, Lord.

Laying a hand upon Madeline's head, Grace said a prayer for the girl's life, her safety, her future, hoping that if God answered any of Grace's recent prayers, it would be this one.

Minutes later, as promised, Nicole returned bearing buttery biscuits and jam, along with hot steaming coffee and plantains. Grace's stomach leapt at the rich savory scents, and when Madeline awoke, the three of them gobbled up the food as if they were old friends sitting around a breakfast table.

Afterward, while Nicole brushed Madeline's hair, Grace stood over the washbowl and attempted to wipe the mud from her face and arms as she regaled them with the story of her capture, and her time aboard *Le Champion.*

"Did you say Capitaine Rafe Dubois?" Nicole's voice rose in surprise.

"Yes. Do you know him?"

Nicole laughed and nodded. "He was here in the tavern last night. Got into one of his scraps with Monsieur Gihon."

Grace halted her toilet and faced her, her blood racing. "You didn't tell him I was here?"

"I didn't know who you were." Nicole scrunched her nose as she battled a particularly stubborn knot in Madeline's hair.

"*Aïe, Maman.*" Madeline cried, her face twisted in a pout.

"*Je suis désolée,* ma chérie." Nicole kissed her daughter on the cheek and continued brushing. "I am almost done." She glanced at Grace. "And now that I know what he has done, I most certainly will keep your secret."

Grace released a sigh.

"I cannot believe Rafe, I mean Capitaine Dubois, would lower himself to commit such a vile task such as kidnapping an innocent lady. So unlike him."

Grace winced at Nicole's use of the captain's Christian name. No doubt they had done business together. Pushing the thought aside as well as the odd feeling of discomfort it caused, she set down the cloth and rolled down her sleeves. "On the contrary, I have spent enough time with him to know he is quite capable."

Nicole stared at her curiously, and Grace continued the story of how one of the crew brought her ashore, and then how all her money was stolen, and how she wandered around town until she was so hungry and desperate that she stole the mango. In a way, hearing the desperation in her own voice as she told the sordid tale aloud assuaged her guilt over the thievery. Almost.

"You poor thing." Nicole let Madeline slip from her lap. The girl grabbed her doll off the bed and approached Grace. "Do you like my doll? Her name is Joli."

Grace bent over and tapped the doll on the head. "Yes, I do very much. She is quite beautiful. Just like you."

Madeline beamed, then she jumped on the bed and began playing.

"What will you do now?" Nicole asked. "You could work here. I do detect a remarkable beauty beneath all that dirt."

Grace's face heated. "Mercy me. No. I could never do—" She caught herself and realized the haughty disdain in her voice had cast a sullen cloud over Nicole's expression. "Forgive me. Again I have offended you. But I have no child to provide for as you do."

Nicole attempted a smile and rose from her chair as someone below began pounding out a tune on the harpsichord.

"You have been so kind to feed me." Grace closed the gap between them and took Nicole's hands in hers. "You are an answer to prayer."

"I don't believe I've ever been anyone's answer to prayer." With the paint removed, Nicole's beauty beamed from her face, and Grace could almost see the innocent little girl she once was peering from behind her blue eyes.

"Well, now you have." Grace squeezed her hands. "And I shall pray for you. That God will deliver you from this life and grant you the money you need to sail to the colonies."

"I fear God will not listen to the prayers of a prostitute." Nicole released Grace's hands and strode to the window.

"I used to believe that, too," Grace said. "But I'm not so sure anymore."

Nicole flipped up the hem of her skirt and snapped open a hidden pocket. Pulling some coins from within it, she offered three to Grace. "Please take these. It won't buy you passage home, but it is a start."

Tears burned behind Grace's eyes and she turned around.

"What is the matter?" Nicole's skirts swished toward her.

"Your generosity overwhelms me." Grace swallowed. This woman, this trollop, had shown her more kindness and mercy than all of the so-called Christian ladies back in Charles Towne. She turned around to see Nicole still handing her the money, a questioning look on her face.

Grace pushed her hands away. "I could never accept that." She wiped a tear sliding down her cheek. "You need that for Madeline."

Nicole flattened her lips in disappointment and studied Grace for a moment before her eyes flashed. "I know what to do."

Grace shook her head.

"I know someone who will gladly help you."

At Grace's inquisitive look, Nicole continued, "A man, a prominent man here in Port-de-Paix."

"I told you I cannot—"

"Non, you misunderstand. A respectable, godly man." Nicole smiled and tapped a finger on her chin. "And someone who would love nothing more than to assist a victim of Captain Rafe Dubois."

CHAPTER 14

Grace leaned out the window of the landau and clasped Nicole's hand. "How can I ever repay your kindness? You saved me from certain death."

"Anyone would have done as much." Nicole squeezed her hand and then released it and bent down to pick up Madeline.

"Yet no one else did." Grace's eyes burned. She felt as though she were abandoning her only friend in the world.

"Be good for your mama, Madeline. She loves you very much." Grace slid a finger over the child's soft cheek.

Madeline giggled and leaned her head on Nicole's shoulder. "*Je l'aime aussi.*"

Thunder rumbled and Grace gazed up at the darkening sky, praying the incoming storm was not a portent of bad things to come. Black, swirling clouds swallowed up the afternoon sun, and Grace offered Nicole a weak smile. "I will pray for you. God is the only One who can truly deliver you from this life."

"You are kind to give me hope." Nicole smiled—a sad, desperate smile that bespoke a wounded heart too familiar with pain and disappointment.

A blast of wind blew in from the harbor where a bell tolled. The breeze danced among Nicole's golden curls, and Grace shook her head at the vision of this woman, this trollop, who was the epitome of humility and kindness.

"*Êtes-vous prête*, mademoiselle?" The footman snapped in disdain as he leaned over from his perch atop the carriage seat above her. His

116

obvious disapproval of her filthy attire had been evident by his twisted features and the lift of his nose when he had opened the carriage door for her. Which only added to Grace's uneasiness about her destination. Would her benefactors be equally repulsed? But what did it matter? She had no other choice but to accept their hospitality.

"Oui," she replied with reluctance. And with a snap of reins, the carriage lurched and lumbered on its way. Grace waved out the window at Nicole and Madeline who were standing in front of the tavern until a curve in the road stole them from her sight.

As she sat back against the cushioned seats, loneliness fell upon her as thick and dark as the clouds overhead. Who was this Monsieur Henri, to whom Nicole referred? That he was an honorable man, Nicole had assured Grace. That he had sent his landau as soon as Nicole's note had arrived in his hands was indisputable, but it still did little to stop Grace's nerves from tightening into knots at the thought of going to an unknown man's home. Yet, this must be God's answer to her prayer for rescue. Mustn't it?

The carriage careened and jolted over the rocky path, twisting and turning around bend and over stream. Tall cedars, lush rosewoods, and the biggest ferns Grace had ever seen passed her window in a pageant of stunning greens and browns. Air fragrant with the sweet perfume of logwood flowers and pimento filled her nostrils. Normally, Grace would have enjoyed such natural beauty, but in her present state of mind, the shadows of the forest seemed like dark and nefarious creatures reaching out for her, trying to pull her into their wooded labyrinth to be lost forever.

"Oh, Lord, let this man be friend and not foe," she whispered as thunder growled in the distance.

Soon the greenery parted to reveal a vast parcel of cultivated land. Rows and rows of sugar cane extended as far as the eye could see. The heads of African slaves working the fields barely poked above the tall, spindly plants. Palm trees lined a gravel road that extended to a large house beyond the fields. Their fronds swayed in the heavy wind like foppish courtiers, gesturing Grace onward to the palace. And a palace it was. The massive structure perched upon a hill lording over its subjects below.

As the landau rumbled down the path, Grace couldn't keep her eyes off the house, or her heart from feeling a deep sense of dread that mounted with each turn of the carriage's wheels. Eight white columns guarded the front of the house, which boasted a full-length porch on both first and second floors before extending up to a steep hipped roof. French doors opened onto the upper porch where urns filled with orchids, lilies, and begonias bounded in a colorful display.

The carriage halted before a wide span of stairs leading to an ornately carved wooden door. Slipping from his seat, the footman snapped open the door and stood at attention but did not place a step down for her. Grace stumbled from the carriage and, avoiding his gaze, began inching her way up the stairs. She grabbed the chain around her neck, seeking its comfort and questioning the wisdom of putting her trust in Nicole. She halted, her throat closing. Hot wind tore at her muddy shirt and matted hair, bringing with it the sting of rain and the sweat of the oppressed. Perhaps she could convince the driver to return her to town. She started to turn around when the heavy door swung open and a man in a green waistcoat appeared in the doorway. "Mademoiselle Grace?"

Grace nodded, and he gestured for her to enter, but he kept his distance as if she had leprosy. Then with a *humph* he abandoned her to stand in a massive foyer that reminded Grace of Lord Somerset, Earl of Herrick's estate she'd visited once in London. An enormous chandelier hanging over Grace's head chimed in the rain-scented breeze that had forced its way in through the open door. Afraid to move lest she muddy the pristine marble floor, Grace glanced over the room, admiring the marble-topped salon table; butler bench, above which hung a gilt cameo mirror; the tall case clock; and console table flanked by two matching oil paintings of the same woman. A wide staircase led up to the second floor then split in two, ascending up either side of the house.

Shoes clipped on the marble, and Grace looked up to see an older gentleman, perhaps in his early fifties, heading her way. He marched with a pompous authority that grated over her, yet his initial look of repulsion quickly faded beneath the veneer of a smile. Stylishly dressed in a suit of black camlet with buttonholes richly bound in silver and his neck swathed in white silk, he halted before her and hesitated as if awaiting homage. His blue eyes glittered in the candlelight, but their lack of warmth caused Grace to shudder.

"Mademoiselle Grace Westcott." He bowed. "Nicole was not exaggerating about your appearance. Non?" He scanned her from head to toe and chuckled.

Grace drew a shaky breath and dipped the curtsy his comportment seemed to demand. "I thank you for your offer to help me, Monsieur..."

Grace looked up into those cold eyes, not wanting to use his Christian name but knowing no other.

"Monsieur Dubois. Monsieur Henri Dubois."

~

Rafe pressed the heels of his boots to the steed's flanks and leaned forward in the saddle, prodding the horse to as fast a canter as possible around the twists and turns leading to the Dubois plantation. Behind him, Monsieur Thorn's horse pounded an ominous cadence in the mud as the night wind laden with the spice of impending rain blasted over them. Rafe's hair loosened from its tie and whipped on his shoulders. Lightning sliced the dark sky, flinging a grayish hue upon the forest and granting Rafe his bearings. In his haste, he'd forgotten a lantern, but he knew this path—every bend and turn—as well as he knew the Caribbean currents. Like a long, spiraling fuse, the trail seemed harmless in its appearance and windings. That was until a man reached the end and found himself in the presence of a deadly explosive.

Thunder growled and it began to rain. Rafe urged more speed from his mount, every muscle within him drawn as tight as the halyard of a full sail. When he had returned to his brig the night before, he had taken to his bed, too exhausted and too inebriated to either set sail or deal with the mademoiselle. It wasn't until he finally woke the next morning, near midday, that he discovered her missing. What was the foolish girl thinking? Wandering the streets of one of the most dangerous port towns in the Caribbean, surpassed only by Tortuga and Petit Goave. And for five days! Zut alors, it was a miracle she had survived unscathed.

If he believed in miracles anymore.

Of course his men had claimed ignorance in her escape. All except Monsieur Thorn, who'd said he discovered her missing four days ago and for fear of invoking his captain's wrath had not told Rafe, but had instead been searching for her frantically on his own. *Les ruses, les déceptions.* Which was why Rafe insisted his first mate accompany him. If Rafe couldn't trust him, it would be best to keep him close.

As soon as he had left the ship, Rafe remembered Nicole's story of harboring a lady dressed as a boy, so he had made haste directly to the tavern, his fears temporarily subsiding—until he'd discovered where Nicole had sent her. Now they resurged all the more, for it would be better for Mademoiselle Grace to be on the streets than in the clutches of his father.

Nudging the horse onward, Rafe ignored the rain stinging his face. He swerved around another bend in a path that was fast becoming a muddy stream and emerged from the thicket onto the wide expanse of the Dubois estate, made all the more hideous by the gray shroud cast upon it from the storm. Pulling the horse to a stop, he wiped the rain from his eyes and stared at the eerie mansion he had called home for one and twenty years, a place he'd sworn he would never set eyes on again.

Monsieur Thorn reined in beside him and tugged his hat down on his forehead. The rain pounded over the trees, the sugar cane, the mud, its cadence sounding like the taunting laughter of a dissident mob.

Thunder rumbled a warning for the men to retreat while they could. Rafe's horse stomped in the mud and snorted, then it pranced sideways as if spooked by some unseen malevolent force. And though every ounce of Rafe longed to turn around and flee back to his ship, he steadied his mount, staring at the house in the distance, the white vision blurred by the constant stream of rain. Within the walls of that mausoleum, a treasure existed—a lady who had become Rafe's responsibility by his own foolish actions. And he could not abandon her to the fiendish devices of this plantation's master.

With a jab of his heels to the horse's flanks, Rafe brought the beast to a gallop over the muddy path, making quick work of the remaining distance. As he approached the front of the house, he shook off his apprehension, reined in the steed, and slid off the animal before it came to a halt. Taking the ostentatious stairs in two leaps, he gripped the pommel of his rapier and pounded on the door before he changed his mind.

⁓

Grace sipped the hot tea, savoring its sweet lemony flavor, and set the cup down with a clank that rang through the room. "Forgive me." She clasped her trembling hands together, still finding it hard to believe she sat in the same room with Rafe's father—the man Rafe had called a monster. "I can't seem to stop shaking."

"Understandable, Mademoiselle Grace." Monsieur Dubois smiled from the cream-colored Louis XIV settee centering the parlor. "You have been through more than a lady should endure." Lightly powdered chestnut curls streaked with silver hung well past his jaw. He shifted his broad shoulders and examined her with dark blue eyes that carried no trace of Rafe within them.

Lowering her gaze beneath his perusal, Grace pressed the folds of her gown—borrowed from Madame Dubois's wardrobe. "I am indebted to you for your kindness, monsieur."

Though shocked at meeting Rafe's father, Grace had found the man to be none of the vile things his son had indicated. He had accepted her into his home with open arms, provided a private bedchamber and a hot bath for her, and given her a lady's maid in attendance. Though she felt a bit uncomfortable sitting alone with him in his parlor, they were not entirely on their own as a footman stood at the door, awaiting his master's command. Besides, Monsieur Dubois had given her no indication his intentions were anything but pure.

So unlike his son.

"Ah, it is my pleasure to help a lady in need, especially one who has suffered beneath my son's bitter hand." He sipped his port. "I feel a sense of obligation to correct the ills which have come about by my offspring."

"That must keep you quite busy." The words flew from Grace's mouth before she realized the insult they contained. And although she meant the statement quite seriously, it drew a chuckle from the elder Dubois.

"I see you have become well acquainted with Rafe."

Grace blushed. "Only enough to observe that he holds to no moral code in his affairs, nor does he speak fondly of you, monsieur."

Monsieur Dubois stood, his imposing frame towering over her, and sauntered to the mantel, gazing up at a painting of a beautiful young woman. "Why would he? My son has abandoned the morality, the honor, the godliness with which I attempted to raise him."

Grace stared into the crackling flames of the fire as the rain tapped on the roof. She thought of her own mother's admonition on her deathbed, entrusting Grace with the responsibility of ensuring the salvation of her sisters. And what a task that had proved to be. She could well relate to Monsieur Dubois's anguish over his son's sinful behavior.

"Mais, let us not think on such things, mademoiselle." Monsieur Dubois sighed and straightened his black waistcoat. "Dinner shall be served shortly. I'm sure you're famished, and tomorrow I shall place you upon one of my merchant ships. I believe Captain Christoff will be traveling north up the coast with a hold full of sugar and coffee and can deliver you safely to Charles Towne."

Hope flooded Grace. She would finally be safe at home and could put the nightmare of Captain Rafe Dubois behind her. She shifted in her seat. Then why did she still feel so unnerved? "I don't know what to say, monsieur. You are too kind. I'm sure my father, Admiral Westcott, will reward you handsomely."

He waved a jeweled hand through the air and threw back his shoulders. "There is no need. Consider it a favor from one Christian to another."

Grace snapped her gaze to his, her heart leaping in her chest. "Then you follow the Savior, Jesus?"

"Oui." He clutched the lapels of his camlet waistcoat. "I and my family are Huguenots. We fled the persecution in France twenty-eight years ago."

Grace's heart soared. The Lord had brought her another Christian. "Did your tribulation not follow you here to the French colonies?"

"Non. Far from the mainland where many struggle simply to survive, not many care which faith one clings to." His mustached lip lifted in a smile devoid of warmth.

Pound. Pound. Pound. A loud banging filled the room from the foyer. *Pound. Pound. Pound.*

Monsieur Dubois's curious gaze shifted to the door. "Who could that be this time of night?"

Footsteps sounded. A door opened. Shouting in French that Grace couldn't understand. She didn't have to. She knew that voice.

Monsieur Dubois excused himself and exited the room. Unable to remain seated, Grace followed him out the door, down a short hallway, and into the vestibule.

She halted. There, just inside the open door, wind howling in protest around him and water dripping from his waistcoat and sash, stood Captain Dubois. He shook his head, spraying droplets over the marble floor, then ran a hand through his hair and met her gaze. Intense emotion flashed within his eyes before he shifted them to the elder Dubois.

"Bonjour, *Père*." One corner of his mouth lifted in a grin, but his voice carried the sting of spite.

CHAPTER 15

Bile rose in Rafe's throat at the sight of his father. The dried beef he had consumed on the ship rebelled in his gut.

"Je suis désolé, Monsieur Dubois." The butler's voice took on a fear-laced apologetic tone. "He forced his way inside."

Footsteps splashed behind him, and Rafe turned to see Monsieur Thorn stop just outside the door. Doffing his hat, the first mate shook the water from it before entering.

"Très bien, Francois." Monsieur Dubois dismissed the butler with a wave, and the man shut the door, raised his aquiline nose at Rafe and Monsieur Thorn, and left the room.

Rafe's father approached him, a carping smile on his lips and his arms extended. "Rafe. How good to see you. How long has it been? Years."

Rafe tightened the corners of his mouth. "Not long enough." He held up a hand to stop his father's advance. "Spare me the pleasantries, Père. I have come for the girl." The sight of Mademoiselle Grace in that exquisite jade gown, her raven hair pinned tightly atop her head, delighted him more than he wanted to admit. And helped soften the blow of seeing his father again.

"You mean Mademoiselle Westcott?" his father said innocently and gestured behind him at Grace. "I don't believe she wishes to accompany you." He turned toward Monsieur Thorn. "Forgive my son's ill manners, monsieur, I am Henri Dubois. Et vous?"

"Justus Thorn, monsieur." Thorn bowed slightly. "You son's first mate."

"Ah, you've brought your nefarious crew along." Rafe's father raised a graying brow.

"This is none of your affair." Rafe stroked the hilt of his rapier, his fingers itching to draw it.

"C'est mon *affaire* when I discover you have kidnapped an innocent lady from her home and intend to sell her to a Spanish don." Monsieur Dubois shook his head and stroked his pointed beard. "To what depths have you sunk, mon *fils*? Do you try to break an old man's heart?"

Ignoring his father and the sharp barb twisting in his gut, Rafe marched to Mademoiselle Grace and took her by the arm. "I see you've already bribed her with fripperies, Père."

"She came to us wearing a torn, filthy shirt and breeches of all things—a product of your hospitality, I believe?" His voice sharpened in sarcasm.

Rafe pulled on her arm, but Grace yanked from his grasp and shot a fiery glare his way. "I will not go with you."

Rafe ground his teeth together. "Believe me when I say you are in far more danger here than with me."

His father laughed. "Yes, choose, mademoiselle. A warm home, clothing, hot food, and a chance to go home to the safety of your loved ones, or"—he gestured toward Rafe and shook his head in disgust—"back to the hold of my son's brig."

Rafe glared at Mademoiselle Grace. Her fresh scent swirled about him, setting aflame his senses and igniting an urgency within him to protect her—to keep her safe from men like his father. Little did she know that here in this house she was but an innocent lamb among the wolves. How could Rafe make her understand? "You will come with me now," he ordered her as if she were one of his crew. He grabbed her arm and tightened his grip, resorting to the only method he knew to ensure his will was accomplished. He felt a rush of heat to his head when instead of obeying she winced and widened her eyes in horror.

He loosened his grip and softened his tone, forcing his features into what he hoped was a pleading look—a look that sat most uncomfortably upon his face. "S'il vous plaît, mademoiselle. You are not safe here."

Confusion rumbled across her features. "And I am safe with you?" She backed away from him, clutching the chain around her neck as if terrified by his very presence. Rafe cringed beneath the sudden ache in his heart.

"I will not allow you to take her, Rafe." His father's sanctimonious voice stabbed him.

Fury gripped Rafe as he swerved about and stared at his father's arrogant stance: one jeweled hand on his hip, the other fingering his beard, his broad figure standing guard over the closest avenue of escape. And history replayed itself in Rafe's mind. Suddenly, he was a young man again, standing before his father—his hero—trying to come to grips with why his own flesh and blood had committed the ultimate betrayal against him.

But Rafe was older now, stronger, and he would not allow his father access to his heart, nor would he allow him to tarnish another innocent woman. Rafe squeezed the hilt of his rapier and took a step toward the man who had sired him.

Henri Dubois crossed his arms over his chest and smirked. "Will you draw a sword on your own father?"

Rafe would love nothing more. The man hadn't changed one bit in the past five years. The same pretension, the same arrogance, the same evil he remembered burned within his father's gaze. But he saw something else in those malicious blue eyes. Rafe saw his mother. And that one vision of her soft, loving face caused him to release his grip on the weapon. She wouldn't want him to harm his father.

"I didn't think so." His father gave him a condescending smile then he looked to Monsieur Thorn as if for approval, but Rafe's first mate maintained his stoic stance.

"I have an idea." A smile curved his father's lips. "Rafe, why not stay with us for a few days? Go upstairs. Your old chamber is still available. Change into some dry and"—he wrinkled his nose—"more appropriate attire, cool your temper, and we can discuss this over dinner. Your stepmother would love to see you again."

Stepmother. Rafe's gut curdled.

His father gloated in the victory of that one word, but Rafe only stared at him unflinching as he pondered his next course of action. He had three choices. Murder his own father—extremely tempting—abandon the foolish Mademoiselle Grace to the fate she had chosen, or accept the invitation to dine with them and await an opportunity to convince the lady to trust him.

Rafe clenched his fists. He could not allow another woman to be trapped in his father's web. Especially since she would not be here but for Rafe. "Très bien. I will stay." The words stung his lips as they flung from his mouth.

"I protest!" Mademoiselle Grace shouted from behind Rafe, and he turned to see her storming forward, her face flush. No doubt realizing the impropriety of her outburst, she halted and softened her tone. "Forgive me, Monsieur Dubois, but if the captain resides here, surely he will attempt to kidnap me again." The fear on her face sliced through Rafe's conscience, but how could he blame her?

"Never fear, mademoiselle." His father's voice boomed through the foyer as if he were giving a speech. "I shall hold myself personally responsible for your safety while you are under my roof." He hesitated and glanced over them all. "Well, that settles things." He rubbed his hands together as if he were anticipating a good meal. No doubt he hoped Rafe would be the main course.

Grace stood at the window of her chamber and stared into the darkness. Raindrops splattered against the panes of glass and slid down in random paths, some twisting and turning, some going straight, others gliding alongside other drops and collecting in a pool at the bottom. Much like people wandering through life. She pondered the odd path her own life had taken of late and the other drops she'd been forced to slide beside. Drops she would have never associated with just a month ago. Drops like Father Alers, Monsieur Weylan, Nicole, Madeline, and of course, Captain Dubois. Yet she knew God had a plan for each person, each path, no matter how chaotic it all seemed. A plan to touch their lives for His glory. A plan of which Grace seemed lately to fall so short.

She sighed and rubbed the jeweled cross in her hand. "Am I bringing You glory, Lord? Have I led anyone to You since this whole horrid venture began? No one seems to listen to me. And now I find myself with an opportunity to go home, but what have I accomplished? What has all this misery produced?"

She thought of Captain Dubois, how his volatile presence had filled the foyer. He had come for her. But the burning flash in his eyes carried no wicked intent, no anger, no malice, but simply concern. She could make no sense of it, nor of the way her heart had leapt at the sight of him. Her cheeks burned in shame. The man was a rogue, a villain. Why did he affect her so? Up until this night, she had felt naught but repulsion, pity, and righteous anger toward him. Yet there was something behind those dark eyes, something that made her think there was much more to this man than his actions toward her intimated.

"Father, I'm sorry for this strange feeling that comes over me in his presence."

A firm hand covered her mouth. Grace's blood froze in terror.

A strong arm grabbed her waist. She struggled against the iron grip, but to no avail. The man forced her back against his muscled torso. "I hope it is a pleasurable feeling, mademoiselle." The deep voice flowed like warm silk over her ear.

Captain Dubois.

Heat stormed through Grace, the heat of embarrassment, the heat of anger. She tried to free her elbows to jab them into his stomach, but his strength forbade her.

"If you promise not to scream, I shall release you. I wish only to talk." His warm breath, edged with brandy and tobacco, tickled her neck.

Grace nodded and his hand fell away from her mouth. "How dare you sneak into my chamber and listen to my personal petitions." She jerked from his grasp, veered around, and raised her hand to slap the grin off his face.

He caught her arm in midair and his smile widened, reaching his eyes in a twinkle of playfulness.

Tugging away from him, Grace retreated into the shadows, praying the captain could not see the blossom of red creeping up her neck.

But by the mischievous look on his face, she knew he had. Not only seen, but he seemed to enjoy her discomfort. With his hair combed and slicked back, and wearing a black silver-embroidered velvet coat and breeches, he appeared more a French gentleman than a rogue. Almost. For a dark purple shadow circled one eye, no doubt from a recent brawl.

"This feeling you speak of, I hope you find it pleasing." He grinned.

"I was not speaking of you." Grace tucked the cross back into her gown and looked away, wincing at her lie.

"Of course not." The lilt in his voice spoke of his disbelief.

Grace stormed away, desperate to put enough distance between them to quell the odd stirring in her belly. "What do you want? To kidnap me again?"

He shrugged. "The idea has, how do you say, crossed my mind."

"I will scream."

"And my father will come to your rescue like the hero he is," he said nonchalantly as he circled the bed and made his way toward her, his boots thumping on the wooden floor. "But beware, mademoiselle, of wolves in sheep's clothing."

Thunder boomed overhead then drifted into a rumble, and Grace backed away from him, her chest tightening. "You are the only wolf I see in this house."

He halted and raised a brow, but she saw no anger in his eyes, only hesitancy, as if he cared that he had frightened her.

"You should not be here alone in my chamber." Grace filled the uncomfortable silence. "'Tis most improper."

At that he chuckled and stepped toward the fireplace. "I believe we are past such formalities, oui?" He laid a hand on the mantel, stomped his jackboot atop the footing, and stared at the burning embers. "I hear you spent five days on the streets of Port-de-Paix. Foolish."

Grace slid behind a settee, effectively using the sofa as a barrier between them. "What did you expect? For me to sit aboard your ship and await your return?"

He smiled. "Oui. Most women would not have the courage to leave." He stepped toward her and his brow furrowed. "Were you harmed?"

Grace swallowed, her stomach constricting at the look of concern in his expression. "I survived, as you can see. God took care of me."

"God?" He snickered. "It was a trollop, I believe, who rescued you."

"God can use whomever He wishes," Grace shot back, realizing Nicole had betrayed her confidence. "You didn't harm Nicole, did you?"

For a second, he seemed genuinely pained that she considered such a thing. "Non. I would never harm her. We are friends." Captain Dubois frowned then looked down at the silk Persian rug beneath his boots. He pressed a finger over his mustache as he took up a pace across the chamber. "Ah, the opulence of my father. What do you think of it?" He gestured toward the walnut bed frame, the pair of matching mahogany nightstands, the oak dressing table with three beveled mirrors, the French tapestries lining the wall.

Baffled by the captain's fluctuating moods, Grace eyed him curiously. "What do you have against him? He seems an honorable man to me."

The captain snorted. "You do not know him." He stopped his

pacing and studied her, an odd mixture of frustration and hunger in his expression. "You must leave with me tonight."

Grace opened her mouth to protest, but he held up a hand to silence her. "I will take you back to Charles Towne."

Her breath caught in her throat. "Surely you don't expect me to believe you?"

"Non. I do not expect you to, but I would like you to." The hard sheen over his eyes softened.

"Why?" she stuttered and shook her head. "Why return me now after all this time? After all you have put me through? And what of the fortune you stand to make from my sale?"

"Things have changed."

"What has changed?" Grace dared to take a step toward him.

He swallowed and looked down, his jaw stiffening. "I was wrong to take you, mademoiselle. I thought you were someone you are not. I thought you deserved the fate I led you to."

Grace tried to make sense of his words, but they clattered around in her mind like pieces of broken china. "But you didn't know me. How could you know—"

"I know you, now." He lifted his gaze to hers.

The sincerity in his eyes sent a jolt through Grace, and she turned her back to him, not wanting to see this side of him, not wanting to believe the words he spoke. "You know nothing of me."

She heard his boots thud over the carpet toward her. "I know you are kind, generous, and courageous, that you stand true to your convictions, that you forgive those who insult you, that—"

"Stop." She held up a hand, unable to listen to the praises that slithered like lies around her ears. Was she any of those things? How could she claim such piety when she'd done naught but doubt God's love for her?

He placed his hand on her shoulder, and she spun around and stared into his dark eyes, longing to know what had caused this villain to drop his guard, to lower his devil-may-care facade. Yet all the while chastising herself for being enamored by what she saw behind them.

Rafe's hungry gaze swept over her, and Grace splayed her fingers over the bare skin beneath her neck. The maid had given her Madame Dubois's most modest gown, but still she felt exposed within its silken folds—especially when the captain's smoky eyes took her in so ardently.

As if sensing her discomfort, he took a step back. "My father has no intention of returning you to Charles Towne, mademoiselle."

"Mercy me. You expect me to take the word of a rake, a scoundrel, over that of an obvious gentleman, a man of rank and wealth."

His jaw stiffened and his right brow began to twitch. The glass wall dropped over his gaze again. Perhaps nothing had changed at all. Yet when she thought of his charitable acts in town, a spark of hope ignited. "There is good within you, Captain Dubois, I know it." Grace smiled and took another step toward him. "Your father is a Christian man. If you but follow God as he does, you can have joy and peace in your life again."

Rafe narrowed his eyes and turned away. "You do not know what you are saying."

"I know he is kind and lives an honest, respectable life, and has the blessings of God that come with it."

The captain snapped stormy eyes her way. "How do you know that? When you have just met him?"

"I am a good discerner of people." Grace raised her chin.

Rafe snorted. "Do you know what I think, mademoiselle? I think you know nothing of people, except for the religious imposters who, in the name of God, flap their tongues in judgment on everyone around them, but cannot see the darkness of their own souls."

Grace's cheeks flamed. "I know that you are a French rogue."

"And you are a prude pieuse," he spat.

"What did you call me?"

"It means pious prude."

"I know what it means." Grace's eyes burned, and she hated herself for it.

The captain released a sigh. "You will come with me now." He closed the distance between them and grabbed her arm. Pain burned across her shoulder.

She whimpered. His face softened.

"Please, mademoiselle." He loosened his grip. "I do not wish to hurt you."

A knock on the door startled Grace. "Mademoiselle, le diner est prêt."

"I must go." Grace tugged on her arm, but he did not release it, nor did he release the lock his eyes had upon hers. A strand of black hair grazed over his stiff, stubbled jaw. His dark eyes perused her face, drifting over her cheeks, lingering at her mouth, then meeting her gaze with such intensity it stunned her. Lowering her lashes, Grace watched the rise and fall of his chest beneath his coat and felt his hot breath on her skin even as her own breath took on a rapid pace. The scent of tobacco and leather swirled around her. Blood rushed to her head.

Tap tap tap. "Mademoiselle?"

Grace shook her head, trying to break free from the spell he had cast upon her. She jerked from his grasp. Throwing a hand to her chest, she looked away, her cheeks flaming. Had he noticed her reaction to him? *Oh Lord, forgive me. I do not know what is wrong with me.*

"*Une minute,* s'il vous plaît." Her voice emerged breathless.

He leaned toward her ear. "Your French improves, mademoiselle." He gave her a grin of defeat before retreating into the darkness behind the door.

A cold breeze swept over Grace as the shadows took him from her view.

"Mademoiselle?" The maid's voice rose in concern.

"Oui." Grace grabbed the door latch and turned to peer into the gloom behind the door, but she no longer saw his dark shape. He had left.

Thunder roared outside her window, echoing the silent roar inside her heart at the thought she might never see him again.

CHAPTER 16

Grace entered the dining hall, her shoes clicking on the Spanish tile. Oil paintings of ships at sea and the French countryside, along with wood-framed, hand-beveled mirrors, decorated the walls. A white marble fireplace spanned the wall to her right. The heat emanating from its smoldering red embers swirled around Grace even from across the room. Two candlelit chandeliers hung from the high ceiling, setting the long dining table aglitter in silver and gold. Swirls of steam rose from platters, spreading their aromas throughout the room. Grace's stomach leapt at the savory scents of cheese, fish, coriander, and cayenne.

In the center of the room Monsieur Dubois and a lady in a blue camlet gown conversed with none other than Mr. Thorn.

"Ah, Mademoiselle Grace." Monsieur Dubois broke away from the first mate and approached Grace, leading the lady on his arm. "May I introduce you to my wife, Madame Claire Dubois." Not much older than Grace, the petite woman with hair the color of candlelight and stark blue eyes dipped her head then rose to display a smile on her lips so tight, Grace feared it might crack her porcelain skin.

"A pleasure, mademoiselle." Her voice sang like the soft music of a harp.

"Thank you for having me in your home, Madame Dubois," Grace said. "Your husband has been most generous."

"That is Henri's way." Insincerity rang in her laughter, but Monsieur Dubois seemed to take no note of it. Behind them, Mr. Thorn nodded a greeting in Grace's direction.

132

"And you know Monsieur Thorn, I believe." Monsieur Dubois gestured toward the first mate, who looked quite dapper in his damask waistcoat.

"Yes." Relief swept over Grace at the sight of a friend. After her unsettling encounter with the captain in her chamber, coupled with her own forebodings of her future course, her nerves had snarled into tight knots. But surely, the presence of an honorable man such as Mr. Thorn spoke of Monsieur Dubois's sincerity to help her. Though she longed to cross the room and relay to the first mate all the escapades of the past five days and to thank him again for risking the captain's wrath to help her, propriety demanded she merely smile instead.

Madame Dubois stiffened, and Grace heard boots thumping on the floor behind her. She recognized the reaction in the lady, and knew Captain Dubois had entered the room.

"*Bonsoir.*" His voice, heavy with confidence, eased over Grace. "Père." A pause and then "Claire" spewed from his lips like venom.

Grace flinched at the curt tone he took with his stepmother, but the woman made no reply. Rafe slipped beside Grace and gave her a coy look as if they shared a secret. Her heart skipped a beat, and she clenched her fists, wondering why she felt relieved that he had not returned to his ship. *Why am I reacting like a common hussy, Lord? Please forgive me.*

Madame Dubois raised her thick lashes and gazed up at the captain as if he were a priceless statue. "Rafe." His Christian name floated from her pink lips, but the captain offered only a curt nod. He turned to acknowledge Mr. Thorn instead. Madame Dubois lowered her chin, and Grace thought she saw her shoulders quiver.

The hair on Grace's arms bristled at the odd relationship between stepmother and son as the tension stretched like a taut line between them.

"What happened to your face?" Monsieur Dubois pointed toward the purple, puffy skin circling the captain's right eye.

"It had an encounter with a man's fist, if you must know."

Monsieur Dubois snorted. "Brawling amongst the ignorant rabble again, Rafe? I thought you would have outgrown such childish behavior by now."

"What do you have to drink, Père?" Captain Dubois headed toward a teakwood *vaisselier* laden with bottles of all sizes and shapes.

"Same old Rafe, I see," his father mumbled.

"And you expected me to change?" The captain snorted and halted before the vaisselier. "Have *you* changed, Père?" His sarcastic tone lit the air like a fuse between them.

Monsieur Dubois frowned. "Your brandy is in its usual spot. But let us put aside our differences for one night, shall we? We have guests."

The captain smirked and poured himself a drink, and Grace felt like scolding him for being so flippant to his father when the man made every attempt to be kind.

"Shall we sit?" Monsieur Dubois led his wife to her place beside his at the head of the table.

The captain returned, a glass of brandy in his hand, and sank into a chair across from Grace but deliberately leaving an empty chair between himself and his stepmother. Madame Dubois frowned.

After they were all seated, and much to Grace's pleasant surprise, Monsieur Dubois inclined his head and led them in a prayer to bless the food. When Grace opened her eyes it was to the captain staring at her, drink already raised to his lips.

Averting her gaze, she stiffened her resolve to not allow his intimidating glances to ruin a much-needed meal or the generosity of his father.

Platters were passed and food dispensed in a much more orderly manner than on board Captain Dubois's brig. Blocks of cheddar cheese, sweet rolls, pea soup, red beans and rice, and some kind of fried shellfish passed beneath Grace's nose. She spooned a portion of each onto her plate.

"Mr. Thorn, how long have you served on my son's ship?" Monsieur Dubois asked.

"One year, monsieur."

"You are British, are you not?" Monsieur Dubois cocked his head, then at Mr. Thorn's hesitancy he added, "Ah, do not worry on my behalf. Madame Dubois has British blood in her. That is why Rafe and I are so proficient in your language."

Mr. Thorn nodded and tossed a bite of fish into his mouth, avoiding the older man's gaze. "Aye, sir. I am."

"And do you agree with my son's chosen profession?" The elder Dubois lifted a spoon of soup to his lips, which rose in a superior grin before he slurped the broth.

Mr. Thorn glanced at the captain, then back at Monsieur Dubois.

"I need the work, monsieur, and your son is a good captain. I don't give much thought to how we acquire our profit."

"Profit, ha! A man can only claim a profit from honest, hard work." Monsieur Dubois tugged upon the foam of Mechlin around his neck. "And your lack of conscience in the matter only proves you have spent far too much time in the company of my son."

"As I have spent in yours, Père." The captain sipped his brandy through clenched teeth.

She gazed between father and son, expecting a fight to break out at any moment. A chunk of cheese lodged in Grace's throat before dropping into her stomach like a rock. Madame Dubois's eyes grew wide and her face paled. Setting down her spoon, she retrieved her crystal glass and took a large gulp of burgundy wine.

"And yet"—Monsieur Dubois pointed his spoon at his son—"when I brought you and your mother here from France, I had barely two livres in my pocket. Now I own one of the grandest sugar plantations on Saint Dominique as well as two merchant ships. All acquired by honesty and the sweat of my brow. Not thievery and murder." His blue eyes turned cold.

Captain Dubois's lips slanted. "Greed and malice hidden behind your so-called respectable business is still greed and malice, mon Père. Just like wickedness cloaked beneath a shroud of piety is still wickedness. What did your Jesus call your type, 'whited sepulchres'?"

Monsieur Dubois coughed, nearly choking on his food. "You go too far, Rafe." His voice rasped even as his face turned a bright shade of red.

Grace flinched and longed to kick the captain beneath the table the way she used to do with her sisters when they misbehaved. Instead, she gathered her wits and spoke in a calm voice. "He addressed the Pharisees as such, to be sure, Captain. But to call someone else that name is to say his faith is in vain, and certainly that is not the case with your father. Besides, he is not a religious leader."

The captain chuckled and raised a brow. "I believe he would question your assessment, mademoiselle."

"I try to be an example among the community." Monsieur Dubois, having regained his breath, toyed with the fish upon his plate.

"These beans and rice are delicious." Mr. Thorn made an obvious attempt to ease the rising hostility. "My compliments to the chef."

"The Africans introduced the dish, monsieur." Madame Dubois spoke her first words since they had sat down, and Grace hoped her soothing tone would cool the men's humors. But she ceased the explanation and instead poured herself more wine as her eyes gravitated to the captain like flowers toward the sun.

But Captain Dubois kept his gaze on the brandy swirling in his glass.

Monsieur Dubois stroked his beard. "It is my duty as a *grand blanc* and a Huguenot to ensure the truth of our Lord is held in high esteem in these savage lands."

Grace faced the elder Dubois and smiled, happy to hear his priorities were in line with scripture. "I agree, monsieur. It is important to use your position to glorify God. 'Tis what I have been attempting to do in Charles Towne."

"Before my rogue son tore you from your home." Monsieur Dubois snorted and plucked a sweet roll from the tray. And for a second, Grace thought he intended to toss it at the captain.

"What is a grand blanc?" Grace asked, hoping to allay that action.

"It means *big white* or *powerful white*," the captain's voice pitched in disdain, his jaw so stiff, Grace thought it would explode. "As opposed to *petits blancs*, the merchants and tradesmen, and then the *gens de couleur*, mulattos and freed slaves, and of course, the African slaves at the bottom. You know how the civilized have need to group people according to wealth and position in order to feed their pride." His dark eyes flashed toward the elder Dubois. "And my father finds himself on top, as usual." The captain took a swig of his brandy.

Grace shook her head at him, hoping he'd see her admonition at his overindulgence in drink.

But he took no notice of her warning. "How is business, mon Père?"

"Très bien. Très bien. I've expanded the plantation lands, acquired another twenty Africans, and should produce the largest sugar crop in Port-de-Paix this year." His face grew troubled. "The only problem I have is with the maroons."

"Maroons?" Grace took a bite of the rice and beans, savoring the unusual spicy, sharp flavors.

Mr. Thorn leaned toward her. "Runaway slaves, miss. Troublemakers and rebels."

"Oui," Monsieur Dubois added. "They raid my barns and steal my livestock and crops."

"No doubt they are hungry," the captain offered with a sneer.

"Then they shouldn't have left their masters," the elder Dubois retorted.

The captain's sharp eyes swerved to his father. "No man should have a master."

Grace gave the captain a venomous look, incredulous at his statement. "And yet you intended to enslave me."

Monsieur Dubois lifted his glass, a triumphant grin on his lips. "Touché, my dear, touché."

But Rafe ignored him and kept his gaze upon Grace. "That was different." He scowled.

"I do not see how," she retorted, returning his stare with equal intensity.

A shadow of remorse passed over his gaze as seconds of tension ticked between them. All eyes shot to the captain, awaiting his response, but it was Mr. Thorn who broke the silence.

"If they were unhappy as slaves, I do not fault them for leaving." He sipped his wine and rubbed the scar on his neck. "We must do what we can in this world to provide our own justice."

"There are some ordained by God to rule, and some meant to be slaves." Monsieur Dubois wiped the crumbs from his cultured beard. "You both would understand that if you read your Bible."

"If it says that, I want no part of this God of yours," Captain Dubois shot back.

Grace's heart shriveled, both at the misunderstanding of God's Word and the captain's declaration. "I beg your pardon, Monsieur Dubois, but the Bible does not condone slavery. It merely mentions it as part of the culture at the time and suggests to those caught in its trap to rejoice that they are free in Christ."

"*Exactement.* These rebellious slaves should have rejoiced in their state and not abandoned it." The elder Dubois said this with such finality as to close the argument, and then offered Grace a spurious smile.

She took a bite of fish, deciding not to press the point, and noticing no one else enjoyed the food besides her and Mr. Thorn.

Madame Dubois passed the captain a platter of fried seafood. "Please eat, Rafe."

He pushed her hand away and held up his glass. "I am eating."

She cleared her throat and seemed to be having trouble speaking then laid a hand on his arm. "You look well. How are you faring in your life upon the sea?"

The captain stiffened. He moved his arm away and stared at his plate of uneaten food but offered her no reply.

"You are no better than a pirate, a brigand," his father muttered peevishly under his breath. "Just like that scoundrel, Jean du Casse."

The captain grimaced and leaned forward on the table. "Jean Baptiste du Casse was a hero. Governor of our island and an admiral in the French navy. If you compare me to him, I accept the compliment." He raised his glass.

Monsieur Dubois scowled. His brow grew dark. "He pillaged and plundered like any pirate, without a care for which nation he served." He snapped his drink to the back of his mouth then slammed the glass on the table. "Regardless, I do not approve of your life, boy, nor your part in it, Monsieur Thorn."

On that point, Grace found herself in agreement, yet she cringed at the harsh tone in the man's reprimand. Had she sounded equally as unforgiving when she chastised her sisters' sinful behavior? No wonder they paid her no mind.

As Mr. Thorn was doing now. With a shrug, he continued eating, obviously willing to endure insults in order to fill his belly.

The captain huffed out a sigh of impatience. "And I do not approve of your life, Père. So here we are."

"Ha! How can I expect you to approve of the honorable life I lead?" Monsieur Dubois plucked a silk handkerchief from his pocket and dabbed at the sweat on his brow. "Why is it so hot in here? Monsieur Ballin!" he barked at the servant standing at the door. "Douse those coals immediately." The man scurried to do his master's bidding while Monsieur Dubois turned steely eyes upon his son. "You were always rebellious. So much like *ta mère*."

Stunned by Monsieur Dubois's cruelty, Grace raised a hand to her mouth to stifle a gasp and then shifted her gaze to the captain, her heart aching for the pain he must feel.

But, instead of sorrow, his face reddened in anger. He slowly rose to his feet. "You may call me what you will, but you will not malign my mother's good name."

His father stood, his chair scraping over the tiles behind him. "Do you dare challenge me in my own home, boy? I should have silenced your impudence the last time we dueled."

"I was but sixteen, Père." That slow grin that so often graced the captain's lips now rose again. "I have learned much since then. And as I recall, it was I who would have bested you, if not for ma mère's intervention."

The food in Grace's stomach soured. She'd never witnessed such hatred in a family. A father and son dueling? Unheard of. She glanced at Madame Dubois, hoping to find a voice of reason, someone to step between these two, but the woman stared numbly down at her lap.

Mr. Thorn grabbed his glass and leaned back in his chair as if ready for the night's entertainment.

Gathering her courage, Grace stood. "Gentlemen, please."

Finally, Madame Dubois struggled to her feet as if weak from some disease and shifted pleading eyes to her husband. "Henri, s'il vous plaît. Do not."

He waved at her as if dismissing a servant. "Sit down and have some more wine. It is what you do best."

The food in Grace's stomach soured at the man's treatment of his wife.

Madame Dubois's shoulders slumped, and she collapsed into her chair in a shroud of despair.

Grace gripped the chain around her neck and said a silent prayer, shifting her gaze between the two men. Monsieur Dubois, her would-be rescuer—the man who only moments ago had proclaimed a devotion to spread the love of God—glared at his son, while the captain's dark eyes brewed with more anger and hatred than Grace had ever seen from a son toward his father.

Mr. Thorn finally spoke. "If I may, Monsieur Dubois, might we put the hostilities aside? Your son and I shall be gone soon enough."

"Back to the trade, eh?" Monsieur Dubois sneered, grabbed his glass, and took a swig.

The captain narrowed his eyes. "I have reasons for what I do. What are yours?"

"Ah, oui. The great Rafe Dubois, champion of those in need. I've heard enough of your praises throughout the city." Monsieur Dubois sank to his chair.

"Perhaps you should heed them and garner some praises of your own. There are many who would benefit from the riches you lavish upon yourself." The captain gestured toward their luxurious surroundings, and Grace heard naught but sincerity in his tone, and perhaps a speck of pleading, ever so slight, as if he truly cared for the poor and wished his father would do likewise.

His father guffawed. "I have no need of the praises of commoners. Besides, it is foolish to help people who by misfortune of birth, circumstance, and a propensity to slothfulness will not fend for themselves. It is the way of the world."

Madame Dubois groaned and took another drink.

Grace eyed the haughty disregard marring Monsieur Dubois's expression and could keep her tongue no longer. "But surely you understand that is not the way of God."

He gave her a cursory glance. "There is much about laziness and hard work in the Bible, mademoiselle."

"There is also much said about caring for those in need."

Monsieur Dubois's face soured, but he made no reply.

Grace could not comprehend how a man who professed faith in Jesus could be so callous. Her glance met Captain Dubois's, and he smiled at her. The smile of a friend.

She lowered her gaze, disturbed by the turn of events that had placed her on the same side as this villain.

"You will never reach my father's heart with your platitudes, mademoiselle." Captain Dubois sighed. "The man possesses no heart."

"Spoken by a man who, no doubt, has a heart." Grace said, hearing the sarcastic bite in her voice. "A heart that thinks nothing of kidnapping innocent women? Is that the type of heart my platitudes would reach, Captain?"

Without looking at her, the captain downed his brandy, rose, and headed for the vaisselier.

Monsieur Dubois grimaced and set down his fork with a clank, All emotion drained from his face as if a curtain had fallen upon it. "Mademoiselle Grace," he began in a tone of formality. "Forgive us for exposing our family contentions in front of you and Monsieur Thorn. I love my son, but as you can see, we do not agree on many things."

Madame Dubois leaned an elbow on the table. "Henri, I am not feeling very well."

The elder Dubois cast his wife a look of scorn and stood. "Pardon me, but my wife seems to have had too much to drink—yet again." He bowed to his guests then glanced at his son as Rafe returned to his seat with more brandy. "You and Monsieur Thorn may stay the night if you wish, but I want you both gone in the morning. Grielle!" He snapped his fingers, and a tall, dark man entered the room. "Escort the mademoiselle to her chamber." He inclined his head toward Grace. "For your own protection, mademoiselle. There are villains afoot." He swept a narrowed gaze over the captain and Mr. Thorn.

Then he assisted Madame Dubois from her chair and led her from the room. After their departure, a shadow fled from Captain Dubois's features. He sipped his brandy and eyed Grace as Grielle came and stood by her side.

She rose. "If I do not see you again, Captain, please know I shall be praying for you." She faced Mr. Thorn. "And you as well."

Mr. Thorn nodded. The captain stood but made no comment. Yet as Grace left the room, she felt his gaze searing her back. Resisting the urge to glance at him, she continued down the hall. She should be happy to be free of Captain Dubois, free from his plans to sell her as a slave, free to return home to Charles Towne. Then why, with each step away from him, did she feel as though she walked out of a prison only to step into a fiery furnace?

CHAPTER 17

Bong. Bong. The clock's chimes echoed through the dark halls of the Dubois home. Two in the morning. Rafe ran a hand over the back of his neck and took up his pace again over the silk-embroidered rug centering the library. Unable to sleep, he'd gone to the only room in the mansion that held more good memories than bad. A place where he and his mother had spent hours reading and playing her favorite game of *vingt-et-un.* His father detested this room. Said the flowery patterns on the chairs and walls made him squirm and softened his manliness. So it had become a ladies' parlor as well as the library, and as Rafe glanced over it now, even in the shadows, he could tell little had changed.

He ground his fists together, thinking that Claire must be using the room now for the same purpose his mother had. But he preferred to dwell on only the pleasant memories invading his mind. Breathing deeply, he could almost smell the *rose de mai* of his mother's *parfum,* which she imported from Grasse each year. Though he knew that would be impossible. She'd been dead these six years. But the pain was all too fresh.

He patted his coat pocket for a cheroot, took one out, and lit it from the embers in the fire then stood and took a puff. He glanced above the mantel where the massive emblem of the Dubois crest hung—two black lions battling against the backdrop of a red coat of arms. Rafe should have felt pride at the family insignia, yet only shame assaulted him.

His thoughts drifted to Mademoiselle Grace. When he had first seen her in his father's foyer, her raven hair wound in her usual tight bun, adorned in that satin gown that gave her an air to match her name, an unexpected thrill had sped through him. At that moment, he had been glad he had broken his vow never to return to this horrid place.

Then the meeting in her chamber. He grinned as he remembered the flush creeping up her face at his close perusal, and the petulant lift of her nose as she stood her ground against him. It had taken every ounce of his strength not to take her in his arms. He was, after all, alone with her in her chamber. But for once in Rafe's life, he cared more about not frightening a lady than he did for his own pleasure—an odd sensation that settled on him like an ill-fitting garment.

And he wasn't sure he liked it one bit.

Then after he'd restrained himself on her behalf, she had refused to listen to him; sacre mer, femme exaspérante! Rafe took another puff of his cheroot and tucked a lock of his hair behind his ear. He had given her another chance at dinner. A chance to see the true *caractère* of his father. And the man had not disappointed Rafe in his performance. Rafe shook his head. Where most women would have cowered before his father's commanding opinions, Mademoiselle Grace had expressed her own with polite bravado. The sanctimonious woman was no weakling. Yet despite the disgust Rafe had seen on her face at his father's boorish behavior, she still intended to accept his offer to return her home.

Rafe must convince her otherwise. She had no idea the danger she was in. Oui, his father may return her to Charles Towne, but it was in what condition that worried Rafe. For his father never met a person or object that he did not try to either possess or destroy.

"Rafe." His Christian name spoken in a desperate female tone swerved him about. Claire stood in the doorway in a white nightdress, her golden hair spiraling around her like a fallen halo. She floated toward him, a haunting apparition from his past.

He took a puff of his cheroot and looked away. "What do you want?"

"So *sévère*, so unfeeling. After all this time." Her voice was both melodious and melancholy like a sorrowful ballad. She halted beside him. Moonlight floating in from the tall French windows accentuated the sorrow etched upon her face.

Rafe let out a sarcastic chuckle. "Moi, sévère?" Drawing another puff, he slowly exhaled the pungent smoke, making no attempt to avoid her with the fumes.

She coughed and batted it away. "Since when do you smoke?"

"Many things have changed." He placed his boot on the fireplace.

"All things?" She stepped toward him.

Her scent of lavender swirled around him like an intoxicating elixir. "Oui." He pushed from the mantel and walked toward the window, his boots thumping his annoyance over the floor.

"I see you have recovered from your wine," he snorted.

"And you, your brandy." She paused. "It is difficult seeing you again, Rafe. Having you so close. I thought perhaps it was difficult for you, also."

Her words knifed toward Rafe, trying to slice through his heart, but he threw up his shield—the hard crust he had built bit by bit over the past five years. He turned to face her. "Je suis désolé for causing you distress, madame, but you are mistaken. You made your choice."

She approached him, her blue eyes brimming with hopeful tears. "A decision I have regretted." The moonlight shimmered over her creamy skin. She eased beside him in that alluring, feminine way, like a cat snuggling up to its owner, trusting, begging to be coddled and loved.

Rafe swallowed, his body reacting to her closeness. He had missed her. He could not deny it. "We all live with regrets."

She laid a hand on his arm, and a spark shot through Rafe. "But must we live with this one?" Then planting a kiss on her finger, she dabbed it on his bruised eye.

Her touch, her scent, the sweet sound of her voice combined in a swirling pool of memories that played havoc with his senses. For a moment, he felt like a young man again, newly in love with the most beautiful woman in the world. Mais non. Too much had happened since that mystical time. He grabbed her hand and jerked it from him. "Sacre mer. You are my father's wife."

She lowered her gaze. "If that is what you call me."

"Oui, that is what I call you, madame. It is a truth that has invaded my worst nightmares these long years."

"Then you *do* still care?" Her voice cracked as she raised her chin.

Rafe clenched his jaw and averted his gaze from her pleading eyes. A battle brewed within him—a battle filled with desire, love, betrayal, and hatred, each emotion struggling for dominance.

"He is cruel to me, Rafe."

"You knew what he was like."

SAINT

Rafe took a final puff of his cheroot, walked to the fireplace, and flicked it into the coals. He must leave before he gave in to every base impulse within him. "I suggest you return to your bed before my father wakes and finds you missing." He turned and stomped out.

⁓

Grace rose from the dining table and pushed back her chair. "Merci." She nodded her thanks to the servant manning the buffet laden with croissants, orange marmalade, and coffee. More exhausted than she realized, she had overslept and missed breaking her fast with Monsieur Dubois and his wife. An event she was not at all unhappy to have escaped.

She'd learned from the butler that Monsieur Dubois had business to attend to and Madame Dubois had taken to her chamber with a headache. Passing through the dining room out into the hallway, Grace couldn't shake the overwhelming cloud of despair that permeated the walls of the Dubois home. Rather than succumb to the weighty oppression, she headed out the front door for some fresh air. Making her way down the stairs, she squinted against the sun hovering above the eastern hills, not yet high enough to inflict its searing rays upon the inhabitants of the island.

Movement caught her eye, and she glanced to her right where Monsieur Dubois stood with his back to her, speaking with another man beneath a ficus tree. They huddled together as if exchanging a grand secret, only whispers of which drifted past her ears. She started off in the other direction, not wanting to intrude, when Monsieur Dubois chuckled. It was a maniacal chuckle that sent a shudder through her and drew her gaze back to the men. Monsieur Dubois slapped the other man on the back and stepped aside, giving Grace a view of his identity.

It was Mr. Thorn.

Slipping behind a hedgerow, she inched her way closer to the men.

"So everything is in order, then?" Monsieur Dubois said.

"Yes, I will meet you as planned."

The sound of hands slapping against each other filled the air. "Finally I will put Rafe in his place." Monsieur Dubois chuckled.

"And I will have my revenge," Thorn growled. "But what of Miss Grace?"

"What of her?" Monsieur Dubois's voice held a nonchalant lilt.

Grace couldn't help the gasp that escaped her lips. The men grew silent, and she could see through the leaves of the bush that their gazes had shot in her direction. Covering her mouth, she inched her way along the hedgerow away from them. Boot steps thudded toward her. In a frenzy, she plucked her handkerchief from the sleeve of her gown and tossed it to the ground just as Mr. Thorn and Monsieur Dubois cornered the bush.

Mr. Thorn's frown darkened. "What on earth are you doing, Miss Grace?" He studied her face, no doubt searching for evidence that she had heard their conversation.

"Mr. Thorn. Monsieur Dubois." Grace forced a smile to her lips and then lowered her gaze. "Oh, there it is." Bending down, she picked up her handkerchief. "This silly thing blew away from me in the breeze and I was just retrieving it."

Monsieur Dubois narrowed his eyes upon her. "I was on my way into town to arrange your passage back home, mademoiselle, when I ran into Monsieur Thorn. He has some amusing stories of his time in the British navy."

"No doubt he does." Grace smiled again. "Though I daresay I wasn't close enough to hear them." With her statement, both men's shoulders seemed to lower in relief. "I cannot thank you enough for procuring me a ship home, Monsieur," she added.

"My pleasure, mademoiselle." Monsieur Dubois nodded.

"Good day to you both." Grace excused herself and started on her way.

"Good day, mademoiselle."

It wasn't until she turned down a narrow pathway that Grace realized her heart was in her throat. What plans had the men been discussing? From the sounds of it, they were up to no good. Stuffing the handkerchief back into her sleeve, she hugged herself as a chill struck her. Her name had been mentioned and then batted away as if she were of no consequence. Did Monsieur Dubois still intend to escort her home?

Weaving around the corner of the house, Grace drew in a deep breath of air laden with moist earth, tropical flowers, a hint of the sea, and the sharp scent of sugar cane. She halted for a moment and watched as a group of slender white birds with long tail feathers and black markings on their heads flitted from tree to tree above her, their joyful warble helping to ease her tension. Perhaps she was making too much of a conversation she had heard only parts of. Careful to avoid the puddles formed from last night's storm, she silently gave thanks to God for bringing her to safety and for being faithful when her own faith had waned. She thought of Monsieur and Madame Dubois and sent up a petition for them as well, for it was obvious they were unhappy together. "They need You, Lord. They need Your forgiveness and love."

To her left, a vine of red and pink flowers spread over the side of the house as if trying to mask the misery within. How could she help this family? Monsieur Dubois had voiced his intent to serve God, although Grace had seen little to validate that claim. Perhaps all the man required was a bit of guidance on the scriptures, and in particular instruction on how to love his wife as the Bible commanded. Grace could certainly provide that.

Continuing on her way, she clutched her skirts to avoid another puddle and gazed out into the distant fields where the dark shapes of slaves tending the sugar cane bowed and rose in the rising sun. The crack of a whip sliced the air. She shuddered. She'd seen mistreated slaves back in Charles Towne, but the sight never failed to send a ripple of revulsion through her.

A path appeared through a patch of pine trees and Grace followed it, unable to shake the sorrow that had attached itself to her that morning before she'd even arisen from her bed. She was going home tomorrow. She should be happy. And though she tried to focus on her good fortune, her traitorous thoughts kept drifting to Captain Dubois. He had no doubt left the plantation at dawn and was at present preparing *Le Champion* to set sail.

She had been delivered!

But knowing she would never see the captain again left a gnawing ache in her soul. She didn't know why. *Please, forgive me Lord. Why am I obsessed with this miscreant who would no doubt sell his own sister for a profit?* Several minutes passed as shame hung heavy on her shoulders, weighing them down as she made her way along the muddy path.

And then she saw him.

The object of her thoughts, standing in an opening up ahead—a small graveyard—his cocked hat in hand, head bowed over a gravestone.

Her heart leapt, and she halted, wanting to call out to him. But not wishing to intrude, she turned to leave.

"Mademoiselle." That deep voice sounded through the clearing, easing over her like warm silk, turning her around.

"Forgive me, Captain. I did not know you were here."

"Of course not. How could you?" He attempted a smile.

She inched toward him, noting the moist sheen covering his dark eyes. "I thought you would be gone by now." He had replaced his gentlemanly attire with his buccaneer garb once again: purple and gold sash girding his waist, rapier hung at his hip, and his baldric strapped across his white shirt.

He dropped his gaze to the grave, and Grace read the markings on the stone:

MADAME ROCHELLE DUBOIS

NÉE LE CINQUIÈME OCTOBRE EN L'AN DE GRÂCE MILLE SIX CENT SOIXANTE-TREIZE

QUITTÉE LE MONDE LE SEIZIÈME MAI EN L'AN DE GRÂCE MILLE SEPT CENT DOUZE

"Your mother." She raised a hand to her throat. "Forgive me. I should leave."

He reached out and touched her arm. "Stay, s'il vous plaît." He glanced down again. "I have not visited her since they laid her in the ground."

"You haven't been home in six years?"

"Five, but the year after her death, I could not bring myself to see her—not like this." He shifted his stance and stomped his boot atop a rock as if trying to crush it. "She was a good woman. Kind, generous, a lady of great honor."

A sudden breeze blew in from the cane fields, stirring a pile of leaves beside the grave into a frenzy and loosening a coil of hair from Grace's bun. She hugged herself, unsure how to respond to this side of the captain that seemed so vulnerable, so troubled—a side that touched her heart in a way she had never thought possible. A villain, a thief, yet giving his wealth to the poor. Rebellious, disrespectful to his father, yet possessing such honor and love for his mother. His grief reopened an old wound in Grace's heart at the loss of her own mother some seven years ago.

"She was murdered," Rafe said, answering the question burning in Grace's mind.

"Mercy me." She clasped her chain, tears bidding entrance into her eyes.

"In a British raid."

Grace felt as if she'd swallowed a stone that now sank to the bottom of her stomach.

The captain gripped the pommel of his rapier. "In retaliation for Jean du Casse's raid upon Cartagena in ninety-seven, the British and Spanish raided Cap-Francais and Port-de-Paix, burning our homes, stealing our produce, slaves, and women. My father was away and I was"—he grimaced—"occupied in town. By the time I arrived home, she was dead."

"You found her?"

"Oui." His lips tightened. "She suffered greatly before she died."

The agony he'd endured made Grace long to reach out to him. But then something cold gripped her heart. "What year was it?"

"1712."

Tears blurred Grace's vision. Her father had been in command of a fleet in the Caribbean at that time. She remembered it clearly because her mother had been dead less than a year and she had been angry at her father for leaving her and her sisters alone so soon. Her head began to spin. Dare she ask? Did she want to know? She threw a hand to her throat to ease the fear and agony burning within it. "Was my father involved?" Agony garbled her voice.

The captain drew in a ragged breath, but he did not look at her.

"Tell me it isn't true?" Grace laid a hand on his arm, drawing his tortured gaze to hers.

"He was in command of the fleet." Rafe's brow darkened. "The captain who attacked Port-de-Paix reported to your father, but I do not know whether he followed your father's orders or not."

All the air escaped from Grace's lungs and she hung her head. Now she understood why Captain Dubois had no qualms about kidnapping her. She was the daughter of Admiral Henry Westcott. The blood of his worst enemies, the people who ravished and murdered his mother, flowed in Grace's veins. She longed to apologize but knew the words would fall meaningless into the mud at her feet.

"So that is why, then," she said as more of a statement than a question.

He shook his head and his shoulders sank. "It was the encouragement I needed to perform a task I normally would not have undertaken."

Her heart jumped. "So you don't normally kidnap innocent women?"

She attempted a weak smile and was rewarded with the slight lift of his lips in return.

"The money would have provided a hospital for the poor." He shrugged, then his eyes grew serious. "There are many sick on this island. Many die each day." He swept his pained gaze toward the sugar fields. "I made a promise to a good man."

Grace's mind swirled in confusion. "One good deed is not enough to negate a wicked act."

"Perhaps." He gripped the pommel of his rapier. "But at the time I did not consider selling you to the don to be wicked, only recompense for the actions of your father."

"And now?" Grace's breath quickened.

He looked at her. "As I have said. Things have changed. You are not what I expected."

His words sang sweetly in her ears. She had misjudged him. He was not the rogue he often pretended to be.

Bending over, the captain plucked a small purple flower from a bush and laid it gently on his mother's grave. "*Reposez-vous en paix, Maman.*"

A tear slid down Grace's cheek. Captain Dubois faced her, his stormy gaze filled with pain, not the anger she expected. His brow wrinkled, and he raised a hand to wipe her tear away then allowed his thumb to caress her cheek. "Do not cry for me."

Grace closed her eyes beneath his touch. Her breath lodged in her throat. She heard him move closer, and she stepped back.

He dropped his hand, the features of his face hardening. "You must come to the brig with me."

Only then did Grace realize her precarious position. With no servants around and Monsieur Dubois away from the house, the captain could easily capture her again.

"Your father has promised to deliver me to Charles Towne," she muttered a bit too fast.

"The price will be too high."

"He charges me nothing, Captain."

He huffed and ran a hand through his hair. "Not yet." He rubbed the purple and black bruise around his eye, and a strange desire overcame her to plant a tender kiss upon it. Pushing the thought away, she turned aside.

"I can see that there is bad blood between you. It saddens me to see a father and son fight so viciously." The shrill voice of a taskmaster and the snap of a whip in the distance only accentuated her statement. "Regardless of what your father has done to you, Captain, you have a Father in heaven. He is the Father of all—especially those whose earthly fathers have disappointed them." But the scowl on his face told Grace that her words bounced off his hard heart and disappeared into the air. "Perhaps I can help you reconcile your differences."

Captain Dubois gazed over the cane fields. "There is no reconciliation, mademoiselle, with or without God's love."

Grace swallowed at the finality of his tone. Yet by his father's words and actions the night before, she believed the elder Dubois suffered from the same hopelessness. "I must admit I feel a sense of unease in your father's presence." Truth be told, Monsieur Dubois's behavior toward his wife, his son, and his general attitudes about position and wealth did not indicate a changed heart within. "And I did not care for his behavior last night."

"Then come back to *Le Champion* with me."

His urgent tone startled Grace. She wanted to believe him—to believe he wasn't a villain, a scoundrel. But perhaps he was only toying with her.

He grabbed her arm. "If you come with me now, I promise to take you home."

Grace searched his dark eyes for some shred of truth. He had kidnapped her, insulted her, held her captive, and intended to sell her as a slave, yet naught but sincerity burned in his gaze now. "What is the promise of a rogue worth?"

"At the moment?" He raised a brow and grinned. "Everything."

"What of your hospital?"

He shrugged. "I will find another way."

Grace studied him. The wind whipped a strand of his dark hair across his jaw, yet the firm press of his fingers on her arm offered her more comfort than threat. *Lord, what do I do?*

He reached up and fingered the curl that had loosened from her bun. "Why do you hide this *beaux cheveux* in such a tight knot?"

Grace's breath escaped her. "To keep myself from vanity," she managed to mutter.

He leaned and whispered in her ear, "I doubt you could ever be vain, mademoiselle." His warm breath sent a shiver down her back. "But why deprive others of your beauty?"

Tugging from his grip, Grace threw a hand to her throat and stepped back. Her thoughts and emotions spun in a whirlpool of confusion that left her numb.

The captain gripped his baldric. "I know you have no reason to trust me. But I am begging you to believe what I say."

Gathering her wits, Grace snapped her eyes to his. "What concern is it of yours what your father does with me?"

"Because you have fallen into his hands on my account."

Grace frowned. Was Monsieur Dubois truly that dangerous? Or was the captain only playing a game? She gazed at him, enjoying the way the soft lines of concern had replaced the hard arrogance on his face. If he was lying to her, he was a master at deception, for Grace had always been good at discerning the intentions of others. Rafe made no pretensions about his lifestyle and seemed to exhibit shame at his mistakes. But Monsieur Dubois's actions defied his proclamation of Christian love. Not to mention the odd exchange she had heard between him and Mr. Thorn. Perhaps he did intend to do Grace harm. She closed her eyes for a second to drown out the sights around her—especially Rafe—and decide what to do. Neither man invoked her trust, but if she had to choose based on the leaning of her heart, she would choose the captain.

Perhaps it was Captain Dubois she was supposed to help after all. During their journey home, Grace would have time to recite scripture and expound to him the goodness of God. Yes, surely that was her mission. Elation surged through her at the thought of bringing this man to redemption.

"Very well. I will go with you." She gave him a weak smile as her stomach folded in on itself. Why was she putting herself back into this rogue's hands? Had she gone mad?

"I have your word, then?" He took a step toward her and looked down at her with more intensity than she had ever seen in his eyes. "Your promise. A promise that will not be broken."

"You have my word." She nodded. "I am not one to break a vow, Captain."

"Non. I would not expect so." He smiled.

"But please allow me to express my gratitude to your father and stepmother for their kindness and bid them farewell."

Disapproval shadowed his face. He scratched the stubble on his jaw. "Not a good idea."

"It is the right thing to do, Captain."

He grinned. "You realize I could kidnap you right here if I so desired."

"It has crossed my mind, Captain, and the fact that you haven't has convinced me of your sincerity."

He grunted in disappointment. "Très bien. But I will not set foot in that house again."

"I will meet you here, in this same spot, at seven tonight." A bead of perspiration slid down her back.

He cocked his head and examined her. "I will be here, mademoiselle." Then he bowed, donned his plumed hat, and strode away.

Grace's legs would not move. Her skin tingled where the captain's fingers had touched her arms. Glancing down at Madame Dubois's grave, she longed to ask the woman about her son. Could he be trusted? Should Grace go with him?

But it was too late for that. The woman was not here, and Grace had already given her word. She had willingly submitted herself back into the hands of a man who had given her no reason to trust him. Either this was truly God's will or she had gone completely mad.

CHAPTER 18

Grace swept a final gaze over her chamber and wondered why. She had no belongings to take with her, save the gown on her back. And even that didn't belong to her. Though a trifle low in the neckline, it was a far more beautiful gown than any of her own back in Charles Towne. And somehow the shimmering green satin embroidered with silver braided ribbons that laced across her ruffled bodice made her feel beautiful. Besides, she liked the way it sounded when she strolled across the room. Mercy me, what was wrong with her? She'd never cared about such fripperies before. Regardless, she'd promised to return the gown as soon as she arrived home.

If she arrived home.

Her discussion with Monsieur Dubois and his wife had gone better than expected. Though the captain's father could not understand Grace's decision to trust his son and not accept his free offer of transport to Charles Towne, he finally acquiesced to her wishes. But only after pleading with her most adamantly to change her mind.

Which she nearly had.

Especially when Monsieur Dubois kept referring to his son as a liar and a blackguard.

Yet after thanking the couple for their kindness, Grace had withdrawn to her chamber to await the appointed time she had agreed to meet the captain. Now, as the hands on the clock sitting atop the mantel inched toward seven, her heart cinched. Her stomach soured, and she found herself regretting her decision.

Lord, am I doing the right thing?

No answer came. No noise, save the swaying of the wind outside the window and soft footfalls outside her door. The oak panel creaked on its hinges, and Madame Dubois peered around the edge. Tearstains marred her pink face. "Bien, you are still here. May I speak with you a moment, Mademoiselle Grace?"

"Of course." Grace gestured her inside.

After slipping through the opening, Madame Dubois closed the door then leaned her ear against it as if listening to see if she had been followed.

"Whatever is the matter, Madame Dubois?" Unease rumbled over Grace's already agitated nerves.

The elegant woman lifted a finger to her lips, waited a moment, then released a deep sigh. Crossing the room, she eased onto the bed and dropped her head into her hands. Her golden curls bobbed as a sob racked through her.

Grace sat beside her, her heart breaking as it always did in light of someone else's anguish. "Is there something I can do?"

Lifting her head, Madame Dubois raised a handkerchief to her nose as tears rolled one after the other down her cheeks. "I cannot bear it another minute."

"Bear what, madame?" Grace longed to grasp her hand but didn't dare.

"My husband." She sobbed. "He is a cruel man. *Certainement,* you can see that."

Grace stiffened at the woman's confession. Did all French women speak with such alarming honesty—especially to a stranger? Yet Grace could not deny what she had witnessed. "He possesses a quick temper. I have noticed as much."

"It is far worse than that." Madame Dubois hesitated then squeezed her eyes shut against another wave of tears. "He beats me. He has many mistresses, many of whom he parades daily before my face."

The announcement struck Grace like a cold slap in the face. This man who declared that his purpose on the island was to glorify God. Could it be true? But why would Madame Dubois lie? Despite Grace's attempt to think well of her benefactor, she had witnessed his callous behavior firsthand.

"I'm so sorry, madame." Against propriety, Grace took the woman's delicate, soft hand and gave it a squeeze. Minutes passed as they sat in silence, and Grace wondered what to say to comfort the lady. "I have a sister, Charity, who married a beast of a man," she finally said. "She lives in agony every day of her life. But I cannot help her. I can only pray for her. As you must do, madame." Grace knelt before the woman and peered up into her swollen face. "Pray for God to change your husband's heart, to convict him of his sin. If he would but repent and turn back to God, his heart would change."

A look of disbelief crossed Madame Dubois's delicate features. Outrage followed it. "I have prayed, Mademoiselle Grace. For many years. And I believe God has answered by sending you to me."

"Me? What can I do but pray for you?"

"You can help me leave him." Madame Dubois leaned forward and enfolded Grace's hands with her own. "If you go to him and tell him you've changed your mind and wish to take him up on his offer, I will convince him that we should accompany you to Charles Towne."

"Accompany me?" Grace blinked. "But why would he agree?"

"He has been meaning to see to some business dealings he has in New France." Madame Dubois's blue eyes sparkled like the sea in bright sunlight. "Then when we reach Charles Towne, I will get off the ship with you."

Grace's head swam beneath the woman's suggestion—a suggestion that if Grace followed would change everything.

"I would not dare escape on my own," she continued. "For I have nowhere to go, no money. But perhaps your family could grant me lodging until I contact my mother's brother in Virginia."

The desperation flaming in Madame Dubois's eyes burned through Grace's resolve. She could not reject this poor woman's plea for help. Hadn't Grace prayed for someone to come alongside Charity should her sister ever decide to leave her husband? Someone who would help her get away to safety? How could she do any less for this pitiable lady?

But she'd given her word to Captain Dubois.

Madame Dubois awaited her answer, her eyes pooling with pleading tears that tore at Grace's heart.

"But I promised Captain Du—"

"Of what value is a promise made to a liar and a thief?" she snapped.

"A promise is a promise, madame." Grace lowered her chin, wondering at the woman's sudden disdain for her stepson when she seemed quite enamored with him last evening.

Madame Dubois patted Grace's hand as one would a little child. "Do you think he intends to honor his promise to take you to Charles Towne? Silly girl."

Grace stood. "Yes, I do." She surprised herself with the confidence of her tone.

Madame Dubois began sobbing again. "Then I am lost." She dropped her head into her hands. "Monsieur Thorn told me you were a kind woman."

"Mr. Thorn? What has he to do with this?"

"It was his idea that I come to you." She lifted her swollen, puffy face to Grace. "For both our well-beings, he said."

"But I am to meet the captain soon." Grace glanced at the clock. Ten minutes past seven. No doubt he was already waiting for her. She bit her lip. "Why do you not come with us?"

"With Rafe?" Madame Dubois's eyes widened as if Grace had asked her to jump out the window. "Even if he plans on taking you to Charles Towne, he would never allow me on his ship. He hates me."

"I doubt that, madame." Although as Grace recalled, the captain had been less than cordial to his stepmother.

Madame Dubois gripped Grace's hand again. "Please do not abandon me, mademoiselle. You are my only hope." The despair in her voice sent a shiver through Grace and drew her down beside the woman, where she wrapped an arm around her shoulder. Rafe had said his father was not to be trusted. This woman's tale only further endorsed that report, so how could Grace leave her in the hands of a monster? "What happened between Rafe and his father?" She could not help the question for she had to know the truth.

Madame Dubois glanced toward the window. "There has always been competition between them. From when Rafe was very little. Henri challenged him constantly. Everything was a contest. Then he would lash and humiliate Rafe afterward—especially if he won. Vraiment, I do not believe he loves his son. He treats him as if Rafe were not his own flesh and blood." She dabbed at her tears. "At least that is what Rafe has told me, and I have not seen evidence to the contrary."

A sudden pain gripped Grace's stomach, and she pressed a hand upon it. The sorrow of such a childhood was beyond her comprehension. But even more confusing was Madame Dubois's actions. "If you knew this, why did you marry Monsieur Dubois?"

"I was a foolish young girl who thought wealth would solve all my problems." She waved her handkerchief through the air, then turned anxious eyes to Grace. "Please do not leave me with him."

Grace felt as if a war raged within her members. Break a vow or save a life. Which was more important? Which one would God have her choose? She squeezed the madame's hand. "I will not abandon you, madame."

"Merci. Merci," the woman sobbed. "You are too kind."

Maybe, Lord, this is the reason You have brought me all this way. To save this poor girl from the horrors of her marriage.

"I must tell the captain of my change of plans." Grace rose and turned toward the door.

"Non. Mademoiselle." Madame Dubois grabbed her arm. "If you go to him now, he will kidnap you again. You do not know him as I do." She gave Grace a look that intimated she too had affections for Rafe, and the sight of it took Grace aback.

"Monsieur Thorn said he would inform him if you agreed," she continued and dabbed the handkerchief beneath her puffy eyes. "And Captain Dubois must never know why you changed your mind."

"Why not?"

Madame Dubois's blue eyes turned to ice. "Because if he knew what his father had done to me he would kill him."

Every step Rafe took over the muddy street sent a thunderous ache through his head. Doffing his cocked hat, he wiped the sweat from his brow and trudged forward. Irksome noises assailed him from all directions. Bells chiming, people screaming, horses clomping, the grating crank of carriage wheels, the lap of waves, and the incessant chatter of the mob, all increased in a cacophony of clatter in his pounding head.

Greetings and hails shot his way, but he dismissed them, in no mood for talking today. The fetor of manure, stale fish, and rotten fruit curled beneath his nose, causing his stomach to heave and nearly spew its contents—if there had been any.

Last night was a dismal, nightmarish blur. But beside his aching head and a knife wound on his arm, Rafe suffered no permanent damage.

When Monsieur Thorn had met him at the graveyard and informed him that Mademoiselle Grace had changed her mind and would be leaving with his father on the morrow, Rafe had ordered him to make ready the ship, then he leapt upon his horse and galloped to his favorite tavern at the edge of town. After he had downed the first several drinks, the rest of the evening transformed into broken memories floating in his mind, none of which fit into any sensible pattern.

Femme exaspérante. Non. Liar, deceiver, *traître*. Just like all women. Why had he been foolish enough to expect this one to keep her promise? Why had he not known she would run into his father's arms just as Claire had done? Rafe clenched his fists as he sidestepped a passing horse and rider. He heard his name called from a shop to his left, followed by another shout, but he ignored them.

Such intimacies he had shared about his mother with the mademoiselle at the graveyard; his face heated. And the way she had cried for him. A ploy? Another feminine trick to soften a man's heart into mush? He spit onto the ground and shoved his way through a mob of fishermen, ignoring their protests. Like her father, like all British, she wore a cloak of honor and kindness that did not exist once circumstances tore it from her.

Rafe had been duped again.

After he had vowed never to allow another woman access to his heart. The lovely raven-haired mademoiselle had pretended to care about Rafe only so he wouldn't kidnap her on the spot. Rafe kicked a rock across the road. *Je suis un imbécile!*

But it wasn't too late. If the mademoiselle could toss her vows so quickly to the wind, why couldn't he?

His father had won again. He had stolen another woman from Rafe. The thought sent waves of searing fury through him. He needed to leave this place as soon as possible. He must bid *adieu* to Abbé Villion, wipe the mud of Port-de-Paix from his boots, and head out to sea where he belonged—away from devious women and his depraved father.

Edging around the stone church, Rafe headed toward an oblong brick building. He shoved open the heavy door; its slam against the stones echoed through the building. Rafe stomped inside, squinting as his eyes grew accustomed to the dim light.

Then it hit him. A blast of hot, fetid air that smelled of human waste and mold.

And death.

His anger fell from him like an overused cloak.

Boxes, barrels, and crates flanked him, lit by four small windows, two on each side of the oblong structure. He recognized some of the goods he had recently delivered and began weaving his way down a narrow path between them toward a lighted area at the far end. Moans of pain slinked their way toward him as Abbé Villion appeared from amidst the clutter.

Despite the bloody rag in his hand, the abbé smiled. "Rafe. How are you?"

"Très bien," he lied, scanning the area behind the abbé where the sick lay on cots lined against the wall. An African woman dabbed a cloth on a young mulatto's forehead. "I have come to bid you *au revoir*. I set sail today."

"I am sorry to hear it, my friend." Abbé Villion's eyebrows pulled into a frown. "When will you return?"

A rat scrambled across the dirt floor by Rafe's boots while another moan sounded from the cots, drawing his gaze back to the sick child. "Who is that?"

Abbé Villion's face seemed to sag. He sighed and turned around, gesturing toward the cot where the woman tended the young boy. "Young Corbin, an orphan. He has the ague, I believe."

Rafe glanced from the boy to the other patients, noting how young they were, all except one giant African man curled up in a ball like a baby. "And the others?"

"Different ailments." Abbé Villion shrugged. "I am no physician."

"This is no place for the ill, in this squalor." Rafe's heart shrank, even as his frustration rose.

"At least here they are safe from the rain."

Brushing past the abbé, Rafe gazed at the sick, his already ailing stomach curdling within him.

From one of the cots, the dark brown eyes of a boy who looked to be no more than six years old stared blankly up at Rafe. In the child's vacant eyes, he saw a hopelessness so intense it made him shiver.

And in that instant, no matter the cost, Rafe felt a renewed sense of urgency. He could not delay his promise to the abbé any longer.

CHAPTER 19

Yellow and orange flames thrust their bony fingers toward the black sky, lunging, leaping, as if trying to escape their dark prison. Grace's heart seized and she whirled about. More flames shot up around her like blasts from a cannon. The heat scorched her gown, her skin, her hair. Pain seared through her. Pain that never ended. Pain that was never satisfied.

Because nothing ever burned.

She peered beyond the circle of flames. More fires flared, illuminating the massive jagged rocks strewn across the barren landscape. Balls of burning pitch and ear-piercing wails shot from black craters. Grace darted in the direction of one of them and peered over the side. Naught but molten blazing rock met her gaze. Yet the screams continued. Nothing had changed.

Always hearing, but never seeing anyone.

No, Lord, not again. Grace collapsed to the sharp rocks that made up the floor of the hideous place and she dropped her head into her hands. A soft voice slid over her. Wiping the tears from her face, she looked up. Not five paces from where she sat stood her sister Hope, her honey blond hair tossing this way and that in the hot blasts coming from the crater. Hope reached out her hand toward Grace and smiled.

Jumping to her feet, Grace darted toward her. "Hope! Hope!" But just as their fingertips grazed, Hope disappeared. "No! Come back! Hope!"

Grace's chest heaved, and she opened her eyes. Darkness everywhere.

No flames, no moans, no screams. In place of the heat, a chill swept over her. She rubbed her eyes and saw the curtains fluttering at the window of her chamber.

Her chamber at Monsieur Dubois's house.

She released a deep breath. Another nightmare. Shivering, she hugged herself, dabbed at the perspiration on her forehead, then swung her legs over the side of the bed. Had she left the window open?

A form emerged from the shadows. A man's form. Grace tried to scream, but he grabbed her arm, twisted her around, and flattened his palm over her mouth.

The smell of tobacco and leather swirled beneath her nose. *Captain Dubois.* She struggled, but this time he didn't release her, didn't remove his hand, didn't allow her to speak. And though he didn't hurt her, his touch was firm, determined.

He turned her so she could see him in the mirror and motioned for her silence. His hand fell away. Grace opened her mouth to ask him what he was doing but before she could utter a sound, he shoved a handkerchief into it and tied it behind her head.

Terror consumed her. Why was he so angry? Mr. Thorn had told her that the captain had accepted her decision and had ordered him to prepare the ship to sail. He had reassured her all was well as he bade her farewell.

Grace groaned as loudly as the cloth in her mouth allowed and reached up to loosen it. But the captain grabbed her hands and tied her wrists behind her. Then hoisting her over his shoulder, he sat on the window ledge, grasped a rope he must have tied to her bedpost during her dream, and flung them both out the window.

"Stay still." His voice was stern, emotionless. Grace's head dangled against his back. The ground loomed in the shadows some thirty feet below her. He released his grip about her legs. Her heart froze as she realized she could fall if she moved the wrong way.

Bracing his boots against the side of the house, he grasped the rope with both hands and inched his way down. Grace squeezed her eyes shut, trying to keep her balance over his shoulder. The muscles in his shoulders and back flexed and strained as he ambled down the siding. Then he clutched her legs again and jumped to the ground with a thud that slapped her cheek against his back.

Grace's head gorged with blood, blurring her vision and making her upside-down world seem more like a dream than reality. Or rather, a reoccurring nightmare as the musky smell of his waistcoat brought back memories of the first time this man had stolen her from her home.

Taking her by the waist, he lifted her up to sit sideways on a horse then leapt behind her. Tugging the reins, he nudged the beast, and they dashed into the darkness.

Wind, heavy with moisture and the scents of forest and flowers, swept over her, flinging the loose wisps of her hair back over the captain. The heat from his body and the touch of his arms as he manipulated the reins alarmed her to the realization that she wore only a thin nightdress. An ache tugged at her throat. Her mouth parched until she could hardly breathe as once again all her hopes were obliterated beneath this brigand's volatile moods. And what would happen to Madame Dubois? Who would come to her rescue now?

The next hour passed in such stunning familiarity that if not for the gag in her mouth, Grace would have thought she only dreamed about the journey to Port-de-Paix, her frightening time alone in town, and finding freedom with Monsieur Dubois.

At the docks, Captain Dubois led her into a small boat, manned by two of his men, and in minutes Grace found herself once again staring at the dark hull of *Le Champion*. The captain pulled her to her feet. Grace tried to meet his gaze, desperate to discover his intent, desperate to find some shred of the concern she'd grown accustomed to seeing in his eyes of late. But he kept his face averted, refusing her a glimpse of his thoughts.

Up the rope ladder and down the companionway he carried her. Then, lowering her to the deck, he shoved her into her cabin. Grace's eyes filled with tears as he untied the gag and tore it from her mouth then freed her hands.

Slowly she turned to face him. His dark eyes blazed like the fires she'd witnessed in her nightmare. She swallowed. A tear escaped her lashes and slid down her cheek.

His chest heaved beneath his white buccaneer shirt, whether from exertion or anger, she couldn't tell. Strands of his ebony hair had loosened from their tie and wandered over his cheek as if seeking an anchor in this madness.

Grace shivered beneath his perusal and wrapped her arms over her nightdress.

His breathing slowed, and he shifted his jaw. "Who is Hope?"

"Why have you taken me again? Let me go!" She stormed toward him and tried to squeeze past him out the door, but his body might as well have been one of the ship's masts as strong and sturdy as it was. Sobbing, she retreated.

"Who is Hope?" he asked again.

"My sister." Her voice came out as if her mouth were stuffed with cotton. "I had a nightmare about her. She was in hell."

He stared at her, his eyes a glass wall, the twitch in his eyelid the only indication of any emotion.

The captain's bold gaze refused to leave her. Grace's face heated. "Now I'm wondering if I am not there as well," she added, trying to cover more of her nightdress.

The captain shrugged off his gray coat and handed it to her. As she reached out for it, a flicker of concern softened his eyes, giving Grace a moment of hope.

But then it was gone.

She held his coat up to cover her chest. "Why?"

He grabbed his baldric. "I thought you were something you are not."

"What am I, then?"

"You are the price of a hospital." Then he stepped out and slammed the door, leaving Grace alone in the darkness.

Rafe bunched his arms over his chest and gazed across the indigo sea. A half-moon sitting a handbreadth over the horizon flung bands of glittering silver upon the waves, lending a dreamlike appearance to the scene. He inhaled a deep breath of the salty air, the smell of fish and life and freedom. Beneath him, milky foam bubbled off the stern of the ship before vanishing into the dark waters beyond—like everything beautiful, everything good. Anything worthwhile in this life turned out to be but a dream, a vapor; if one dared try to grab hold of it, it simply vanished.

The ship pitched over a swell, and Rafe braced his boots against the deck. He plucked a flask from his pocket and took a gulp of brandy before replacing the cork and slipping the container back into his coat. The liquor took a warm stroll down his throat as the sound of a fiddle and the voices of men playing cards blared from behind him. His crew seemed happy to be at sea once again and on their way to procure a fortune.

Rafe wished he could share their mirth.

But the vision of Mademoiselle Grace shivering in her cabin would not obey his order to vacate his thoughts: the braids of her long raven hair swinging over her white nightdress like liquid obsidian on cream; her emerald eyes moist with tears; her bottom lip trembling. And all he had wanted to do was take her in his arms and comfort her. Sacre mer, what spell had la femme cast upon him? Even after her betrayal, even after a day out at sea, he still couldn't get her out of his mind. He shook his head, scattering his thoughts of her. This time he must not allow himself to become attached to her. This time he would keep his distance.

Shoes scuffed over the deck behind him, and Rafe flattened his lips. He craved no company on this dark night, preferring to torment himself with the shame and guilt that had become his friends since he had stolen Mademoiselle Grace from his father's house.

"Mon ami." Father Alers eased beside him and folded his hands over his prominent belly. "You have been hiding from me."

"Apparently not well enough."

Father Alers chuckled. "The crew told me you were in a foul humor. And no wonder after what you have done."

"And what is that, mon vieux?"

His friend gave Rafe a reprimanding look but said nothing, only gazed over the dark waters.

"I had no choice."

"We all have a choice."

"She chose my father over me. She broke her vow."

"Vraiment?"

"I would have returned her home." Rafe fingered his mustache.

"And for one lie, you send her to her death instead?"

"Not her death."

"Ah, but a fate worse than death." Father Alers's tone carried the convicting ring of truth.

"She betrayed me. She intended to go with my father to Charles Towne."

"Oui, I heard votre père was involved. That explains much." Father

Alers scratched his wiry gray beard.

"What do you mean?" Rafe reached for his flask, uncorked it, and took another sip.

"Only that I fear you are more angry at your father than at the mademoiselle."

"Absurde. I know what to expect from my father. But the mademoiselle...I thought she was different."

"I see nothing changed in her." Father Alers shrugged.

"She deceives you with her saintly behavior, but inside she is a snake like my father, like Claire." The thunderous clap of a sail sounded above him, and Rafe took another swig of brandy. "Not to be trusted."

"Hmm."

"Lives will be spared from the doubloons she will bring me." Rafe bristled as the words sounded more like an excuse than a reason. "Besides, the men haven't been paid in over a month and they start to complain."

"Is that how you justify your actions?" Father Alers coughed his disapproval and glanced into the dark sky above them. "The sacrifice of one for the many?"

Rafe scowled. "What do you want, mon vieux?" he barked. "Does the mademoiselle require something?"

"Non. She is well." Father Alers fixed Rafe with a withering stare. "More kind and accommodating than one would expect in her situation."

Rafe corked his flask and returned it to his coat. "Then excuse me." Turning on his heel, he marched across the quarterdeck, bunching his fists together—angry at Father Alers, angry at himself, angry at the world.

Not even the brandy seemed to numb his fury this night as he leapt down the companionway. Nor as he stormed down the narrow hall to his cabin and blasted through the door. He slammed it and stomped to his desk. Striking flint to steel, he lit a lantern and rummaged through the closet for another bottle of the brandy.

A soft scraping sound met his ears. Rafe froze. Slowly tugging his pistol from his baldric, he cocked it, then he spun around, pointing it toward the source. Out of the shadows drifted a lady in an azure gown.

"It is me, Rafe." Her soothing voice penetrated the haze that covered his mind.

She took another step, and the lantern light shifted across her face. Rafe lowered his pistol and rubbed his eyes as her form swirled in his vision. *It could not be. I have had too much brandy.* He opened his eyes expecting the apparition to have vanished. But she remained. A sweet smile lifted her lips, and she reached out for him.

Claire.

CHAPTER 20

"Claire, sacre mer, what are you doing here?" Rafe tucked his pistol back into its brace and narrowed his eyes upon the last person he expected to see aboard his ship.

She sashayed toward him, the swish of her blue gown setting his nerves on edge. Lifting her thick lashes, she gazed at him with all the love and adoration he remembered. "Are you not happy to see me?" She placed a hand on his arm.

Rafe jerked from her touch, turned around, and grabbed the bottle of brandy he'd been searching for. "I asked you a question." A question to which his alcohol-hazed mind could not fathom any rational answer.

"I could stand it no longer."

Rafe circled her, opened the bottle, and searched for a glass, not wanting to look into those crisp blue eyes. Spyglass leapt from the window ledge and landed on a chart stretched across his desk. Where had *le chat* come from? Ignoring the feline's nudge on his arm, Rafe found a glass, poured himself a drink, and faced Claire.

"What could you not stand, Madame Dubois?"

She drew her lips together in a pout. "I liked it better when you called me Claire."

He cocked a brow. "That was a mistake. Like many things between us."

"Oh, Rafe, must it always be so?" She fingered the lace atop her bodice. Her golden curls bounced around her neck with her every movement.

"What are you doing here?" He tipped back the brandy; if he

drank enough, it would render him unconscious and put an end to this miserable night.

Inching toward him, she grabbed the edge of his desk, her delicate fingers kneading the rough wood as they had oft rubbed the stiff muscles in his neck. He swallowed.

"I ran away from your father."

Rafe jerked. Though her presence here had precluded any doubt of that fact, hearing the words aloud caused his blood to boil.

She reached out to him. When Rafe lurched away, she clasped her hands together and looked down. "He is a monster, Rafe. I could tolerate his abuses no longer."

"What business is that of mine?" Rafe slammed the liquor to the back of his throat.

Her eyes glistened. "I thought you might still care."

Spyglass rubbed against Rafe's back, vying for his attention.

He snorted. "How did you get on board?"

"I hired a man to row me out to your ship." She shrugged, sending her gold jeweled earrings shimmering in the lantern light. "I have no one else to turn to."

"I am the last person to whom you should run, madame." He clanked the glass atop his desk as his muscles tensed in anger. "Your presence here is unwelcome. Do you know what I do with stowaways?"

She eased beside him. Her lavender scent rose to tantalize his nose. "Help me, Rafe. I beg you. Help me escape him."

Rafe stepped back, his stomach knotting. "I toss them overboard."

"You would never harm me, Rafe." Tears pooled in her thick lashes and a shudder swept through her.

"And yet you had no qualms about harming me."

"I was young and foolish."

"And you are so much wiser now, I see."

"Let us forget the past." She toyed with a curl dangling about her cheek and pouted her lips. "Can I please stay? I will be no trouble. I've brought my lady's maid to attend to me."

Rafe's throat went suddenly dry and he cleared it. "I see you have planned well. I seem to have no choice. For now."

She gave him one of those sweet, seductive smiles that in times past melted his resolve. Rafe fought against the haze in his mind that prompted him to take what she so freely offered.

He licked his lips.

Spyglass batted Rafe's glass off the desk. The shrill crash jarred him from the woman's trance, and he glanced down at the glittering shards strewn across the deck. Spyglass pressed her head against his arm and he hoisted the cat onto his shoulder, thankful for the interruption.

A knock sounded on the door.

"Entrez-vous."

Rafe's helmsman entered, his eyes alighting upon Claire and widening in admiration.

"What is it, Monsieur Atton?" Rafe ground his teeth together. What fools men became in the presence of a beautiful woman.

The helmsman jerked from his trance. "Capitaine, Monsieur Thorn wishes to inform ye that the brig is sailing trim, the horizon is clear, and he's putting Weylan on watch."

"Très bien." Rafe nodded. "Tell Monsieur Thorn to come to my cabin before he retires."

Claire flinched at the mention of his first mate's name, and Rafe looked at her curiously. "You do not approve of Monsieur Thorn?"

She looked away. "I hardly know him."

Monsieur Atton turned to leave.

"Leave the door open, monsieur," Rafe ordered. Better not to be alone with this vixen.

"Aye, Capitaine." Atton's boot steps faded down the companionway.

Rafe patted his pocket for a cheroot. "You have placed me in a precarious situation, Madame Dubois."

She frowned.

"Sans doute, my father will come looking for you. And he will believe I stole you away."

"I wish that you had." Her voice was laden with sorrow, but instead of invoking Rafe's sympathies, it had the opposite effect. He picked up the lantern, lit his cheroot in its flame, then inhaled the pungent smoke, allowing it to filter into his lungs.

Turning, he glared at her, searching her eyes for a hint of the real reason for her sneaking aboard his ship. Whatever it was, she was up to no good. And now, on top of everything else, he must deal with this spoiled, self-centered woman.

She swallowed and flitted her gaze about nervously. "Why call Monsieur Thorn?"

"To escort you to your quarters." Rafe swung about and stared out the stern windows at the star-studded sky bobbing up and down beyond the panes.

"But I thought...I thought I could stay in here with you." The swish of her gown followed him.

She eased beside him. Feigned innocence beamed from her blue eyes as her lips once again drew together into that pleading pout. Rafe's blood heated at her salacious offer as memories swirled in his mind—pleasurable memories of their past together.

Spyglass leapt back on the window ledge, and Claire jumped, wrinkling her nose in disgust.

"You wished to see me, Captain?" Monsieur Thorn's voice rescued Rafe from his thoughts.

Claire stiffened beside him and looked down.

"Oui, Madame Dubois will tell you where her lady's maid is hiding. Then please escort them both to Mademoiselle Grace's cabin."

Monsieur Thorn nodded but oddly withheld his glance from Claire.

"Mademoiselle Grace?" Claire's normally soft tone ascended to a screech. Her eyes widened and her nostrils flared.

"*Quel est le problème?*" Rafe asked.

Claire planted her hands upon her hips. "What is *she* doing here? I thought she was leaving on Henri's ship tomorrow."

"There has been a change of plans." Rafe eyed Claire curiously, wondering what difference the mademoiselle's presence made to her.

Madame Dubois stared at Monsieur Thorn as if he had the answer, but he shifted nervously and gazed into the dark sky beyond the window.

She swept seething eyes to Rafe. "I will not share a cabin with that woman."

⌒

Grace rose from kneeling beside her bed and rubbed her aching knees. The brig creaked and moaned as it navigated another wave—sounds that had become her constant companions since Captain Dubois had kidnapped her the night before. With the exception of brief visits by Father Alers, she'd not spoken to a soul, especially not the captain, though she'd heard him storming through the companionway outside her door often enough. She knew it was him because his thick jackboots made a distinctive angry *th-ump* when he marched about.

Grace moved to the porthole. Stars winked at her from their posts positioned across the dark shroud covering the earth. Perhaps they guarded more than the night sky. Perhaps they were God's army of angels watching over her. It brought her comfort to think so.

She wove around her cot and glanced over the cabin. The lone lantern perched upon the table cast eerie shadows across the bulkhead, shadows that hovered over her heart and brought her to her knees in prayer. All day she'd been asking God why—when she had been so close to rescue—He had brought her back into captivity. When she received no answer, she prayed for Hope instead. The vision of her sister in hell had jarred Grace to her very soul and reminded her of the brevity of life here on earth and the urgency of bringing others to Christ.

Grace lowered her chin, ashamed that her anger and judgment at Hope's willful rebellion had caused her to cease praying for her sister. But from now on, she promised to pray for Hope every day. She'd also said a prayer for Madame Dubois—that God would heal her heart and her marriage, and only as a last resort, provide an escape from the brutality of her husband. And for her sister Charity and her marriage as well.

Yet heaven remained silent.

Grace sank to her bed and removed her shoes, then she began loosening the ties of her bodice on yet another borrowed gown that Father Alers had provided for her. Where he procured all these gowns, she didn't want to know. She did want to know, however, why she was here on this brig. Every time she thought she knew what God's plan was for her, every time she thought she knew who she'd been sent to help, everything changed.

The door crashed open, slamming against the bulkhead with a jarring crunch. Grace splayed her fingers over her loosened ties and slowly rose as none other than Madame Dubois entered the cabin. A mulatto woman, her face lowered, followed on her heels, and Monsieur Thorn completed the entourage, a trunk hoisted over his shoulder.

"Madame Dubois." Grace darted toward her, thinking that the captain must have kidnapped her as well.

But the woman ignored her to swing about and face Mr. Thorn. "This is all your fault," she snapped.

Mr. Thorn chuckled. "Zooks, madame. I do not see how." He lowered the trunk to the floor then shot a quick smile Grace's way. "Have a pleasant evening." Then looking as if he couldn't escape quickly enough, he left and closed the door.

A chill filtered through the stifling hot room, lifting the hairs on Grace's neck and arms.

Madame Dubois faced her. Gone were the soft tranquil lines of innocence and humility Grace had witnessed in Port-de-Paix, and in their place marched an army of defiance, petulance, and perturbation.

Grace blinked at the drastic transformation. Perhaps the woman was angry that Grace had failed to keep her promise to help her. "Madame Dubois. I was quite worried about you." Grace stepped toward her. "I fully intended to help you, but as you can see Captain Dubois stole me against my will."

"Of course I can see that." She waved toward the mulatto woman. "Annette, stop cowering in the corner, unpack my things, and hang them up." Then shifting her glance over the cabin, she thrust out her chin. "How are we all to fit in here? *C'est impossible.*" Her eyes landed on Grace's cot. "And there is only one bed." Her face drained of all color.

"Madame Dubois, sit down. You don't look well." Grace led her to the chair, and she flounced into it with a huff.

"Would you like some lemon juice?" Grace poured some of the sour liquid from her pitcher into a mug and handed it to Madame Dubois, but she batted it away.

Taking no offense, Grace set the glass down and gazed at the mulatto opening Madame Dubois's trunk. Tall, slender, with ebony hair and skin the color of bronze, her dark exotic eyes shifted toward Grace before she snapped them away.

Grace smiled. "I am Grace Westcott. And you are?"

"She is nobody," Madame Dubois barked from her chair.

The mulatto woman backed away from Grace. She glanced at Madame Dubois. "I am Annette."

"Pleased to make your acquaintance, Annette." Grace shivered beneath another chill, still baffled at its source, as a heaviness settled on her.

Madame Dubois turned in her chair to look at them. "Annette is my husband's child."

Grace blinked. "Your daughter?" She studied Annette, whose gaze had lowered once again to the deck. The young lady looked nothing like Madame Dubois.

"Non, *vous imbécile*. My husband's and one of our slave's," Madame Dubois shot back, her voice firing with spite.

Grace gulped. The more she discovered about Monsieur Dubois, the more his claim to be a man of God shriveled.

Madame Dubois clicked her tongue. "My husband, along with many of the grand blancs on Saint Dominique, is attempting to create a race of exotic beautiful woman by breeding with the African slaves." She gestured toward Annette. "They are called *les Sirènes*."

Grace clutched her throat, abhorring what she heard. "I cannot believe it."

"It is an acceptable practice among the grand blancs, mademoiselle, one which I despise."

"But why is she your slave? And what of her mother?"

"Annette is free, but at her father's request, she serves me. As for her mother"—Madame Dubois looked down—"Monsieur Dubois maintains a relationship with her." A vacant glaze covered her blue eyes then sharpened when she looked at Grace. "Now do you see why I must leave him?"

Grace's heart melted. She had heard of such practices in Charles Towne but had hoped they were rumors. How could any woman endure such infidelity? She rushed to Madame Dubois's side and knelt before her. "Of course. I understand. But how did you come to this ship?"

Madame Dubois took a deep breath but did not take Grace's outstretched hand. "I climbed aboard. How else?"

"But I understood you to say that Rafe hated you and would never allow you aboard."

"He had no say in it." Madame Dubois's tone sank.

Annette began unfolding her mistress's skirts, bodices, and petticoats and hanging them on knobs in the open armoire.

Grace rose and sat on her bed. "I don't understand."

"No, I suppose you wouldn't." Madame Dubois straightened the lace at her sleeves. "When I found you missing, I had no other option but to appeal to my stepson for help."

Grace thought back to the events of the prior night. "But how could you know I was missing when I was taken in the middle of the night?"

Madame Dubois's face flushed, and she stood, waving a hand through the air. "I could not sleep and went to your chamber to speak with you and found you gone."

"But we set sail as soon as the captain came on board. There would have been no time." Grace furrowed her brow and wondered why Madame Dubois would not meet her gaze.

The mulatto continued her work, but Grace did not miss the furtive glance she cast her way.

"Oh, what does it matter?" Madame Dubois's voice sharpened and she huffed out a sigh. "I am here now."

Grace grasped her chain. "Then you should be happy, madame. You are free from your husband."

"Except Rafe is angry and refuses to listen to me." Madame Dubois began to pace, the swish of her gown slicing through the cabin.

"We have that in common, madame."

Madame Dubois halted and raised a curious eye to Grace. "Why did he kidnap you again?"

"I betrayed him. I didn't keep my promise to return. You should have allowed me to speak to him about our plans."

Madame Dubois cocked her head, sending her golden curls bobbing. "What does he intend to do with you?"

"I don't know." Grace's stomach tightened. "Perhaps sell me to the don as he originally planned."

A hint of a smile appeared on Madame Dubois's lips as if the information pleased her.

Grace could make no sense of the woman. She seemed as volatile and unsettled as the captain. Perhaps the abuse she had endured at the hand of her husband made her that way. Could she be the one Grace had been sent to help? "Perchance if we explain to Captain Dubois our plans, he will understand your desperation to come aboard since he kidnapped your only means of escape. Surely then he would forfeit his anger against you."

The woman stormed toward Grace as if she'd asked her to jump overboard. She grabbed Grace's hands and shook them. "Non. You must promise never to tell Rafe of our prior plans. Remember what I said?"

Grace remembered. Madame Dubois said he would kill his father. Perhaps he would. Perhaps he wouldn't. Nevertheless, she had made a vow once to this woman, and she intended to keep it. "I promise."

CHAPTER 21

Rafe marched toward the door, intending to storm into the cabin, give his instructions, and leave as soon as possible. And he would have done just that, save for Father Alers's staying hand on his arm and the look of reprimand the former priest shot his way. "A gentleman does not enter a lady's chamber without knocking, Rafe."

"I am no gentleman. And this is a cabin aboard *my* ship, not a lady's boudoir." Rafe jerked from his grasp, but the old man forced himself in front of Rafe and tapped on the oak door. "Mademoiselle Grace, Madame Dubois, *pouvons-nous entrer?*"

Rafe folded his arms over his chest and shook his head while Father Alers waited for a reply.

"Une minute, s'il vous plaît," came a soft response.

Rafe stomped his boot and huffed in impatience as Spyglass scurried down the hallway and began scratching the door for entrance. "Le chat does not wait for permission." He smirked.

The door opened, and Claire's gaze passed over Father Alers and landed upon Rafe. She smiled and gestured them inside.

Stepping around the father, Rafe brushed past Claire, trying to avoid any contact with the woman, but she laid a hand on his arm in passing. Instead of his normal heated response to her touch, he felt nothing.

Putting distance between them, he glanced across the cabin. Claire's maid, Annette, stood, head lowered in the corner. On the other side of the room beneath the porthole, Mademoiselle Grace clung to a bundle of blankets as if she had just picked them off the floor. Her eyes met his, convicting green eyes tinted with anger and fear that bristled over his conscience.

Spyglass scampered inside and leapt onto the table beside a lantern set aglow by rays of morning sun beaming in through the porthole. The cat nibbled upon the few crumbs strewn over the plates that had held the ladies' breakfast.

Claire leapt back in disgust. "Take that filthy beast away!" She waved her hand toward Spyglass as if she could brush the cat from the scene.

"She is my pet, madame, and as such, you will not address her as a filthy beast."

Mademoiselle Grace giggled, drawing Rafe's gaze to her, to her wrinkled gown and disheveled hair. "Did you sleep on the floor, mademoiselle?" He inclined his head toward the blankets bundled in her arms.

She scrunched them closer to her chest then curled a stray lock of her hair behind her ear. "Madame Dubois was quite distraught last night."

"So you abandoned your bed to her?" Rafe did not like the odd sensation that welled within him at the revelation.

"Why shouldn't she?" Claire snapped. "She is your prisoner while I am your guest."

Rafe faced the woman, radiant as always in the morning light, her golden curls spiraling like gentle waves over her neck, lace abounding from her tight silk bodice that flowed down to an azure skirt. No doubt Annette had already spent hours fussing over her mistress. "You are many things, madame, but my guest is not one of them."

Claire drew her lips into a pout as Spyglass jumped into the chair beside her, giving her a start. The lines of her face folded in repugnance.

"I have brought two hammocks." Rafe retrieved the brown bundles from Father Alers, who remained in the doorway, and handed them to Claire.

She held them out from her body as if they were covered with mud then shoved them back at him. "You cannot be serious. This cabin is far too small for all of us." She threw a hand in the air. "It is stifling in here and it smells as if something has died. And I ache from that infernal thing you call a bed." She pressed her delicate fingers on her back.

A lump of disdain balled in Rafe's throat. "The other ladies slept on the deck, and yet, I do not hear them complaining."

"Humph," she snorted. "No doubt they are used to such conditions, while I am not." Claire laid the back of her hand to her forehead. "I am feeling faint." She attempted to bat Spyglass from the chair, but the cat hissed at her, sending her reeling backward.

A giggle escaped Mademoiselle's lips again, as one did Annette's. Claire glared at her maid. Tossing a hand to her throat, she threw back her shoulders. "Please, Rafe." She sidled up to him and fingered the lace atop her bodice, drawing his attention to the low neckline. "Surely you can find more suitable accommodations for me."

And by the seductive lilt to her voice, Rafe knew exactly to which accommodations she referred.

"Why, there is not enough room for my trousseau." Claire glanced at the armoire from which a multitude of colorful gowns overflowed.

"In fact, I can barely move in these cramped quarters." She continued her performance, and Rafe released a heavy sigh. Like a bad play, her theatrics became irksome.

He cocked a brow, wondering if Claire had always been this peevish, or had she been polluted by spending too many hours with his father? "And yet this is the only cabin I have to offer you."

"Not all." She gave him a pleading look that fell short of its intended mark on his heart.

Father Alers coughed.

"I am famished." She pressed a hand over her stomach. "Do you intend to starve me as well?"

"Father Alers brought you food this morning." Rafe gestured toward the empty tray atop the table.

Claire turned up her nose. "You cannot expect me to eat such slop."

Father Alers coughed again and shuffled his boots over the deck.

Rafe turned to his friend. "Would you show Madame Dubois and her maid to the galley? Perhaps she can find something more to her liking there." Although he knew she would not, knew that nothing aboard this ship would be to her liking, he longed to relieve himself of her company and speak with Mademoiselle Grace in private.

Father Alers gave him a look that said he'd rather be boiled in oil, but he nodded and gestured for Claire to follow him.

"Very well." She gathered her skirts and sauntered past him, brushing against his arm, and leaving her scent of lavender behind—a scent that used to delight him, but now turned stale in his nostrils. En fait, with her exit, fresh air filled the cabin, and a heaviness lifted from his heart.

He exhaled a ragged breath, set the hammocks on the chair, and turned toward Mademoiselle Grace. "You should not be so kind to her," he said, pointing to the blankets still in her arms. "She will not return the favor."

"I seek no reward." She placed the blankets on the bed and pressed the wrinkles out of a gown she had obviously slept in. Yet regardless of the creases in her skirts, regardless of the strands of raven hair that had escaped her pins and the shadows beneath her eyes, she was the most beautiful thing he had ever seen.

She splayed her fingers in modesty over the skin above her gown, so different from Claire who so blatantly tried to attract him by her physical charms. "Do you intend to sell me to the Spanish don, Captain?" Her bottom lip quivered as she leaned toward Spyglass. The cat willingly leapt into her arms, and Mademoiselle Grace stroked the gray fur atop her head.

Rafe clenched his jaw and rubbed the stubble upon it. Everything within him screamed non. He could never do such a thing. But then he remembered her lies, her betrayal, and the faces of the sick children in Port-de-Paix that constantly haunted his nightmares. "You betrayed me."

"How?" A delicate line formed between her brows—a tiny wrinkle in her otherwise lustrous skin.

"You did not meet me. You broke your vow." Rafe must always remember that, especially now when she looked at him with such sorrow and naïveté.

"But I sent Mr. Thorn—"

"Sacre mer. I heard what he had to say." Rafe held a hand up to stop her. He remembered it all too clearly. *The mademoiselle sends her apologies,* Thorn had said with a bit of scorn in his tone, *but she prefers the comforts which your father can offer her on the journey home rather than the inhospitality of your brig.* Rafe clenched his jaw. "Can you deny that you lied to me—that you dishonored your oath?"

She bowed her head, and Spyglass nuzzled beneath her chin. "I had good reason."

Rafe thumped his boot on the hard deck. "What reason?" If she would but give him an explanation, any explanation that made sense, any explanation that would appease the throbbing wound that had reopened in his heart. If she would do that, he might forgive her, he might take her in his arms as he longed to do, he might return her home safely, or take her anywhere she wanted to go.

If she would but speak the right words.

"I am not at liberty to say." She swallowed, and her hands began to tremble.

Rafe bunched his fists. "Not at liberty, or do not wish to admit that you received a better offer?" Just as Claire had done to him so many years ago.

Mademoiselle Grace lifted her chin, her eyes filling. "I am sorry." And in those eyes he saw no reason to believe otherwise.

"It is not enough." He grabbed the pommel of his rapier, rubbing his thumb over the silver until it ached.

"For now, it is all I can give you," she said softly.

"Then I fear it is all I can give you as well. I am sorry, mademoiselle, but oui, I must sell you to the don as planned."

"I break one vow and my sentence is to be a lifetime of slavery?"

Rafe ground his teeth together. "It is more than a broken promise, mademoiselle. All my life, not one person has kept their word to me. Not ma mère, not mon père, and not Claire."

Her eyes widened at the mention of Claire, but he continued, "Does a person's word mean nothing anymore?" He stormed toward her and she flinched at his anger. But he could not stop. "I will tell you what a broken promise means. It means there is no honor within, no decency. It indicates a heart filled with selfishness and deceit." He gripped the pommel of his rapier and tried to collect his emotions as her eyes grew moist. "You had me fooled, mademoiselle, with your pious act. But no more." He shook his head. "No more. And I, too, will keep my word— the vow I spoke to Abbé Villion."

Tears spilled from her lashes down her cheeks as she continued scratching Spyglass. Rafe knew he had better leave before he changed his mind.

"I bid you adieu." He nodded, stomped out, and slammed the door behind him. Then leaning back against the oak slab, he slammed his fists against it, trying to collect his raging emotions. Even in her betrayal, the woman still bewitched him.

⤜≈⤛

Grace clung to the railing amidships and gazed over the rippling turquoise sea. The afternoon sun cast bands of glittering diamonds atop the waves as they frolicked on their course without a care in the world. She envied them. White billowing clouds cluttered the horizon but rarely passed over the broiling orb to offer the ship's inhabitants any respite from the heat. Perspiration trickled down her neck and back and beaded on her forehead, relieved only by the continual salt-laden breeze wafting in off the sea.

Grace closed her eyes as the brig rose and plunged over another swell. A burst of wind clawed at her hair, freeing a strand from her tight coiffure as she listened to the swish of the foamy waters against the hull and the thunderous flap of sails above her. Not to mention the ever-present creak and groan of the planks and the shouts of the crew as they went about their tasks. All familiar sounds to her now, replacing the pleasant music of home: the chirp of birds outside her window, the laughter of her sisters, Molly singing hymns as she prepared supper, the swish of the angel oak leaves dancing in the breeze in front of their home. Every place created its own unique music, and though the music aboard this ship carried a pleasant tune, the place to which it carried her would not be so pleasant.

Opening her eyes, she stared at the foam purling off the ship, and her thoughts drifted to Madame Dubois and her spiteful, curt behavior. Not at all like the charming hostess who had befriended Grace at the Dubois estate. The change in her demeanor had completely baffled Grace—that was until Captain Dubois entered the cabin and the lady transformed into an amorous coquette before Grace's eyes.

Mercy me. The captain was her stepson. Grace rubbed her eyes and dabbed at the perspiration on her neck. Apparently Madame Dubois was much more than his stepmother. Or had been at one time. Now Grace understood the hatred spilling from Madame Dubois's eyes. Jealousy. She was jealous of Grace. Though Grace could not imagine why. The captain intended to sell her to the don and be done with her. He had reassured her of that fact in the cabin that morning.

Yet right before he had declared her doom so vehemently, she had glimpsed a softening in his otherwise hard gaze, as if he wished their journey could take another course. And she longed to tell him the truth, the real reason she had broken her vow to him, if only to erase the anguish from his eyes. But she couldn't. If only she could go back in time and do things differently. But it was too late for that. She had wanted so much to help him—to help everyone, but instead, she had made a mess of things.

"Good day to you, Miss Grace." Mr. Thorn slipped beside her and tipped his hat.

Grace forced a smile despite her dismal thoughts. "Good day, Mr. Thorn." With his pristine blue waistcoat, white breeches, boots, and tricorne, the young first mate reminded Grace of a painting of a young British seaman hanging in her father's study—quite in contrast to the rest of the bawdy crew.

"I've been meaning to thank you again, Mr. Thorn, for helping me escape at Port-de-Paix."

He flattened his lips. "A lot of good it did, eh?"

Grace drew a deep breath. "It would seem God wishes me to remain on this ship for some reason."

He snorted. "I believe that is the captain's wish, not God's, Miss Grace."

A heaviness settled on her at the man's lack of faith. But how to reach him? Mr. Thorn behaved every bit the godly man: honorable, moral, kind. Yet without faith, where could it lead? "I suffered greatly while in town. I lost the money you so generously gave me, and I nearly starved to death. If not for God's help, I would have surely died."

"And yet, it would appear that He saved you only to imprison you again." Mr. Thorn brushed dirt from his waistcoat.

"We do not always understand the ways of God."

"I would say we never can and never will." He gripped the railing as the brig canted over another wave.

Two sailors passed behind them, laughing and cursing as they leapt up the foredeck ladder. Grace recognized them as Mr. Legard, the bosun, and Mr. Weylan, the man who had accosted her below deck. She shuddered, but could not miss the knowing glance they exchanged with Mr. Thorn. When she looked at the first mate in confusion, his face mottled. "Forgive their blasphemy, miss. I grow so tired of the crass language aboard." He glared after them as they continued across the foredeck. "Scoundrels, profligates all."

Grace examined him, curious at his extreme censure of his fellow sailors—men he must work and live with in such close quarters.

"And the captain is no better," he added. "You are fortunate he curbs his tongue in front of the ladies."

Grace raised her brows, surprised that Captain Dubois possessed the manners to restrain himself at all. "Aren't you and the captain friends?"

"Friends? I work for him, 'tis all."

"And yet he speaks much more fondly of you than you do of him."

"Can you blame him?" He chuckled.

Shielding her eyes from the sun, Grace studied the baffling man and wondered where his true loyalties lay. If not with the captain, and not his own countrymen, then where? "Do you have family somewhere, Mr. Thorn?"

"Yes, on Nassau. A mother, father, and younger sister." He clenched the railing.

"A sister? How nice." Grace had always wanted an older brother—someone to stand up for and protect her and her sisters when their father was out to sea, as he so often was.

Mr. Thorn took a deep breath and gazed out over the glistening water. "Yes. Her name is Elizabeth." The tone of his voice carried fervent love along with deep sorrow, giving Grace pause.

She laid a hand on his arm. "Is she well?"

He shifted his brown eyes to her, and the anguish she saw in them took her aback.

"As well as can be expected," he said. His gaze hardened into stone, and he swept it over the deck as if in search of some remedy.

Grace didn't know what to make of it. No doubt something horrible had happened to his sister. "What does she suffer from?"

Withdrawing his arm from beneath her hand, Mr. Thorn threw back his shoulders as if tossing aside some cumbrous memory. "Forgive me, miss. I misspoke." Then, he directed his gaze at a sailor sitting atop a barrel. "Bear a hand aloft, Mr. Fletcher!" he bellowed and watched as the man grunted then flung himself into the ratlines. Plucking a handkerchief from his pocket, Mr. Thorn dabbed the perspiration on the back of his neck. "Abominable heat. What brings you on deck, miss?"

Truth be told, when Madame Dubois and Annette returned, Grace found she couldn't escape their company fast enough. Between Madame Dubois's barbed looks of disdain and Annette's skittish demeanor, the atmosphere had become intolerable. Grace liked the mulatto woman, but could not shake the unease that slid over her in the maid's presence. Just that morning, Grace could have sworn she heard the woman chanting something in her dark corner before sunrise. "My cabin has become quite crowded as of late."

"Ah yes, the resplendent Madame Claire Dubois." He swirled his hand in the air like a courtier's bow.

Grace found his reaction odd. "You do not approve of her?"

"Do you? Vainglorious peacock, ill-tempered shrew," he spat in contempt. "She and her husband are suitably matched. Yet here she is seeking the affections of the captain."

"So my assumption is correct." Grace shook her head even as the man's words grated over her. Was she so quick to label others in such cruel terms? Though the accusations may be true, and she could not deny thinking them herself, hearing the acrid criticisms on another person's lips sliced deep into Grace's conscience.

Mr. Thorn leaned toward her as if he shared a juicy secret. "Aye, apparently they have quite a past."

The brig lurched, sending a cool spray over Grace, jarring her from participating in the man's gossip, though she longed to know the story. "But didn't you befriend her at the Dubois estate? Were you not involved in convincing her to elicit my help to escape to Charles Towne?" Though Grace had promised Claire she would not tell Rafe of their plans to escape to Charles Towne, surely it was safe to discuss the matter with Mr. Thorn since he was involved in the scheme. Besides, Grace wished to gain an understanding of the connection between Madame Dubois and Mr. Thorn.

His face reddened, and he drew out his handkerchief again and dabbed the sweat on his brow. "She sought my help, to be sure. Like you, she had me fooled into believing she truly wished your assistance to get to Charles Towne." He shrugged and gazed off to his right. "Apparently she had other plans."

Grace eyed him, sensing he knew much more than he was saying. She remembered the conversation she'd overheard between Mr. Thorn and Monsieur Dubois—something about revenge. "Mr. Thorn, may I ask you a personal question?"

He nodded, though hesitancy shadowed his expression.

"I still do not understand why you sail with Captain Dubois. You don't approve nor associate with the crew. And you have not hid your disdain for the captain, at least not from me."

He laughed. "Can you blame me? Sailing with such miscreants? I am indeed as out of place as a nobleman in a brothel."

His chuckle faded as his eyes focused on something behind Grace. Silence invaded the ship. Grace turned to see Madame Dubois emerge from the companionway, Annette on her heels. Shielding her eyes from the sun, the woman gave Grace a cursory glance before heading toward the other side of the ship, barking at Annette to follow her. The crew quit their ogling and returned to their duties.

"She is quite beautiful," Grace admitted.

"Yes, she is." Mr. Thorn's eyes remained locked upon the ladies as they took up their spot on the larboard railing. Then he jerked. "Oh, you mean Madame Dubois?" He snorted. "She is tolerable, I suppose."

Grace blinked. "Do you speak of Annette, then?"

"She is exquisite." His tone sang with admiration as his eyes never left the young mulatto.

Grace bit her lip, not wanting to disclose that Annette was Rafe's half sister. "Yes, she is."

Annette opened a parasol and held it over her mistress to shield her skin from the searing rays of the sun. Grace touched her own cheek and felt the heat emanating from it. In no time she'd be as tan as these sailors. Most unappealing. But then again, when had she cared for her appearance? Movement caught her eye and she swept her gaze to the companionway where Captain Dubois emerged. Their eyes met and he halted, his white buccaneer shirt flapping in the wind beneath his gray coat. Unsettled by his perusal, she faced the sea again.

Boots thumped toward her. "Monsieur Thorn, do you not have something better to do?" His deep voice tumbled over them.

"Nay. Not at the moment." Mr. Thorn raised an eyebrow that did not have the intended effect as Captain Dubois's expression remained as hard as stone.

Grace gazed between the two men. Captain Dubois fingered the hilt of his rapier, yet said nothing.

"Very well, then." Mr. Thorn ran a thumb along the scar on his neck. "I am sure I can find some of the crew to order about." He touched the tip of his hat and nodded to Grace. "Good day to you, miss." Then he left.

Silence spread between them.

"Why must you be such a bully?" The words came out of her mouth before she considered their content.

Instead of anger, his lips curved into a grin. "A bully? Moi? I am so much more than that."

"Yes you are. Kidnapper, rogue, and scoundrel are a few other titles that come to mind."

He chuckled. "The pious prude has acquired some pluck. But we have already discovered a few flaws hidden behind your proper facade, have we not, thief?"

Horrified, Grace turned away from him as a blast of wind raked over her hair, her gown, as if trying to peel back her saintly layers in order to reveal the darkness of her heart.

A scream from across the deck brought their gazes to Madame Dubois, who was swatting at Spyglass with her parasol. "Infernal beast!" she shouted, but the cat was far too swift, darting across the bulwarks back and forth as if taunting the lady.

Captain Dubois chuckled and leaned his elbows on the railing.

"Aren't you going to rescue your pet?" Grace asked as laughter erupted from the crew.

"Non. Spyglass does quite well on her own." His eyes met hers, playful mirth dancing across them, and again Grace thought she saw a hint of kindness lurking behind the hard shield. He took one last look at Claire and his features stiffened.

He faced Grace, studying her with that intensity that seemed to peer into her soul. He fingered a lock of her wayward hair.

She slapped his hand away. "You may be selling me as if I were cargo, but I do not belong to you, Captain."

"Do you not?" He gave her a rakish grin.

Grace attempted to stuff the loose curls back into her bun, but the traitorous strands refused to be pinned. She knew he could play with her hair if he wanted. Truth be told, he could do whatever he wanted with her.

Thunder bellowed in the distance, drawing the captain's gaze to the horizon.

"A storm approaches, mademoiselle."

She eyed him. "Yes, Captain, I fear it does."

CHAPTER 22

The brig rolled. Grace stumbled and raised her hand to the bulkhead to keep from falling. Rain pounded on the deck above her, sounding more like grapeshot than drops of water. Clutching the chain around her neck, she withdrew her cross and wobbled toward the porthole. Through the glass, lightning wove a smoky trail across the darkened sky. "Just a tiny squall," Father Alers had reassured her. "Nothing to worry about. This brig has been through much worse." Grace rubbed her fingers over the cross. Thunder growled. "Protect us, Lord," she whispered. A moan sounded from the other side of the cabin, reminding her she was not alone.

Turning around, Grace held her arms out in an effort to keep her balance over the teetering deck and ambled toward the mulatto woman who sat on the floor in the corner by the armoire—where she had been for the past two hours. Grabbing the table, Grace sank into the chair beside her.

Annette smiled but continued her work. In the light of a lantern she had tied to the armoire, Annette arranged a series of articles across a multicolored flag: an amulet, a string of beads, a rattle, and various polished stones.

The hairs on Grace's arm bristled. "May I ask what you are doing?"

The lady frowned but said nothing, as she had every time Grace had attempted conversation with her during the long night.

"There is no need to be frightened of me," Grace assured.

Annette's dark eyes lifted to hers as if searching the validity of her statement.

187

Grace forced a smile to her lips and wondered why the lady, who must be near her own age, held such a timid manner toward her. The brig pitched over a swell and Grace gripped the arms of the chair. Thunder hammered overhead, drowning out the sound of her nervous breathing, but only increasing the weight of heaviness that had fallen on her since the storm began.

"Living aboard this brig is quite a change from living at the Dubois estate." Grace once again attempted a light tête-à-tête with the woman. So often maligned by Madame Dubois and ignored by everyone else, Annette appeared lonely, withdrawn, in need of love and encouragement. And to think she was Captain Dubois's half sister. Did the captain know of the relation? If he did, he certainly made no attempt to acknowledge Annette.

The lady nodded and completed her arrangement. Black hair the color of coal tumbled over her left shoulder onto her plain cotton gown. With full lips, an aquiline French nose, and dark, mysterious eyes, the woman's beauty was unquestionable. The fact that she had been bred for that very quality made Grace's stomach sour. Yet, she reminded herself, regardless of the nefarious purposes for which man chose to bring life into the world, God had His own glorious plan for each precious soul. And this woman was as much a child of His as anyone else.

The sea roared against the hull. The deck rose and plunged, and Annette laid her hands over her trinkets, keeping them in place. Then staring at her display, she muttered words in a language Grace could not understand.

Words that sent a chill coursing through her.

Grace hugged herself as another blast of thunder rumbled through the planks of the brig.

"I cause the storm to cease," Annette said.

Grace eyed the lady, waiting for the smile, the laugh that would accompany such an astonishing statement, but with her lips in a firm line and her eyes staunch with sincerity, Annette remained unmoved.

"What do you mean?" Grace finally said. "How can you stop the storm?"

"With these charms." Annette waved a hand over her treasures. "And my prayers to the spirits of my ancestors."

Grace's stomach shriveled. The lady engaged in some kind of primitive religious ritual. No wonder Grace had felt a darkness, an oppression whenever she'd been in her presence, for she had learned from Reverend Anthony, her pastor in Charles Towne, that many of these ancient religions were mere covers for the worship of demons. An urge to rise and dash from the cabin surged within her, but she willed her breathing to steady and her face to remain placid.

Lightning flickered a deathly pale over the scene. Perhaps this was why the Lord brought Grace all this way—to deliver this girl from spiritual bondage. Grace's heart thumped wildly in her chest.

"Annette, I serve a God more powerful than the spirits of our ancestors."

The woman stared blankly at Grace. "I know. I felt His power when I met you."

Grace flinched even as a thrill went through her. "You did?"

"Why do you not pray and sacrifice to Him to stop the storm?"

Grace fingered her cross, appealing to God for the right words to say to this girl. "I have been praying. But there is no longer a need to offer sacrifices to God, because He offered His own Son as a final sacrifice for all people everywhere."

"He sacrifice His Son?" She shook her head, her brow pinching. "Why would He do that? C'est fou."

"He did it because He loves us all so much." Grace reached out her hand to Annette. "He loves you, Annette."

Refusing Grace's hand, Annette lowered her gaze. "No one loves me. I am a possession: one of Monsieur Dubois's prize mares. I am caught between two worlds, the ones of my ancestors and the world of the whites."

She said the last word with such hatred, it made Grace jump. "God loves you, Annette. Of that I am sure. He wants you to become part of His family. And if you do, you'll never feel lost again."

Annette tossed her long hair over her shoulder and sighed as if considering Grace's words. She lifted her chin, and her eyes glistened with tears.

The door crashed open and in flounced Madame Dubois. Turning, she slammed the oak slab in the face of whoever had escorted her to the cabin and then flung herself onto the bed.

Grace slouched in her chair at the woman's poor timing. A few more minutes and she may have been able to lead Annette down the path to a new life.

Instead, Annette's eyes widened as she shoved her trinkets into a burlap sack and jumped to her feet, no doubt in expectation of her mistress's command.

Which came within seconds. "Annette, come here. Help me undress. These bindings are squeezing the breath from me."

Grace cringed at the fear on the mulatto's face. "How was your dinner?" She turned to face Madame Dubois, who stood and clung to the bulkhead while Annette began untying the laces of her bodice. "Horrible. Simply horrible," she sobbed. "Rafe was in such a foul humor, and he barely spoke to me at all." Annette removed the ties from Madame Dubois's skirt and began unlacing the stomacher as the woman continued her groaning, only exacerbated by the rise and swoop of the brig that nearly sent her tumbling to the plank floor.

After regaining her stance, Madame Dubois shot a fiery gaze at Grace. "It was as if he blamed me for your not attending."

Grace laughed. "I am his prisoner. What does he expect?"

"That is exactly what I told him." Madame Dubois batted Annette away and sank onto the bed. "He barely touched his food—which was the same vicious sludge they serve us here, je vous assure—and his crew was quite *désagréable*."

Grace could well attest to that. "At least you are free from your husband's brutality, madame. Isn't that what you wished?"

She dabbed at her tears. "Oui."

Thunder roared from a distance, and the rain faded to a light tapping. Grace leaned toward Madame Dubois, trying to squelch her anger at the woman's selfishness. "Captain Dubois will not allow you to go back to such suffering, I am sure of it."

Madame Dubois nodded, her curls bobbing. "He intends to put me on a ship to Virginia when he makes anchor at Kingston."

"That is good news, is it not? Then you can live safely with your relatives."

"Non!" she shouted, causing Annette to jump. "I do not want to live with them." Her blue eyes turned to icy daggers. She waved Grace away. "Zut alors, what do you know?"

Grace closed her eyes beneath the woman's scorn as the depth of her deception became all too clear. "Then your plan was never to go to Charles Towne with me." She muttered the words without question.

In reply, Madame Dubois lay back upon her bed and resumed her sobbing.

Forcing down her rising fury, Grace stood, grabbed her blankets, and began arranging them into a makeshift bed on the floor beneath the porthole. Though she had tried to sleep in the hammocks the captain had provided, she'd been unable to get comfortable, preferring the hard deck to the swaying confinement of the tight bands of cloth. Finally she lay down, ignoring her stiff back, and soon drifted to sleep to the rumbling sound of receding thunder, the pitter-patter of rain, and Madame Dubois's incessant whimpering.

Hours later, Grace stirred, alerted by whispers across the room. Recognizing the voices as those of Madame Dubois and Annette, Grace's heart settled to a normal beat, and she attempted to fall back asleep, but the content of those words kept her awake.

"Do you promise me this will work?" Madame Dubois asked.

"Oui, madame. It works for many generations."

Silence for a minute. "Uhh, it tastes terrible."

"Oui, what is that compare to love?" Annette said.

"How long before it begins to take effect?"

"It work right away, but you must also give this to the captain."

A sigh. "I do not see how, but I will find a way."

Shuffling, swishing of a nightdress, and Grace heard the creak of Madame Dubois's bed as she crawled beneath her coverlet. Within minutes the sound of her deep breaths filled the room. Grace had just begun to ponder the meaning of what she had heard when footsteps tapped over the deck. The door creaked open and then thumped closed. Annette had left.

Grace sat up and braced her back against the bulkhead, gathering her blankets to her chest. Fear gripped her for the woman's safety. Perhaps Annette had never been on a ship before. Perhaps she didn't realize the dangers lurking among the less-than-scrupulous crew. Grace prayed for her. Minutes passed, and she stood and began to pace. But when Annette didn't return after an hour, Grace donned her bodice and skirts, checked to ensure Madame Dubois slept peacefully, and slipped into the companionway.

Though the storm had long since passed, the lanterns in the hallway had not been relit, and Grace chided herself for not bringing one of her own. Groping her way along the bulkhead toward Captain Dubois's cabin, she drew a shaky breath of the stale air. The scents of moist wood, tar, and a hint of tobacco filled her nose. Thunder growled in the distance, and Grace halted and hugged herself. A thick blackness crowded around her. Up ahead, a blade of light sliced the darkness beneath the captain's cabin door. He was awake. A knot formed in her throat. She knew it was not only improper but dangerous to go to his cabin alone late at night, but she didn't dare search the ship on her own, and she feared something terrible had befallen Annette.

CHAPTER 23

Rafe propped his boot on the ledge of the stern windows and stared at the retreating storm, barely visible in the predawn gloom. Yet as each cloud rolled from the sky, one by one the stars appeared, clear and sparkling against the ebony backdrop. He wished for the same clarity in his thoughts. Yet they remained as cloudy and turbulent as the storm that had just passed.

He took a swig from his bottle, the taste of brandy souring in his mouth. He set it down and pressed a palm against his forehead, trying to stop the incessant droning in his head. Too much liquor again. When Mademoiselle Grace had not appeared at dinner, his mood had grown peevish. He could not explain it. Perhaps it was because her absence had left him at the mercy of Claire's attentions. Attentions that had only further soured his mood. Attentions that had become nauseating to him. Six months ago—non, even two months ago—he would have sold all he had to win back Claire's love. Now, he was not so sure. He was not sure about anything.

Rafe began to pace. Yet Claire's obvious pursuit of him presented him with the perfect opportunity—an opportunity for *la vengeance*. He could steal Claire back from his father and cause the man as much suffering as he had caused Rafe. The impending victory—so close he could taste it—turned to ash in his mouth when he thought of Mademoiselle Grace.

Next to her, Claire was a spoiled schoolgirl with her vain mannerisms and constant bickering. Had she always been that way? Or perhaps

Mademoiselle Grace made Claire seem abhorrent by comparison. Everyone paled in comparison to the mademoiselle.

But she betrayed you. The icy voice chanted in Rafe's head, stabbing his heart.

Oui, she did. Just like Claire. Rafe rubbed his temples. Maybe she was no different after all.

Then why did Mademoiselle Grace's actions and her words lead him to the opposite conclusion? The conclusion that she was an angel—a pure, kindhearted angel sent by God.

Wolves appear in sheep's clothing.

Rafe plucked a cheroot from his pocket and lit it in the lantern. He took a puff and plopped down on the ledge. But he was no imbecile. And he would not allow himself to be fooled by her charms.

Spyglass jumped onto the ledge and swung her one eye upon him—a reprimanding eye, a condemning eye. Rafe winced beneath a stab of unfamiliar conviction, and he waved the cat away. "She has you fooled, le chat stupide."

The cat yawned and licked her paws, unmoved by his accusations. Then, slinking by his leg, she crawled into his lap. With his free hand, Rafe caressed her. "So you wish to make friends again, non?" The fresh scent of the mademoiselle filled his nostrils, sealing the cat's betrayal even as the smell brought visions of her flooding into his mind.

"You have been with her!" He pushed the cat away. "Traître."

Spyglass gave him a cursory glance then leapt onto his desk and turned the other way.

But too late; Rafe could not force the mademoiselle from his mind. He took a draught of his cheroot and stared out the window, wondering what it would be like to be loved by such a woman.

Tap tap tap.

Rafe groaned, not wishing to leave his dream world just yet. "Entrez-vous."

The door squeaked open and light footsteps sounded, but Rafe continued staring out the window, hoping whoever it was would see he was occupied and go away. When no voice beckoned him, he swung around, ready to spew a string of blasphemies at the sailor who dared disturb him.

It was no filthy sailor who met his blurry gaze, no unkempt man, but a lady dressed in shimmering silk with skin the color of pearls and hair the color of the night—a glowing vision of the woman who hounded his dreams.

She jerked back at what must have been a look of desire on his face.

"Mademoiselle Grace." The words slid like silk off his brandy-drenched lips. He rose from the ledge and stamped his cheroot onto a tray.

"Captain." She clasped her hands together and took a step toward him.

Her shapely form spiraled in his gaze like smoke from a fire, and he inhaled a deep breath, hoping her scent would find its way to his nose. But all he could smell was the sting of his own tobacco and brandy.

"I came to. . ." Her bottom lip quivered. "I mean to say. . ." Fear skittered across her green eyes. "Forgive me. I shouldn't have come." She whirled about.

"Non. Please do not leave." He took no care to remove the pleading from his voice.

She slowly turned to face him. "You have been drinking."

Rafe wove around his desk, approaching her slowly so as not to frighten her off. "When am I not drinking?" He grinned.

She frowned as Spyglass jumped from the desk and began slinking around the lacy hem of her skirts.

Rafe continued toward the apparition, wondering if his brandy-hazed mind had only conjured up the focus of his recent thoughts. Where was his anger when he needed it? She had lied to him, betrayed him, and with the worst possible person—his father. But right now he could think of nothing else but that he must touch her. He must discover if she was real. And if she was, what other reason could she have for coming to his cabin at this hour of night besides the one that heated his blood?

He halted before her. She lowered her chin, and he allowed his gaze to soak her in from head to toe.

She cleared her throat and shifted nervously, then started to take a step away from him. Rafe touched her arm. The warmth of her soft flesh rose from beneath her sleeve to his fingertips.

Oui. She was real.

In that moment, he would forgive her betrayal, would forgive her deception, if only. . .if only she would love him. If only she would take away the emptiness in his soul.

Rafe ran his thumb over her cheek. Breath escaped her parted lips, but she did not retreat. Lifting her thick black lashes, she gazed at him with those emerald eyes, searching his face for something—if he knew what it was, he would gladly give it to her.

"Please do not sell me to the don, Captain," she whispered in a pleading tone, perhaps sensing his weakened condition.

Rafe ground his teeth together to keep from proclaiming what his heart longed to shout—that he would never do anything to harm her.

She lowered her gaze. "Is there naught I can do to persuade you to change your course?"

"Perhaps." He grinned, allowing his thoughts the freedom to roam into dangerous seas. Had she come to offer herself to him? Though every ounce of his flesh yearned for it to be true, a part of him would die of disappointment if it were. He took a deep breath, trying to clear his swirling head, and cursed himself for drinking so much brandy. Her womanly scent tickled his nose, and his body warmed at her closeness. He reached toward her. She flinched but did not back away. He fingered a lock of her raven hair, relishing the silky feel.

"You wear your hair loose for me, non?"

"No." She started to retreat, but Rafe touched her arm again, halting her.

He swept the back of his fingers over her neck, her jaw, her chin, lifting it. The look in her eyes nearly sent him reeling backward. Where was the hatred that had burned within them the last time they were on this brig? He would have expected it to have returned in full force after he kidnapped her again. But all he saw in its place was concern, admiration, and dare he hope, a shred of ardor.

"You have not answered my question," she said.

"En fait, I have had my doubts as to my present course." It was true enough, although he had not changed his mind about selling her. His fury had continued to fuel his resolve to do so, but at the moment he felt both weakening.

She placed a hand on his arm but immediately lowered it. "Perhaps God is convicting you of your wrongdoing."

Spyglass meowed as if in agreement.

"Oui." Rafe continued caressing her chin, wondering why she allowed him such liberties. Peut-être he had been wrong about her innocence.

As he had been wrong about Claire's. "Or perhaps I can be persuaded to choose the right course." He swallowed against a burst of desire.

She regarded him with cynicism and a flicker of hope. "How so?"

He brushed a curl from her face. "Stay with me tonight."

A tiny line formed between Mademoiselle Grace's brows. It deepened. Her chest heaved, and she took a step back. Anger flashed across her eyes.

"How dare you suggest such a thing?" She raised her hand and slapped him across his cheek.

Rafe could have stopped her, but somewhere deep down inside, he knew he deserved her scorn. The sting radiated across his jaw and over his face, but it did nothing to ease his roaring conscience. He rubbed his cheek and grinned. If she had been any other woman, he would have dismissed her immediately, angry that his passions had been aroused for no reason. But not this woman. Delight surged within him at her rejection, for he would not have expected any other reaction.

Rafe stomped to his desk and took a swig from an open bottle. "Do you find me so repulsive that you would rather become a slave than spend an evening with me?" The thin gray line of dawn spread across the horizon. Wiping his mouth with his sleeve, he turned to face her. "I thought I saw some attraction, even longing in your eyes, non?"

"No." She snapped. "'Tis the drink that clouds your mind." She hugged herself. "You are naught but a French rogue. And you will not add me to your list of conquests."

He shrugged. "You may regret that decision someday."

"You flatter yourself, Captain."

"There are many women who would count themselves fortunate to receive my affections."

"Then they may have you."

"And yet you came crawling to my cabin late at night. What am I to think?"

Spyglass meowed, and Mademoiselle Grace scooped her up and held her against her chest.

Rafe leaned back onto his desk. "Sacre mer, you give more affection to my cat than to me."

"Spyglass isn't going to sell me to a don."

"Peut-être, if you give me the same attention, I will not either."

"'Tis not the same affection you seek."

"Oui, mais a much more enjoyable one." Rafe grinned at the way his words made her squirm.

She stiffened her jaw and met his gaze. "The affections of which you speak are sacred and meant only for marriage, not as a bargaining tool." She set Spyglass onto the floor. "I have never even kissed a man and do not intend to do so until I am betrothed."

Never kissed a man. Sacre mer. Her innocence stunned Rafe. "How difficult it must be to keep such strong passions contained."

"Strong?" She huffed. "You fool yourself, Captain. And it is not difficult to do the will of God."

"For la prude pieuse as you are, perhaps, mon petit chou."

She stiffened her lips. "So now I am a pious prude and a cabbage?" He grinned and stroked his mustache.

"You are a brute when you drink." She swept her sharp eyes to his.

A twinge grated over Rafe's conscience.

"It does not become you, or any man, to benumb himself with alcohol. How can you behave like a gentleman when your senses, your very soul is thus bewitched?" The haughty reprimand faded from her gaze, replaced by one of appeal.

Grabbing the half-empty bottle of brandy, Rafe studied the amber liquid. It had always brought him relief from the pains of life. It had always been his friend when no one else cared. Yet at that moment he would gladly abandon it to see the approval swim back into Mademoiselle Grace's green eyes.

He made his way toward his bed and poured the contents of the bottle into his chamber pot. "Anything for you, mademoiselle."

She blinked and clutched the chain around her neck.

He started toward her, but she held up a hand. "Enough of this. Captain, I have forgotten myself. I came to tell you that Annette has disappeared."

Rafe halted. "Annette? Claire's lady's maid?"

Mademoiselle Grace nodded. "She left the cabin more than an hour ago and has not returned. I thought you should know."

Rafe sighed. This lady cared for everyone, regardless of status. "You were right to tell me." He grabbed his rapier, slung it into his sheath, and then added his pistols. "I will escort you back to your cabin." Rafe held out his arm, hoping she'd take it, but not expecting her to after his performance.

She hesitated, then started to raise her hand, giving him a flicker of hope.

Monsieur Thorn barreled into the room. His wild gaze shifted curiously between them before he inclined his head toward Rafe.

Mademoiselle Grace lowered her hand.

Rafe ground his teeth together. "Sacre mer. What is it, Monsieur Thorn?"

"A ship, Captain, a mile astern and bearing down upon us fast. And from the looks of her, 'tis Captain Howell again."

Rafe shook his head and ran a hand through his hair, trying to shake away the alcoholic daze. "How did he find me again so soon?"

"Bad luck, perhaps, Captain?" Monsieur Thorn's grin sent a sliver of unease through Rafe that he had no time to question. While in Port-de-Paix, Rafe had sent a post to Governor Woodes in New Providence, demanding an explanation for the misunderstanding, but of course he wouldn't have received it yet.

In the meantime, Rafe would have to deal with this imbecile Howell or any other captain, who dared try and sink him for piracy.

CHAPTER 24

Slowly closing the door so as not to awaken Madame Dubois, Grace crept across the squeaky deck toward her bedding. The faint glow of dawn filtered in through the tiny window and alighted upon Annette, who was sitting on the edge of Madame Dubois's cot.

Grace jumped, not expecting to find anyone stirring at this hour, least of all Annette, who she supposed was still wandering about the brig. Taking a breath to still the rapid thumping of her heart, Grace opened her mouth to question the mulatto, but Madame Dubois's shrill voice from the bed interrupted her.

"There you are. Where have you been?" Her tone lacked the usual sharpness, almost as if the energy required to speak the words stole her breath away.

Ignoring her, Grace moved to the chair and took a seat. "Annette, you are safe! I was so worried."

"Worried? About me?" Annette circled her fingers around a small vial in her hand.

"I heard you leave last night." Grace tried to rub the heaviness from her eyes. "And when you didn't return, I went to beg the captain's assistance to find you." Grace gestured toward the door where she'd parted ways with Captain Dubois, the warmth of his touch still lingering on her fingertips.

"You were with Rafe?" Madame Dubois struggled to rise, but sank back onto her pillows with a moan.

Shouts blared from above, followed by the booming snap of sails catching the wind. The brig canted, and Grace clasped the arms of the chair.

"I was not *with* the captain." Grace's harsh tone surprised her as did the unusual guilt grinding over her conscience. She had done nothing wrong. Except be alone with the captain in his cabin. Except allow him to caress her cheek and glide his fingers through her hair.

Annette stared aghast at Grace as the same oppressive heaviness that always surrounded the mulatto woman filled the cabin and clung to Grace like a dense fog. She hugged herself and ran a wary gaze over the shadowy bulkheads, expecting to find the source of the eerie feeling in the form of a hovering specter.

Madame Dubois laid a hand on her forehead and moaned. "Why worry about Annette? I am the one who needs *l'assistance*."

Grace sank to her knees beside the cot, chiding herself for not noticing the woman's distress. "Are you ill?" She lifted her hand to lay it upon Madame Dubois's cheek, but the woman swatted it away.

"Non, je suis *affligée*."

"Madame suffers from a broken heart," Annette offered, shoving the vial into the sleeve of her cotton gown.

A broken heart? The captain's history with Madame Dubois became all the more obvious as time went on. Grace's stomach curled at the thought of what must have occurred between them, before or after her marriage to his father. She didn't want to know. She bit her lip, shifting her thoughts back to the present and the suspicious vial stashed in Annette's sleeve.

She looked at Annette. "And you have the cure?"

The woman made no reply. She gazed at her mistress, then grabbed a damp cloth from the table and dabbed it on Madame Dubois's forehead.

Grace rose from her chair and went to gather her bedding. The ship pitched, and she threw a hand against the bulkhead to keep from falling. The mad gurgle of the Caribbean dashing past the hull filled the room, unsettling her nerves. Setting her blankets atop the chair, Grace faced Annette. "Where were you last night?"

The mulatto raised her dark eyes to Grace's, then lowered them again, but not before Grace caught a flicker of fear crossing them. "I stopped the storm."

The hairs on Grace's arm bristled. Indeed the storm had ceased, but whether it had anything to do with Annette's prayers, Grace could not say—did not want to even consider. Though she knew the forces of darkness were powerful, she shuddered to think they could be acting within such close range.

Madame Dubois groaned. "Oh, who cares about Annette! Go get Rafe. I need to see him." She waved a hand toward her maid. "Help me up, Annette. I want to look *présentable*."

BOOM! Cannon shot rumbled through the brig, shaking the timbers and echoing like the voice of God off the bulkheads.

Grace dashed to the window. Black smoke curled past the salt-streaked panes.

"Zut alors!" Madame Dubois shot up in bed. "Are we under attack?"

"Stay here," Grace ordered, rushing out the door and slamming it behind her without awaiting a response. Clutching her skirts, she bolted up the ladder and sprang onto the deck. If they were to be involved in another battle, she intended to face it head-on and not risk being blown to bits below deck without a moment's warning.

Sailors scrambled across the brig, some carrying cannonballs and others muskets, pistols, and axes. Men hauled ropes or flung themselves aloft—all of them mumbling curses as they went. Scanning the raucous mob, Grace's eyes found Captain Dubois. He stood with boots planted firmly apart on the quarterdeck, flanked by Mr. Thorn and Father Alers. His gray waistcoat and purple sash flapped in the breeze behind him. Beneath his hat, black hair streamed like liquid coal. With a spyglass pressed to his eye, he surveyed something off their stern as he bellowed orders to his first mate.

The brig crested a wave, and Grace stumbled but managed to make her way to the larboard railing. Wind too hot for so early in the morning struck her like the opening of an oven. The acrid scent of gunpowder stung her nose. The sun peeked over the horizon, transforming the crest of each wave into sparkling silver. Squinting against the brightness, Grace leaned over and glanced astern. In the distance, the curve of two red sails flamed in the rising sun. White foam swept over the oncoming ship's bow as she closed the distance between them.

Captain Howell's ship, the *Avenger*.

Grace rubbed her eyes as the sun glinted off a slight movement beyond the pursuing ship. Suddenly a pyramid of brimming white sails slipped into view.

"Two sails! Two sails!" A man yelled from aloft.

Grace swallowed, wondering if the other ship could be her sister's. But she knew her hope was in vain. Even if the sailor had kept his word to deliver her post to Charles Towne, Faith would not have had time to catch up with them yet. She gazed at the two ships swooping through the azure waters, fast on *Le Champion*'s stern. *Oh Lord, please be with us.* The brig rose and plunged over a wave, showering her with a spray of seawater and sending foamy water onto the deck, soaking her shoes.

The captain leaned toward Mr. Thorn and said something that sent the first mate leaping down the quarterdeck ladder, Father Alers on his heels. Surprise widened the first mate's eyes as he passed Grace, but he tipped his hat and continued on his way, dropping below deck. Father Alers halted beside her.

"You should go below, mademoiselle." He grabbed her arm, but Grace resisted and shook her head. "Did we fire a cannon?"

"Oui. A warning shot only. Maintenant." He gestured toward the companionway.

"Please let me stay, Father." Grace gave him a pleading look. "I promise I won't cause any trouble."

His shoulders slumped and he quirked a brow. "Only if you stop calling me Father."

Grace smiled. "Forgive me, but the title sits so well upon you."

He snorted and folded his hands over his prominent belly. A hint of a smile slanted his lips. "Très bien. Mais, I will stay with you. Non?"

"Didn't the captain give you some task to do?"

"Oui." He smiled. "To watch over you." The older man took a position beside her.

Mr. Thorn soon returned with a rolled-up chart in hand and rejoined his captain. Together, they spread it atop the binnacle, held it down against the buffeting wind, and examined it for several minutes. Finally, the captain rolled it up and handed it to Mr. Thorn with a nod. He glanced across the main deck, and his gaze found hers.

Delight brightened his eyes for a moment but quickly faded into annoyance. He gripped the hilt of his rapier and turned to face Mr. Atton at the helm. "Set a course west by south, Monsieur Atton." Then shifting to Mr. Thorn, "All hands aloft, Monsieur Thorn!" he bellowed. "Let fall the topsails and gallants!" Mr. Thorn repeated the commands, sending sailors leaping into the ratlines.

With straining cordage and creaking blocks, the ship swung slowly to starboard, and Grace clutched the railing to keep from falling. Above her, men who looked more like monkeys balanced on ropes no thicker than her wrists as they unfurled the white canvas to catch the swift Caribbean breeze. Sails flapped and thundered hungrily but soon found their satisfaction when an influx of wind filled their white bellies. Grace lowered her gaze to Captain Dubois. With Mr. Thorn beside him, he pointed to something off their starboard bow. She glanced in that direction and saw naught but an eternity of turquoise waves.

When she turned back around, the captain stood before her. She let out a gasp and clutched her throat as his dark gaze drank her in. She lowered her chin. Placing a finger beneath it, he raised her face until she was forced to look at him.

"I found Annette. She is safe." Grace winced at the stutter in her voice.

"I am happy to hear it."

His touch brought back memories of their time in his cabin, and shame struck her. Shame she had allowed him such intimacies, shame she had enjoyed the way his touch made her feel. And now as he stood so close to her, strands of his black hair grazing his stubbled jaw, all those feelings came flooding back.

What was happening to her? She should not be feeling such wanton sensations. Sensations that clouded her judgment and befogged her mind so that she did not remember why she'd gone to the captain's cabin in the first place. Not until she had slapped the captain and he'd stepped away from her.

Yet regardless of her inner turmoil, she had not deserved his salacious invitation. She called her anger forward, hoping the force of it would dissolve her shame and confusion.

He released her chin. "Go below, mademoiselle."

"Please, Captain, I do not wish to die in that tiny cabin."

"No one dies today. There will be no battle."

Father Alers shifted his amber eyes between them curiously then scratched his thick beard. "No battle? I have never seen you run, Rafe."

Captain Dubois huffed out a sigh and gazed at the ships bearing down on them. "I have already bested this buffoon in a challenge once. But we are no match for two ships. I know of an island to the southwest with many shallow inlets where we will be able to hide."

Grace followed his gaze to where the ships, though not advancing, had certainly not slackened in their pursuit. "But won't they see where we have gone?"

"*Le Champion* is shallow on the draft, mademoiselle. She can sail places other ships cannot." He doffed his hat and ran a hand through his hair. "Besides"—one side of his mouth lifted in that grin of his that sent her heart racing—"I have precious cargo aboard that I do not wish harmed."

"Yes, we wouldn't want your valuable *cargo* destroyed," she retorted.

"Non. We would not." He lifted a brow and replaced his hat.

"Captain, a moment, please." Mr. Thorn hailed him from the quarterdeck and after inclining his head toward her, Captain Dubois joined his first mate.

Thankful he seemed to have forgotten he'd ordered her below, Grace whirled around, gripped the railing, and closed her eyes. The hot wind, tainted with brine and fish and wood, whipped over her, loosening her hair from its pins. But she no longer cared, having grown long since weary of the battle to keep it properly pinned in place. Besides, she could not deny how free she felt as the wind spread its whispery fingers through her curls. *Mercy me, how I have changed.* But was it for the best?

Father Alers cleared his throat. "*Le capitaine est bien épris avec vous,* mademoiselle."

Grace snapped her eyes open and stared at him aghast, amazed at both his statement and that she had understood it. "He is taken with any female, Fa. . .Mr. Alers."

He smiled, revealing a row of crooked teeth. "Oui, that is true. But not in the same way, je vous assure."

Grace shook her head. "He intends to sell me. Forgive me if I do not believe any interest he has in me goes beyond his own needs or those of his precious hospital." Her words swirled around her, taunting her with their duplicity, and she attempted to bat them away into the rising breeze. But she could not deny the goodness, the deep affection she had seen in Rafe's eyes—beyond all the anger, beyond the pain. Nor could she deny her own growing feelings for him, conflicted as they were.

Father Alers brushed gray spikes of hair from his face and gave her a knowing look. "It is a sin to tell a fib, mademoiselle."

Angry that the man read her thoughts so easily, Grace folded her arms over her chest. "He kidnapped me—twice. What more is there to say?" Yet truth be told, his capture of her this time seemed to spring from some deep pain within him rather than any desire to harm her.

Father Alers raised a sardonic brow. Ignoring him, Grace pursed her lips and glanced behind at the two ships that were fast on their heels. A sudden fear clamped her heart. From what she'd seen of Governor Woodes's men, they were no better than pirates. Glad for a chance to change the subject, she faced Father Alers. "Will they catch us?"

"Non." He laid his hand upon hers on the railing. His warm fingers scratched her skin like rough rope. But she found it oddly soothing. "Rafe is the best capitaine I have seen," he added.

Grace chuckled. "I do not know whether that should make me happy or sad."

Father Alers's golden eyes twinkled in the rising sun as the light cast shadows over the crevices in his face. Yet nothing but warmth beamed from his expression.

"Land ho!" a booming voice echoed from the crosstrees. Grace scanned the horizon, and minutes later a gray mound rose from the azure water like the back of a crocodile. The captain barked a series of orders, sending his men scurrying across deck. Off their stern, the two ships maintained a fast pursuit, and Grace could not imagine how the captain expected to hide from them.

Flying through the water with every inch of canvas set to the breeze, *Le Champion* sped toward the burgeoning mass of land.

"Watch your luff, Monsieur Atton!" Captain Dubois barked, stomping across the deck. Though Grace tried to avoid looking at him, she found her gaze drawn to the captain as if a spell had been cast upon her that only the sight of him could appease. Never once did his voice wobble in fear, never once did he seem confused, unsure, or hesitant. He commanded his men with naught but confidence and authority. Grace faced the sea again, chiding herself for admiring anything about the rogue.

Within minutes, the small island loomed large before them, and Captain Dubois brayed a string of orders that brought the brig on a sharp tack around the western peninsula.

"Trice up, men," the captain bellowed. "Shorten sail!"

Shielding her eyes from the sun high in the sky, Grace watched as the men, dangling in the shrouds, hauled in the canvas on fore- and mainmasts. With only her topsails fluttering in the light breeze, the brig slowed, and without hesitation, the captain sailed her into the entrance of an oblong harbor riddled with sandbars and reefs.

Grace followed the captain's gaze off their stern, but the pursuing ships were nowhere in sight.

"She's shoaling fast, Captain," Mr. Thorn shouted, examining the lead and line that one of the crewmen had just pulled up from the water.

"Keep me informed." Captain Dubois jumped onto the quarterdeck and relieved Mr. Atton of his duty at the helm.

The captain stood at the wheel while his men hung over the bow, directing him which way to steer the brig. Another man tossed the lead and line repeatedly over the side, shouting out the dwindling depths of the sea. Grace leaned over the railing. She could make out the dim bottom of the sandy bay beneath the brig. Sharp, jagged reefs rose from the depths like sharp talons searching for a victim. One slip and their hull would be penetrated and all would be lost.

She raised her gaze to the pristine white shores of the island that framed the small harbor. Sand, sparkling like white jewels in the sunlight, fanned up to a lush web of greens and browns, making up the forest. The scent of tropical flowers and fruit wafted over Grace and she drew a deep breath. The smell of land—land where she was not to be sold. Not yet.

Hushed whistles alerted Grace to another female on deck, and she turned to see Annette dashing toward her. Fear flashed from her brown eyes.

"What is it, Annette?" Grace grabbed her hands.

"Madame Dubois. She is ill. You must come at once."

After Mademoiselle Grace disappeared below, the deck of *Le Champion* groaned as if lamenting her absence. As did Rafe—an internal, silent groan. He had allowed her to remain above for the sole purpose of enjoying the occasional glances he stole of her when she was not looking. Her presence had a calming influence on him that he could not explain.

"Weigh anchor!" Mr. Thorn shouted, and the massive iron hook struck the water with a resounding splash. Within seconds the thick rope snapped taut and the brig jerked to a stop. Captain Dubois jumped down to the main deck, peering over both sides to ensure their safe distance from the reefs. Then raising the spyglass, he studied the wide mouth of the harbor.

"Any sign of them, Captain?" Monsieur Thorn asked.

"Non." He lowered the glass. "If luck is with us, they did not see which inlet we slipped into."

Mr. Weylan approached, a group of sailors following him like a foaming wake. "Capitaine, what is your plan?" The second mate adjusted his feathered hat and put his hands upon his waist. "We cannot stay here forever."

Ayes and grunts tumbled from behind him.

Rafe flattened his lips, feeling his ire rise at this new provocation. "We will wait for an opportunity to slip by them." He forced confidence into his voice then studied his crew. The men's loyalties shifted like waves tossed in a storm, the respect he usually found in their eyes in short supply.

"What if they trap us?" Monsieur Legard asked, peering from behind Weylan.

"They cannot see us from the entrance to the harbor." Rafe pressed a finger over his mustache. "We will leave under cover of darkness."

The lines on Monsieur Weylan's face folded, and he scratched his matted hair.

"What else, Monsieur?" Rafe sighed in frustration.

"The men are unhappy, Capitaine. We have not been paid in over two months."

Rafe gripped the hilt of his rapier, his muscles tensing for a fight. He felt Monsieur Thorn stiffen beside him, but when Rafe glanced his way, a slight smile sat smugly upon his first mate's lips.

"And now we are delayed again," another sailor shouted. "When do we sell the woman?"

Rafe ground his teeth together. "I am to meet the don in seven days." Yet the thought of making that appointment ate away at Rafe's gut.

He eyed his men in turn. "With me as your capitaine, have you not lined your pockets with more coins than you could spend? *Où est votre confiance?*" Rafe frowned. How could he blame them? He was not sure he trusted himself anymore. But to let them see his hesitation, his doubt, would be certain death.

"I am still the capitaine of this brig. Unless one of you wishes to challenge me?" Rafe leveled a stern gaze at each man and then glanced over the sailors on the quarter and foredecks who'd gathered at the first sign of an altercation. "*Personne?*"

Some of his men stared blankly back at him; others shook their heads.

"Non. Of course not, Capitaine." Weylan smiled, but in that slick smile Rafe saw the makings of a mutiny.

Rafe narrowed a gaze upon him then glanced over the men. "Get back to work or I'll slice all of you through myself!" he barked, and the men scattered like flies before the whip of a horse's tail.

Then fisting his hands, Rafe spun around and stomped toward the companionway. In seven days' time he must either hand Mademoiselle Grace over to the Spanish don or face a mutiny—a mutiny he was sure would result in his death.

CHAPTER 25

Grace dabbed the moist cloth over Madame Dubois's forehead and cheeks. Heat radiated from the woman's skin as if it were a searing griddle. A lump formed in Grace's throat. She harbored no deep affection for the woman but certainly did not wish her any harm.

A soft moan slipped from Madame Dubois's lips, and she tossed her head across the pillow. Red blotches marred Claire's normally creamy skin, and dark circles hung beneath crystal blue eyes that were glazed with fever. Grace swallowed against her rising fear, laid the cloth down, and stood. Across the cabin, Annette rested on her bedding as if she hadn't a care in the world.

Making her way to the window, Grace peered out at the black sky, dusted with a myriad of twinkling stars. Her eyes ached from lack of sleep. She rubbed them and whispered a prayer. *Lord, please help me. Please help Madame Dubois.* As usual, God's voice was silent. *Where are You, Lord?* She scanned the endless expanse of night sky, remembering a time when her prayers were filled with faith. Now she couldn't affirm that God even heard her pleas, though certainly He had kept her alive to this point. But for what purpose?

Gentle waves licked the brig's hull. Somewhere up on deck, a fiddle moaned a sad tune, even as laughter bubbled up from the sailors' berth at the forecastle. Everything seemed so peaceful. Yet it was a delusory peace. For not far away lurked two fully armed ships ready to pound *Le Champion* into splinters and sink her into the sea. And within this tiny cabin one woman fought for her life, another lived as a slave, while the third would soon become one.

"Annette." The desperation in Madame Dubois's voice tugged at Grace's heart.

Annette glanced at her mistress, then closed her eyes, feigning sleep.

Grace moved to the cot. "'Tis me, Grace, madame." Retrieving the cloth, she patted it over her forehead. "How do you feel?"

Madame Dubois's lashes fluttered open. Blue eyes, sparkling in the lantern light, alighted upon Grace. "Where is Annette?"

"She is sleeping. But I am here, madame." Grace took the woman's hand in hers, wincing at the heat emanating from her skin, and surprised when the woman received her embrace without recoiling.

Madame Dubois's chest rose and fell, and she lifted a hand to her head. "What is wrong with me? Am I dying?"

"No, of course not." Grace attempted a comforting smile.

Rustling sounds rose from the corner, and Annette appeared beside them. Spyglass ceased her purring. Grace gave the mulatto a cursory glance before returning her gaze to Madame Dubois. "Can you eat something, madame?" The poor woman had not partaken of any food since last night.

"Je ne sais pas." Madame Dubois breathed out words barely above a whisper. "Perhaps."

"Annette," Grace said. "Would you please tell Father Alers to bring up some broth for Madame."

Annette blinked and gazed at her mistress as if she were an apparition before darting out the door.

Spyglass stretched on the table where she lay and began purring.

"My head hurts." Madame Dubois pressed her temples and turned toward Grace. "Where are we? Where is Rafe?"

"We are safe." Grace didn't want to add to the woman's stress by informing her of the two ships following them. "And Rafe, I mean Captain Dubois, is no doubt up on deck." Though Grace had not seen him for several hours.

Madame Dubois stared at Grace as if seeing her for the first time. The haughty sheen had dissipated from her eyes, along with the animosity that always fired from within them. "Why are you being so kind to me?"

Grace squeezed her hand. "Because you are ill. Surely you would do the same for me should I become waylaid by some malady."

Madame Dubois shook her head, a slight smirk upon her lips. "I do not think so."

Grace chuckled, knowing that in her delirium, the woman had spoken the truth. She released her hand and dipped the cloth back into a basin of water. Then wringing it out, she laid it over Madame Dubois's forehead. "It does not matter. I will care for you anyway."

"I do not deserve it," she muttered, her confession shocking Grace.

"None of us deserve anything good, madame." Grace flinched at her own words, wondering where they had come from. Yet tears filled her eyes as she realized how true they were. *For all have sinned, and come short of the glory of God. There is none righteous, no not one.*

The door creaked, and Annette entered, followed by Father Alers, a tray in hand. He ambled in and set it down on the table then eyed Madame Dubois with concern. The scent of lemons and beef broth swirled about the cabin. Annette closed the door and slunk into the shadows against the bulkhead.

Spyglass sat up, her ears perked.

"How is she?" Father Alers sank into the chair.

Grace shook her head. "I cannot cool her fever."

The old priest leaned forward in the chair and scratched his beard as if trying to conjure up a solution.

Grace stood. "It came upon her so suddenly. I've never seen such a thing."

A gasp came from the shadows, and Grace snapped her gaze toward Annette's dark form, wondering at the woman's odd behavior and then remembering the potion she had given Madame Dubois. "Do you know what happened to your mistress, Annette?" Her voice carried more accusation then she intended, and Annette cowered further into the shadows—so far Grace could not see her eyes.

"Non, mademoiselle," came her sheepish voice.

Father Alers gestured toward the tray. "Perhaps the broth will strengthen her."

"Do you have any herbs aboard, any feverfew, peppermint, or elderflower?" Grace clasped her hands together.

"Non."

"No one with medical knowledge?"

"Non." Father Alers shook his head.

A groan sounded from the cot. "Mademoiselle." Madame Dubois reached out her hand, and Grace fell to her knees and took it in her own.

"Yes, I am here, madame." She laid the back of her hand on Madame Dubois's cheek, then flinched at the heat radiating off her skin.

"I am dying." Her voice wobbled, and her chest rose and fell rapidly.

Visions of Grace's mother on her deathbed crept out from hiding and dashed tauntingly across Grace's mind. Madame Dubois looked so much like her: same blond hair, same striking blue eyes, and now the same feverish skin, same raspy voice, same delirium. Grace would not watch another woman die. "No, you will not die."

Father Alers handed Grace the bowl. "Help her drink this."

Gently placing her arm beneath Madame Dubois, Grace tried to lift her. "Madame, please drink this broth."

"Non. Non." She waved it away. "I cannot."

With a huff of defeat, Grace handed the bowl back to Father Alers, her heart sinking lower in her chest.

"Mademoiselle," the woman panted. "I must tell you something."

"You should rest, madame. Regain your strength." Grace wiped a saturated curl from her face.

"Non, s´il vous plaît. I must." She stopped to catch her breath. She peered at Grace below heavy lids and shook her head. "What you must think of me."

"It does not matter."

"I was not always like I am now." Madame Dubois swallowed and tried to gather her breath. "I grew up in France, in the small port town of La Havre. Mon père worked on the docks and ma mère washed clothes to make extra money. She was British like you."

"Shhh." Grace dabbed the cloth on her head, wondering why the woman cared to disclose her childhood now of all times.

"Mon père died in an accident. Ma mère died of the sickness two months later," she rasped.

Grace halted her ministrations. She had lost only one parent. She could not imagine the horror of losing both.

"I exist on the streets for many years." Madame Dubois coughed, and her face pinched in pain. "Then at sixteen I accept the King's offer to come to Saint Dominique to become wife to a planter."

Grace thought of Nicole. It would seem many of the women at Port-de-Paix shared the same past.

Madame Dubois squeezed her hand. "I never had enough *nourriture*. I never had *des belles robes*. I never had someone to love me. Comprenez-vous?" She lifted sincere eyes to Grace, and in that look, Grace no longer saw a vain, pretentious woman. She no longer saw a jealous shrew. She saw a frightened, innocent little girl.

Drawing Claire's hand to her lips, Grace kissed it and smiled. Her eyes moistened at the thought of what this woman had endured. "I cannot say that I completely understand, but I do empathize with your pain, for I too, have suffered loss." Grace wiped a tear pooling at the corner of Madame Dubois's eye. "Now you must rest and get well." Though by the rising heat on the woman's cheeks, Grace began to doubt that would happen.

Madame Dubois's breathing grew ragged and her lids closed. She turned her head and fell asleep. When Grace tried to wake her there was no response, not even a whimper. Leaning her head on the cot, Grace allowed her tears to fall. "Please, Lord, heal this woman. Please."

"She will not live." Annette's words pierced the air like a rapier.

Grace snapped her gaze toward the mulatto. "How can you say such a thing?"

Annette stepped out of the gloom into the lantern light. Malevolence, but also a spark of dread, burned in her brown eyes as she gazed at her mistress. Grace shivered.

Father Alers stood, the legs of his chair scraping over the planks of the deck.

"What have you done?" Grace asked as she rose and took a step toward her. Spyglass darted to the edge of the table, and shifted her one eye onto Annette.

The mulatto swallowed, her wide eyes sparking in the lantern light. "I gave her what she want, what she beg for."

Father Alers glanced over the cabin as if he, too, felt the darkening presence within, then he narrowed his eyes upon Annette. "And what did she ask for?"

"*Un philtre d'amour.*" She laughed. "To make her irrésistible to Captain Dubois."

Grace grabbed her arm. "A love potion? What was in it?"

"Nothing that would do any harm." Annette trembled, her gaze skittering to her mistress. "Except to one who has no heart."

If Annette had poisoned Madame Dubois, what hope did they

have to save her? She thought to insist the mulatto give her an antidote, but from the look in her eyes, Grace didn't dare allow the woman to administer any further potions to her mistress. Blood surged to Grace's head even as her stomach knotted. "If Madame Dubois dies, her death is on your hands."

Tears swarmed into Annette's eyes, and she drew a ragged breath. "I gave her what she asked for," she repeated, her voice raised in fear. "It is the gods who decide if she deserves to live." She shuddered, tore her arm from Grace's hand, and dashed from the cabin, sobbing.

Grace started after her, but Father Alers held her in place. "Let her go. Our concern must be for Madame Dubois."

Spyglass curled into a ball again on the table.

Grace eyed the cat curiously then clutched the chain around her neck. "Yes. We must get her to port. We must find an apothecary."

"We cannot. Le Capitaine spotted one of Woodes's ships just outside the harbor entrance. Until they are gone or we have a moonless night, we are trapped in this cove." Father Alers pressed down the coils of his gray hair, but they sprang back into their chaotic web as soon as he withdrew his hand.

"So there is naught we can do for her." Grace glanced at Madame Dubois.

Father Alers crossed himself. "Nothing but pray."

❧

Thorn rubbed the back of his neck and took another turn across the foredeck. Unable to sleep, he'd dismissed the sailor on watch and took his place. He squeezed the muscles in his arms and stretched his back. Why was he so tense? Everything was going according to plan.

He slid his thumb over the scar stretching down his cheek and neck, a constant reminder to stay the course—to forge ahead until the vengeance that gnawed hungrily in his gut was satisfied. Glancing over the ebony waters of the bay, her shallow waves christened in silver moonlight, he smiled at the fortunate turn of events. Movement on the deck below caught his eye. A dark form ducked within the shadows by the starboard railing. One of the crew? No, the shape was far too small. Muffled sobs filled the air.

Thorn made his way down the foredeck ladder then crept across the main deck, trying not to alert whoever it was. But as he grew near, her sobs grew louder—for he could now tell it was a woman—a woman with hair the color of the night tumbling down her back. His heart leapt.

Annette.

He took another step toward her. His boot thumped. She whirled around to face him and let out a gasp, backing away.

He lifted a hand. "Don't be afraid. I heard you crying."

She glanced toward the companionway hatch then back at him, swiping the moisture from her cheeks.

"May I?" Thorn motioned to the spot beside her, hoping she would accept his company.

She said nothing. He slipped next to her and grabbed the railing. Trying to appear nonchalant, he glanced over the dark waters. "Beautiful night."

She sniffed and faced the harbor. "Oui."

Thorn took a deep breath, trying to still the thumping of his heart. He'd wanted nothing more than to speak to this dark beauty ever since she had boarded the brig, but her position and color created societal obstacles that had prevented him. Now, as she stood beside him, smelling of citrus and cedar, his senses inflamed. And all he wanted to do was discover the cause of her distress and stop her from crying. "Are you ill, mademoiselle?" He dared a glance at her. Her dark, thick lashes lowered to her cheeks that looked more like creamy *café* in the moonlight.

She shook her head. "My mistress is ill."

He nodded and leaned his elbow on the railing, trying to make out more of her exquisite features in the shadows. "I am sorry."

"Pas moi. I am not." Her French accent sharpened.

Thorn chuckled. She clicked her tongue and started to leave, but he grabbed her arm. "Please forgive me. I was not laughing at you. It is just that, well..." He released her, thankful when she stayed even though her suspicious gaze signaled she could bolt at any minute. "Your mistress is not a person to evoke much sympathy, non?" He mimicked her French, hoping it would please her and was rewarded with a tiny smile that set his heart soaring.

"Why do you, a white man, speak to me?" she asked, her sweet voice barely audible over the creaking of the ship.

Realizing he must look a fright, Thorn adjusted his coat and brushed dirt from his sleeve. "I have wanted to speak to you ever since you came aboard."

Her delicate brow folded. "*Pourquoi?*" She took a step back as if suddenly afraid of him.

He lifted a hand in an effort to assuage her fear but it only sent her farther away. "You misunderstand, mademoiselle. I have no untoward intentions. I only wish to get to know you."

"To know me?" She shook her head as if he'd said the moon were made of flour and milk.

"Yes. That is all." Thorn opened his palms in a gesture of innocence.

She faced the bay, the breeze dancing through her hair that reminded him of black silk. He longed to sift his fingers through it. "You are very beautiful."

She huffed in disgust. "Oui. It is what I was made for."

"Not all you were created for." Thorn laid a hand on her arm, but she snapped from his touch and shot fiery eyes his way. A cloud strayed over the moon, stealing Annette from his sight.

"Non? Mon père treats me as a slave. Ma mère is his mistress. And Madame Dubois despises me. I am half black, half white. The blancs shun me. The Africans are repulsed by the white blood in my veins. I live *suspendue* between two worlds, and I belong to none. I am nothing without my beauty. And if that is all you want from me, you must speak to Monsieur Dubois. I am sure you and he can make a good deal." Turning, she started to walk away, but Thorn jumped in her path, blocking her. He hoped she couldn't see the grin on his lips at her spirited oration. The woman was not only beautiful but full of pluck as well.

She tried to weave around him, but he grabbed her arm.

"Do not leave, Annette." His throat constricted beneath a sudden sorrow. Sorrow at a life so enshrouded with misery and rejection. "I assure you, I want nothing from you but your friendship." He peered in the darkness, longing to see her face. "I, too, find myself between two worlds. I am an Englishman on a French brig. I am a man of education and honor among a bevy of crude, ill-mannered sailors." He leaned toward her. The cloud abandoned its post, allowing the moon to bathe her in milky light. "We have much in common, mademoiselle."

She lifted her moist brown eyes to his. And in them he saw a spark of hope.

But then she looked away. "I must go," she said.

Thorn released her, and she dashed to the companionway ladder.

Then casting one last glance his way, she disappeared below.

Thorn smiled and gazed up at the half-moon. If God listened to prayers, Thorn would thank Him for the moon tonight that kept them imprisoned within this cove. For if the white orb had not made an appearance, they would have attempted an escape in the darkness, and he may not have had the chance to become better acquainted with the alluring Annette.

In fact, each day they remained in this cove provided an opportunity for their refuge to be discovered.

Which could only bode well for Mr. Thorn.

And very badly for Rafe.

CHAPTER 26

At Father Alers's gruff "entrez-vous," Rafe entered the small cabin, Spyglass bounding in on his heels. The putrid stench of *infirmité* assaulted him and drew his eyes to the lithe, ghostly form lying on the cot amidst a tangle of blankets and golden hair. Thunder clapped outside, sending the brig aquiver with a sense of impending doom. Although storm clouds covered the tiny island, a few resolute rays of sunlight pierced the porthole into the tiny cabin.

Father Alers gazed at Rafe with those intense golden eyes, now filled with concern.

"*Comment va-t-elle?*" Rafe asked. When he had heard of Claire's illness, he assumed it was just another one of her tricks to get his attention.

Claire moaned and shifted on her coverlet.

Apparently, this time, Rafe had been wrong. He glanced across the cabin. Spyglass lapped broth from a bowl on the table. A jumble of blankets lay stuffed in one corner by the armoire alongside a candle, a necklace, and some stones.

"Where is Mademoiselle Grace?"

Father Alers stretched his legs out before him and folded his hands over his belly. "The mademoiselle went above for some air."

"Grace went above? *Sous la pluie?*" Rafe glanced at the porthole, where streaks of rain flattened beneath the prevailing wind.

Father Alers shrugged. "It stopped raining, and the poor mademoiselle has been attending Madame Claire throughout the night."

"Vraiment?" Though Rafe knew of the mademoiselle's charitable heart, he felt a twinge of shock that she would care for a woman who had done nothing but reproach her.

"Oui, the mademoiselle has been most *aimable* to Madame Dubois." Father Alers shook his head. "She returns each of Madame's insults with kindness."

Rafe scratched his jaw as his muscles stiffened in defiance of Grace's forgiving heart. Yet for as long as Rafe had known Father Alers, the man had dispensed his approbation of others as sparsely as he did the prize claret hidden in his trunk.

Claire moaned, and he stared at the red blotches marring her sweat-laden face. She had always been so beautiful. Even now, consumed with sickness, she still displayed the feminine charm he had once been unable to resist. Yet lately her beauty seemed more akin to a lovely gown of silk and lace—a garment one put on and took off and that faded and stained and wrinkled over time.

Rafe shifted his stance and spotted a cockroach scampering away. He smashed it with his boot, hoping to alleviate his aggravation.

"Where is Annette? She should be attending her mistress."

Father Alers's eyes took on a haunted look. "She ran out after Mademoiselle accused her of poisoning her mistress."

"Poisoning?" The word rebounded through Rafe's mind like round shot but found no place to land.

"Oui, un philtre d'amour." Father Alers snorted. "A potion to win your heart."

Claire moaned again and clamped her lips together. Spyglass finished lapping up the broth and begin licking her paws and washing her face.

A deep sorrow fell upon Rafe like the weight of an anchor, even as his anger burned. Why now? Why did Claire want so desperately to win back his heart now? When he no longer felt anything but pity for the woman. When his thoughts were constantly on another.

"Do you think Annette poisoned her?"

"*Qui sait?*" Father Alers quirked a brow. "For now, we must get Madame Dubois to an apothecary."

Claire's lashes fluttered, and she groaned. Father Alers wrung out a cloth and laid it atop her forehead.

Rafe stomped to the porthole. "We cannot. Woodes's ships cruise outside the harbor waiting to strike us as soon as we set sail."

Claire's eyes opened to tiny slits, and Father Alers removed the cloth. "We are trapped?"

"Non, I will think of something." Rafe flattened his lips and made his way to the cot.

"Rafe." Claire lifted a shaky hand toward him, and he knelt beside her, taking it in his. Whatever animosity he harbored against this woman, however much she had ripped out his heart and trampled upon it, he did not wish her dead.

Father Alers stood and pressed a hand on Rafe's back, then he stepped toward the door. "Can you sit with her for a minute? I need to make sure Yanez is attending his duties in the galley in my absence."

Rafe shook his head. What did he know about tending the sick?

But Father Alers waved him off. "I'll return straightaway." And then he was gone.

Rafe released Claire's hand, removed his rapier, and laid it on the table. Taking the chair Father Alers had vacated, he grabbed his baldric and began toying with the rough leather at its edge. Sweat beaded on the back of his neck as he glanced over the cabin, careful to avoid looking at the sick woman on the cot—the woman he had once loved, the woman he had intended to make his wife. Thunder rumbled outside, emulating the storm that raged within him. Fear, love, desire, hatred—all churned in a massive dark cloud hovering over his heart. A cloud that threatened to unleash a torrent on him at any moment.

Spyglass jumped into his lap, and he caressed her fur, thankful the cat had not completely abandoned her affections for him as everyone else seemed to have done.

"Rafe." Claire breathed his name on a sigh and turned her eyes upon him, once so clear, but now covered with a feverish haze. "You came to see me."

Rafe nodded and leaned forward, placing his elbows on his knees and forcing Spyglass from his lap.

Her breathing took on a rapid pace. "I fear I am dying."

Still Rafe said nothing, for he hated offering people vain hope only to ease their discomfort. And honestly, from the heat he'd felt sizzling from her skin, he could not deny that she spoke the truth.

"Do not look so pleased." She tried to laugh but coughed instead.

Thunder growled, and Spyglass meowed in reply then leapt to the foot of the cot and sprawled across the coverlet.

Rafe looked down at the tiny divots marring the deck. The brig rolled over a wave, its planks creaking and groaning. "I do not wish you to die, Claire."

"Then why can you not look at me?"

Rafe raised his gaze to hers only to see her eyes pool with tears. Sweat glistened on her forehead and neck, and the silky hair he had once adored lay matted in sweaty tangles around her face.

"I wanted you to love me." She swallowed.

Rafe closed his eyes. "I did."

"Did." She said the word with the finality of a judge's mallet.

"What do you expect?" Rafe snorted and sat back in his chair.

She licked her chapped lips. "Something to drink, s'il vous plaît?"

Rafe grabbed a mug from the table, lifted her shoulders, and raised it to her mouth. She took a sip then collapsed back onto the cot.

"Merci." The word escaped her lips as if the effort exhausted her.

Thunder bellowed, echoing through the ship like a mighty gong.

He returned the mug to the table but before he could get away, she grabbed his arm with more strength than he would have assumed remained within her.

"I did this all for you, Rafe."

"Did what?" He knelt on one knee, wanting to tear from her grasp, but the desperation in her eyes stayed him. Raindrops tapped on the windowpane.

"Came aboard your ship. Left your father."

"I did not ask you to come."

"I thought I could change your mind. I thought you may still love me." She gasped, unable to catch her breath.

Rafe shook his head, rummaging through the dunnage in his heart for any remaining feelings for this woman who had betrayed him so mercilessly.

Claire's brow furrowed. "It is Mademoiselle Grace, is it not? You love her."

Rafe plucked the cloth from the bucket and squeezed the water from it as if he were trying to squeeze the truth from Claire's words. "She has nothing to do with this."

Claire raised her hand to her forehead. "I tried to send her home."

"What do you mean?"

"I told her I needed her help to escape from your father's abuse. I begged her"—she drew a shallow breath—"to accept his offer to go to

Charles Towne. . .where I would secretly get off the ship with her."

"You what?" Rafe dropped the cloth into the bucket and stood.

"Please don't be angry with me, Rafe." Claire coughed, her eyes flashing with fear. "I saw the way you looked at her. But I knew with her gone, you could still love me."

Rafe grabbed his baldric and paced before the cot. So that was the reason Mademoiselle Grace had not met him that night. It wasn't his father who had persuaded her to go with him, who had lured her away with his riches. It was Claire. And instead of riches, Claire had lured the mademoiselle with the only thing irresistible to her—the prospect of helping someone in need.

"But you stole her back." Claire laughed then clutched her throat. "I did not expect that."

Rafe hung his head and halted before the cot. Shame tugged upon him. He had believed the worst of Mademoiselle Grace and had stolen her from her bedchamber without giving her a chance to explain.

"Rafe." Claire held out her hand. "Please do not be angry with me."

Kneeling, Rafe took her hand in his. Staring into her blue eyes, he felt no love, no remorse, nor even anger—only pity.

"I am not angry." Rafe sighed and squeezed her hand. "Maintenant, you must get some rest."

And as if his hint of regard was all she needed to usher her into a moment's repose, she closed her eyes and drifted off to sleep.

The door creaked open, and Mademoiselle Grace stepped in, her raven hair hanging in damp tendrils about her face. Her emerald eyes alighted upon him and widened in surprise. She gazed at his hand holding Claire's. "Forgive me." She started to leave.

"Non." Rafe shot to his feet. "Do not go, s'il vous plaît."

She faced him, then swept the cabin with her gaze, carefully avoiding his eyes. Spyglass aroused from her nap and began to stretch. "Where is Father Alers?" she asked.

"In the galley."

"I did not mean to intrude."

"There is nothing to intrude upon."

"It is none of my business if there is." She swallowed and glanced at Claire with concern.

"She just fell back asleep. Will you sit, mademoiselle?"

Grace glared at him as if he were the devil himself. He winced beneath the pain it caused him. "I do not bite, mademoiselle." He attempted a grin.

She cocked a brow. "I am not so sure."

That he frightened her was obvious. That he disgusted her made his heart sink like a lead line. That he should leave her alone and offer her some peace, he knew was the right thing to do. He gestured toward the chair. "I will not torture you with my presence, mademoiselle."

With a hesitant swoosh of her damp skirts, she moved to the chair and sat down. No sooner had she alighted upon it than Spyglass leapt from the cot and jumped into her lap.

Rafe could not help but smile. "You have made a friend, I see."

"Yes, one friend aboard this ship, it would seem." Her voice was laden with sorrow as she caressed the cat's fur, and Rafe swallowed.

Retrieving his rapier, he sheathed it with a metallic *chink* and started toward the door. He gripped the handle, stopped and rubbed his thumb over the cool silver. He could not leave Grace, not with the judgment, the disdain for him, pouring from her eyes.

He swung about.

She swallowed but did not look at him. "I thought you were leaving."

"So did I."

"Claire needs medical assistance, Captain."

Raindrops pounded on the deck above like bullets assailing his guilt. "I am doing all that I can."

He gripped his baldric and cleared his throat. He wanted to tell her about Claire, wanted Mademoiselle Grace to understand why her betrayal had struck him so hard. "Did you know that Claire and I were betrothed?"

She twitched and her chest rose and fell, but she did not look at him. "It is none of my business, Captain."

"Perhaps not. But I want you to know."

She looked at him. "There is no need."

Rafe shifted his boots and glanced at Claire. "We had such great plans. She shared my dreams of helping the poor. We cared about the same things. Or so I thought." He walked to the porthole. Rain dashed and splattered against the panes just like the dreams he and Claire shared so long ago. "When I found her on the street, she was poor and in rags. We were young and innocent and full of hopes and ambitions."

He turned around. Mademoiselle sat quietly petting Spyglass. Only her rapid breathing gave away her emotions.

"Turns out all she wanted was my money." Rafe chuckled. "And when she discovered my father had disowned me and I had forfeited my inheritance, she left me a week before our wedding. And ran straight into my father's bed."

Mademoiselle Grace flinched and pushed a damp curl behind her ear. When she raised her eyes, they glistened with tears.

A wave of heat stormed up Rafe's neck and onto his face, and he felt instantly ashamed. Why had he shared such intimacies with her? He adjusted his coat and strode toward the door.

"Wait." Mademoiselle Grace set Spyglass on the deck and stood. She bit her lip and faced him. "I am sorry."

"I do not want your pity."

"Then what do you want?" she snapped.

Rafe approached her. He didn't know what he wanted anymore. He wanted to tell her he knew why she had betrayed him. He wanted to tell her he understood how convincing Claire could be. He wanted her to not look at him with such condemnation. But right now, all he wanted to do was kiss her.

He raised a hand to caress her cheek and grabbed a lock of her wet hair instead. "I like your hair unbound." He played with the soft, moist tendril.

She swung around, jerking it from between his fingers. "You should leave."

Perhaps he should. Perhaps he should walk out that door and never allow himself to be alone with this precious creature again. Laying a hand on her shoulder, he slowly turned her around. "It is my brig, mademoiselle."

"And I am your property." The sharp tone faded from her voice.

"You are so much more than that." His gaze took in her lips, her flushed cheeks, and those emerald eyes shimmering with tears—and something else. An invitation? He leaned closer until their lips were but an inch apart. The sweet smell of rain mixed with her feminine scent and swirled about his nose. She did not back away, did not slap him.

Instead she breathlessly awaited his kiss.

CHAPTER 27

Grace closed her eyes. Her heart thumped. She could feel the captain's warm breath wafting over her face. His lips hovered over hers.

The door crashed open. Grace opened her eyes and jumped backward, her heart in her throat. Father Alers strode into the room, his curious gaze shifting between her and Rafe. The captain huffed and shook his head.

Clutching her skirts with one hand and covering her mouth with the other, Grace dashed up the companionway ladder and bolted onto the deck. Slipping across the slick planks, she rushed to her favorite spot beside the foredeck where the bulkhead offered some protection from the buffeting winds. The rain had ceased again, but its spicy scent still stung in the breeze that now cooled the tears flowing down her cheeks.

What had she done?

She'd nearly kissed the captain.

She *would* have kissed the captain if Father Alers had not interrupted them.

She touched her lips where she could still feel Rafe's warm breath, could still smell his scent of tobacco and leather. What had come over her? Not only had she nearly allowed his kiss, she'd *wanted* him to kiss her. Horrified, she quickly bowed her head and gripped the railing. *Lord, please forgive me.*

Never in her life had she felt such an overwhelming attraction. Mercy me, she had never even kissed a man before. And there she was like a common hussy, accepting this rogue's advances. And with him on his way to sell her into slavery. Had all reason, all piety fled her mind and her soul when she needed them the most?

She lifted her face to the breeze and gazed at the island. The leaves of palms and banyans whipped this way and that in the wind as if waving to her, beckoning her to come and join them on land. And oh how she wanted to. If only to get away from the captain and the spell he had cast upon her. Perhaps Annette had slipped some of her love potion into Grace's food. She laughed at the thought but could find no other explanation for her unchaste behavior.

Black clouds hung like vultures overhead, making the afternoon look more like night. How long would they be cornered in this bay? How long would she be trapped with the captain, unable to escape? She drew a deep breath and tried to calm her nerves. She must not think of herself. She must think of Claire. The woman needed medical attention. Without it, she would most likely die.

Perhaps that was the reason Grace had been sent on this journey— to help Madame Dubois get well, to befriend the woman, to help her know God's love.

Grace bit her lip, remembering the look on the captain's face when he had shared what had happened between him and Claire. Despair had dragged his features down, dissolving the arrogant shield he sometimes wore until he looked more like a lost little boy instead of a vicious mercenary. Grace hugged herself as the wind whipped over her rain-dampened gown. She trembled beneath the chill. From what she could gather, Rafe had spent his entire childhood beneath the thumb of an unloving and cruel father. Then when he had finally found someone with whom to share his life and dreams, she had betrayed him.

And in the worst possible way.

How did one ever recover from such heartache—when everyone they had ever loved and trusted turned against them?

Grace's heart shriveled. No wonder the captain had reacted so violently to her betrayal. No wonder he had been so angry when he stole her from his father's house. He had assumed she was no better than Claire and his father. Gripping the railing, she closed her eyes, trying to make sense of it all.

Then what had changed the captain's mind? What had calmed his fury? For in that tiny cabin, his dark eyes had burned with such ardor, such warmth, it frightened Grace. Not the kind of fear she had for her life, but a different kind of fear—a fear of the desires that lay hidden in her own heart.

Spotting Grace by the railing beneath the foredeck, Rafe headed toward her. He needed to speak with her. He needed to talk about their near kiss. And why she was so distraught when she rushed from the cabin. Was it possible she held some affection for him? He dared not hope.

He approached slowly so as not to frighten her, but she did not turn around. Her eyes were closed and she seemed in deep thought—or prayer. Not wanting to disturb her, he climbed up the foredeck ladder and found a spot nearby to wait until she finished. A few minutes passed and Rafe was about to peer over the side to check on her when Monsieur Thorn's voice blared up from the spot where Grace stood. Easing toward the edge of the foredeck railing, Rafe listened as he kept himself from their view.

"Miss Grace?" Mr. Thorn's voice startled her, and she flung a hand to her chest as she tucked her private thoughts regarding the captain behind a closed door in her mind. Too late. Her cheeks heated beneath a blush.

"Good day, Mr. Thorn." Her voice sounded husky.

Mr. Thorn slipped beside her and glanced over the choppy waters of the bay. "So you decided to brave the storm as well, I see."

Grace thought of the devilish look on the captain's face when she had leapt out of his arms. "'Tis too hot below." She flustered at the insinuation of her statement. "I mean, 'tis crowded." Any room was crowded with the captain in it. "I mean—" She sighed in resignation of her befuddling verbiage. "Yes, I am braving the storm."

Mr. Thorn gazed at her curiously. "Are you well, Miss Grace?"

She gave him a flat smile. "As well as I can be, Mr. Thorn."

He leaned on the railing and glanced at the island, battered by the gusty wind, but still beautiful in the ashen light. "How is Madame Dubois?" His tone held no concern.

Grace shook her head. "Not well."

"Hmm." He doffed his hat. Shaking the dampness from it onto his knee, he ran a hand through his hair then snapped the tricorne back atop his head. "It must be quite daunting to be so close to land, miss, and have no way to escape."

The lift of his cultured brow and the hint of playfulness in his brown eyes sent a spark of hope through Grace. She narrowed her eyes. "Whatever do you mean, Mr. Thorn?"

He smiled and fingered his chin then glanced at the island. "I believe I recognize this island. Yes. I know I have anchored here before. Careened our ship here once, I believe. Plenty of fruit and water for the taking to last someone several months, or at least until another ship arrived—or say someone *sent* another ship." He gave her a sly wink.

Grace eyed him with suspicion. That Mr. Thorn's last attempt to help her escape had not worked out well was no reflection on him or his kindness. But something about the man set her nerves on edge. Though he appeared a just man, his critical attitude toward others gave her pause. And then there was the odd conversation she'd overheard between him and Monsieur Dubois. The two of them had been up to something, but what? Grace grabbed the chain around her neck and pulled out her cross, rubbing it between her fingers. "You would attempt helping me again?"

"Why not?"

"Why risk invoking the anger of your captain should he discover your treachery?"

"For the same reason I aided you before, mademoiselle. I do not wish to see an innocent woman sold into slavery."

Fury clawed up Rafe's spine, stiffening it and sending a flash of heat to his chest. Liar, traître. He had trusted Thorn—had called him friend. Rafe gripped the hilt of his rapier, holding back his urge to call the man to swords right then and there, but wanting first to hear the mademoiselle's answer.

Grace gazed across the deck toward the larboard railing where a group of sailors huddled beside the quarterdeck, rolling dice. "But with so many men on board, how could we escape their detection?"

"Leave that up to me." Mr. Thorn tugged upon his coat.

Grace rubbed her cross and gazed at the inviting shores. To remain on board would leave her at the mercy of the captain, not to mention her own unexpected passions. To leave would at least provide her a chance to live, to be free once again. Didn't the Bible say to flee temptation and wickedness? She gazed up at Mr. Thorn, unable to discern whether the warmth in his eyes sprang from sincerity or cunning—eyes that carried none of the innocence of his twenty years. Regardless, what choice did she have?

"When?"

"Tonight."

～

Later, back in his cabin, Rafe ground his fists together and stomped with the ebb and tide of a restless pace across the Persian rug centering the floor. Finding the silken threads sufficiently humbled, he stormed toward the stern windows and crossed his arms over his chest. Nothing but a black wall met his gaze, mirroring his mood. Well past midnight, the thick clouds had captured all traces of the moon, casting the earth's inhabitants in complete darkness—or at least his corner of the earth. Dark and barren—like Rafe's heart.

Thorn's betrayal blazed through Rafe like lightning. Was there no one in his life who would not stab him in the back? Rafe plucked a cheroot from his desk drawer and lit it from a candle. Drawing a puff of the pungent smoke, he hoped the tobacco would loosen his stiff nerves and numb the pain in his heart.

Grace was gone. He knew it. Nothing would have prevented her escape. The night was dark. Most of the crew remained below deck sheltered from the rain. No one would have stood in their way. Not even Rafe. For as much as he wanted to keep her with him and lock up his traitorous first mate, Rafe had realized their plan would serve his own purposes quite well. Thorn wasn't the only one betraying Rafe. He had been *trompé* by his own feelings. For the more time he spent with the mademoiselle, the more conflicted he became. He doubted he could sell her to the don or to anyone for that matter. This way, at least he would not have to face a mutiny when his crew discovered their pockets would not be lined with gold anytime soon.

Oui, Grace was gone, and the brig seemed nothing more than a hollow shell without her.

Rafe drew in another drag of sweet tobacco then blew out a cloud of smoke above him. It dissipated into the darkness as the mademoiselle had. He should be thankful to be rid of her.

Then why did his heart crumble within him? He grabbed a bottle of brandy from the shelf, opened it, and took a long draught. A rank of numbing fire marched down his throat. Mademoiselle Grace had told him the liquor turned him into a brute. Did it? The taste of it soured in his mouth, and he slammed the bottle down and wiped his lips.

Rap rap rap.

"Entrez-vous," Rafe barked; then he turned to see Monsieur Thorn stride in, wearing a confident grin of a snake.

"The sails have all been painted black, Captain."

"Très bien." Rafe's stomach clenched. He wanted to inquire whether Thorn had delivered Mademoiselle Grace safely to the island, but now was not the time. He would find out soon enough, and then as soon as they were free of Woodes's ships, Rafe would deal with this betrayer. In the meantime, Grace would be quite safe and well fed on the island until he could send a ship to rescue her and deliver her safely home. "Douse all lights, weigh anchor, and hoist away topgallants and jib."

"A very good plan, Captain, if I do say so." Thorn's eyes held an admiration that Rafe no longer believed existed in the man. "Under these clouds, 'twould be a miracle if we were spotted."

Rafe grunted in response, and Monsieur Thorn touched his hat and backed out the door.

After taking one last puff of his cheroot, Rafe extinguished it on a tray. He blew out the candle, sheathed his rapier, shoved his pistols into his baldric, and followed his first mate up on deck. The night would bring many challenges, not the least of which would be navigating the ship through the reefs of the harbor in the dark. For that he needed a sharp mind and quick reflexes. So he shoved all thoughts of Mademoiselle Grace from his mind—and his heart.

Two hours later, guided by four lanterns hanging over the sides of the ship, two at the bow and two amidships over larboard and starboard rails, Rafe had maneuvered the brig to the mouth of the harbor. "Hoist up and douse the lanterns. Lay aloft and loose topsails," he whispered to Thorn, who then marched across deck to deliver his orders to the men. Voices traveled far at night, especially in the oppressive dank air beneath the cloud-covered sky.

A thunderous *snap* sounded from above, and Rafe glanced up and peered into the darkness but could not make out the black sails that had just been raised to the wind. Planting his boots on the deck, he folded his arms across his chest and allowed the breeze to whip through his hair and bring with it the scent of brine and freedom. He shot one last glance over his shoulder at the bulky shadow of the island, and his chest grew heavy.

Mademoiselle Grace was there somewhere. Was she afraid? Was she lonely? Or was she glad to be rid of him? That she suffered under any one of those emotions saddened him. Turning back around, he thrust his face into the wind, trying to shake her from his thoughts. He must focus on their escape. Up ahead, lanterns blinked from the two ships that guarded the harbor, one to the north and one to the south. *Le Champion* would have to slip through the half-mile gap between them—barely enough breathing room. Was he le fou to attempt such a feat? One shift of the clouds, one beam of errant moonlight, one slip of a word from his crew, and all would be lost.

The mademoiselle's scent tickled his nose. Sacre mer, did her fragrance remain to taunt him?

"Do we have a chance, Captain?" Her soft voice floated on the wind.

Rafe jumped and snapped his gaze toward the source. Grace's outline shadowed beside him. He rubbed his eyes.

She released a sigh. "Your silence speaks volumes, Captain."

"You are here," was all he could think to say as his heart swelled.

"Where else would I be?"

"On the island."

He saw her flinch.

"I overheard Monsieur Thorn's offer," he admitted.

She said nothing.

Rafe scratched the stubble on his jaw. "Why did you not go? Why did you not escape when you had the chance?"

She was silent for a moment. "I could not leave Madame Claire so ill. No one else, besides Father Alers, seems to care about her, and she is in need of a woman to attend her."

Rafe gazed over the inky expanse, unable to discern sea from sky—just as he was unable to comprehend her words. "You refused a chance at freedom for *her*?"

"I may be a pious prude as you say, but I am not cruel, Captain." Her voice stung with offense, but also with a strength that pleased him.

Prude pieuse. Had he called her that? More than once, if he remembered correctly. Sans doute, she could behave like one, but at the moment all he saw was her heart of gold.

Thorn's tall figure emerged from the darkness. "Captain? The men await your orders."

Rafe turned to Grace, unsure what to say. He started to leave, then touched her arm. "A prayer to that God of yours for our success could not hurt."

"Of course." He felt her smile, though he could not see it.

Grace inched her way to the starboard bow and gripped the railing. She'd never been in such oppressive darkness. Behind her, she heard the captain whisper orders to Monsieur Atton. Only the soft flap of sails and purl of water against the hull graced her ears as the ship slipped through the sea. Up ahead, their two pursuers guarded the harbor like sentinels. One lantern hung from the foremast of each ship, illuminating the pathway to freedom between them—much like the narrow gate to salvation. Grace bowed her head. *Lord, grant us safe passage through our enemies. Make us invisible to them and to all forces of evil.*

Raising her head, she nearly chuckled at the irony of her prayer. The shuffling of feet sounded behind her as the crew attended to their captain's orders. Invisible black sails filled with wind overhead. Ingenious. Her admiration of the captain's skills rose along with her conflicting sensations whenever he was near. Why would he have allowed her escape? It made no sense. Could he be having second thoughts about selling her into slavery? Or was he just testing Monsieur Thorn's loyalty? Betrayal was something she had learned did not sit well with the captain.

"You should go below." His deep voice startled her.

"I am praying as instructed." She noted the humor in her own voice.

"Très bien." He leaned on the rail beside her and brushed a strand of hair from her face. "It will not matter should they detect us. A broadside from both sides would sink us within minutes."

Grace swallowed. Sink? A lump formed in her throat as *Le Champion* glided between her pursuers. Silence consumed the ship as if the angel of death floated across the decks, quieting everything with a touch of his scythe: the tongues of the sailors, the creaks and groans of the planks, and the flap of sails. Only the ripple of water against the hull gave any evidence of their passage.

As if sensing her fear, the captain placed a hand on her arm. She jolted but dared not move. The lanterns of the pursuing ships winked at her from her right and her left. They were so close, she heard voices from their decks: laughter, song, and a heated argument.

Minutes passed like hours until finally the lanterns and voices were behind her. Facing the wind, she released a tiny breath.

Rafe tiptoed toward the helm, where Mr. Thorn stood beside Mr. Atton. Whispers echoed back and forth, and several sailors leapt into the ratlines and scrambled above, their dark shadows like evil specters attempting to creep into heaven.

In the distance, the lanterns of the ships faded. They were safe!

A yellow burst of light lit the sea off their stern. Grace stared at it curiously, unsure of its source.

"All hands down!" Captain Dubois yelled and leapt on top of her, forcing her to the deck.

A thunderous boom racked the sea and air.

CHAPTER 28

The captain flung one arm around Grace's waist as he shoved her to the deck before covering her body with his own. The ominous whoosh of the shot heading their way filled Grace's ears, and she squeezed her eyes shut. The crunch and snap of severed wood crackled in the air, followed by a massive splash. Grace gasped to fill her lungs with air. A tingling sensation whirled through her. Rafe lifted his head, but inches from her own, and gazed at her as if he too experienced the odd feeling. Curses and shouts saturated the air.

"Capitaine?" someone shouted.

"Oui." He leapt off her and helped her to her feet. "Are you all right?" His voice rang with concern.

"Yes, thank you."

He shifted his attention to the ship that had fired upon them and instantly stiffened. "Monsieur Legard, take the mademoiselle below." Then he turned and began braying orders to his crew.

Weaving amongst the frantic sailors that scampered across the deck, Mr. Legard escorted Grace below and ushered her into her cabin, closing the door with a thud.

Dropping to her knees beside the cot, Grace held Claire's feverish hand in hers and closed her eyes. Deafening blasts exploded all around her, sending a tremble through the brig that matched the tremble already coursing through her body. Boot steps hammered overhead, accompanied by shouts and curses—all in French. Yet amidst the clamor, Grace could still make out the captain's deep timbre as he ordered his crew about.

The sting of gunpowder seeped through the planks of the cabin to join the fetor of death and disease within. Claire groaned, and Grace peered through the darkness where the woman lay. "Lord, please save us," she prayed as another cannon thundered. Her heart stopped. The blast came from *Le Champion*'s guns as the captain no doubt attempted to stave off their pursuers.

Weaving around Claire on the cot, Spyglass snuggled up to Grace, nudging her hand for a pet. Grace obliged the cat, then pressed her fingers over her right cheek and winced where a bruise formed from her tumble onto the deck. She might have been able to protect her face from the splinters if she'd known the captain intended to pounce on her. She hadn't felt any pain at the time. She hadn't felt anything but Captain Dubois's warm body atop hers and the tingles that rippled through her at such close intimacy.

Sobs filled the air, reminding Grace she was not alone. She scanned the dark cabin but couldn't make out Annette's slight form. "Annette, all will be well." Grace shoved aside her anger at the mulatto. "Come here." Shuffling sounded and Annette emerged from the shadows and knelt beside Grace. Grace put an arm around her, noting her sweet citrus scent and the quiver that sped through her. "I am frightened as well, but Captain Dubois is a skilled captain." She offered the lady a smile that was no doubt lost in the darkness even as she wondered where her confidence in Rafe came from.

Boom! A loud roar threatened to split the timbers of the brig.

Shouts and curses filled the air above them.

The *crack* of wood. Then a crunch. A snap. More shouting shot down from above, "*Prenez garde en bas!*"

Bam! The ship canted to larboard. Flakes of dirt showered on them from above.

Grace glanced aloft. Coughing, she batted away the dust. Silence consumed the brig. Only the mad dash of water against the hull reassured Grace that they still lived. But what of everyone else? Had they all died?

Annette whimpered and Grace drew her closer, embracing her. "Shhh. It will be all right." But would it? She had no idea. Truth be told, she wasn't sure she knew much of anything anymore.

They huddled together in the dark for what seemed an eternity. Madame Dubois's breathing grew ragged, and Grace took her hand again then released Annette and groped around for the bucket. Upon finding it, she wrung out the cloth and laid it atop the dying woman's forehead. How long could she survive? How long would any of them survive with two ships in fast pursuit and hard intent on sinking them to the depths of the sea?

Yet, Grace had not heard a gun fire for quite a while. In fact, she'd not heard anything.

A thin line of light appeared beneath the door and Grace took Annette's hand. A thousand terrifying thoughts rampaged through her mind. Had they been boarded by the enemy? Had the captain been killed?

The latch clicked and the door creaked open to reveal Mr. Thorn, his features distorted in the glow of the lantern he held. His eyes landed upon Annette and remained there for longer than seemed proper before he shifted them to Grace. "The captain wishes me to inform you that we are safe now." He placed the lantern atop the table.

"So he is well?" Grace pressed a hand over her pounding heart.

"Quite," Mr. Thorn replied. His answer sent an awkward rush of joy through Grace.

Annette stood, fidgeted with the trim on the neckline of her gown, and slunk out of the light.

Thorn's gaze followed her. "Are you ladies unharmed?"

"We are fine." Grace rose and brushed the dust from her skirts. "I heard a loud crash. What happened?"

Tearing his eyes from the mulatto, Mr. Thorn straightened his coat. "Our main-topmast was damaged."

Grace clutched her throat. "Isn't that bad?"

"It can be, but no one was injured."

"What of the two ships?"

"We lost them in the darkness." He gave a half smile.

Claire groaned, and Grace dropped to her knees beside the woman. Now doused in light, Claire's sunken cheeks bore the color of sunbaked sand and were just as hot to the touch. Her gray lips smacked in agony, and beads of sweat marched across her face and neck. Grabbing the cloth, Grace dabbed it over the woman's skin. She sighed. "Mr. Thorn, can you please summon Father Alers?"

"Will she die?" His voice was emotionless.

"Please get the father." Grace's exhausted tone bespoke her internal agony. Claire was dying. Grace was all too familiar with the merciless fiend called death—an ugly beast who delighted in torturing his victims, leaving behind a trail of hopelessness and pain. During her mother's tumultuous death, Grace had felt the monster's breath upon her neck, his laughter beating like demon wings against her skin.

She shuddered, and all hope drained from her. The only thing left to do was to ensure the woman's salvation. If Claire regained consciousness Grace hoped she'd at least be willing to speak to the former priest.

With Mr. Thorn's departure, the room chilled. Grace hugged herself and lifted her gaze to Annette who stood beneath the porthole. The mulatto immediately lowered her chin. "Annette, did you poison your mistress?"

Her eyes filled with tears and she lifted a hand to her nose. "It was not only un philtre d'amour."

"What, then?"

The woman squeezed her eyes shut as tears sped down her cheeks. Spyglass ambled to the foot of the cot and directed her one eye upon the maid.

Grace rubbed her forehead. "Then at least tell me if there is some way to save her."

"There is nothing you can do." Annette met her eyes then, and the fear and hopelessness that burned within them frightened Grace. "What will become of me?" she asked.

"I do not know. You have done a terrible thing, Annette."

Claire's troubled cough brought Grace's attention back to her. A heaviness fell upon the cabin as if one of the storm clouds had infiltrated the tiny space. Grace gasped for a breath. Spyglass hissed—at what, Grace couldn't see.

Boot steps thundered in the companionway, and in marched Captain Dubois. His dark hair fell in disarray across the gray coat that spanned his broad shoulders. Black soot smudged his face. His buccaneer shirt was torn at the collar. But other than that, he seemed in one piece. Relief eased over Grace at the sight.

He glanced at Annette before focusing on Grace and narrowed his eyes as if sensing her discomfiture. "How is Claire?"

"Worse, I'm afraid."

He glanced over the cabin as if he, too, felt the dark presence. Father Alers and Mr. Thorn entered behind him.

The priest dashed toward the cot while Mr. Thorn took up a position beside his captain.

"Will she die?" The emotion in Captain Dubois's voice surprised her. Was it possible he still harbored some sentiment for Claire?

Father Alers stooped and laid a hand on Claire's cheek. He swallowed and in his golden eyes, Grace saw that he had reached the same conclusion she had.

She dabbed the cloth over Claire's moist neck. So young, so full of life. Too young. It felt wrong for her to die. An unconscionable betrayal.

"No." Grace spoke the word that was screaming within her. She would not watch another woman die.

Father Alers pressed down his coiled gray hair and shook his head. "Je suis désolé."

"No," Grace moaned and leaned on the cot. Spyglass pressed against her head, her soft purrs rumbling in her ears. *Lord, what do I do? Tell me what to do!*

For we wrestle not against flesh and blood. The verse from Ephesians drifted through her mind. For a moment, she did not know why. But then. . .

She sat up. "This is no sickness."

The wrinkles on Father Alers's face folded.

"At least not a natural one." She glanced over at the captain and then Mr. Thorn—who returned her stare with one of bewilderment. And finally Annette. The guilt pouring from the mulatto's face confirmed Grace's suspicions.

Claire coughed and began to heave as if frantically searching for air. There wasn't much time.

Laying a hand over Claire's forehead, Grace drew in a deep breath. "Father, in Your Son's precious name, the name of Jesus, I bind and cast out from this woman and from this cabin and from this ship, the evil forces that have made Claire ill." The words that slipped from Grace's lips sounded so weak, so human, so powerless. She studied Claire, but the woman groaned and her breathing grew even more ragged. Perhaps Grace should have yelled the words. Maybe she didn't have enough faith. She searched her heart for that mustard seed of faith God said was all that was needed to do anything in His name.

Claire's hand hung limp and cold in Grace's. Grace's stomach soured and she bowed her head.

"Do you believe I am who I say I am?"

The words flowed over her like a gushing waterfall. *Yes, I do, Lord.* Tears burned in Grace's eyes. She stiffened her jaw as anger now welled within her—anger at the wickedness trying to steal this woman's life. She lifted her chin. "Be gone, in the name of Jesus."

Mr. Thorn chuckled, and the captain shifted his boots over the deck. Father Alers met Grace's gaze with one of pity. He laid a hand on her shoulder as if to say, "A noble attempt."

Grace bowed her head and allowed her tears to fall. She had failed. Or maybe it wasn't God's will at all that Claire live. Lifting Claire's hand to her mouth, Grace laid a kiss upon it.

And the woman's fingers squeezed hers in return.

Grace popped open her eyes and stared aghast at Claire. Her breathing had calmed. Her eyelids fluttered.

Annette gasped, and Grace heard the tap of her slippers as she approached the cot.

"Claire?" Grace pushed damp hair from the woman's cheek.

Claire moaned and pried her eyes open.

Grace giggled between sobs of joy. It was only then that she realized the heaviness in the room had left.

Father Alers stumbled backward and plopped into the chair.

A faint smile lifted Claire's lips where a hint of pink peeked from behind the gray. "Grace," she whispered.

Annette backed against the bulkhead, her mouth hanging slack.

"Zooks," Mr. Thorn declared. "I cannot believe it."

Grace gazed at the men over her shoulder. The captain's dark eyes widened and he shook his head.

She smiled. "Thanks be to God, she will live."

CHAPTER 29

Standing at the stern of the brig, Grace drew in a deep breath of the night air, laden with salt and fish and a hint of flowers—the latter of which she must only be imagining. For they had not seen land since they left the island two days prior—in a frenzied dash to escape their pursuers. And she had not seen the captain, save in passing, since God had delivered Claire of the evil forces causing her illness. Grace longed to know what he thought about the incident. Had it convinced him of God's existence? Or did he merely think it coincidental, a bizarre accident, an act of black magic as she'd heard some of the crew declare. Perhaps witnessing the power of God had frightened Captain Dubois. But no, that didn't seem like him at all. Then why did he avoid her?

Due to the southern course the ship maintained, she assumed they were still heading toward Colombia. Yet the captain had known about Thorn's plans to help her escape and he had made no moves to stop them. Why? It didn't make any sense.

The ship bucked over a wave, then creaked and groaned in complaint. But Grace wasn't complaining anymore. She was convinced the purpose of her entire harrowing escapade had been for God to deliver Claire from the forces of death. She had stayed on board for that very reason. And now with that task completed, surely the Lord would rescue Grace. She must only wait and believe.

For two days Grace had stayed by Claire's side, and with Father Alers, had nursed some strength back into the woman, though she still had not risen from her bed. Father Alers was overwrought about

241

the miracle, saying that in all his time as a Jesuit priest, he'd not seen the likes of it. He had told Grace that he'd begun to read the Holy Scriptures again. Grace smiled at the thought. Finally she had done some good.

She gazed out over the ebony sea, lit in glittering ribbons of silver by the light of a half-moon, and released a contented sigh. Nights upon the Caribbean held a mysterious beauty all their own. During the day Grace must not only endure extreme temperatures but also the incessant hammering of the crew as they repaired the mainmast. So she had waited until nightfall to emerge from below, no longer fearing the crew. Aside from a few ribald comments tossed her way—which unfortunately she'd grown accustomed to—they left her alone.

The ship pitched over a wave, and Grace gripped the railing as a spray of seawater showered over her. She shook it off and smiled as the curls that had loosened from her pins tickled her neck. She liked the way they felt. In fact, she relished the absence of the continual headache caused by her tight coiffure.

Annette appeared beside Grace. "Bonsoir, mademoiselle."

Grace caught her breath at the woman's sudden presence. "Bonsoir, Annette." She had hardly seen the mulatto during the past few days. The maid had darted in and out of the cabin, bringing stew and lemon water for her mistress, but never staying long enough to talk. Her actions and attitude seemed to indicate that she felt remorse for what she had done, but Grace needed to ensure that Annette had no intention of harming Claire again. "Where have you been?"

Annette shrugged. The moonlight transformed her skin into dark cream. "Are you angry with me, mademoiselle?"

Grace bit her lip. She had been angry. But she could not find her fury anymore. It had softened into pity and fear—fear for the girl's eternity. "No. I am not angry, Annette. I have been praying for you."

"Praying?" Annette fidgeted with the lace at the cuff of her gown. "My mistress recovers."

"Yes." Grace eyed the lady. "Does that make you sad?"

A moment passed as Annette scanned the dark horizon. "Oui."

As Grace suspected. At least the girl had not lied. "Thank you for being honest, Annette." Grace bit her lip, wondering how to ask her next question, but knowing she must regardless of how audacious it sounded. "Do you plan to hurt her again?"

The mulatto flashed her dark eyes at Grace. "Non. Though she deserves it."

Grace pushed a strand of hair behind her ear and sighed. "I know Madame Dubois is not often kind to you."

Annette gave her a sideways glance.

Grace squeezed the railing, the damp wood still warm from the sun. She longed to know what Annette had done to Claire, to know exactly what Grace had been dealing with. "May I inquire...may I ask what you did to cause Madame Dubois's illness?"

"I cast *un maléfice* on her, a hex."

Grace's breath held tight in her throat.

"A curse from my ancestors," Annette continued in a matter-of-fact tone that sent a chill through Grace.

"Is that who you pray to? Your ancestors?"

"Oui." Annette wrapped her arms around her tiny waist. "My ancestors were strong warriors before my people were stolen from our land."

Grace flattened her lips. An urgency rose within her to help Annette see the dangerous path she was on. But how could she help this girl without offending her? "Your ancestors are dead, Annette. 'And as it is appointed unto men once to die, but after this the judgment,'" Grace quoted from Hebrews. "You are not praying to them, but to demons, to the evil forces that rule this world."

Annette's chest rose and fell rapidly as she stared out upon the sea. Her jaw stiffened, but she said nothing.

A blast of wind whipped over them, and Grace leaned toward Annette. "You cannot deny what you saw."

"Oui. I been thinking of that. Your ancestors are more powerful than mine."

"No, Annette. That power came from God—the one and only God. He is nobody's ancestor. He's the Creator of all. He's *your* Creator."

"If He is the only God, and my Creator, why does He allow my people to be *les esclaves*?" Her words came out in strangled tones.

Grace laid a hand on her arm. "I do not know. But I do know that this world is ruled by God's enemy. Much of the evil we experience is his doing. If you want to blame someone, blame him."

Guttural laugher bellowed from the main deck as if in derision of her statement.

From Annette's expression, Grace gathered she agreed with the sentiment. "I blame the blancs," she snapped. "They have caused my people to suffer. People like Monsieur Dubois and my mistress. They must pay."

"But you are half white, are you not?"

"Monsieur Dubois sired me, but he is not my father." She whipped her hair behind her, giving Grace a venomous look.

Grace's heart shrank beneath the girl's misery. Slavery was a wretched enough institution without enduring the stigma of being bred for beauty and strength like a prize horse. "If you are unhappy, why not run away?"

Annette snorted. "Where do I go? I drift in empty space between my two peoples. Neither wants me."

"God wants you."

Annette snatched her arm from beneath Grace's hand and she backed away, her chest heaving. "He is the God of the whites."

Grace reached out her hand, wanting so badly to help this poor woman. "No. He is the God of all and shows no partiality toward one race or another."

"I do not wish to hear it!" Annette's dark eyes simmered as she swatted tears from her cheeks. "Leave me be!" Then hoisting her shirts, she darted across the deck.

Grace lowered her gaze, her heart sinking. *Lord, where did I go astray? Why wouldn't she listen to me?*

Lifting her face to the humid breeze, she allowed the wind to dry her tears. Then whirling around, she scanned the deck for Annette. Perhaps Grace had been too bold, too forceful in her efforts to turn the woman to God. Determined to comfort her and offer an apology, Grace headed across the quarterdeck to find the mulatto. Passing by the helm, she nodded at Mr. Atton, then carefully made her way down the ladder. She scanned the shadowy deck, lit only by the circle of light coming from the lantern hanging at the mainmast, and spotted a cluster of sailors by the starboard rail passing a bottle. She wanted to ask them where Annette had gone but thought better of it. Averting her gaze, she felt their eyes follow her across deck. Then clutching her skirts, she climbed the foredeck ladder. Perhaps the girl had gone to the bow. She was rewarded when she saw a dark figure standing by the cathead.

Rafe took a sip of brandy then closed the flask. Why did he no longer find pleasure in the pungent liquor? Why did it sour upon his lips when he needed the numbing elixir so badly?

It was the mademoiselle.

Sacre mer, her disapproval of it had tainted it for him. As she had tainted all the pleasures he used to enjoy: his sanity, his reason, his indulgence in other women. Zut alors, even his food had become tasteless. Reaching back, he tossed the flask into the raging sea and watched it sink in the black waters—along with all the passing pleasures that had provided diversions from the futility of his life.

He had avoided Grace, hoping some of those old plaisirs would return. Hoping he wouldn't have to face the evidence of what he had seen in the cabin below. The miracle, as Father Alers kept proclaiming; the battle between good and evil; the way Grace's words, empowered by the name of Jesus, had snatched Claire from death's door. There must be another explanation. And until Rafe could figure out just what it was, he preferred not to speak to Mademoiselle Grace. It was bad enough he had to listen to Father Alers's incessant babbling about God and His power and His presence. Rafe's heart and mind chafed beneath the onslaught of their religious nonsense.

And to compound his angst, Rafe still had to deal with a possible mutiny when his crew discovered that he no longer intended to sell Mademoiselle Grace to the don. Oui, he had finally decided what his heart had known long ago—that he could never harm such a precious angel. Besides, after he had discovered the reason for her betrayal, his anger had swept away like seawater through scuppers. He would find another way to procure the money he needed for the hospital—even if he had to resort to piracy.

Rafe gripped the railing. He remained on course for Rio de la Hacha to keep the crew's suspicions at bay and to give him time to formulate a plan that would assuage their anger and appease their greedy hearts. Yet no brilliant scheme had forged in his mind.

Which was why he desperately needed to drown himself with brandy. His sudden distaste for it only further exacerbated the suffering in which he found himself.

Femme exaspérante!

Shuffling sounded behind him. Rafe's mood soured further at the prospect of company. He wanted no more of Father Alers's religious lectures, nor Monsieur Thorn's placating grins. "Allez-vous-en! Go away!" Rafe bellowed.

"Very well," the soft voice replied.

Rafe swerved about. Mademoiselle Grace's slight figure retreated. "Non. I did not know it was you."

She slowly turned around. "My mistake, Captain. I was looking for Annette." The moonlight sent shimmering waves of silver upon her, transforming her raven curls into glistening onyx.

Rafe swallowed.

She cocked her head. "Have you seen her?"

Gathering his wits, Rafe shook his head.

She nodded and started to leave.

"Do not go."

"Do you wish something, Captain?" A question as loaded as one of his twelve-pounders below. He smiled.

She looked down as if his perusal frightened her. "I have no time for your games, Captain."

"I fear I am done playing games, mademoiselle." He started to reach for her but gripped his baldric instead.

She turned to leave again, but Rafe closed the gap between them in one step and grabbed her arm. Her eyes shot to his as if he'd stabbed her. She jerked from his grasp.

"If there are no more games, then I must assume you still intend to sell me." She took a breath and gazed over the turbulent dark sea. "I cannot say I know much about navigation, but I can tell in which direction you have set your sails."

Rafe could not deny her words, nor could he for some reason find his voice. Her sweet scent swirled beneath his nose as his gaze was drawn to the silken curls of raven dancing over her graceful neck. He could no more hurt this woman than he could pluck out his own eyes. He hesitated.

"Have you been drinking?" She arched one beautiful eyebrow.

"Unfortunately, non." He grinned.

"Then why not answer my question?" A discordant fiddle chimed a sailor's ballad from the main deck, drawing her gaze over her shoulder.

Then facing forward, she released a sigh. "If you'll excuse me." She started to turn.

Rafe grabbed her arm again, rewarded by those emerald eyes shifting to his, searching his face for the answer to her question.

Rafe softened his grip. "I could never sell you, mademoiselle."

She wrinkled her nose. "What did you say?"

He released her and took a deep breath, then dug his thumbs inside the sash strapped at his waist—if only to keep his hands off her. "You heard me."

"I don't believe I did."

"I am not going to sell you." Rafe had expected a bit more appreciation. "*Est-ce que je me fais compris?*"

"I understand your words." She clasped her hands together and stepped toward the railing as if searching for the answer upon the seas. The ship pitched, and Rafe placed a hand on the small of her back to steady her. A spray showered over them, crystallizing into tiny diamonds on her cheeks and neck. She looked at him. Disbelief and a glimmer of hope battled in her eyes.

"What has changed your mind?"

"Do you need to ask?" Raising his hand, he cupped her chin and rubbed his thumb over her cheek, pressing lightly over the red abrasion. She winced.

"Je suis désolé. I did not mean to hurt you."

She swallowed. Fear dashed across her eyes. She lowered her chin. Rafe gently raised it and allowed his gaze to wander over her face: those sparkling emerald eyes, the tiny ringlets dancing over her forehead, and those moist lips. Her breathing grew rapid, and Rafe could stand it no longer. He lowered his mouth to hers.

Ah such sweetness, so soft, so willing. She received his kiss and returned it with a passion he would not have suspected existed within her. Never before had a simple kiss consumed so much of him, making him long to protect and cherish this woman forever.

He withdrew and leaned his forehead against hers. Her warm breath intermingled with his and filled the air between them for one treasured moment.

Before she pushed away from him and dashed across the deck, disappearing into the darkness.

CHAPTER 30

G race halted before her cabin, wiped her tears, and slowly opened the door. Darkness spilled over her. Stepping inside, she clicked the latch shut and waited until her eyes could make out the contents of the tiny space. Deep, steady breathing coming from the direction of the cot reassured her that Claire was still asleep. Annette, however, was nowhere to be seen.

Assured of her privacy, Grace flung a hand to her mouth and sank to the deck in a flutter of billowing skirts. Tears poured from her eyes so fast she could not wipe them away before they slid from her jaw onto her lap. How could she have allowed such a thing to happen? With trembling fingers, she touched her mouth where the press of the captain's lips still lingered, where she still tingled from the passion in his kiss.

Where she had welcomed his advance without inhibition! Even worse, she had enjoyed it—every second of it.

What was wrong with her?

And her suspicion that the captain's promise not to sell her was only a trick to solicit her kiss only increased her guilt. She was smarter than that.

Plucking a handkerchief from the sleeve of her gown, Grace dabbed her cheeks and blew her nose. She hung her head.

I am a trollop. I am a woman of the lowest of morals.

Scenes from her recent past rose like specters to haunt her conscience. The lies she had told in Port-de-Paix, the mango she had stolen, the vow she had broken, the hatred in her own heart for Rafe and the members

248

of his crew who had attacked her, her continual doubts and wavering faith, and now, her immorality. When she had always prided herself on following all of God's laws so faithfully, these infractions had begun to dissolve the very essence of who she believed herself to be. Now she wasn't sure who she truly was anymore.

Grace's tears wove a crooked path down her cheeks. Something furry brushed against her, and she jumped. "Spyglass, how did you get in here?" She lifted the cat into her lap and scratched her head.

"I am a liar, a thief, a murderer, and a trollop, Spyglass," she wailed upon a whisper. "I am undone."

The cat only purred in return.

The darkness of the room closed in on Grace. Claire's rhythmic breathing drummed out the sentence of her guilt. The creak and groans of the brig rose to scold Grace for her fallen state. And the snap of the sails pounded like the judge's mallet, condemning her.

Please forgive me, Lord. Please do not abandon me.

Drawing her knees up to her chest, Grace leaned her head on Spyglass and wept into her fur.

"Though your sins be as scarlet, they shall be as white as snow."

Grace peered into the shadowy room. "I do not deserve it, Lord."

"As far as the east is from the west, so far hath I removed your transgressions from you."

Grace took a deep breath to quiet the sobs still rippling through her. Setting the cat onto the deck, she gathered her skirts, struggled to her feet, and made her way to the window. As the moon washed its milky light over her, she prayed it would wash away her guilt as well, prayed she could accept the mercy so freely offered. *Lord, I do not understand why all this is happening, but I am still Yours if You will have me.*

The door creaked open and a footstep sounded, not the light step of Annette, but the hollow thud of a boot. Grace's chest tightened, and she turned to see Mr. Thorn's dark outline framed by the doorway. Spyglass leapt onto the chair between them.

"Forgive me, Miss Grace, I mean. . ." he stuttered as he glanced over the cabin. "I thought I heard crying. . .I thought perhaps, well, never mind. It was most improper of me to enter without permission."

Yet he didn't leave.

Grace dabbed at her tears and drew herself up. " 'Tis quite all right, Mr. Thorn. 'Twas me you heard."

He withdrew his hat and took a step toward her. "Are you hurt?"

Grace put a finger to her lips and glanced at the cot. "Madame Dubois sleeps."

And when he still remained, she added, "I am fine, Mr. Thorn," hoping he would leave her to her misery.

"I see you are distraught, miss," he whispered.

"It is nothing."

"Has Captain Dubois harmed you?"

Grace touched her lips as renewed tears burned behind her eyes. Quite the contrary. "No more than I have allowed him."

The brig canted, and a beam of moonlight sliced across Mr. Thorn, accentuating the warm sparkle in his brown eyes and the red scar angling down his face and neck.

"You should have escaped to the island." He fingered his chin.

"Then Madame Dubois would not have survived."

"Humph." He gazed at the sleeping woman.

"You do not believe, Mr. Thorn?" Of all the people, besides Father Alers, Grace would have thought the scrupulous first mate would be the first to embrace the miraculous intervention of God.

He shifted his stance. "I heard your prayer. I saw the woman recover, but I cannot connect the two without reservation."

"But you *do* believe in God?" Grace's heart skipped a beat.

"Most certainly, miss. I simply do not believe He takes much care of the happenings on earth." Mr. Thorn fumbled with his hat.

"Yet when presented with proof that He is very much aware and involved, you refuse to believe." Grace instantly regretted her churlish tone, but she was tired, emotionally spent, and suddenly unsure of her ability to do any further good for God.

Mr. Thorn leaned on the door frame. "If what you say is true, why would He waste time on...on someone like Madame Dubois, an insolent mean-spirited shrew?" His voice hardened like steel.

Grace winced at his harsh censure of Claire. "None of us are without fault, Mr. Thorn." The truth spilled from her lips before she realized they were meant as much for her as for the first mate.

"Some are far better than others," he replied.

Grace flattened her lips. If Mr. Thorn would give no credence to her opinions, perhaps he would believe the testimony of a priest. "Father Alers confirms the event as an act of God."

Mr. Thorn snorted. "Begging your pardon, miss, but Father Alers is a silly old fool who turned his back on his true faith and now seeks a sign to confirm what he once believed. He is what your Bible describes as a wave of the sea being driven and tossed to and fro."

Grace grabbed her chain, appalled at the man's assessment. "Is there no one on board who meets with your approval, Mr. Thorn?"

"You may call me Justus, miss. And yes. I find you to be above reproach, which is why I have done all in my power to aid in your escape."

Justus. Grace stifled a chuckle. And like a judge, he wielded his sword of justice on everyone he met.

Like me.

The words stabbed her conscience. Was she like Mr. Thorn? Did she pass such quick and merciless judgments on all those around her?

Thorn glanced over his shoulder. "And Annette, despite her circumstances, appears to be principled and virtuous."

Grace shook her head. Annette, principled? Had the man gone daft?

"Do you happen to know where she is?"

"No. I saw her above earlier." The last thing Grace had seen of Annette was the flash of blue cotton as she ran away after their conversation—a conversation that mimicked the failings of the present one. "What is your business with her?"

"Merely concerned for her safety. Nothing unscrupulous, I assure you." Then bowing, he donned his hat. "I beg leave of you, miss."

"Good evening to you, Mr. Thorn. . .I mean Justus."

After he left, Grace turned to gaze out the window, where the stars began to fade beneath the approach of dawn. Though she hadn't slept, she was thankful for the close of this peculiar night. It was as if the air had been tainted with some maddening elixir, or perhaps they sailed through an aberrant patch of sea where reality became warped.

For the world no longer made any sense.

≈

Annette gripped the backstay and stepped onto the gunwale. Her bare feet slipped on the polished brass, and she clutched the rope tighter until the rough threads burned her tender skin. A gust of wind raked over her, trying to tear her from her perch, but she would not let it.

Not yet.

The fresh scent of dawn approaching filled her nostrils, and she dared a glance some twenty feet below where black waters churned like a malevolent brew. Their foamy fingers clawed at the hull as if trying to grab her. Swallowing, she closed her eyes and prayed for her ancestors to receive her into their arms.

At last she would finally be home. With the people to whom she belonged. Finally she would be at peace. Finally she would be at rest.

All she had lived for these past years, her only purpose, had been to rid herself of Madame Dubois, to send the woman into the underworld and appease the revenge that gnawed daily at Annette's soul. Rochelle Dubois, the master's last wife, whom Annette had served one year prior to her death, had been nothing like Claire. Though the lady had known Annette was the result of her husband's philandering, Madame Rochelle had treated her with kindness. Annette had truly grieved her passing, but no more than when she'd been introduced to her new mistress. Since then, Madame Claire's spiteful insults, self-centered demands, and malicious reprimands had eaten away at Annette until she could stand it no longer.

She had attempted once to run away and join the maroons, a group of Africans who had escaped their masters and lived free and wild in the forests of Saint Dominique. But they would not have her. They treated her no better than they treated the grand blancs, even making the abhorrent assumption that she was one of them because of the white blood flowing in her veins. Beaten, bruised, and heartbroken, she had dragged herself home.

Because she had nowhere else to go.

That was when she dove into the religion of her ancestors, seeking answers. And the answer she kept hearing over and over again was that the woman must die. It was the only way to be free.

But Mademoiselle Grace's God had ruined Annette's plans. A loving God would not do such a thing. A loving God would have allowed Madame Dubois to die as she deserved. A loving God would have granted Annette her freedom. She wanted nothing to do with this cruel God of the blancs. Now all that faced Annette was a future of abuse and hatred—a future of slavery. And she could not bear the thought.

A ribbon of gray settled on the horizon, pushing back the shroud of night. She didn't have much time before the crew arose and the helmsman and night watchman spotted her.

"Receive my spirit, oh great *Loa*. I am coming home." Annette released the rope. Her heart crashed in her chest. Her sweat-laden feet began to slip on the gunwale. The ship pitched and plunged over a wave, and Annette released herself from all fetters of this world.

She fell through the air. Free at last.

Until rough hands grabbed her waist.

She crashed against a warm, hard body, then landed on the deck with a thud. Pain shot up her back. She opened her eyes. A man's dark face filled her spinning vision. "Are you all right, mademoiselle?" Monsieur Thorn's voice.

Annette raised a hand to rub her aching forehead. "What have you done?"

"I have saved you," he said, sitting beside her and taking her hand. "Can you sit up?"

Annette shook off her dizziness and welcomed the anger brewing in her belly. "What have you done?" she repeated and swatted his hand away. Scrambling to her feet—a bit too fast—she wobbled on the shifting deck. "Imbécile."

The gray ribbon expanded over the horizon, taking on a ruddy hue—the same hue that now blossomed upon Mr. Thorn's face. "I save your life and you call me a fool?" He retrieved his tricorne from the deck.

"I did not wish to be saved."

His head jerked as if she'd slapped him. The angry flush faded from his features, replaced by concern. "You did not slip?"

Annette twirled around, not willing to face him, not wanting to see the care burning in his gaze, not wanting to believe it existed. She felt him move behind her. Placing his hands upon her shoulders, he turned her around. "Why?"

The tears she'd successfully kept at bay filled her eyes. "Because my mistress lives to torture me. My father ignores me. My people despise me, and the whites use me. I belong nowhere but with my ancestors in the afterworld."

Monsieur Thorn's jaw stiffened, and the green flecks in his brown eyes brightened. The look within them startled her. A look of admiration, of concern. A look she had never seen directed toward her. He drew her against his chest and wrapped his arms around her. Strong arms that locked her in a cocoon of warmth and protection.

No one had ever hugged her before.

～

Thorn held his breath. He didn't want to frighten away the woman who stood stiff as a bowline in his arms. But at least she had allowed him to embrace her. Slowly, her body softened, and she snuggled into him and released a shuddering sigh. The fear that had surged within him at her mention of jumping overboard now subsided to a tiny squall. Why would such a precious creature wish to deny the world her presence? And why did he feel like he'd died and gone to heaven with her in his arms?

"No matter what, there is always hope, mademoiselle," he whispered in her ear. "Do not give up."

The sun shot golden arrows over the indigo sea and across Thorn's face, announcing the new day. He squinted and tightened his embrace on Annette, not wanting these precious moments to end.

But like all good things in his life, it did end, as she pushed away from him and took a step back. Wiping her damp face, she looked down as if embarrassed. "You must think me *une sotte*."

Thorn shook his head.

She lifted her gaze to his, her dark eyes hardened with bitterness. "Before, I want Madame Dubois dead. I want my revenge. But when it is stolen from me, I believe I have no choice but to die."

Thorn studied her. So she *had* been responsible for Madame's illness. But who could blame her? The woman made Annette's life unbearable. It was justice. It was merited. But not until that moment did Thorn realize how quickly the thirst for revenge could turn on the ones wielding it and end up destroying them instead. He stiffened beneath the revelation but shrugged it away before he was forced to ponder its application to himself.

"There is always a choice. Choose to live, Annette." He gripped her shoulders. "Promise me you won't try to take your life again."

She looked down. "You do not know what you ask, monsieur. You do not know the life I face. No one cares about me."

"I care." He smiled.

She gazed at him, her eyes a mélange of disbelief and hope. But then she rewarded him with a flutter of lashes and the semblance of a smile upon her lips.

Something caught Thorn's gaze over her shoulder, and he stiffened. White sails floated like puffs of cotton on the horizon. Annette saw them too and gave him a curious look. Thorn looked aloft at the watchman in the crosstrees. He had not seen the ship yet. Good.

The more time that passed without detection, the faster they would be caught.

CHAPTER 31

Grace pried her eyes open, still heavy with slumber. The creaking and groaning of the brig she'd grown accustomed to tried to lull her back to sleep, but the dusty ray of sunshine streaming through the porthole told her it was well past dawn.

And she needed to speak with Rafe.

After Mr. Thorn's visit, Grace had gathered her blankets and curled up on deck, hoping to get much-needed sleep and make some sense of the discord bristling through her. But slumber had dashed about the cabin most of the night like a child playing tag, outwitting and outmaneuvering her. Finally, some time before dawn she must have drifted into unconsciousness out of sheer exhaustion.

Spyglass leapt from the chair and sauntered toward Grace. Plopping down on her stomach, the cat began kneading Grace's nightdress and saturating the air with the rumble of purrs. "You never seem overwrought, my friend. Would that I could be like you." Grace scratched Spyglass beneath the chin, and the cat stretched her neck toward the deck above. Closing her eyes, Grace longed to dive back into the ignorance of slumber, but Spyglass resumed her kneading, pricking Grace with one of her claws.

"Ooh!" She grabbed the cat. "Very well, no need to stab me. I shall arise." Sitting up, Grace kissed the cat on the cheek, then set her down on the deck. She glanced over the cabin. Annette's blankets lay folded in the corner.

"Bonjour," a voice coming from the cot startled Grace. She rose and sat in the chair, studying the madame. Though it had been little more than a day, color had returned to Claire's cheeks and her eyes regained their luster. "Good morning, Claire. How do you feel?"

"Stronger." She looked at Grace as if she were an angel. "I owe you my life, mademoiselle."

"No. You owe God your life."

Claire drew in a deep breath and struggled to sit. She pushed a curl from her face. "I never believed God cared for me."

"He does." Grace retrieved the mug of lemon water from the table and handed it to Claire.

Taking it, Claire took a sip. "I am not so sure." She shook her head and dropped her gaze to the mug clasped between her hands.

Grace's vision blurred with tears for the sorrow this woman had endured.

Claire pressed her lips together. "Yet no one could have shown me the love you did after I treated you so horribly, unless God helped them." She chuckled and Grace smiled, unable to respond, her throat closed tight with emotion.

Claire's face reddened. "Forgive me for sharing such personal confidences with you during my illness."

" 'Tis quite all right. I had no idea your life had been so difficult."

"It is no excuse for my behavior." Claire sighed.

Grace clasped her hands together. Indeed, she used to believe there was no excuse for bad behavior. She had always looked down on those who could not control their passions and who chose evil over good. Then why did she find no disdain for this woman before her, only understanding and concern?

"I love him still," Claire said without looking up.

The words shot straight to Grace's heart as Rafe's name drifted through the air, unspoken. "I know."

"But it is too late for us. I see that now." The sorrow lining Claire's face made Grace's heart crumble even as a twinge of jealousy sprang from among the pieces. She shook it off as Claire continued, "And I am married to a monster." She trembled.

Grace took the cup from Claire's hands before she dropped it and placed it back atop the table. "You needn't remain so, madame."

Claire's eyes searched Grace's in confusion.

"Your husband has been unfaithful and continues to flaunt his philandering before you daily."

Claire shrugged. "What is to be done about it?"

"He has broken his covenant with you, Claire."

"Vraiment?" A spark of hope lit her eyes, but then her shoulders sank. "But where would I go?"

Grace leaned over and took her hand. "Perhaps 'tis time to start trusting God for your future and not man or money."

Claire swallowed and her hand trembled. "We shall see."

"Do you feel up to a stroll on the deck?" Happy that Claire seemed slightly open to the things of God, Grace would put off her talk with Rafe if she could continue the conversation. "The fresh air would do you good."

"Non. I am still too weak." She raised a hand to her forehead. "And tired. I believe I shall sleep some more."

"Very well." Grace assisted Claire back down onto the cot. "We will talk later." She brushed the hair from her face.

"Merci." Claire smiled then closed her eyes.

Rising, Grace splashed water on her face from the basin. She donned her petticoat, stays, and skirts and brushed and pinned her hair up as best as she could—no longer concerned with a proper, tight coiffure.

Out in the companionway, she headed for Rafe's cabin. Spyglass pranced beside her as if she knew exactly where Grace was going and thought it was about time.

Ignoring the fluttering in her stomach, Grace approached the captain's door. She must apologize for their kiss and inform Rafe it could never happen again. She did not want him to get the wrong idea about her affections for him. Whatever they may be.

She squared her shoulders and knocked.

"Entrez-vous," Rafe's resonant voice bade her entrance, and she opened the door and slipped inside, Spyglass on her heels.

Rafe's gaze swept over her, and his grin reached his eyes in a sparkle that sent a wave of warmth through Grace.

Spyglass leapt upon the captain's desk and began batting the feathers of a quill pen.

The door thudded shut, and suddenly Grace found herself alone with the captain. He leaned against his desk, arms folded across his waistcoat, but the grin that had taken residence on his lips, a grin that contained a mixture of admiration and hunger, caused her heart to flutter.

Grace clasped her hands together and she looked down. The hollow thud of his footfalls pounded over the deck. Black leather boots appeared in her vision. His body heat radiated over her, carrying with it his scent of tobacco and the sea. And her heart felt as though it would crash through her chest. Placing a finger beneath her chin, he tipped her head up until their eyes met. "You wish to speak to me, mademoiselle?" His tone was playful, inviting.

"Oui, I mean yes." Grace pressed her moist palms over her skirts. "But if you please, could you back away a bit? I cannot seem to breathe."

Chuckling, he took a step back. "Oui, bien sûr. Mais does my presence disturb you?"

Gathering her wits and her resolve, Grace stood and faced him. "Yes." She might as well be honest. "It does."

"C'est bon."

"There is nothing good about it."

"A matter of perspective."

Grace sashayed away from the door, putting some distance between them. What was wrong with her? She'd come here to tell Rafe she would not receive his affections again. But instead all she wanted to do was feel his arms around her and his lips upon hers. Her cheeks heated until she had to withdraw a handkerchief from her sleeve and wave it around her face. "It grows warm below deck."

"Feels quite cool to me." He raised his brows.

Grace swallowed and looked up at him. He wore his black hair tied behind him, revealing a jaw peppered with stubble that reminded her of crushed charcoal. The fading purple of a bruise circled one eye. He stretched his shoulders back, only a hint of their strength discernable beneath his gray coat. To the left of his long black breeches tucked into his cordovan boots, hung the rapier that rarely left his side. And suddenly as she gazed into his dark, penetrating eyes, all rational thought dashed away in fear, leaving her standing there speechless.

He stepped toward her. "Mademoiselle?"

Grace held up a hand and averted her eyes to the contents of his desk. A full bottle of brandy glittered amber in the morning sun. "I do not believe I've ever seen an untouched bottle in your cabin, Captain. Have you given up your drink?" She hoped her playful tone would douse the heat that rose between them.

"I have, but I will pour one for you if you wish." His gaze brushed over Grace, and she thought she detected a slight grin on his lips.

"I would never touch such a vile drink."

"Ah, mademoiselle, vile it is not. Mais that it offends you has become the bane of my existence."

"I am pleased to hear it, Captain."

He bowed. "I live for your approval, mademoiselle."

Spyglass jumped to the deck and began to circle her skirts.

"You mock me, Captain."

He cocked his head. "Never."

She turned her back to him. "Will you return me to my home?"

"As I have said."

Grace grabbed the chain around her neck and pulled out her cross, then moved toward the cannon in the corner. "What of your hospital?"

"I will find another way."

"What changed your mind?" The words were out before she realized the implication of what she asked. The only thing that mattered was that he *had* changed his mind. Then why did her heart cinch within her chest awaiting his answer? She must be truly daft. For if he spoke the words she yearned to hear, she feared it would be the end of her.

Rafe rubbed his jaw and stomped back to his desk, the bottle of brandy luring him like glittering gold. Memories of their kiss last night warmed his body. Even though she'd fled with a look of horror on her face, Rafe had kissed enough women to know that Grace had enjoyed every moment of their embrace. And that thought alone had caused a spark to ignite in his heart—in a place long cold and dead.

Turning, he stared at the mademoiselle's back, green skirts flowing around her, trimmed in gold lace at the hem and waist. Coils of loose raven curls danced over her neck, taunting him like bait.

Why had he changed his mind? He shook his head, unable to deceive himself any longer. He knew why. He should tell her how he felt. Fear began a frantic pounding within him, erecting barricades, reminding him of the pain of rejection. It was bad enough he had allowed himself to fall in love again. But he would be a bigger fool to allow another woman to break his heart.

He straightened his shoulders. "I decided the don would most likely return you. Such a shrewish tongue would never survive a Spanish overlord."

She whirled around in a cloud of green silk, disappointment tugging down the corners of her mouth. "Shrewish?" Her face paled. "Of all the. . ."

Rafe's heart sank as the ardor, the affection, drained from her eyes, replaced by fury and pain.

"Very well. That makes what I have to say much easier." She lifted her chin, clutched her skirts, and headed toward the door, where she halted and drew a deep breath. "I came to inform you that I was remiss in accepting your. . .your"—she looked away—"kiss. And that it must never happen again." She gave him a venomous look, and he instantly longed to make things right.

Rafe moved toward her, his voice low. "I heard no objection while your lips were on mine."

She fanned her red face with her handkerchief. Tiny scratches lined one cheek and Rafe swallowed, longing to kiss them away.

"I am voicing them now." She took a step back. "Promise me you will not take advantage of me again, Captain."

"Take advantage, sacre mer." Rafe ran a hand through his hair, feeling his ire rising. "Mademoiselle, you have my word that I will take no further liberties with you."

Her lip trembled. "I shall hold you to that, Captain." She swerved about and opened the door. "Come, Spyglass," she called over her shoulder, and the cat promptly obeyed, stopping to hiss at Rafe on her way out.

He slammed the door shut after them and leaned back against it. The woman had not only stolen his heart but his cat as well.

CHAPTER 32

Grace leaned on the railing amidships and gazed as the setting sun spread a plethora of brilliant colors: persimmon, violet, saffron, and coral across the horizon. Yet the beauty was lost on her. For clearly she had gone mad. After her encounter with the captain, she had been unable to stop crying. For what reason her mind could not fathom. Finally this harrowing adventure would be over. She would be safe in her home in Charles Towne. She should be the happiest woman alive. Then why did tears continually spring from her eyes and her heart feel as though it had been mauled by a grappling hook?

A light breeze wafted over her, cooling the perspiration on her arms and fluttering her curls about her neck. Perhaps the fresh air was all she needed to clear her head and heal whatever ailed her heart. Soon the darkness would drive her back to her cabin. She drew a deep breath of the tropical air, allowing it to fill her lungs with its spicy aroma. She would miss it. The sea held a different scent than the harbor in Charles Towne.

Charles Towne. Where she would no longer have to deal with the French rogue Captain Dubois. The captain had not only called her a shrew, but he had claimed it was the reason he refused to sell her to the don. That she had been hoping for another reason, a more personal reason, brought her shame. That he seemed equally anxious to return her home and be rid of her himself caused her heart to shrivel.

Am I a shrew? Grace's eyes burned. What did she expect? Did she expect this Frenchman, this mercenary, this man who kidnapped her, to declare his love for her?

I am a silly woman, Lord. A silly woman who has been no good to anyone. Done nothing right except perhaps step out of the way so You could save Claire. At least I can go home with some dignity.

Footfalls sounded and Grace turned to see Annette inching across deck, a bundle in her hands. Behind the mulatto, the crew's eyes brushed over her, then swept away. In one corner, Monsieur Weylan, Mr. Fisk, Mr. Holt—the three sailors who had assaulted Grace below—and one other man huddled together as they often did when on deck.

"Bonsoir, mademoiselle." Annette moved beside her. The setting sunlight cast a rainbow of colors over her tawny skin, making her look far more innocent than Grace knew her to be. Yet Grace no longer felt angry with the lady.

"Good evening, Annette. How is Madame Dubois?" Grace asked.

Annette flattened her lips. "Madame rests. She will recover." The sting of hatred so oft in her voice when she spoke of her mistress had lost its potency. "You did not tell her what I did?" She gazed down at the choppy waves pounding against the hull.

Grace shook her head. "No need, since you promised not to harm her again."

"You are very kind, mademoiselle." Annette unwrapped the bundle in her hands, revealing the stones, beads, rattle, and amulet she used in the rituals of her religion.

The hairs on Grace's arms bristled, but she resisted the urge to leave. She needn't be afraid of such things. She only hoped the girl didn't intend to use them again—especially right here in front of her.

With a flick of the cloth, Annette tossed them all into the sea. They splashed one by one into the dark waters and disappeared from sight. Then she uttered a sigh of resignation, folded the cloth, and slipped it into a pocket in her skirt.

Grace tipped her head curiously. "Why did you do that?"

"I have been thinking. Compared to your God, the religion of my ancestors is weak and harms others. I no longer wish to pray to my ancestors."

Grace nearly leapt out of her shoes. "I'm very happy to hear that, Annette." She stared out to sea again, where the sun sank further behind the horizon, and pondered what to say next, not wanting to fail again. "Perhaps you would like to pray to my God?"

"Non." Annette's reply disappointed Grace. "I do not, mademoiselle. If He is the one true God, then I want nothing to do with a God who enslaves my people."

"But you are mistaken, Annette." Grace laid a hand on hers. "He is—"

A deep, buoyant chuckle drew Annette's attention behind them to where Mr. Thorn had joined Weylan and his friends. The mulatto's dark eyes latched upon the first mate, and Grace nearly gasped at the ardor she saw within them. Turning, she studied the odd group curiously. They spoke in whispered tones and bore a camaraderie that could only be fostered by long acquaintance or a bond of common goals. Yet, how often had Mr. Thorn scorned these very men.

"Bonsoir, mademoiselle." Annette scurried away, dropping below deck before Grace could continue their conversation. Frustration joined her already troublesome thoughts and she turned back around.

The sun disappeared behind the sea, dragging with it the last traces of its brilliant glory and leaving the world in a shroud of gray that soon faded to black. Yet Grace could not pull herself from the railing. She did not want to face the captain. She did not want to spend hours in idle chatter with Madame Dubois. In truth, she wanted to be alone to sort out the chaotic emotions whirling within her.

An hour later, the tread of boots and bare feet sounded, followed by hushed voices. Familiar voices that caused her to slink further into the shadows beneath the railing. A group of sailors made their way to the capstan amidships, their dark gazes scouring the deck for any intruders. They didn't seem to see her.

Grace held her breath and craned her ear toward the group, trying to make out the words over the slap of waves against the hull.

"So, we are in agreement?" Weylan said.

"Aye."

"Oui, I have informed the others." A third voice.

"When?"

"The ship should arrive tomorrow at sunrise." Weylan again.

"The captain will not go down easily."

At the sound of Mr. Thorn's voice, Grace tossed her hand to cover her mouth.

"He will have no choice."

The men grunted their approval and then dispersed across the deck, some heading up to the quarterdeck, others to join sailors lumbering by the larboard railing. The rest dropped below hatches. Grace clutched her throat and released her breath. Her thoughts whirled with the content of the men's conversation. Though her mind refused to accept it, she knew what she had heard. Plans for a mutiny.

But Mr. Thorn, of all people?

Grace trembled.

She must warn Rafe. She dared not move for several more minutes, at least until her heart no longer pounded in her ears. Then slowly, she tiptoed out from her hiding spot and slipped down the companionway.

And barreled right into Mr. Thorn.

Wearing the grin of a panther who had just caught his prey. "What do we have here, a little ship mouse?"

Grace tossed a hand to her throat. "Mr. Thorn, you gave me such a fright. I was just going to my cabin." She heard the tremor in her voice and tried to skirt around him, but he blocked her way.

"Indeed? And where have you come from?"

"I was. . .I was up on deck getting some air." She tried to shove him aside. "Now if you please, sir."

He grabbed her arm. His tight grip pinched her skin and sent pain down to her fingers. "I cannot let you warn him, miss. You know that."

Grace lifted her gaze to his. Determined brown eyes with a hint of sorrow met hers. Her heart thrashed in her chest. She kicked him in the leg. He let out a moan and bent over to rub the wound. Grace gathered her strength to shoulder him aside when something hard hit her head with a *thunk*. A burning pain seared down her neck and back. The companionway spun in her vision and the last thing she remembered was Mr. Thorn's contorted expression before everything went black.

~⁀↝~

Rafe sat up in bed and rubbed his aching eyes. Sunlight poured in through the stern window setting everything aglow in its path. Rising, he tossed a shirt over his head, feeling more hopeful than he had in years, despite his lack of sleep. During the wee hours of the night Rafe had paced across his cabin—had suffered beneath the pain that, upon delivering Grace to Charles Towne, he would never see her again. And he had concluded that it would be worth the risk of confessing his love to her, if there was but the slightest chance she might love him in return.

Which was why Rafe must seek out Mademoiselle Grace straight-away. It was time to risk his heart again. He had been betrayed by everyone he'd loved, but maybe, just maybe, Grace would be different. Perhaps her God truly did exist and by following Him, she had become incapable of dishonesty and betrayal.

Donning his waistcoat, boots, and baldric, he strapped on his weapons and headed out the door when Monsieur Fletcher nearly barreled into him. "A ship, Capitaine!" the man said in an urgent tone. Setting aside his task for now, Rafe followed him above.

"Where away?" Rafe shouted as he burst forth upon the deck.

"Two points off the starboard stern!" brayed a sailor.

Plucking out his spyglass as he went, Rafe leapt upon the quarterdeck and drew it to his eye before reaching the helm. Only a hint of the cool night remained in the morning wind that whipped through his hair. He focused the glass on a trio of sails, their bellies gorged with wind, not more than a league off their stern.

Monsieur Thorn appeared beside him.

"What do you make of her?" Rafe handed him the glass and braced himself on the deck as the ship pitched over a swell. Still angry at his first mate for offering to help Grace escape at the deserted island, Rafe decided to let the matter go and relieve the man of his duties the next time they weighed anchor at some port. Sans doute the man suffered from a concern for Mademoiselle Grace's welfare. How could Rafe blame him for that?

Thorn pressed the spyglass to his eye and shrugged. "A merchant, perhaps? She flies the ensign of France." He lowered the glass and squinted into the rising sun. "Nothing to cause alarm, I am sure."

Rafe eyed him curiously. "Then why does she give chase?"

"Perhaps she needs our help."

"I see no *signal de détresse*." Rafe snatched the glass back, examining the narrow lines of the hull, the shape and position of her sails. At least she was not one of Woodes's two ships that had pursued them earlier. Sacre mer, was every ship in the Caribbean after him?

Lowering the glass, he turned to Thorn, surprised by the grin tugging at his first mate's lips. "All hands aloft. Loose topgallants. Clear away the jib."

"But our main-topmast, Captain." Thorn seemed in no hurry to obey.

"I am aware of the damage, Monsieur Thorn. Raise what sails we have left." Rafe ground his teeth together and gripped the hilt of his rapier. "And have Monsieur Porter clear the tackles and load the guns."

"Zooks, Captain, is that quite necessary?" Thorn chuckled and brushed specks of dried salt from his coat.

Scowling, Rafe turned a cold eye upon his first mate, a man who had never hesitated to obey him. "Do as I say, Thorn, or I'll find someone who will."

The first mate touched his hat, gave Rafe a grin laced with indignation and turned to bellow orders to the crew. Ignoring Thorn's impertinence, Rafe narrowed his eyes upon the ship that dared to intrude upon his waters.

Spyglass leapt into his arms and draped herself over his right shoulder. Purring filled his ears, and Rafe stroked her fur, releasing a familiar scent that delighted him. "So you have been with the mademoiselle." He grinned. "I do not blame you." His thoughts shot to the look of pain on Grace's face when he had called her a shrew. He had not meant to cause her any suffering, but only to cloak his true feelings. But he must not think of that now. For now he must shake this snake from his leg—this ship that dared to pursue him.

An hour crept by, and Rafe still was unable to determine either the ship's identity or her purpose.

The sun climbed midway between wave and topmast, and already the heat sent streams of sweat down his neck and back. The thunderous snap of sails glutting with wind sounded above. Shielding his eyes, he glanced at the line of men balancing across the foretop yard, as they adjusted sails to catch the shifting trade winds. At Rafe's direction, Monsieur Atton altered course repeatedly in an attempt shake off the nagging ship. But to no avail. "Zut alors, what does le irksome mongrel want?"

Rafe shrugged off his coat and tossed it to the deck by the railing, allowing the salty breeze to cool him. He stormed toward the taffrail and raised his spyglass again.

"She gains on us," Thorn shouted from behind him.

"Je sais!" Rafe wondered at the lack of concern in this first mate's voice.

Father Alers approached and squinted in the sunlight. The wrinkles around his eyes folded like the threads of an old rope.

Rafe adjusted the glass, bringing the ship into clearer view. A bark. Three-masted, fore- and aft-rigged. The French flag flapped lazily upon her bowsprit.

Shifting the telescope aft, Rafe focused on the ensign upon the mainmast. His heart leapt in his throat.

The figure of two black lions battling against the backdrop of a red coat of arms. The Dubois crest. Rafe lowered the glass and slammed it shut. "Sacre mer, my father's ship."

"Votre père?" Standing at the quarterdeck railing beside Rafe, Father Alers flinched, his gray hair puffing around his head like a turkey displaying its feathers.

"Oui." Rafe's blood boiled.

Father Alers grabbed the glass and examined the ship himself. Lowering it, he scratched his gray beard. "I suppose he wants his wife back."

"He can have her," Rafe spat; then he marched to the quarterdeck railing.

"Egad, your father. How on earth did he find you?" Thorn appeared beside him.

"I wonder." Rafe shot an accusing glare at his first mate. In light of his impudent behavior toward Rafe, Thorn's recent deception regarding Grace began to reek of treachery rather than mere concern for the mademoiselle.

Rafe turned to the helmsman. "Hard to larboard, Monsieur Atton. Let's keep aweather of him. Perhaps he'll grow bored as he does with most of his intrigues."

"Hard to larboard, Capitaine," Monsieur Atton replied and adjusted the wheel.

Le Champion swept over the rolling waves under a full press of sails, at least the sails that remained. Rafe cursed. With his main-topmast damaged, he'd have trouble outrunning his father's ship.

"Perhaps you should see what he wants?" Monsieur Thorn lifted one brow.

"If he has come for his wife, I am happy to hand her over. Otherwise, I have nothing to say to him."

Rafe marched to the bulwarks, annoyed with his first mate's cavalier attitude. A gust of wind struck him, yanking strands of his hair from his tie. The ship bucked, and he gripped the railing until the wood bit into his fingers. Rafe had spent a childhood buried beneath his father's shadow, and the next several years of his life digging out from under it. Aside from his last unavoidable visit, he had vowed never to see the man again—the man who ruled the Dubois estate and most of Port-de-Paix with the iron scepter of cruelty.

But the sea was Rafe's territory. Was it not enough the man had stolen Rafe's childhood? Was it not enough he had stolen his fiancée? Did he want the sea as well?

Rafe grunted and gripped the pommel of his rapier. Whatever mischief his father was about, it would only end in disaster. Of that he was sure.

As the minutes passed, Rafe grew more agitated. His father's ship furled tops and mainsails, stripped to mizzen and sprit, and was now within one half mile of *Le Champion*, so close Rafe could make out her crew, as well as the yellow plume fluttering atop his father's cocked hat. Yet still Rafe waited. Waited for a signal to parley, a salute of the flag, anything to announce the man's intentions.

Finally, when the ship sailed just a quarter mile off their starboard stern, the flag atop her foremast dipped in a signal requesting a parley. Rafe narrowed his eyes, his gut churning with distrust. "Return the signal, but ensure our guns are loaded and ready. And man the swivels," Rafe ordered Mr. Thorn.

"But 'tis obvious he means us no harm," the first mate replied.

Rafe's jaw hardened, and blood surged to his fists. "Do as I say!"

"As you wish, Captain." Thorn's voice carried a sneering bite as he touched his hat and left.

Rafe shook his head. What was wrong with the man today?

Father Alers grunted and laid a hand on Rafe's arm. "Be patient, my boy."

"Never fear." Rafe sighed and crossed his arms over his chest. "Regardless that my father has never given me a reason to trust him, I will not fire upon him without cause. I shall wait to see what he wants."

His father's ship plunged through the turquoise sea, sending a foamy squall over her bow as she tacked alee then came even on *Le Champion*'s keel. Without warning, her larboard gun ports popped open one by one and the charred muzzles of ten guns spewed out from them like ravenous black tongues.

Father Alers gave a sordid chuckle. "Your wait is over, Capitaine."

"Zut alors." Rafe swerved on his heels. A string of rapid orders exploded from his lips, sending his men flying across the deck. "Helm's lee! *Adieu-va!*" he bellowed. Above him the sailors scrambled to let go the foresheets.

"Rise tacks and sheets!" Rafe braced himself on the deck as *Le Champion*, with straining cordage and creaking blocks, swung to larboard. She pitched over a swell, and foamy spray swept over the deck, slapping Rafe's boots. Lugsails flapped thunderously until the sails caught the wind in an ominous snap. *Le Champion* veered promptly about on an eastern tack, flashing the pursuing ship her rudder.

Boom! A volcano of hot metal fired from his father's ship, sending the air aquiver.

"All hands down!" Rafe dove to the deck. The crunch and snap of wood grated over his ears, and he looked up to see a gaping hole of jagged shards marring the taffrail. Rafe jumped to his feet. The other shots plunged harmlessly into the churning wake off their stern. He released a sigh and lifted a contemptuous gaze toward his father's ship.

Ten puffs of gray smoke curled upward from her hull like snakes beneath a charmer's flute. His father had fired upon him. After requesting a parley. Had the man no decency?

"Bring her about!" Rafe shouted to Monsieur Thorn, who was struggling to rise. "And ready the larboard guns."

The ship yawed widely to port as Rafe leapt down the quarterdeck ladder and marched across the main deck. Fury fanned his hatred into a roaring flame. His father may have oppressed him in his youth. He may have belittled him and defeated him, but Rafe was no longer a little boy, and he'd be keelhauled and strung from the yardarm before he'd allow his father to best him upon the seas.

Bracing his boots upon the slanted deck, Rafe glanced aloft as his crew worked furiously to complete another tack. Pride swelled within him at their skill and efficiency. He had taught them well. In a few minutes they'd be in position to deliver a well-deserved broadside to his father's ship.

A ship that now floundered in an effort to veer away from *Le Champion* as the crew no doubt sensed their imminent danger. Rafe grinned. He glanced over his shoulder. From the quarterdeck, Monsieur Thorn gazed at their enemy with the look of expectancy, rather than anger. Father Alers made his way over the teetering deck to Rafe.

Le Champion rose and swooped over the turquoise swells. The creak of her blocks and the rattle of flapping sails filled the air along with the silken rustle of the sea along the hull. The sting of gunpowder tainted the morning breeze. Rafe ordered top and studding sails reefed as they swung around and hove to, athwart the ship's bow.

His father's crew darted frantically across the deck and up into the ratlines, attempting to find the wind and turn their ship. Amidst the chaos, her larboard guns had not been reloaded and still hung from their ports in impotence.

Rafe had them. "Monsieur Thorn!" he bellowed.

"Yes, Captain."

"On my order."

"On your order, Captain." Thorn shifted his stance, not meeting Rafe's gaze.

Facing forward, Rafe studied his prey. Within seconds, they'd be in perfect position to loose a broadside. Within seconds, he would finally beat his father, sink his ship, and take the man prisoner. A tingle of elation ran through him at the prospect.

He opened his mouth to give the order.

"Wait, Captain. They raise a white flag," Monsieur Thorn said

Rafe glanced at the white cloth climbing toward the blue sky.

Father Alers turned to him with a look of censure. "They surrender, Rafe."

"He surrenders because he knows I have the advantage and could blast him from the water." Rafe grabbed his baldric. Yet a thread of relief wove through his knotted insides. No matter what his father had done to him, no matter the beatings, the humiliation, the belittling, the hatred, no matter the way he treated Rafe's mother, it was wrong to fire upon one's father.

Besides, Grace would not approve. Scanning the deck, he searched for a glimpse of her, but she was nowhere to be seen. She had admonished him to be a better man than he was. And right now, he wanted more than anything to prove to her that he could be. He turned around. Off their larboard side, his father's ship slipped through the sea, already positioned board by board. On her foredeck, the man who sired him stood awaiting his fate. If Rafe intended to loose a broadside, he must do so immediately or forfeit the chance to prove that his father had been wrong about him.

To prove that Rafe was not a failure.

Rafe clenched his fists until they hurt. "Stand down."

Mr. Thorn smiled. "Very well, Captain."

Shoving aside the angst churning in his gut, Rafe released a ragged sigh. "Arm the men and then signal my father to come aboard."

CHAPTER 33

Grace woke with a start. Pain burned through her head. Her lips ached. The taste of sweat-laden cloth filled her mouth. Why couldn't she move her hands and legs? She sprang up, and her head crashed into something hard. A crate? A barrel? Hard to tell in the darkness. Panic took over. She wrestled to free her hands, but the more she struggled the more her wrists stung until something warm seeped from them. Blood. She tried to scream, but her voice came out a muffled groan from behind the cloth stuffed in her mouth. *Lord?* As her mind cleared, she tried to recall how she ended up in this dark prison.

Mr. Thorn. The last thing she remembered was bouncing off his thick chest and the furtive look of treachery on his face.

The mutiny! They planned to mutiny!

Inching her backside over the rough planks of the deck, Grace used her bound hands to locate the door. She must be in some kind of storage room. She must get to Rafe. She must warn him. She had no idea how long she'd been in here. Lifting her legs, she kicked the door. *Pound. Pound. Pound.* She groaned a muted call for help. For several minutes, she repeated the process until her legs ached and her throat swelled.

Boom! Boom!

Cannon blasts fired in the distance. Grace's breathing took on a frenzied pace. Who was firing at them? Footsteps sounded on the deck above her like methodical drums. Muffled shouts and curses trickled down to taunt her ears. Grace screamed again and thumped her feet against the door. Nothing.

She would not give up. She must warn Rafe before it was too late.

~

Within minutes, Monsieur Dubois and several of his crew had boarded a cockboat and with oars to water, made quick work of the distance between the two ships. Rafe's father stood at the bow with arms at his hips and yellow feather fluttering from his hat as if he were the conqueror of the world.

Familiar with his father's ostentatious display, Rafe ignored him, though he could not deny the fury that pulsed through every vein. "Steady, men." His piercing gaze scoured his crew as they stood armed with rapiers, pistols, and axes.

The cockboat thumped against the hull, and two of Monsieur Dubois's crew climbed over the bulwarks. Each gripped a pistol in one hand and drew their sword with the other. Three of Rafe's crew took a step forward, taunting the men with their blades and angry curses. Rafe stayed them with a lift of his hand.

Finally, his father clambered aboard, his face plump and red. "Infernal ladder," he grunted; then glancing at Rafe's crew, he lengthened his stance, adjusted his velvet waistcoat, and replaced his look of frustration with a veneer of confident insolence. He turned cold eyes toward his son. "No stomach for a fight, Rafe?" He waved a ruffled handkerchief in the breeze. "So much like your mother."

"If it's a fight you want, Père, it's a fight I'll give you. My men are well trained," Rafe replied, his statement confirmed by thunderous grunts behind him.

Monsieur Dubois shot his beady gaze across the deck as the remainder of his men jumped over the bulwarks and joined him. That made twelve men to Rafe's thirty.

"Have your men stand down, Father. I seek no battle between us." And that was no lie. He wanted his father to state his business, take his wife, and be gone. Rafe glanced across the deck, wondering why Grace had not come above but was thankful when he did not see her.

Monsieur Dubois tugged on the white swath of silk at his neck and directed his gaze to Mr. Thorn. The first mate shook his head and looked down.

"Very well, Rafe." Monsieur Dubois gestured for his men to lower their weapons.

Rafe glared at his father, questioning his decision to allow him aboard. "You should thank me for sparing your life, Father. For it was only our relation and our common bond to ma mère which stood between me and the cannons that would have sunk you to the depths."

"C'est vrai? I am more inclined to believe it was your cowardice that failed you." His father laid a hand on his hip and took a turn about the deck. "How you have succeeded as a mercenary I shall never know. Well, perhaps that is why you saw fit to steal my wife from me. Intending to sell her as well?"

Monsieur Thorn slipped from beside Rafe and disappeared behind him. Was the man so much a coward that he could not stand beside his captain in time of need?

"I did not kidnap Claire," Rafe shot back as he slid his fingers over the warm pommel of his rapier. One false move and he would silence his father's insolent tongue.

"Non? Is she not on your brig?" Monsieur Dubois's tone rose in sarcasm.

Rafe flexed his jaw. "Oui, but not by my doing."

"Then by whose? I suppose she stole away in the night and hired a boatman to bring her aboard?" He chuckled. "She has neither the brains nor the bravery for such an act."

A moan sounded from the companionway, and all eyes shot in the direction of the woman emerging from below.

"Ah there you are, ma chérie." Monsieur Dubois's features sharpened, but he made no move to aid his wife.

Claire walked across the deck, her blond hair shimmering in the noontime sun. The color had returned to her skin though her chest rose and fell from the exertion of climbing abovedecks.

Claire reached his side. "Henri. What are you doing here?" Disbelief and anger rang in her tone.

"I came to rescue you, ma chérie." His smile sent ice through Rafe.

Claire's face scrunched, and she eyed him with disbelief.

"What has Rafe done to you, ma chérie?" he went on. "Are you injured?"

"She has been ill," Rafe said. A gust of hot wind tainted with human sweat tore over the deck, tossing his hair.

Monsieur Dubois took Claire's arm and tried to draw the woman into an embrace. She stiffened, but he forced her against him. "Are you so inept, my son, that you cannot take care of one woman?"

Rafe snorted. "No more inept than a man who cannot hold on to his own wife."

Father Alers coughed.

Monsieur Dubois huffed and directed his gaze behind Rafe where Rafe heard the thudding of bare feet on the deck. He stole a quick glance over his shoulder but only Monsieur Thorn and a band of Rafe's men met his gaze. He faced forward. "How did you find me?"

"You are not the only one with skills upon the sea."

"Which is why your broadside splashed impotently into the water."

A vein pulsed on his father's sweaty neck. "Yet I believe it is I and my men who have boarded your ship."

"Only by my leave." Rafe groaned and stomped his boot on the deck. "Assez! If you have come for your wife, take her and go." He waved a hand in dismissal.

"No, please, Rafe," Claire cried. Fear and desperation scampered across her blue eyes.

"Silence, woman!" Rafe's father put his arm around Claire's shoulders, forcing her against him. Her face pinched. He glared at Rafe. "And leave her kidnapper unpunished?" Monsieur Dubois's eyes searched the deck. "And where is your other victim? I assume you stole Mademoiselle Grace as well?"

"Rafe did not kidnap me, Henri." Claire swallowed and stared at the deck. "I came of my own will."

Henri's face mottled in blotches of red and white. The veins in his neck pulsed. Rafe feared he would explode, but then a flash of anguish peeked out from behind the anger in his eyes. He shoved Claire to the side. "It matters not."

"Of course it matters, Father." Rafe shook his head. "We have no quarrel now." At least none Rafe cared to address. Then why did the hairs on the back of his neck suddenly stand on end?

Footfalls pounded on the deck behind him. Muffled voices bounced through the air.

The *ching* of sword against sheath. The cock of pistols. Rafe froze. The taste of metal filled his mouth.

Slowly he turned around. The tips of ten rapiers shot toward him. Sunlight glared from their blades and bounced over the deck like grapeshot. Toward the forefront of the mob of Rafe's own men stood

Monsieur Thorn, wearing a look of haughty disdain. Beyond them, the remainder of Rafe's crew halted beneath the leveled aim of blades and pistols.

Rafe threw back his shoulders and lengthened his stance to cover up the fear tying his stomach into knots. He swung back to his father, whose blue eyes glowed with cruel deception. "What is this about?"

His father grinned. "This is what I believe you call a mutiny."

CHAPTER 34

Grace stopped pounding the door to catch her breath. Perspiration streamed down her face and neck. Her head ached. Blood dripped from her wrists, and her mouth was stuffed with cotton. But at least the cannons had ceased and the ship had slowed to a near halt. In light of what she'd overheard, however, that might not have been a good sign at all.

She continued battering the door with her feet and groaning through the saturated cloth in her mouth.

Finally, she heard shuffling in the hall. "Mademoiselle?" Annette's sheepish voice squeaked through the oak.

Grace groaned and kicked the door again. The latch clicked, and light spilled in around the mulatto's thin form.

"Mademoiselle!" Annette dropped to the deck and plucked the handkerchief from Grace's mouth. "Who did this to you?"

Grace coughed and tried to speak but her words emerged in a grating rasp.

Annette battled the ropes around Grace's wrists and feet. "When you not come back to the cabin last night, I worry, and come looking for you."

"Thank you, Annette," Grace managed to say. Tearing the loosened ropes from her ankles, she rose. A wave of dizziness swirled her vision, and she leaned on the bulkhead.

"Are you all right, mademoiselle?"

Grace gripped Annette's shoulders. "Where is Rafe?"

278

"Captain Dubois is on deck, mademoiselle." Annette's brows drew together.

"Come, we must hurry." Grace swept past her.

"It is not good." The *tap tap* of Annette's shoes behind Grace only added to her rising fear. "You should not go above, mademoiselle."

Ignoring the lady and the sinking feeling in her gut, Grace navigated the narrow hallways and companionway. Then clutching her skirts, she climbed up the ladder and emerged into the sunlight, Annette fast on her heels.

A growling mob undulated over the main deck, and Grace ducked into the shadows beneath the quarterdeck. She strained to see through the horde of cursing sailors. Drawing Annette to her side, she circled around the mob until she spotted the yellow feather fluttering atop Monsieur Dubois's hat. Bright flashes caused her to squint and focus on their source.

Swords. Drawn swords. All pointed at Rafe. She was too late.

Rafe cursed himself as every muscle within him grew taut. How could he have been such a fool? He eyed his father, longing to draw his rapier and etch a permanent frown over his caustic grin. *Stupide.* Rafe shifted his gaze from his father to Monsieur Thorn. Despite the anger boiling in Rafe's gut, a sharp twang struck his heart. "So you joined mon père against me?" He formed the words his mind still refused to believe. That the man who had sailed with him for a year, the man he considered his friend, had committed the ultimate betrayal. But why not? Everyone betrayed Rafe in the end.

Thorn raised one shoulder. "So it would seem."

"And all of you!" Rafe yelled over their shoulders to those of his men who had joined the traitorous mob. "Have I not served you well?" He scanned their faces. Weylan, Holt, Fisk, Porter, Maddock, and a dozen other men who had been his companions. Some lowered their gazes, others gave him a sheepish look of apology, while others twitched their fingers over their weapons as if anxious to be done with him.

He turned back to Thorn. "Why involve my father in this?"

Thorn cocked a brow. "In the event there were not enough men willing to turn against you, Captain. And as it turned out, I needed his crew." He shook his head. "Even when I informed the men that you reneged on your promise to sell the mademoiselle and line their pockets, most still would not join us. A testament to you, I suppose. Though for the life of me, I find their loyalty confounding."

Movement on the fore- and quarterdecks drew Rafe's attention to groups of sailors who gathered at each railing, shock and fear tightening their features as some of their own companions held them at gunpoint. Even Monsieur Atton, normally a solid rock of composure, stared at Rafe with a look of horror.

Weylan stepped forward, tugging upon the lace at his cuffs. "It's about her." He wagged a thumb toward his left, and Rafe glanced to see Mademoiselle Grace huddling in the corner beside Annette, her eyes wide, and her bottom lip quivering.

Zut alors, the woman always chose the most inopportune time to come on deck. His stomach tightened. What would happen to Grace now? "We heard you had grown soft on the woman," Weylan added with a sneer.

Rafe faced him. "What is that to you?" He gripped the hilt of his rapier, causing the swords pointed his way to jerk to attention. Grace gasped.

"Easy, messieurs." Rafe released the weapon and narrowed his eyes upon his father. "This has nothing to do with your wife." Rafe huffed as understanding dawned. "You planned this mutiny all along."

"Ah, gentlemen." His father glanced over the mob. "At last my son has regaled us with a smidgen of his acclaimed wisdom." His blue eyes flashed. "I had begun to doubt you possessed it."

Ignoring him, Rafe directed his attention to Thorn. "And you told him where to find us."

Thorn grinned.

Rafe nodded toward Claire who leaned against the foredeck, her eyes laced with horror. "Was she also a part of this?"

"My faithless wife?" Henri chuckled. "Non, she is merely a pawn. En fait, she believed she was running away to be with you. Had I known I was marrying a *souillon*, I would have allowed you to keep her."

Rafe gripped his baldric as a blast of wind tore over him. "But you did marry her. You won, Father. Why come after me?"

"Because I could not stand that she still wanted you, still loved you." Rafe's father shot a look toward Claire that burned more with pain than hatred, then he stomped toward Rafe, his eyes bulging. "Just like your mother. It was always about you. Smart, quick-witted, capable Rafe. Stronger, wiser, better." He spat to the side.

Rafe winced beneath the man's fury. He could find no cause for it. Nothing he had done in his childhood except succeed at all he did. Shouldn't a father be proud of such a son? "I was never in competition with you."

Henri snorted, his face reddening. "Oh, but you were. Every time you succeeded. Every time you won the affections of a lady I coveted, every time Claire's eyes lit up at the mention of your name. Every time I heard of your grand successes upon the sea and was bombarded by the people's praise for you in town." He snorted. "Assez!"

The loathing that twisted his father's features stunned Rafe. "So you devise a plan for me to appear to kidnap your wife so you can come after me and kill me?"

"How else to be rid of you within the bounds of the law? I am not a murderer." Henri lifted his shoulders as if shrugging off his anger, shrugging away his son.

"My crew will testify otherwise." Rafe said.

"Who would believe them over me?"

Rafe's heart collapsed into a ball of lead. His father was right. "I did not realize your hatred of me ran so deep."

Henri glared at Rafe for a moment. He licked his lips and looked away. "You are not my son."

A drop of sweat slid down Rafe's back. The sun fired hot arrows upon him. Waves slapped against the hull. Claire gasped.

Rafe's fingers went numb. "What did you say?"

Henri gazed over the sea, his stony face holding a trace of sorrow. "I said you are not my son."

"Then whose son am I?"

His father met his gaze. His eyes glinted like steel. "You are the son of the pirate Jean du Casse."

CHAPTER 35

Jean du Casse? Blood dashed from Rafe's head. Blinking, he caught himself before he stumbled backward. Jean du Casse, the admiral of the French navy? The man knighted by Louis XIV, the governor of Saint Dominique? The buccaneer who led the raid on Spanish forces at Cartagena? That Jean du Casse? The incredulous possibility swirled in Rafe's mind. Could it be true? Could he be the son of such a great man? Rafe raised a furrowed brow to Henri as his jumbled thoughts fled to his mother.

"I see where your mind takes you, Rafe." Monsieur Dubois stroked his pointed beard. "Straight to the source. En fait, I only discovered the truth after your mother died. Evidence of her duplicity in a letter I found stuffed in a drawer. I regret to dash your virginal memory of her, but she was nothing more than a souillon, a prostituée."

In a flash, Rafe drew his rapier and leveled its tip upon Henri's throat. "You will take that back, monsieur. If my mother found love in the arms of another it was because you drove her to it."

Blades flashed his way. A sharp tip pressed against his side. Rafe glanced in the direction to see Thorn's furious face at the end of the gleaming hilt.

"Stand down," Thorn ordered. "Or I'll run you through."

"Not before I slit his throat." Rafe pressed the point harder, and blood blossomed on Henri's white cravat as his eyes became transfixed in horror.

Thorn chuckled. "Go ahead. It matters not to me. "You may fall atop his dead body if that is what you wish."

Silence swallowed all sound aboard the ship except Henri's hurried breathing. Rafe's hand began to shake. Not from fear or even rage, but from the overwhelming desire to destroy this man who had destroyed Rafe's life.

"No, Rafe." Mademoiselle's quivering voice spilled over him from behind, followed by Claire's sobbing, "S'il vous plaît."

Lowering his blade, Rafe stepped back. Though he cared nothing for his own life, or for the life of Henri Dubois, he had Grace to consider. And as long as he lived, he would do his best to protect her. But he must live. He glanced her way. Green eyes, pooling with fear, met his. Claire, her face red and puffy, clung to Grace's left arm, while Annette stood as rigid as a mast off her right.

Father Alers's gray hair flared about him. He gripped the pommel of his blade and stepped forward from beside the three women. "Say the word, Capitaine, and I will fight by your side."

Henri chuckled. "How noble. Can you invoke no more loyalty than that of one old man?" He grinned, and the sailors joined his laughter.

"Non, mon ami," Rafe spoke to the former priest as he inclined his head toward Grace. "Stay with her. Keep her safe."

Father Alers nodded his understanding and took a step back.

Tears spilled from Grace's eyes.

Wrenching his gaze from her, Rafe thrust the tip of his rapier into the deck and leaned on the handle. "So, Henri, what will it be? Keelhaul? Hanging from the yardarm, or will you toss me to the sharks?"

"Such imagination!" Henri laid a finger on his chin. "Non, nothing so colorful. Monsieur Thorn has requested the honor of a duel to the death."

Rafe couldn't help the chuckle that escaped his lips. "To the death?" He directed a challenging gaze toward Thorn. "And what happens when I win?"

Henri smirked. "It depends on how long you can swim."

Rafe narrowed his eyes upon Henri, then plucked his sword from the deck and faced Thorn. "If you dare to challenge me, Thorn, you are a bigger fool than I thought."

But his words did not have the intended effect on Thorn. Instead, his first mate returned his gaze with hauteur. "You forget, Captain,

I learned swordsmanship in His Majesty's Navy. And I have kept my skills sharp. Have you?"

Rafe grinned. "We shall see."

⊱❧⊰

A duel to the death.

Grace's stomach lurched, and she realized if she'd had anything to eat in the past twelve hours, it would now be upon the rolling planks beneath her feet.

One hand on his hip, Thorn raised his blade and twirled it around Rafe's chest, taunting him. The captain stood his ground, a smug look on his face that was surprisingly devoid of fear.

Claire threw a hand to her chest and began wheezing then melted into Grace's arms. Father Alers helped lead Claire to a nearby barrel in the shade before he took a stance beside the women.

Rafe doffed his hat and flung it to the deck. "Are you going to fight or twirl your blade through the air like a woman?"

Thorn squinted, tightened his lips, then lunged toward Rafe. The captain leapt to the side and lifted his own blade to strike Thorn. Thorn recovered and met his thrust hilt to hilt. The *chink* of metal sliced over the ship.

Monsieur Dubois retreated to the railing as the crowd withdrew, allowing the combatants room. Shouts and jeers trumpeted through the air heavy with heat and sweat.

Grace's throat went dry. What if Rafe lost? What if he died? Horror stiffened her back. She could not imagine a world without Captain Rafe Dubois. She could not imagine this ship without him. And she could not imagine her life without him. The last realization stunned her the most. That, along with the awareness that her own welfare had not been foremost in her thoughts.

Rafe swung aside and drove his rapier in from the right. "We were friends once."

"We were never friends." Thorn dipped to the left and brought his blade up to strike the captain in the leg.

Rafe swerved about to avoid the thrust and circled his opponent. "Then you are a good liar."

Above them, loose sails flapped beneath a blast of wind as the brig rolled over a swell.

Thorn matched Rafe's stride until the two rotated over the deck like the spokes of a wheel. "Indeed I am a liar, but you are a murderer."

Rafe cocked his head, wiped the sleeve over his moist brow. "I am. But who do you say I murdered?"

Thorn charged him, his face a jumbled mass of red. "My sister."

Grace's breath halted in her throat.

Rafe met his attack and the clank of swords filled the air. "I have never killed a woman," he ground out with exertion.

The two men grunted, their swords slammed together. Rafe freed his blade and swept down on Thorn, nicking his right shoulder.

Thorn winced, a slice of purple forming on his blue waistcoat. He stared at it as if it were some strange occurrence, then his face grew hard and stiff.

"Who is your sister?" Rafe charged him again.

Thorn met his attack and gave Rafe a venomous look. "You do not remember her, then?" He pulled back. His lips curled in disgust and he charged Rafe like a mad bull, but his effort spent itself idly against the captain's skill. Rafe met each blow, each strike, with a calm defensive maneuver. Thorn stumbled, panting heavily, his mounting frustration evident on his face.

"You can take 'im, Thorn," one man yelled.

"Don't let that *cochon lâche* get the best of you!" another brayed.

"Finish 'im off, Capitaine!" Mr. Atton bellowed from the quarterdeck, echoed by several cheers, and Grace was thankful at least some of Rafe's men remained loyal.

Her eyes slipped to Monsieur Dubois. One of his hands clutched the larboard railing, the other was stuffed within his coat, as he watched the duel as if it were an afternoon's entertainment.

Even so, a measure of ease settled upon Grace's nerves. Rafe was indeed well skilled with the sword. Truth be told, in all her years of watching her father's swordplay with his friends in Portsmouth, she'd seen none to compare. But now her fear shifted to Mr. Thorn. For even though he had betrayed his captain—and her—she did not wish for him to die.

❧

Rafe eyed his opponent, noting that the look of insolence had spilled from his face along with the sweat that now ran like streams over his cheeks. "I know nothing of your sister."

Thorn stormed toward Rafe, brandishing his blade high.

Rafe met his thrust with a counter-parry, then he danced to the side and came in from the right. Their swords crashed, steel on steel, the sun glinting off their blades.

Pushing back, Thorn spit to the side and shook the sweat from his face. "Remember when you frequented Nassau upon your father's merchantman?"

Rafe kept his rapier aimed upon the rogue as his thoughts sped back in time. "Oui, I remember Nassau." A time long ago when his mother still lived. A time when Rafe believed that if he worked hard enough he might make his father proud.

"Elizabeth. Elizabeth Grayson," Thorn growled.

Rafe halted, his chest heaving. A vision of a young woman with eyes the color of lilacs rose from his memories. "Oui, Elizabeth." He furrowed his brow. "Your sister? Thorn is not your real name?"

"Does that surprise you?" Thorn lunged at Rafe, but Rafe batted his sword aside.

"I did not kill her." He'd had enough of this foolishness.

"Perhaps not her body." Thorn raged, his brown eyes flashing. "But her life, her future."

With a shake of his head, Rafe allowed his gaze to drop. All this had been caused by a woman's broken heart?

"Allow me to extend to you her compliments." Thorn swept down upon Rafe, and before Rafe could react, his arm exploded in searing pain.

At the sight of blood, the horde of sailors pressed in on them, assailing them with the stench of sweat and the clamor of shouts and curses.

Rafe pressed his hand over the wound and leveled his rapier at Thorn. "That is what this is about? Your sister?"

"You used her. You told her you loved her." He leapt toward Rafe and met his sword hilt to hilt. Pulling back he swung at him again. They inched over the deck, parrying back and forth. "Then you left her." Thorn heaved out in between breaths. "And destroyed her."

Suddenly the rapier felt as heavy as an anchor in Rafe's hand, as heavy as his heart. "I was but twenty. A foolish young man. I never meant any harm to her."

"Harm?" Thorn twisted, then came about and sliced his blade across Rafe's leg.

The sailors crowed in delight.

A thousand hot needles stabbed Rafe's thigh, and he stumbled back.

Grace screamed.

Thorn grinned, wiped the sweat from his brow, and halted to catch his breath. "You ruined her so no one else would have her."

Tightening his grip on his rapier, Rafe shoved aside the pain in his leg, the pain in his heart. He could not allow his emotions to weaken him now. Not when Grace needed him the most. "Enough of your games, monsieur." Rafe clenched his jaw and set his mind on the task at hand. "Let us finish this."

Thorn rubbed a thumb down the red scar on his face and neck. "You don't remember me either?" He lunged toward Rafe.

Lifting his blade, Rafe met his parry with equal intensity. "Should I?"

"Do you remember the boy you fought after you left Elizabeth sobbing in the parlor? The boy who challenged you as you headed out to your ship to leave her forever?" In one swift move, Thorn dove at Rafe from the left. The chime of their blades rang over the deck.

Rafe halted. He swallowed. "Vous? That boy was but eleven or twelve. He drew a sword on me."

"I was thirteen."

Rafe shook his head, his frustration rising with the heat of the day. "I was defending myself."

"Now the boy has grown and you defend yourself again. Only this time you will not be so lucky."

Rafe fought off his advance. "I do not wish to fight you, Thorn. What I did to your sister was wrong. And for that, je suis désolé. Let us end this now."

"As you wish." Thorn charged him in a ball of red fury.

Rafe swept his blade up to receive him. Their swords clanked. Rafe slashed back and forth. Thorn stumbled, warding off each blow with difficulty. The sailors parted as Rafe forced Thorn backward through their ranks.

They shoved their fists in the air, cheering Thorn and cursing Rafe.

With one final blow, Rafe struck Thorn's blade, flinging it from his hand and sending it clanging to the deck. A look of horror branded the first mate's reddened face. He gasped for air.

Rafe leveled the tip of his rapier over Thorn's chest.

Monsieur Dubois appeared beside him, hands on his hips, and glared at Monsieur Thorn. "I thought you said you could beat him, monsieur." He huffed. Then turned to Rafe. "Well, be done with it. Kill him."

Thorn gulped. Rafe was baffled at the cruelty of the man he'd called Father.

The crowd parted, a flash of green crossed Rafe's vision, and Grace dashed to his side, Father Alers on her heels. She grabbed his arm and shook her head.

"Kill him. Kill him," the men began a new chant.

Thorn closed his eyes.

Henri adjusted his neckerchief and sighed in impatience. "Do you intend to kill him or not?"

Rafe eyed his trembling first mate. The man he'd considered his friend. The man who had betrayed him—like everyone else. For that, he deserved to die. Rafe blinked sweat from his eyes and gripped his hilt tighter as every ounce of him twitched to do the deed—to gain some recompense for the all the treachery Rafe had endured.

But then he glanced at Grace's pleading face. She did not approve. Her God would not approve. Perhaps there was a better way to live.

Rafe dropped the tip of his blade to the deck. "I do not."

Thorn's eyes popped open.

Henri snorted in disgust. "Très bien." He snapped his jeweled fingers. "Take le capitaine below."

Two sailors shoved Grace out of the way and grabbed Rafe's arms, twisting the rapier from his grasp.

Tossing one of the men off, Rafe drove his fist into the other's jaw and sent him reeling backward. But more hands latched onto him. He struggled, but to no avail.

Henri waved a hand. "Lock him in irons."

"No! Rafe!" Grace pushed her way back through the crowd. Her delicate hand stretched toward him from amidst the filthy mob.

But he could not reach out to touch her.

Would probably never touch her again.

He had finally seen a gleam of ardor in her eyes. But now they would be separated forever. He would lose Grace, lose his ship, and possibly his life. And his father—or rather this brute who had pretended to be his father—would once again win. Forcing his anger aside, he turned toward Henri. "Promise me you will take Mademoiselle Grace back to her home."

"I fear I cannot do that." His lips writhed in a crooked smile. "How do you think I arranged this mutiny?" He waved at the men in dismissal as he did all his slaves. "Non, I will sell her to the don and divide the money among the crew."

To which a cheer arose from the men.

He leaned toward Rafe, a maniacal spark in his eyes. "And then I will take you to Roger Woodes in Nassau. Where I am sure you will be tried and hanged, as the son of a pirate deserves."

"My father was no pirate." Rafe found a moment's joy in associating the word *father* with someone other than the man who stood before him now.

"Hmm. But you are kidnapper, non?"

"And you are a mutineer."

"Moi? Non." Henri laughed. "Monsieur Thorn and I have merely rescued these ladies from your brutal hands and relieved a criminal of his ship."

"Some of my crew know differently. You cannot kill them all."

Henri grinned. "A pocket full of gold does much to temper one's tongue. Non. They will not speak on your behalf. And those few who do will not be believed."

CHAPTER 36

Grace clung to the side of the cockboat and swallowed a knot of fear. A sliver of a moon frowned at her from above the gray horizon that wreathed a sea of ebony. The small boat crested a wave and water sloshed over the side. It soaked her slippers and sent a chill through her, despite the air thick with heat and moisture. The salt stung her raw ankle, and she tugged at the rope that bound her.

Monsieur Dubois perched at the bow, lantern in hand and face to the wind. His chest swelled as he peered through the darkness toward a shadowy mound up ahead. Behind him, two of his men grunted as they shoved oars through the churning water, sending the boat gliding toward its destination.

The coast of Colombia.

Where Grace would be sold to Don Miguel de Salazar.

She took a deep breath of the night air. The smell of earth and sea mingled in a fragrant symphony that would have otherwise soothed her nerves. But instead, her stomach coiled like a bundle of rope and her mind reeled with terror.

What would become of her? She could hardly consider it without breaking into a violent tremble.

For two days she'd been locked within her cabin. Twice a day, one of Monsieur Dubois's men had brought her food and changed her chamber pot, offering her only grunts and leers in response to her pleading questions. Then torn from her cabin in the middle of the night, she'd been lowered into this boat and shoved off without explanation.

But she knew where she was going.

Even in the gloom of the night, she could make out the pyramid of land looming ahead.

Oh Lord, how did it come to this? Please help me.

Amidst the fear, her thoughts veered to Rafe, as they often had during the past few days. The look on his face as he had been dragged away to the hold would forever be carved in her memory. His dark eyes had locked upon hers, gulping her in as if she were a dying man's last drink. And though she tried to do the same, tears had filled her eyes and the vision of him had grown blurry. Just like her hope.

Would Henri turn over the man he'd raised as his own son to be hanged?

Grace drew out her cross and rubbed it as a blast of night wind tore over her. The splash of the oars and purling of water against the hull increased in both pace and ferocity. Moonlight glittered off the waves' rising crests as they crashed ashore in bands of light that marched ahead of her, leading her to her doom.

"Hold on, mademoiselle," Henri shot over his shoulder.

Grace lifted her slippers and placed them on the thwarts as they crested another swell. The wet rope chafed against the raw skin of her ankle, and she winced. The other end was tied to one of the oarlocks to prevent her escape over the side. Not that she would dare attempt it since she couldn't swim. Although drowning was beginning to seem preferable to the fate that awaited her at the hands of the Spanish.

How did I get here, Lord? She tightened her lips. *Whatever reason You had for sending me on this harrowing journey, I was open to Your will. I wanted to be used for Your glory.*

The croak of tree frogs and the call of the night heron met her ears. They were close now.

Grace's throat burned. She had done no good at all. She had not saved one soul, nor brought one person closer to God, save perhaps Father Alers. And even though Claire had been delivered of the curse Annette had cast upon her, she wavered in softening her heart toward God. Now Rafe would be hanged, Annette would remain a slave, Claire would go back to Monsieur Dubois, and Thorn would have his revenge.

The boat pitched over a wave then plunged down the other side. Seawater splashed over her, and she shook it off as tears filled her eyes. *I have done nothing good, Lord. Nothing. In fact, I have done worse.* She had stolen, lied, judged, broken a vow, faltered in her faith, and not only felt desire for Rafe but allowed him to kiss her. Some godly woman she was. How she had boasted back in Charles Towne of her righteous ways. How she had wagged her finger and flapped her tongue at others, so quick to point out their faults and failings and weaknesses.

Yet when faced with the same temptations, she had failed. She had sinned. She was no better than anyone else. She had judged people by their actions alone when she had no idea the path their lives had taken, the struggles and heartaches they'd suffered.

Nicole filled her thoughts. A trollop. A woman Grace would never have spoken to before. Yet she had been naught but kind to Grace. And Mr. Thorn, ever the presentation of propriety. Monsieur Henri, a godly man, a leader in his community—a man who spoke all the right words, who knew his scriptures. Both these men Grace would have gladly befriended a month ago. Yet inside, they were not godly men at all, but filled with hatred, jealousy, and revenge. And then there was Rafe. The ruffian, the rogue, but deep within, despite his cruel childhood, he possessed the heart of a saint.

How quick she was to judge others when it was her own heart that needed scrutiny.

Lowering her chin, she allowed her tears to fall. The boat canted over another wave, and she gripped the side, wishing they would capsize. She deserved nothing more than to drown beneath these foaming black waves.

The sailors adjusted their oars against the raging swells that came faster and more furious as they approached shore. Salty water crashed over her. She shivered as the boat struck land with a jolt. Splinters jammed in her fingers, and her knee struck a thwart. Pain etched up her thigh.

The sailors hopped out on either side. Waist deep in water, they dragged the bow of the boat onto the sand. Grace's breath heaved. Terror stiffened every nerve, every fiber.

Monsieur Dubois stepped onto the shore, fisted his hands at his waist and glanced about as if he were king. One of the crew untied the rope around Grace's ankle and offered her his hand.

Clutching her skirts, she splashed into the cool water. Her slippers sank into the sand as another wave crashed over the back of her legs, nearly toppling her. Grace froze as if the wave carried a serum of revelation. All through this harrowing journey, she had assumed that God had sent her to help someone else. She had assumed that once she had completed that task, she could go home. But now as she stood on the shores of Colombia, the jagged cliffs rising from the beach like ominous judges on a bench, the realization struck her just like the waves at her back. She hadn't been sent to help anyone else see the light. She'd been sent so that she would see the light. The light of her judgmental, prudish ways. The light that revealed deep down she was no better than anyone else.

"Come, come. *Dépêchez-vous*." Henri held the lantern aloft and motioned for the men to bring her along.

Each sailor grabbed one of her arms. They dragged her out of the water and up the beach.

In the distance, beyond the rhythmic crash of waves, horses snorted and three men emerged from the dark forest.

"Captain Dubois." One of them approached Henri. The high-crested Spanish morion atop his head glimmered in the lantern light.

"Oui." Henri assumed Rafe's role with the ease of a man practiced at trickery.

"Is this Admiral Westcott's daughter?" the man said in a perfect Castilian accent.

"Oui, bien sûr." Henri laid a hand upon the hilt of his rapier. "As promised."

The other man approached Grace. He wore a suit of black taffeta with silver lace over which hung a corselet of black steel beautifully damascened with golden arabesques. A Spanish musket hung over his shoulder. He swept a contentious gaze over Grace and snorted before turning toward Monsieur Dubois.

"Then let us be about our business."

Thorn leaned on the starboard railing and clasped his hands together. Beneath him, the sea lapped against the hull, pointing foam-laced fingers toward him—accusing fingers. In the past few days, instead of celebrating his victory with the crew, Thorn had sunk into a mire of despair, barely able to arise from his hammock each day. Wasn't this what he wanted? What he had worked for, for so long?

"Bonsoir," Annette said as she slipped beside him.

"Good evening." Thorn could not look at her—had been avoiding her for two days, too afraid to discover that she hated him for what he had done.

"Are you well?" She pointed toward the bloodstain on his right shoulder.

Her concern sparked hope within him. "Yes. It is not deep." Not as deep as Rafe could have made it if he had truly wanted to hurt Thorn. The thought chafed Thorn's conscience.

"Revenge is not so sweet, non?"

Thorn met her gaze, those dark, clear eyes that spoke more of understanding than condemnation. "No, it is not."

"Not for me either." She attempted a smile.

"I wanted to kill him for what he did to my sister. Can you understand?"

"Oui." She laid a hand on his. He squeezed it and held it tightly within his own.

"You do not fault me then?" he asked.

"How can I after what I did?" She gazed over the onyx sea then shrugged. "Perhaps it is not up to us to set things right in this world."

Thorn clenched his jaw. "My sister is still ruined."

"But the captain has changed, non?" Annette rubbed her thumb over his hand. "He is not the same man who did such atrocious things to your sister."

"People don't change."

"The captain did not kill you when he had a chance."

That fact had haunted him day and night for the past two days. Releasing her hand, Thorn gripped the railing until the wood bit into his fingers.

"Ever since Mademoiselle and her God have come on board." Annette shook her head and gave him a bewildered look. "I've seen many things I would not have believed before."

Thorn swallowed. "Indeed." He followed her gaze to the dark mound of Colombia in the distance.

"I miss her." Annette whispered then her voice grew hard. "You should not have let him take her."

Thorn shoved aside the agony he had endured since Monsieur Dubois had rowed away with Grace. "She was part of the bargain. I had no choice." He knew it was an excuse, but it was a good one.

But instead of agreeing with him, Annette gave him a look of censure that cut through his excuses straight into his heart.

"How am I to fight an entire crew?" he snapped.

She narrowed her eyes upon him, studied him for a moment, then shook her head and walked away.

Thorn leaned his elbows on the railing and dropped his head into his hands. Before the mutiny, he thought he knew exactly what he wanted—knew exactly what was the right thing to do. Now, nothing made any sense anymore.

❧

Rafe yanked once again on the iron manacles clamped around his ankles. But he received the same result as he had the last time. And the time before that. Cramping pain searing over his feet and clawing up his legs. Blood dripped from his scraped ankles. The patter of tiny feet filled his ears, and he swatted away the rats.

He'd lost track of time. Two days? Four days? He had no idea how long he'd been chained in the hold. With nothing to gaze at but a darkness so thick it seeped into his soul, he'd begun to lose all hope.

That the ship had sailed for a few days, he could tell by the roar of the sea against the hull and the undulating roll that had tied his stomach in knots. But the thunderous sound had softened to the gentle slap of waves, and the grating of the anchor chain and ominous splash of iron had told him they had arrived at their destination.

Had his father truly sailed to Colombia to deliver Grace? Rafe ground his teeth together and grabbed the chain again. Groaning, he yanked upon it, straining the muscles in his arms. With nothing but putrid water, unfit to drink, for two days, Rafe could feel his body weakening. Soon, he would be unable to keep the rats at bay. He lay down on the damp planks of the hold, hoping for a moment's rest before the ravenous creatures crowded in on him, but the tap of a multitude of little feet drummed over his ears in warning. He sat back up and swatted them away.

Stripped down to his breeches, Rafe stood and fisted his hands, digging his nails into his palms. The stench of human waste and mold and decay clung to him like a garment. He tried to pace, but the chains forbade him. His swollen ankles cried out in pain. Bien. The pain kept him awake. He yanked his hands through his hair and thought of Grace.

Sold to a Spanish don. A life unimaginable. Yet hadn't it been his fault, his doing, his idea?

What an imbécile Rafe had been. Fooled his entire life by a man claiming to be his father. Rafe didn't even look like Henri. Now this man, this imposter, who had ruined Rafe, and probably his mother. . .

Would finally win in the end.

Rafe shouted into the darkness, scattering the approaching rats and shaking the timbers of the hull.

When he had spent himself, he sank to the deck and lowered his head. Thoughts of the past month flooded his mind. Grace, sweet Grace. Even chained in the hold, he smiled at the thought of her. How she had changed him. How she had opened his heart again. Though her tongue was quick to judge, she'd had the best intentions—to love and care for others. If there was a heaven, Rafe suddenly wished to go there so he would see her again.

God, if You are there, save me.

Rafe surprised himself at his prayer. He heard the rats circling him. One of them chomped upon his toe. Pain spiked through his foot, but Rafe hadn't the energy to brush the rodent away. Then a hiss, scampering of paws, and the rats retreated. Something furry landed in his lap and began purring. Spyglass. Rafe drew the feline to his chest and scratched beneath her chin. "So you have come to my rescue, petit chat."

Or God had answered his prayer.

He set Spyglass down by his legs, and the cat stood guard, hissing and pouncing upon the rats who dared draw near.

A breeze blew over Rafe, and he rubbed the sweat from the back of his neck even as the hairs stood at attention. A breeze? In the hold? He peered into the darkness.

"I am here, son."

Rafe jumped at the silent voice. His heart hammered a frenzied beat. He shook his head. "I must be going mad."

He had wanted nothing to do with God. Not the God his father worshiped. Not the God whose rules his father had strapped to Rafe's back ever since he could walk. Not the God who blessed men like Henri with wealth and power and left good people poor, helpless, and starving.

Yet hadn't he seen Claire delivered from her illness? And what of Grace? She worshiped this same God. Through her eyes, this God was love and joy and light and goodness. Through her eyes, Rafe found himself yearning to know Him.

If only...

"God, are you there?" Rafe whispered then suddenly felt foolish.

Nothing.

Spyglass meowed.

Rafe caressed the cat's fur.

"I am here, son."

Rafe swallowed. Either God spoke to him, or he had become fou. Perhaps he was already dead. If so, Rafe had some questions for the Almighty. "Why has this happened?"

"I love you, son."

"Then why did You allow Henri to torture me all those years?"

"I love you, son."

"Why did You allow my mother to die?"

"I love you, son."

"Why did You allow Claire to betray me? And Thorn?"

"I love you."

Where frustration should have risen within Rafe at each repetitive answer, instead he found comfort in the words.

"Son."

Rafe scanned the darkness. *Son.* Did that mean God was his father? His real father? Hadn't Grace told him that God was the Father of all, especially those whose earthy fathers had failed them?

"Father?"

A presence descended on him. It swirled around him. It filled him. Joy and love as he'd never known. Rafe's throat burned. He rubbed his eyes. And in that moment, he knew that all his searching, all his yearning, had been in vain. This was what he wanted. No praise of man or praise of a father could surpass this feeling—this Presence. But then he saw himself as he was. Selfish and greedy and filthy. Even his charity toward the poor, if he admitted the truth, was done more to receive the praise of the people than for their ultimate good. To prove to everyone that his life had value, that he was not a failure.

"Leave me," Rafe cried out. "I have done so much wickedness."

"I love you, son."

A squeaking. A pinprick of light appeared above him. It blossomed, and footfalls sounded on the ladder. Spyglass nudged Rafe's side as if urging him to rise.

A circle of light advanced down the ladder, scattering rats in its path. Then a pair of brown boots followed. Not the boots of Weylan, who had been bringing Rafe his daily water.

Rafe stood.

And stared straight into the face of Monsieur Thorn.

Thorn approached him, holding a finger to his lips. His eyes landed on Spyglass, and he smiled then lifted his gaze to Rafe. An emotion flickered within his brown eyes that Rafe could not determine.

"Come to gloat?" Rafe hissed.

"No, Captain." He set down the lantern and clipped a set of keys from his belt; then he knelt and unlocked the irons around Rafe's bare feet.

CHAPTER 37

Rafe tossed the white buccaneer shirt over his head and thrust his arms into the sleeves, all the while keeping a wary eye on Thorn, who stood penitently beside Rafe's desk.

"Why are you helping me?"

Thorn released a heavy sigh and shrugged. "You did not kill me when you had the chance."

But Rafe had wanted to kill him. Even when Thorn had released him down in the hold, Rafe had wanted to throttle the man and lock him in the irons that had held Rafe captive.

But he didn't. Something had changed within him. He couldn't describe what it was. But he no longer harbored the same fury, the same hatred, toward those who had betrayed him. He donned the waistcoat, fastened the silver buttons, and shifted his shoulders. A weight had been lifted from them, a weight he'd been carrying around for years.

"Yet you betrayed me, lied to me all this time." Rafe strapped on his baldric and pistols while studying Thorn's expression.

Thorn scraped one boot across the deck planks and looked down. "I did."

Rafe buckled his belt about his waist. "I ruined your sister and scarred your face."

"You did."

"Then what has changed?"

Thorn fingered his chin and raised his gaze. "I have discovered revenge does not taste as sweet as I first assumed." He glanced out the stern windows into the darkness beyond. "You are a good man, Rafe. I saw true remorse in your eyes when you discovered what you had done."

Plucking his rapier off his desk, Rafe sheathed it with a metallic *ching*. Finally, he felt safe. If Thorn intended any *traîtrise*, he would not have allowed Rafe his weapons.

"Besides"—Thorn tugged at his once-white cuffs, now dirtied from their journey—"in the past few days, I have come to realize that what Miss Grace said was true. It is not for me to seek revenge. As with Annette's attempt to enact retribution upon her mistress, we only make things worse. I must trust in God's justice."

When Thorn faced Rafe, only sincerity burned in his eyes.

"Can you forgive me, Captain?"

Rafe stared at the bottle of brandy on his desk, his throat longing for a sip, yet his soul cringing at the thought. Forgive Thorn? For the lies, the betrayal, the intent to kill Rafe? Could he? Yet how couldn't he, after God had forgiven Rafe of things equally repugnant.

"I should ask your forgiveness for my beastly behavior toward your sister." Rafe sighed and ran a hand through his hair. "It was horrible of me." He gestured toward Thorn's face. "And to be so careless with a young boy."

Thorn rubbed his scar, and a spark of malice flashed in his eyes. But then it was gone. "I hope we can once again be friends."

Rafe cleared the emotion from his throat and spotted his boots perched in the corner. In one stride, he picked them up and took a seat. He did not have time to ponder Thorn's request. "I must rescue Grace. How long ago did Henri take her ashore?"

"Over an hour." Thorn's tone dove in despair, but Rafe would not allow his own hopes to follow. Cringing in pain, he tugged his boots over the raw scrapes on his ankles then stood. He glanced out the stern windows. Still black, but dawn would be here soon. It was a three-hour ride by horse to Don Miguel's mansion in Rio de la Hacha. But the horses would move slowly due to the darkness and the thick vegetation. Rafe would not. He pressed the wound on his thigh and winced. He must not let it hold him up. "You told Henri the signal?"

"Weylan did." Thorn pressed his lips together, his eyes heavy with guilt. "Don Miguel's men were waiting, just as you said."

A rap sounded on the door, and it creaked open to reveal Father

Alers, tray of food and drink in hand. The old man gave Rafe a wide smile, revealing a full row of crooked teeth, and Rafe thought it the most pleasant sight he had seen in days. Father Alers set the tray down on the desk, and Rafe grabbed his arms and shook him. "It is good to see you unharmed, mon vieux. Monsieur Thorn informed me that my father. . .I mean Henri had chained you to one of the guns."

"It was nothing." He chuckled. "Besides, who would harm an old priest like me?"

"And the rest of the crew?" Rafe asked Thorn.

"Those loyal to you were forced to swear allegiance to me and Monsieur Dubois or be tossed in the hold." He waved a hand through the air. "An act of preservation. They are still with you, I am sure."

"Bien." Grabbing one of the mugs from the tray, Rafe gulped down the rum-flavored water until it ran down his chin onto his shirt. The liquid, though warm and bitter, filled his mouth and trickled down his parched throat as if it were from a bubbling spring.

"Easy, my boy," Father Alers said. "You will make yourself ill."

Rafe smiled and wiped his sleeve over his mouth. "Merci." Then he chomped down on a hard biscuit. Normally he hated the crusty, bland flavor, but after not eating for days, it melted like butter in his mouth. "Are you sure my father will not return to the brig tonight?" Crumbs shot from his lips.

"Yes," Thorn replied. "As soon as he came back from shore, he gathered two of his men and rowed back to *Le Vainqueur*. To ready her for sailing at first light."

"What did he order you to do?"

"To sail with him back to Port-de-Paix." Thorn lifted his brow.

"He trusts you with *Le Champion*?"

"Why wouldn't he? I am his ally. Besides, he left five of his crew here, plus the men from your crew who joined him."

"Scalawags!" Father Alers spat then gave an apologetic look upward. "Forgive me, Lord."

Rafe drained the second mug of water and set it down with a *clank* on the tray. He flexed the muscles in his arms and back, allowing the nourishment to settle in and bring back his strength.

Swishing sounded and Claire flounced into the room, Annette following behind her. "You are well, Rafe. I was so worried. . . ." She grabbed his arm and squeezed him as if to make sure he was real.

Rafe stiffened as Claire's familiar scent of lavender filled his nose. "I feared Henri would kill you." She lifted moist eyes to his.

"I believe that is still his intent, madame." Rafe pushed her back, noting that her close presence no longer affected him. Behind Claire, Annette and Thorn exchanged a glance of affection that startled Rafe.

He faced Claire. "Why did Henri not take you with him?"

"He is a proud man. Do you think he wants a wife who would betray him as I have?" She sighed. "No. Better for his reputation if he can say that he cast me aside."

Thorn stepped forward. "Monsieur Dubois will expect us to set sail with him. He has claimed this ship as his own."

Rafe studied his first mate, noting the gleam in his eye. "Mais, I suspect you have another plan?" He raised a brow.

Thorn exchanged a furtive glance with Father Alers. "Yes. Once out at sea, we fire upon your father's ship and take him by surprise."

Father Alers punched the air with his fist in excitement. "Then we board him and take both his ship and the doubloons he received for the mademoiselle."

Claire sank into a chair. "You will not harm my husband."

Thorn bowed toward her. "No, madame. Our only intent is to make him pay for what he has done."

Rafe eyed Thorn and Father Alers curiously. Perhaps he wasn't the only one who had gone mad. "The crew will never allow it."

"We have promised them double what Henri intended to pay them out of the money he received from the mademoiselle's sale." A pleased look overtook Thorn's features.

Grabbing a silk ribbon, Rafe tied his hair behind him and grinned. "I thought you were going to allow God's justice to prevail?"

Father Alers leaned toward him with a sly look. "Sometimes God uses men to enact His judgment."

Rafe chuckled. "And what will you do with all that wealth?"

Father Alers folded his aged hands over his belly. "I will give it to Abbé Villion in Port-de-Paix. I believe there's a hospital that needs building." His golden eyes sparkled with satisfaction. "En fait, I may join him in the effort. I feel God tugging me back into His service."

Rafe blinked. "When did this happen?"

"Mademoiselle Grace has opened my eyes. I no longer wish to run from God."

The ship creaked beneath a wave, and Rafe glanced out the window. A hint of gray spread across the horizon. He could afford no further delay.

Rafe started for the door and stopped to place a hand on Claire's shoulder. "When you reach Port-de-Paix, if Henri changes his mind and insists you come home, you do not have to obey him."

She nodded. "I do not intend to."

"A good decision." Rafe looked at Monsieur Thorn, hoping to elicit his help in settling Claire somewhere safe, but the man's eyes were riveted onto Annette.

Thorn cleared his throat. "Since you no longer need a maid—"

"She is free to go." Claire waved a hand toward Annette. "I cannot take care of her."

Annette's eyes widened, and she exchanged a glance with Thorn.

Rafe leaned toward Claire. "But who will take care of you, madame?"

She let out a tiny laugh. "Go save Mademoiselle Grace." Pain darkened her blue eyes. "We can talk about this when you return."

Rafe shifted his gaze over his friends, allowing the change in Claire, in Thorn, in everyone, to sink into him. What had happened during the two days he had been below? Had something been added to the water to make everyone so amiable? Or was it his sweet Grace and her God—his God now—who had changed them?

Thorn stepped forward, his brown eyes troubled. "Captain, we need you here. I need your expertise in sailing and in battle." His face grew tight. "This is your chance to beat your fa—Henri—to finally win."

Rafe hooked his fingers onto his baldric. *To finally win.* To finally best the man who had spent a lifetime battling Rafe—torturing Rafe, beating Rafe. The urge to stay and fight mounted within him, setting his senses aflame. A chance like this would never come again. And if things went wrong without him, Rafe could lose his brig, his livelihood, his means with which to provide for the poor. And with that, his purpose to live.

Mais non. What would any of that mean without Grace?

"I will not leave her." Rafe's tone conveyed the conviction of his heart.

"She is already in the hands of the Spanish, Rafe." The sorrow dragging upon Father Alers's face threatened to destroy Rafe's remaining hope.

"If you go ashore, we cannot wait." Thorn tightened his lips. "If we do not sail with your father, he will become suspicious."

Rafe gripped the hilt of his rapier. "Then go."

Father Alers gave him a sympathetic look. "Je suis désolé, Capitaine, but it is too late. If you attempt to rescue her, you will die."

CHAPTER 38

Grace shifted her legs over the leather saddle, trying to relieve the ache in her right thigh from sitting astride the horse for hours. In front of her, two Spaniards led their thickly muscled steeds down the narrow trail, chattering in Castilian as if they were on a Sunday outing. Behind her, the third rode quietly, save for the squeak of his armor and the clank of the metals adorning his horse.

With naught but a lantern to guide their way, they had forged through the thick undergrowth, following a path that wound deeper into the green mesh of vegetation. For hours, Grace had fought off vines and branches that struck her face as well as the insects that bit her tender skin. All around her, life teemed and buzzed. Frogs croaked and katydids droned. At one point during the night a deep, guttural roar sounded in the distance, raising the hair on her arms.

Quite possibly, she may not survive to meet her new Spanish lord. The thought, though alarming, did not distress her overmuch.

Slowly, the hulking shadows around her—that she'd imagined to be monsters in the darkness—formed into trees, vines, and shrubs as dawn lifted its curtain over the Colombian forest.

Grace pressed her fingers over the scratches marring her face and ducked just in time to avoid another assault from a low-hanging vine. At least now she could see the attacking plants coming at her.

A myriad of birds took up a chorus of praise, ushering in the new day as if they didn't realize the horror that transpired beneath them. Grace glanced up to see patches of gray sky appear amidst the tangled mass of the canopy.

Her mouth went dry, and she gulped. She'd kept her fear at bay during the night by praying. Somehow it was easier to believe God was with her in the darkness, easier to imagine Him walking beside her, leading her horse, whispering comforting words into her ears.

But in the daylight, the reality of her situation struck her like the ray of sun gleaming off the morion of the Spaniard in front of her.

She drew a deep breath. Earth and life and air, perfumed with spice and flowers, filled her lungs, mocking the shroud of death that hung heavy over her heart. *Lord, where are You?*

One of the Spaniards cast a glance at her over his shoulder. His eyes were as hard as the steel breastplate he wore. He said something to his companion and they shared a chuckle. No doubt at her expense.

Something stung her neck, and Grace slapped the insect breakfasting on her flesh. Wiping away a trickle of sweat from her forehead, she tried to force her thoughts to good things. At least these men seemed disinterested in her. That was something to be thankful for. But then her thoughts sprang to Rafe, as they had often done during the night. And she took up her pleas to heaven for the French captain again.

Please, Lord, do not let him die. Help him to come to You. And forgive Thorn and Henri. Help Claire and Annette. And Lord, please save my sister Hope and bring her home. And help my sisters and my father to follow You always. Since Grace did not know how long she would live, she thought it best to cover all her loved ones with God's blessing before she passed from this world.

She also added a plea that her passing would occur soon. For the Spanish were notorious for their cruelty. Especially toward those they deemed infidels, heretics to Catholic Spain. Add to that whatever grudge this Don Miguel de Salazar had against her father, and her future appeared bleak.

Perspiration streamed down her back, and she gasped for air amidst the rising humidity. *Lord, forgive me for being such a Pharisee. Please grant me the strength to accept whatever consequence You send my way.* For she knew she deserved it. And much worse.

Thud.

A scream of pain.

The Spaniard who led the way toppled from his horse. With a snort, the steed bolted down the trail. The other horse reared and clawed at the air, screeching. The man on its back held on to the pommel of his saddle, trying to control the beast. He yanked on the reins and cursed. Finally calming the horse, he grabbed his musket and dismounted. A string of Castilian spewed from his mouth to the man behind Grace.

Grace's heart thundered. Her mind reeled. What was happening? Her horse started prancing about nervously.

The man behind her grabbed her reins. With one quick motion, he yanked her from the animal and tossed her to the ground. Pain shot up her back. She glanced at the Spaniard who had fallen from his horse. Blood oozed from an ugly wound on his head.

He wasn't moving.

More Castilian shot through the air. The man who'd knocked her down drew his pistol and sword, dragged Grace behind him, and crouched among the leaves. His comrade dove into a shrub on the other side of the trail.

The crack of a pistol sounded.

Two of the horses spooked and bolted down the trail.

Grace's heart bolted off with them. Her head spun. Who attacked them? Spain had many enemies. The French, the British, natives—a shiver ran through her at that final thought. Whoever they were, she wouldn't allow herself to hope that they were there to rescue her.

One of the men shouted something into the forest.

Grace scanned the mass of tangled green. No movement. Nothing.

"We travel on the order of Don Miguel de Salazar. Show yourself." The Spaniard attempted the command in English.

A flash of gray and black. Something pounced on the man across the path.

Grace shrieked and peered through the underbrush. *Rafe! It was Rafe!*

Grunts and curses flew through the air along with flailing limbs. The man beside Grace stood, pointed, and cocked his pistol upon the tumbling men.

Rafe clutched the man by the collar of his ruffled shirt. With his face red, his veins pulsing, his black hair flying about his face, the captain looked more like a wild animal than a man. He flatted his fist on the man's jaw then tossed him against a tree trunk. The Spaniard's eyes rolled up in his head, and he slid down the bark and landed on the damp ground with a *thump*.

The man beside Grace halted in fear at this unearthly apparition. Recovering himself, he pointed his quivering pistol at Rafe.

"Rafe!" Grace screamed and barreled into the man's legs. He stumbled to the side. The pistol fired. The blast echoed through the forest.

Wiping the sweat from his brow, Rafe met her gaze briefly and smiled.

The Spaniard tossed his smoking pistol to the ground, and drew his sword. But before he could point it at his assailant, Rafe had drawn his own rapier. With one swift strike, he sent the man's blade twirling through the air. The polished steel glittered in the rays of sunlight that had made their way to the forest floor before the tangled forest swallowed it up.

The Spaniard stood aghast as if he could not process how one man could have defeated three of Spain's finest soldiers. His chest began to heave beneath the decorated steel breastplate.

Rafe leveled the tip of his rapier at his neck. "Go tell Don Miguel de Salazar that I have changed my mind. Mademoiselle Grace Westcott is not for sale."

The man's dark eyes skittered about as if he were deciding whether it would be preferable to die at his attacker's sword or face the wrath of his master.

"Allez-vous-en!" Rafe barked.

At which the man turned and fled down the trail.

Grace tried to move but found her limbs had frozen. From fear, from shock, she didn't know. Perhaps she was afraid that if she moved, if she entered this vision, it would dissipate, and she would be back on her horse heading toward Rio de la Hacha.

Rafe sheathed his rapier. His dark eyes found hers.

"Are you real?" Grace asked.

"Come and see." He gave her a rakish grin.

Struggling to her feet, Grace rushed toward him. She fell against him and was comforted by firm, strong arms and his scent of tobacco and leather. She trembled.

"Shhh. . . You are safe now." He caressed her hair. Then holding her face between his hands, he brought her eyes to his.

The ardor, the affection, she saw within them both frightened and delighted her. "You came for me."

"Of course." He kissed her forehead.

"But you were locked in the hold."

"Oui, I seem to recall that."

A slight giggle escaped her lips, at odds with the tension of only a moment ago. Then as if a spigot had been opened, tears spilled down her cheeks.

Rafe wiped them away with a gentle thumb, and he gazed at her as if she were the most precious thing in the world.

Grace's belly fluttered. She knew she should back away from him. She knew she should resist the intense feelings bursting within her. For she had no idea where his intentions lay. Rafe was a man accustomed to the lavish affections of women. His charm, his virility, drew them to him like ships to a protective harbor. She would not become another one of his conquests. This ruffian, this French rogue. The man who had stolen her from her home.

But not until that moment did she realize he had also stolen her heart.

He ran his finger along her cheek and dropped his gaze to her lips. Yearning tingled across her own and she closed her eyes, wanting nothing more than for him to kiss her.

But no. Grace shot backward, tripping over a root. He grabbed her arm to steady her, and she lowered her chin, not wanting to be mesmerized by those dark eyes again.

She crossed her arms over her stomach and glanced down the trail. "You have no horse. How did you catch us?"

"I am a fast runner." He smiled. "Especially when there's something worth running to catch."

❧

Grace was alive. Rafe's heart soared. He silently thanked God for helping him deliver her from the Spanish soldiers. Now all he wanted to do was kiss her. He sensed her longing, but she had demanded he refrain from kissing her ever again. Though every fiber of him longed to do so, by the grace and strength of God, Rafe would honor her request.

He studied her, wondering whether the ardor brimming in those lustrous green eyes was because she was grateful for her rescue or because she loved him. He supposed it didn't matter. As long as she was safe.

He grabbed her shoulders, noting they still trembled slightly. "Did they hurt you?"

She shook her head. Rafe drew her close again. He must get her out of here as soon as possible. These were Spanish lands—enemy lands. He must get her back to shore where they had a better chance of escape. Perhaps Thorn would win his battle with Henri and come back for them. If not, Rafe would do what he could to keep them hidden and alive until he could figure out a way to get off the coast.

Or God would provide. Surely the Almighty hadn't gotten them this far to have them die. Rafe smiled. He could get used to depending on an all-powerful God. He had always believed such subservience would weaken a man. Now he discovered the opposite to be true.

After lifting Grace atop the remaining horse, Rafe leapt behind her and took the reins. She leaned back onto his chest. Her scent soothed his nerves. During the ride back to shore, Rafe regaled her with the tale of what had occurred in her absence: how Monsieur Thorn had delivered him from the hold, how he had changed his ways, how Madame Claire was finally free of Henri, how Father Alers planned on returning to God's service, and the strange love that had sprouted between Monsieur Thorn and Annette.

Grace smiled. "And I thought God had not used me at all."

"Mademoiselle, God has done more good through you than you know."

She sat up and stretched away from him, meeting his gaze. "Did you say God?"

Rafe smiled as he nudged the horse onward. "Hmm. Did I leave out the part about my conversation with God in the hold?"

"Why yes, monsieur, I believe you did." Delight sparkled in her green eyes. A lock of raven hair danced over her face, and Rafe brushed it aside.

"Let us just say, He and I have made our peace."

She nearly leapt from the saddle, and Rafe had to grab her waist to keep her from falling.

"I am most pleased." She kissed him on the cheek, sending a spark of warmth through him. He wrapped one arm around her, reveling in the feel of her in front of him.

Several minutes passed in silence, except for the thump of the horse's hooves and the buzz and chirp of insect and birds. Despite the sweltering heat, despite the danger, with Grace in his arms, Rafe wished this journey would never end.

Grace strolled along the beach. She dipped her bare feet into the cool waves, allowing the bubbles to wash over her legs. A gust of salty wind wafted over her from the sea, twirling her loose hair about her waist. Relishing the feel of it, she glanced over her shoulder at Rafe. He had spent the day building a makeshift shelter with banana leaves, and now he assembled logs for a fire to protect and warm them through the night. Beside him lay the cockboat he had dragged up on shore and the kegs of water he'd brought with him. Stripped down to his white shirt and breeches, his black hair grazing his shoulders, he looked every bit the dangerous mercenary he claimed to be, and Grace's heart swelled with love for him.

She shook her head, still having trouble believing all Rafe had given up for her. He had risked his life to rescue her, had forfeited an opportunity to beat Henri Dubois and retrieve the money for his hospital. He had abandoned himself on the shores of enemy territory, and quite possibly lost his ship, along with his livelihood. But was he prompted more out of guilt for his own duplicity in her situation or from his love for her? Rafe was a man of strong desires, to be sure. But Grace had no experience distinguishing fleshly longings from true love.

He raised a hand to shield the glare from his eyes and glanced at the sun sinking below the western horizon. His eyes met hers. He smiled, dropped the log he'd been using to prod the flames, and trudged through the sand in her direction.

Grace's breath caught in her throat, and she faced the sea again, dropping her skirts to cover her bare legs. She tried to focus on the ribbons of violet, gold, and crimson that spiraled over the horizon and not allow Rafe's presence to affect her. But to no avail. Her stomach tightened as he took a spot beside her and folded his arms over his chest.

"There is nothing like a Caribbean sunset." His nonchalant tone implied that her presence did not have the same effect on him.

Grace nodded. A wave caressed her feet, tickling her skin and loosening the sand beneath her toes. She dug them into the cool grains, seeking an anchor for her traitorous emotions. "How long do you think it will be before we are rescued?"

He turned to her, a wounded look in his eyes. "Do not fear, we shall not be here long."

"I would not mind if we were."

He cocked his head. "Vraiment? At one time you detested my company."

"Can you blame me?"

"Non." He chuckled and kicked the sand with his boot, staring at the turquoise waves. "What has changed?"

"*I* have changed."

He faced her. A warm breeze danced around them, fluttering Grace's hair, and Rafe ran his fingers through the strands. "En effet, you have changed. When I met you, you wore these curls so tight upon your head, I thought your skull would crack from the strain."

Grace laughed. "'Tis true." She studied him, wondering if she should abandon her safe shores and plunge into the deep. "That is not all that has changed."

"What else?" His tone was cavalier.

Grace bit her lip. "I have seen what a judgmental prude I have been."

"Oui."

"You do not have to be so agreeable." She mocked offense.

He grew sober. Lifting his hand, he slid a finger over her cheek. Grace's pulse raced. "What else has changed, mon petit chou pieuse?" He searched her eyes like a man digging for buried treasure.

"Can you not tell?" She gave him a coy look.

"Hmm, your face has tanned from the sun."

Grace ground her teeth together. "Not that." He taunted her. *The rogue!* Grace huffed. She turned to leave, frustration broiling in her stomach.

Rafe grabbed her arm. A mischievous grin lifted his lips. "Peut-être, have your affections changed for me?"

Grace narrowed her eyes at the man's presumptuous arrogance. "I suppose you are accustomed to women declaring their love for you."

"Oui, a common occurrence." He shrugged then grew serious. "Mais there is only one woman from whose lips I long to hear it declared."

Grace's body tingled with joy. She ran her fingers over the black stubble on his jaw. "Then you must know, Rafe Dubois, that I love you."

His dark eyes sparkled, and he knelt on one knee and took her hand in his. "My sweet prude pieuse, I have loved you since the moment I first saw you." He placed a kiss on her fingers and smiled. "Will you do me the greatest honor of becoming my wife?"

"Yes!" Grace could hardly contain her joy. She fell into his embrace before he could fully right himself. Stumbling backward, Rafe picked her up and swung her around as their laughter joined the crash of the sea.

When he placed her down on the sand, Grace puckered her lips and closed her eyes.

Nothing but a sharp wind scraped over her mouth. She pried open one eye and peered at Rafe.

He cocked a brow. "You ordered me never to kiss you again, mademoiselle."

"And of course that's the only one of my orders you obeyed." Grace huffed.

He licked his lips. "Do I have your permission?"

"You have it, monsieur. Now and forever."

He gave her that roguish grin that sent her heart aflutter and lowered his lips to hers.

EPILOGUE

Grace wiggled her toes into the sand and leaned back against Rafe's thick chest. He wrapped his arms around her waist, and his warm breath caressed her skin as he nibbled on her neck. She giggled and snuggled closer to him, amazed at the providence of God. A God who surely had a grand sense of humor. For who would have thought someone as pious and proper as her would be betrothed to a rogue like Rafe? Not only betrothed but enjoying every minute she had spent with him the past two days,

Boom! A cannon blast thundered.

Grace snapped her gaze to the sea where the puff of gray smoke clung to the red hull of a brig. The ball splashed harmlessly into the waves. A warning shot. Or. . .

Grace threw a hand to her throat. "I know that ship! That is my sister Faith's ship, the *Red Siren!*"

The cockboat crunched against the shore, and Grace could barely restrain herself from dashing into the waves to greet her sisters. Yes, *sisters*. Both Hope and Faith sat among the stern sheets of the tiny craft. Lucas and another sailor leapt over the side, but before they could hoist the boat farther upon the sand, Faith bounded into the water, followed by Captain Waite. Waves crashed over her as she waded toward shore, splashing her brown breeches and white shirt. When she reached dry sand, she rushed toward Grace with a beaming smile upon her face and her red hair flaming behind her. The scent of lemons rose to Grace's nose as she clung to her sister.

"I cannot believe we found you!" Faith stepped back and examined Grace, her nose wrinkling slightly. Behind her a man that looked oddly like Mr. Nathaniel Mason, the shipwright from Charles Towne, carried Hope from the boat and set her upon the sand. Lifting the skirts of her yellow gown, Hope rushed into Grace's arms, sobbing. "Oh, Grace. We were so worried. So very worried."

"Hope, Faith." Tears overran Grace's lashes and spilled down her face. "I thought I would never see you again. Oh, thank God for bringing us all together." Grace hugged her sisters and kissed them repeatedly on the cheeks as they laughed with delight.

Clank. Clink. The sound of steel on steel rose above the crashing waves.

Grace withdrew from her sisters and glanced up to see Mr. Waite holding his sword, hilt to hilt with Rafe, while Mr. Mason aimed a pistol to her beloved's head.

"No!" Grace dashed to Rafe's side.

"Relatives of yours, mademoiselle?" Rafe's insolent grin never faltered. "Is this how *les anglais* greet one another?"

Mr. Waite narrowed his eyes. "I saw this scoundrel accosting you on shore."

Grace cleared her throat. "This scoundrel is my betrothed, Mr. Waite, Captain Rafe Dubois."

Hope gasped and Faith flinched backward as if she'd been struck.

Mr. Waite's blue eyes shifted between Grace and Rafe. Finally he lowered his blade.

Nathaniel, however, kept his pistol aimed. "Then what, pray tell, was he doing?"

Rafe sheathed his sword and winked at Grace.

"Please lower your pistol, Mr. Mason," Grace said. "He was doing me no harm, I assure you." She couldn't help the flush that heated her face.

But Nathaniel would not be appeased. "Isn't this the Frenchman who kidnapped you?"

Grace gave Rafe an adoring look. "Yes."

Hope laid a hand on her hip. "You do have much to tell us, dear sister." Her gaze swept to Grace's loose hair. "I see this journey has done you some good."

Grace clutched her sister's hand. "More good than you know, Hope.

I've been praying for you, dear sister. You left with Lord Falkland. We had no idea where to search for you."

" 'Tis a long story," Hope said. "I have been praying for you as well."

"You, praying?" Grace blinked.

"Part of that long tale." Hope's eyes sparkled with more life than Grace remembered ever seeing within them.

"We all have stories to tell." Faith made her way to Mr. Waite. He put his arm around her.

With a huff of resignation, Mr. Mason stuffed his pistol into his belt and exchanged a loving look with Hope that sent the girl sashaying to his side. "It is fortunate we found you."

Rafe inched his way beside Grace. "How did you know where we were?"

Captain Waite folded his arms across his chest. "When we stopped in Charles Towne for supplies, we received your post, Miss Grace."

"And set sail straightaway for Port-de-Paix, but you had already left," Faith added.

"A local fisherman thought he saw a woman matching your description being brought aboard Captain Dubois's ship." Mr. Waite gestured toward Rafe. "Then of course we knew from your missive that you were headed to Rio de la Hacha."

Faith beamed "And here we are."

Grace shook her head at the providence of God. *Thank You, Lord.*

Lucas ambled forward, floppy hat in hand. "Good to see you, Miss Grace." He nodded her way, his dark hair coiling about his brown face.

"And you, Mr. Lucas," she replied.

"We have more good news." Hope almost leapt in the sand. "Along with yours, we also received a post from Father." She exchanged an excited glance with Faith before facing Grace again. "He is bringing Charity home and in fact, they may already be there now."

Grace blinked and glanced at Hope. "What of her husband?"

Lowering her gaze, Hope clung to Mr. Mason's arm.

"He is dead." Faith's tone held no emotion. "Killed in a duel over his entanglement with the wife of an earl."

"Oh my." Grace clasped her throat. How oft had she prayed for Charity to be delivered from the beast, but she certainly had not wished him dead. But Charity was coming home! And she would be finally free from the man's abuse. Grace could hardly contain her excitement. *Another praise to You, Lord.* "I shall be so glad to see her!"

Lucas glanced toward the west where the last traces of light fell below the horizon. "The sun sets, mistress."

"Aye, I don't feel safe this close to the main." Mr. Waite eyed the sea with caution. "There are Spanish *guardacostas* about."

But as quickly Grace's joy had risen, a sudden realization struck it down. She gazed up at Rafe. "Surely you wish to return to Port-de-Paix?" It was his home, after all, and he had friends there. Would she have to be separated from him until they could be wed? She could not bear the thought.

As if sensing her fear, he brushed a curl from her cheek and caressed her skin with his thumb. "Oui. I need to get word to Monsieur Thorn that we are rescued. And to make sure his plan worked and that everyone is safe."

Faith turned to her husband. "I am sure Captain Waite would be willing to make a brief stop there to drop you off, Mr. Dubois, would you not, Captain?"

"Of course." Mr. Waite tipped his tricorne at Faith. "Anything for my first mate."

Grace gazed down at the mounds of crystalline sand at her feet and clasped the chain around her neck, seeking anything to cling to besides the sorrow overwhelming her. "How long will you stay there?"

Placing a finger beneath her chin, he lifted her to eyes to his. "You have attempted to escape me twice, mademoiselle, do you think I would allow it again? Non, you will not leave my sight." He smiled and raised his brows. "Ever."

Grace thought her heart would burst as Rafe took her hand and placed a gentle kiss upon it. She gazed up at him, tears of joy filling her eyes.

Mr. Waite cleared his throat. "Well, that being the case, I assume we will have no choice but to wait for you until you conclude your business at Port-de-Paix, sir."

Grace sent Mr. Waite a look of gratitude.

"I thank you, monsieur," Rafe nodded in his direction.

"Then it is settled," Faith said.

"And afterward we shall all go home." Mr. Mason held his arm out for Hope, and the couple turned and made their way to the boat. Mr. Waite and Faith followed.

M. L. TYNDALL

Home. The word wrapped around Grace like a warm blanket. A gust of wind dashed over them, filling the air with the aroma of salt and brine and flowers—the scent of the Caribbean. Closing her eyes, Grace thanked God for seeing her through this harrowing journey step by step, for changing her judgmental heart into one of love, and for the incredible man standing before her.

She glanced up at Rafe, his black hair tossed by the breeze. He smiled at her, his sultry dark eyes burning with such love and admiration that her knees began to tremble. Then sweeping her up into his arms, he carried her to the cockboat to begin their new life together. Grace smiled. And what a life it would be, being married to Captain Rafe Dubois.

Sniffles (aka Spyglass) 1988–2009

ABOUT THE AUTHOR

M. L. TYNDALL

MaryLu Tyndall dreamed of pirates and seafaring adventures during her childhood days on Florida's coast. She holds a degree in math and worked as a software engineer for fifteen years before testing the waters as a writer. Her love of history and passion for story drew her to create the Legacy of the King's Pirates series. MaryLu now writes full-time and makes her home with her husband, six children, and four cats on California's coast, where her imagination still surges with the sea. Her passion is to write page-turning, romantic adventures that not only entertain but expose Christians to their full potential in Christ. For more information on MaryLu and her upcoming releases, please visit her Web site at www.mltyndall.com or her blog at crossandcutlass. blogspot.com.

Books by M. L. Tyndall

Legacy of the King's Pirates series
The Redemption
The Reliance
The Restitution

The Falcon and the Sparrow

Charles Towne Belles series
The Red Siren
The Blue Enchantress
The Raven Saint